S0-AAZ-461

DEADLY ANNIVERSARIES

DEADLY ANNIVERSARIES

A COLLECTION OF STORIES FROM CRIME FICTION'S TOP AUTHORS

EDITED BY MARCIA MULLER AND BILL PRONZINI

*Sue Grafton, Laurie R. King,
Lee Child, Margaret Maron,
S. J. Rozan, Max Allan Collins,
Wendy Hornsby, Jeffery Deaver,
Bill Pronzini, Carolyn Hart,
Peter Lovesey, Meg Gardiner,
Marcia Muller, Julie Smith,
William Kent Krueger,
Peter Robinson, Naomi Hirahara,
Doug Allyn, Alison Gaylin,
Laura Lippman*

THORNDIKE PRESS
A part of Gale, a Cengage Company

Copyright © 2020 by Mystery Writers of America, Inc.
Introduction Copyright © 2020 by Marcia Muller and Bill Pronzini
If You Want Something Done Right . . . Copyright © 2020 by Sue Grafton
Ten Years On Copyright © 2020 by Laurie R. King
Normal in Every Way Copyright © 2020 by Lee Child
The Replacement Copyright © 2020 by Margaret Maron
Chin Yong-Yun Sets the Date Copyright © 2020 by S. J. Rozan
Amazing Grace Copyright © 2020 by Max Allan Collins
Ten Years, Two Days, Six Hours Copyright © 2020 by Wendy Hornsby
The Anniversary Gift Copyright © 2020 by Gunner Publications, LLC
The Last Dive Bar Copyright © 2020 by Bill Pronzini
Case Open Copyright © 2020 by Carolyn Hart
The Bitter Truth Copyright © 2020 by Peter Lovesey
Unknown Caller Copyright © 2020 by Meg Gardiner
April 13 Copyright © 2020 by Marcia Muller
Whodat Heist Copyright © 2020 by Julie Smith
Blue Moon Copyright © 2020 by William Kent Krueger
Aqua Vita Copyright © 2020 by Peter Robinson
The Last Hibakusha Copyright © 2020 by Naomi Hirahara
30 and Out Copyright © 2020 by Doug Allyn
The Fixer Copyright © 2020 by Alison Gaylin and Laura Lippman
Thorndike Press, a part of Gale, a Cengage Company.

ALL RIGHTS RESERVED

This is a work of fiction. Names, characters, places and incidents are either the product of the author's imagination or are used fictitiously. Any resemblance to actual persons, living or dead, businesses, companies, events or locales is entirely coincidental.
Thorndike Press® Large Print Mystery.
The text of this Large Print edition is unabridged.
Other aspects of the book may vary from the original edition.
Set in 16 pt. Plantin.

LIBRARY OF CONGRESS CIP DATA ON FILE.
CATALOGUING IN PUBLICATION FOR THIS BOOK
IS AVAILABLE FROM THE LIBRARY OF CONGRESS

ISBN-13: 978-1-4328-7914-3 (hardcover alk. paper)

Published in 2020 by arrangement with Harlequin Books S. A.

Printed in Mexico
Print Number: 01   Print Year: 2020

To All the Mystery Readers
Who Made This Volume Possible

TABLE OF CONTENTS

INTRODUCTION

This year, Mystery Writers of America celebrates its 75th anniversary.

Founded at the close of World War II, MWA began as a small association of professional writers dedicated to promoting higher regard for mystery and detective fiction, and to the principle espoused by the slogan "Crime Doesn't Pay — Enough." Over the years since, the organization has grown and expanded dramatically to include aspiring crime writers and individuals devoted to the genre, as well as professionals allied to both crime fiction and nonfiction. It currently has more than 3,000 active, associate, and affiliate members worldwide.

Each year at its annual banquet in New York City, MWA presents the Edgar Allan Poe Awards for the previous year's best adult and young adult crime fiction, true crime, reference works related to the genre, and television productions; the Raven

Award to nonwriters who have made notable contributions to the mystery genre; and other awards established in recent times such as the Ellery Queen Award, the Robert L. Fish Memorial Award, the Simon & Schuster Mary Higgins Clark Award, and the G. P. Putnam's Sons Sue Grafton Memorial Award. Also bestowed is the organization's highest honor, the Grand Master, in recognition of those authors whose body of work has been deemed significant and of consistent high quality.

Since its inception, MWA has sponsored many excellent anthologies of stories by its members. This volume commemorating its diamond milestone differs from most previous ones in that all those invited to contribute are Grand Masters, Edgar winners, or have served as MWA presidents. The authors and their honors:

Grand Master: Sue Grafton, Marcia Muller, Bill Pronzini, Margaret Maron, Carolyn Hart, Max Allan Collins, Peter Lovesey

Best Novel: Julie Smith, Margaret Maron, S. J. Rozan, William Kent Krueger

Best First Novel: Laurie R. King

Best Paperback Original: Laura Lippman, Naomi Hirahara, Meg Gardiner, Alison Gaylin

Best Short Story: Wendy Hornsby, Doug Allyn (2), Peter Robinson, S. J. Rozan

President: Margaret Maron, Sue Grafton, Laura Lippman, Lee Child, Jeffery Deaver, Meg Gardiner

Each of the nineteen stories presented here involves, directly or indirectly, an anniversary of one kind or another — wedding, birthday, law enforcement, military, sporting event, others rare and sinister. They encompass a wide range of historical and contemporary U.S. settings — New York, Chicago, New Orleans, San Francisco, Southern California, the Pacific Northwest, the Nevada desert, Iowa, northern Michigan, Texas, North Carolina — as well as London and other U.K. locales. The types of stories also differ widely: detective tales featuring prominent series characters, stories steeped in Chinese and Japanese culture, narratives of domestic intrigue, psychological suspense, dramatic irony, black humor, swift action, quiet horror — and for good measure, one with a supernatural twist and another with an appended recipe. Something, in short, for every taste in crime fiction.

It has been a privilege and a pleasure for us to serve as guest editors of *Deadly Anniversaries.* May the reader derive as much enjoyment as we have from reading (and writing) these stories.

— Marcia Muller and Bill Pronzini

■ ■ ■ ■

IF YOU WANT SOMETHING DONE RIGHT . . .

BY SUE GRAFTON

■ ■ ■ ■

Lucy Burgess waited her turn at the Rite Aid pharmacy counter. The pollen count had soared and she'd gone to the drugstore to pick up Burt's allergy medication, his bronchodilator inhaler, and a new brand of antihistamine he'd seen on TV. What a baby. Apart from his being an alcoholic and chronically unfaithful, he was becoming tedious. He was constantly misplacing his personal belongings — cell phone, car keys, glasses, wallet — making it her responsibility to locate the lost items. Really, there was no excuse for his being so disorganized. He was a high-profile divorce attorney who battled for his clients as though his life depended on it. He said that in the fight-or-flight stakes, he was all fight, which was what made him such a dangerous opponent. He claimed his stress levels were what kept him on top of his game.

His high blood pressure did actually worry

the doctors, and the asthma he'd suffered all his life was hard on him, but the rest of his ailments were ridiculous. Burt was highly suggestible, but she hadn't realized how paranoid he was until the trip to India came up. This would be their twenty-fifth wedding anniversary, and for years he'd promised her a trip to India. They'd reserved a large stateroom on an elegant cruise line that would take them from the Bay of Bengal around Cape Comorin to the Arabian Sea. Burt had set aside the time — two full weeks in August — which he hadn't done in years. She thought everything was fine, but then he'd started kicking up a fuss. First he worried about exposure to infectious diseases. Then he fretted about the filth, the vermin, tainted food, and the risk of contaminated water.

Then, just last week, he'd canceled his reservation altogether, leaving her to go by herself. What kind of anniversary celebration was that? Not that she cared. Why pay good money just to hear him complain? He was probably carving out time for his latest lady-love, but how could she call him on it when she had no concrete proof?

The most irksome consequence of his cancelation was that now, in addition to her preparations, she had to make sure he'd be comfortable on his own, which included two weeks' worth of meals, refills on all his medications, and a list of emergency numbers as long as her arm. Orderly as usual, she'd bought a slim pocket-size notebook in which she kept a running tally of all the errands she had to run. The notebook was perfect for slipping in and out of her handbag, allowing her to utilize time that would otherwise go to waste. Standing in line at the gourmet market, she worked on her "to do" list, checking off the stops she'd already made.

Bank. Check.
Drugstore. Check.

The journal was divided into two sections. The first was devoted to things to be accomplished before she left town. In the second section, she kept a running list of ways to kill Burt. She'd come up with the idea as a form of idle amusement. Imagining his demise helped her tolerate his many loathsome qualities, among them his need to always be right and his tendency toward verbal abuse. He would never lay a hand on her, but he put her down every chance he got.

Under **Possibilities**, she'd written:

19

Gun? Where to acquire?

Poison? Possible, but how to administer?

Car wreck? Also possible, but difficult given ignorance of auto mechanics. Who to consult?

She didn't write down **garrote**, because she didn't have the strength.

She and Burt had no children. She was ten years younger than he. Early on he'd lobbied for a child, but thank God she'd had the sense to say no. Turned out Burt demanded her total focus. Moody, petulant, and self-centered, he was a man who'd do anything to maintain control. She suspected infidelity was his means of tranquilizing himself, because every time he launched a new affair, his temperament improved. Suddenly, he would become kinder and more attentive, much as he'd been in recent months.

The first indication of a new dalliance was his staying late at the office, where a series of soon-to-be-divorcées paraded past his desk. These women were vulnerable. He had the power to make or break them financially, which made them oh-so-eager to suck up, so to speak. His current extramarital fling had lasted longer than usual. Burt was easily bored, so most of the women he bedded disappeared within weeks, but this liaison had gone on for months. Lucy had begun scrutinizing his phone bills, looking for a pattern of frequently called numbers. She didn't want to learn the woman's identity, because she knew from experience that once a name and face were attached, the affront would be harder to ignore.

In the interest of keeping tabs on the situation, she searched his desk drawers at home. She checked his calendar for initials and cryptic references. She steamed open the bank statements, studied his expenditures, and then made copies of his canceled checks and all his credit card bills. She kept a record of the hotel rooms, the many expensive meals out, and the flowers he lavished on his paramour. If nothing else, he'd taught her the value of documenting items for later use as ammunition. The week before, she saw that he'd made a cash withdrawal of five thousand dollars, probably to buy jewelry, his modus operandi. Lucy was relieved. Usually, the jewelry came close to the end, like a form of severance pay.

She'd assumed she was home free until she ran into Laird Geiger, their estate attorney, as she emerged from the dry cleaners that day — yet another item she could check off her list.

He'd greeted her warmly and bussed her on the cheek. They chatted amiably and were on the verge of parting when Laird said, "Oh, I nearly forgot. I ran into Burt last week and he said he needed to come in for a chat. Have him give Rachel a call and we can set something up. I gather he wants to bring his will up-to-date. Is everything okay?"

"Oh, we're fine. You know him. We're leaving on a cruise, and he wants to make sure he has all his ducks in a row. I'll deliver the message. Better yet, I'll call Rachel myself and get it on the books."

"Do that," he'd said. "I'll be out of town this next week, but Rachel can slot you in as soon as I get back."

Before he was even out of sight, Lucy could feel the chill descend. They'd had no discussion at all about their wills. Clearly, Burt was up to no good. All she needed was for him to cut her out of his estate, removing her as his executor and prime beneficiary. For the first time, she understood he must be serious about the woman, whoever she was. If talk of divorce was not far away, he'd make sure she got creamed.

That night in bed, Burt watched *CSI* while

rubbing salve on an imaginary rash. Smelling the ointment, she began to think in more concrete terms about killing him. She propped her journal against her knees, tapping her lip with her pen as she analyzed the choices.

Hit-and-run? Hard to pull off without witnesses.

Bludgeoning? Ugh. All that bone and splattered brains? No, thanks.

During a commercial, she caught Burt peering over at her. "You've had your nose stuck in that thing for weeks," he said. "What's so fascinating?"

She closed the journal, a finger on the page to save her place. "Just some ideas I had about the silent auction for the charity luncheon next year. I wasn't happy with the format."

"They suckered you into *doing* that again?"

"I insisted. Brenda was in charge this year and completely botched the event. She was all over the place, dropping the ball right and left. Pathetic. We could have made a lot more money if she'd done as I said."

He gave her the indulgent smile he used when he was systematically betraying her. "I have to hand it to you, kid. You may be a cold fish, but you're efficient as hell."

"Thank you, Burt. That means a lot to me."

Burt had the good grace to laugh while she went back to her list. **Stabbing** would be nice.

On Tuesday, she drove into Beverly Hills to Saks Fifth Avenue. At the makeup counter, she watched as a saleswoman named Marcy smoothed a drop of liquid foundation on the back of her hand. She and Marcy discussed the virtues of "Ivory Beige" versus "Medium Beige." Lucy made her selection and when she reached for her wallet, she realized her handbag was gone. For a moment, she stood perplexed. Had she set it down somewhere? Left it in the shoe department when she was buying her Ferragamos? Most certainly not. She remembered distinctly that she'd placed the bag on the glass counter near the perfume display. Someone had come along and lifted it. A wave of intense irritation swept over her as she thought how much work it would take to replace her driver's license and close all her credit card accounts. Fortunately, she'd put her car keys in her jacket pocket so at least she could get home.

Marcy called store security and in the confusion that followed, Marcy admitted with embarrassment that they'd had a rash of purse snatchers working in the store. Lucy scarcely listened because the contents of the journal had just popped into her head. She could feel dampness forming at the nape of her neck. How explicit were her notes? The only items she could remember with absolute clarity were her name, address, and phone number neatly printed on page one. Anyone finding it could read the lengthy scribbled debate about the virtues of **electrocution** versus **miter saws** and other woodworking tools. Dear god. Marcy was chattering away, apologizing for not warning her, but Lucy was intent on the possible ramifications of the theft.

The answer came soon enough. The next day, the phone rang and a man with problem adenoids introduced himself as Mr. Puckett. He told her he'd found her purse in some shrubs and he thought she might want it back. She assumed he'd swiped the bag himself, removed all the cash, and would be angling for a reward for returning the very bag he'd stolen. He didn't sound very bright, but neither did he sound sinister. She suggested they meet at the public library, where there was no danger of running into anyone in her social circle.

She waited in the reference department,

as agreed. At the first sight of him, she nearly laughed aloud. He was such a bandy-legged little jockey, he should have been wearing silks. He couldn't have weighed more than 122 pounds. He was in his fifties, his sparse hair combed straight back, widow's peak kept in check by a malodorous gel. He seemed perfectly at ease as he passed the bag across the table. She murmured a word of thanks, wondering if a twenty-dollar bill would suffice, when he pulled the journal from his pocket. "The name's Puckett," he remarked.

"So you said on the phone," she replied with all the chill she could muster.

He smiled, leaning toward her. "Mrs. Burgess, I'd cut the attitude if I was you. What you got here ain't nice. Doubtless, you'll intuit the subject matter to which I refer." He opened the journal and read a few telling lines in a theatrical tone. Two patrons at nearby tables turned to stare.

"Please keep your voice down."

He dropped into a whisper. "Excuse me. I must've forgot myself in my haste to communicate."

She held out a hand. "I'll have that now."

"Not so fast. You got a real problem here, judging by what you've wrote."

She tried to stare him down. "There's a

very simple explanation. I'm writing a play."

"You ain't writing a play."

"Well, I'm thinking about one."

"You're an amateur at this, right?"

"I don't know what you're referring to."

"You're gonna blow it *big*-time. Just my opinion as one who would know."

Voice low, she said, "Not to contradict you, Mr. Puckett, but I've done years of community service, and my planning skills are highly regarded. Once I've made up my mind to do something, I never fail."

"Mrs. B, it's dirty work whacking someone. Much trickier than puttin' on a charity lunch. Murder's a serious crime, in case you hadn't heard."

"You're a purse snatcher. You're a fine one to talk."

"Correction. You left said reticule on the counter at Saks. Thinking it was lost, I sought to return the alleged bag to its rightful owner. In casting about for some means of identifying same, I inadvertently disinterred some data that would suggest you're formulating a plan that might be expeditionary to your hubby's untimely end."

One of the two nearby library patrons gathered his belongings and moved to a table some distance away.

Lucy said, "You made copies, I'm sure."

"Strictly for my own protection. Any individual who'd ponder such acts might decide to eliminate a person like myself, who now has advanced and intimate knowledge of same. I hope you don't mind my asking, but what'd hubby do to generate such rage?"

"Why is that any of your business?"

"Because I'm in possession of certain tangible information that I'd be distressed to see fall into the wrong hands, namely his. Such an unfortunate turn of events might result in a failure to activate."

"I'm sure we can come to an understanding. I'm willing to pay you . . . within reason . . . if you'll return the journal and any copies you made."

"You misunderstand. My taking your money in return for this here would constitute the *corpus delecti* of the crime of blackmail. You're hoping for a corpus of another kind, or so I surmise."

"I wish you'd just say what you mean."

"I have a suggestion."

"I can hardly wait."

Her sarcasm seemed to go right over his head.

He said, "Keeping my remarks entirely famatory, every matrimonial association is defeasible, am I right? So why not take that route? I'm talking divorce here, in case you're not getting my drift."

"Thank you for the clarification. Divorce has a cost attached that I'd prefer not to pay. California is a community property state. Most of our assets are tied up in real estate. Burt's ruthless. If we divorce, I'll be crushed underfoot."

"So what I hear you saying is that you and him are engaged in a parcenary relationship of which you'd like to see his participation shifted to the terminus."

"Precisely. He's a drunk and he's had numerous affairs. He's also on the verge of changing his will. He had a chat with our estate attorney, who happened to mention it earlier this week. I pretended I knew what was going on, but that was the first I'd heard of it. If Burt cuts me out of his will . . ."

"Lady, I'm way ahead of you. You're hoping the turd will expire before such changes are made."

"Close enough."

"I think you might find me a valuable ancillary to your ruminations. Once we come to an agreement, you show me a picture of the man you want severated, and I'll handle it from there."

"Severated?"

"You know, like his head from his neck."

He drew a line across his throat.

"Decapitated? That's vile. I couldn't live with myself."

"I don't mean to sound misapprobative, but you're favoring a claw hammer. I seen it on your list."

"It was the only thing I could think of at the time."

"If you wouldn't take unkindly to some direction, I have at my disposal a certain pharmaceutical substance which if mixed with a certain foodstuff or perhaps inculcated into a common household product changes from inert to extremely ert. It's like a certain particle of speech that in itself may not look like much, but in conjecture with its opposite can have a deleterious effect."

"Meaning what?"

"Ingest one iota and the recipient susperates his last. The only known unction is extreme."

"If he's stricken, why wouldn't he use his cell phone to dial 9-1-1?"

"Easy. Turn off the ringer and toss it in the trash. Next question."

"Will he suffer?"

"Not that much. On the other hand, you wouldn't want to be there. This form of expiration is often accompanied by encopresis."

"Enco . . ."

". . . presis. Victim shits himself."

"I see."

"A further advantage to this toxic substance? There's no known anecdote. And the best part is this — no one will ever know. It looks entirely natural, like a sudden heart attack or a massive stroke."

"You mentioned putting this substance in food. Won't he taste it?"

"Negatory, but if it worries you, I can add a dollop to one of his personal hygiene products, like maybe his shaving gel."

"Or maybe the container of wet wipes," she said, helpfully. "He's always swabbing down the counters because he's phobic about germs."

"Now you're thinking like a champ. So what do you say? Are we in this together or are we not?"

She considered his proposal, quickly assessing the pros and cons. As crude as he was, she could see the virtue of delegating this particular job. She was a capable woman, but she wasn't at all certain she'd be good at murder. She might get rattled and betray herself. On the other hand, if Puckett was experienced and had access to an undetectable poison, she could avoid doing anything distasteful.

31

Cautiously, she said, "The police are thorough. How can you be sure the poison will defy detection?"

"Because I've seen to such situations in the past. The forensic experts can expiscate all they like. They'll never cop to this."

"And you'd do this in exchange for what?"

"Why don't we say equipotent compensation."

"Which is how much?"

"Ordinarily, we're talking five grand . . . a bargain, even if I say so myself."

"I'm sure it is, but if my husband dies —"

"Correction. *When* hubby dies . . ."

"Suppose I come under suspicion? The police will examine my bank accounts. I can't afford to show a large cash withdrawal. How would I explain?"

A flash of annoyance crossed his face. "I'm not asking for dough. Did I say a word about that? Jesus, lady. That would be unpropitious, to say the least."

She put a finger to her lips, shushing him again.

He lowered his voice. "You're an educated woman, am I right?"

"I graduated from Smith. I assume you've heard of it."

"Of course. With a common name like that? So what it ain't Harvard? It's nothin' to be ashamed of. Now me, I'm a self-educated sort."

"I never would have guessed."

"It surprises a lot of people, but it's the truth. I've been studying you. Just while we been sitting here, I'm picking up clues. You may be hoity-toity, but you're not a bad egg. You got a good life that you're just trying to protect. If hubby don't treat you right, you gotta take the situation in hand. I got no quarrel with that."

"I appreciate your support."

"So I'm thinking there's more than one woman in your position. We could make a deal on the if-come. I do for you and in exchange, you give me a referral should another housewife of your acquaintance express an interest in the process of spousal peroration."

"Like a loss leader."

"Right. I'm out the bucks on this one, but the deal will be effective at bringing in the trade."

"How do I know I can trust you?"

"How do I know I can trust *you*? Truth is I do. You know what I sense about you? You're a nice lady. I mean, aside from your desire to take a lead pipe to hubby's skull, I'd say you're a peach."

She studied him briefly. "I leave on Tues-

33

day for two weeks in India. Our anniversary trip. If you can take care of this while I'm away, I'll have the perfect alibi."

"Good move."

"So how do we proceed?"

"Simple. You have an alarm system at your place?"

"Yes, but we hardly ever use it."

"Fine. You give me a house key and the code. I already got the address off your driver's license, so I know where you live. I'll keep an eye on the place, and at some point when hubby's out, I'll let myself in and insinuate a generous serving of the you-know-what where it'll do the most good. And don't pin me down. The less you know the better. When the time comes, you want to be able to fake your genuine surprise."

"And my genuine horror and grief."

"That, too."

"Perfect. I'll give the housekeeper the time off, as well, so you won't have to worry about her." She removed the house key from her key ring and dropped it in his palm. "One more thing. How will I know when the job is done?"

"Easy. I'll leave the key underneath the doormat in front. The key ain't there, you know the job ain't been done. It's there, then all your troubles evaporate."

34

■ ■ ■ ■

For Lucy Burgess, the cruise was magical. Knowing the pesky business with Burt was finally under control, she felt lighter and freer than she had in years. She slept late, alone in the luxury of her stateroom. She made friends, sunned herself, danced, played bridge, and sat in the bar drinking pricey champagne. On the various shore excursions, she scarcely noticed the loathsome lepers and crippled children begging her for coins. She was dreaming of what awaited her when she got home: the properties, the house. She could get a dog, now that she didn't have Burt's allergies to worry about.

She did entertain the faintest whisper of uneasiness where Puckett was concerned. There was no guarantee that he would do what he said. She believed in backup plans, keeping a little something in reserve. Delegating work was all well and good, but if the other person failed to perform, you had to be prepared to step in. She pondered this for days with no clear sense of how to protect herself. Then in Goa, on the final day ashore — her silver anniversary of marriage to Burt, by happy coincidence — she

35

went on the tour of a local factory, and the answer presented itself.

On her return that Saturday, when Burt wasn't at the airport to meet her plane, she was thrilled. Wonderful! Divine! He was doubtless *d-e-a-d*. Giddy, she took a taxi to the house. Once her luggage was on the porch and the driver had pulled away, she lifted one corner of the mat. There lay her house key, glinting in the sun. *Hallelujah,* she thought. *It's over.* The deed was done.

She unlocked the door, breathing in the familiar scent of the rooms. The house felt gloriously empty. Colors seemed brighter and every surface shone. The very air seemed sweet. She made a cautious circuit, knowing the body was somewhere on the premises. She hoped he wasn't sprawled on the bedroom floor, where she'd have to work around him when she unpacked her bags. She was also hoping he hadn't been dead so long that putrefaction had set in, though they probably had cleaning services to eradicate the ooze. She found herself tiptoeing, as though playing a game of hide-and-seek, peeking around corners to make sure the coast was clear. Guest room, hall, foyer bathroom. Really, how aggravating. She was running out of rooms.

"Hey, babe. Why didn't you tell me you were getting home today?"

She whirled, shrieking.

There stood Burt, alive and well, and apparently in perfect health. In addition to looking fit, he seemed rested, probably from screwing his brains out the whole time she was gone. Her heart was pounding and she thought she'd weep from disappointment, but she had to carry on as though everything were fine.

She recovered sufficiently to fake her way through the rest of the day. Sunday came and went. She waited, but there was no sign whatever that Burt was on the brink of death. He must have spent every minute at his girlfriend's place. Clearly, he hadn't ingested or applied poison of any kind. She wondered where it was. Puckett had mentioned food, personal hygiene items, and common household products, but he hadn't said which. How could she avoid poisoning herself by mistake? He could have put the fatal dose in anything. She realized with dismay she had no way of reaching him. Originally, he'd called her — and had neglected to give her a contact number in return. Whatever he'd done, wherever he'd put the poison, she was now as vulnerable as Burt.

When two more days passed and they continued to coexist, her anxiety began to mount. Burt showered and shaved, slapped cologne on his face, and went merrily off to work. When he came home, he'd fix himself a drink while she prepared dinner as she usually did. While his appetite was hearty, she couldn't eat a thing. The only products she used were those she removed from her own suitcases, sitting in the bedroom still packed and kept under lock and key. She bathed with newly opened bars of soap and ate all her breakfasts and lunches out. She avoided room fresheners, laundry soap, and scouring cleanser, even though the sinks were turning gray. No shampoo, conditioner, or styling spray for her. She made certain no toothpaste, dental floss, or mouthwash crossed her lips.

Meanwhile, Burt was in the best of spirits. Lucy was mystified. What if he'd already been exposed to the poison and somehow managed to avoid harm? Maybe he was naturally immune to whatever it was. Occasionally, she thought he might be toying with her. He'd start to eat a handful of nuts, and then change his mind. Or he'd fix himself a sandwich and end up throwing it in the trash. The suspense was getting on her nerves.

By the weekend she decided it was time to move on to Plan B.

Saturday night, the two retired early. Lucy read the paper, catching up on the news while Burt lay beside her, watching one of his boring TV shows. She noticed him wincing as he cleared his throat. "Scratchy. I think I'm coming down with a cold."

"Poor you," she said.

"Yeah, poor me. There's all kinds of shit going around these days. Client came in yesterday and coughed all over me. Office was a cesspool of germs. I sprayed everything as soon as she left."

Lucy snapped the paper, folding it back so she could check the weather page. "Highs in the nineties tomorrow. How unpleasant is that?"

"What's the pollen count?"

"Way up," she said.

He looked over at her. "They're talking weeds?"

"Weeds and grass. Molds are moderate, but trees are off the charts."

"Shit." He got out of bed and padded barefoot into the bathroom where she heard him opening the medicine cabinet. Lucy rolled her eyes.

Sunday morning, Lucy went into the big

39

walk-in closet and got out her walking shoes. She couldn't bear it. She had to leave the house or she'd go stark raving mad. She was beginning to regret the agreement she'd made with Puckett, which was harebrained at best. The man was a moron. She took off her robe and was pulling on her sweats when Burt stuck his head in. "So, how about Sunday brunch? I thought you could rustle up some bacon, eggs, and toast."

"I was just going for a walk."

"Come on. Indulge me. It'll be just like the old days. I'll walk with you afterward. How's that for a deal?"

She shoved her feet down into her running shoes and laced them, then followed him down the stairs. His proposal was the first nice thing he'd come up with in recent memory. Eggs must be safe. Surely, Puckett hadn't used osmosis to get poison through the shells. She didn't give him credit for the imagination it would take to inject a dose into the hermetically sealed package of bacon they'd had for a month. She made a pot of coffee. She poured Burt a glass of orange juice while he sanitized his hands and downed his echinacea. For once, his fussiness seemed more eccentric than annoying. She had quirks that probably annoyed him no end. She cooked his bacon, eggs, and toast. She opened a jar of his favorite strawberry jam and spooned it into a dish.

She put his plate in front of him, and then sat across the table watching as he read the Sunday paper and wolfed down his meal without saying a word. He was still in his robe and pajamas. He didn't shave on Sundays so he was disheveled — unusual for him.

He looked up, noticing for the first time she wasn't joining him. "You're not having anything?"

"I'm not hungry."

"Something wrong with you? You've hardly touched a bite since you've been home."

"I haven't been feeling well. My digestion's off. I'll fix something for myself later on."

He wiped his mouth and crumpled the paper napkin as he pushed his plate aside. "You picked up a bug. I hear some parasites can live in your guts for life. I warned you about that. You better have the doc run some tests."

Lucy took his dirty dishes and put them in the sink. She ran water, but she couldn't bring herself to add detergent, which might be the agent Puckett had selected to deliver the you-know-what. On second thought, she added detergent. No danger there. Puckett must have known Burt had never washed a dish in his life. Behind her, she heard him snicker. She assumed he was reading the funnies, but when she turned she saw him looking at her with barely suppressed mirth. She turned off the water. "What's so funny?"

"Nothing," he said solemnly, and then cracked up again. "No, wait. This is rich. This is killing me. Maybe it's time to end your misery."

"Misery?"

It took him a minute to compose himself. Finally, he took out a handkerchief and mopped his eyes. "Whew. I didn't mean to lose it there. I just couldn't help myself. This past Friday, I ran into a pal of yours, who said to tell you hello."

"Oh? And who was that?"

"A fellow named Puckett. He says the two of you had a meeting before you left town." Burt was making an effort to keep a straight face.

Lucy frowned. "The name doesn't ring a bell." She leaned her backside against the counter and crossed her arms, keeping her distance from him. "How do you know him?"

42

"He was referred by one of the other attorneys in the firm. I said I needed a little job done and his name came up."

"What sort of job?"

Burt left her hanging for a moment while a smile played across his lips. "Let's put our cards on the table for a change, okay? Just this once."

"Fine. Go ahead. I'm fascinated." In truth, she felt a touch of uneasiness settle in her gut.

"I knew you were up to something so I paid this guy Puckett five thousand bucks to steal your purse and hand it over to me. You might have noticed the cash withdrawal when you were snooping in my desk."

"I don't know what you're talking about."

"I was curious why you were so engrossed in that journal of yours. Every time I turned around, you were scribbling away."

"That's how I'm able to stay organized. You know how I am."

"Come on, Luce. I read it from beginning to end. You were planning to have me iced. Puckett spilled the beans about the deal you made."

"Burt, I'd never heard of this Puckett fellow until you mentioned him just now."

"Get off it. The cat is officially out of the bag. He left the key under the doormat like he said he would. When you got home from the cruise, you thought I was dead. I watched you creep around the house with me ten steps behind. You should have seen the look on your face when you turned around and spotted me. You screamed like you'd seen a ghost."

Lucy smiled politely. The joke was always on her. She wanted to protest, but she couldn't see the point.

"You want to know how I survived?" He began to laugh again, so tickled with himself he started to snort. "The guy's an actor. He does improv. There isn't any poison. That was all bullshit." On he went, chortling to himself while she stared, her smile fading. "Sorry, but I got such a kick out of watching you this past week. You were so worried about poison you wouldn't sit down on the toilet seat. You had to squat to pee."

Lucy faltered. "An actor?"

"Get a clue. With all that phony lingo, you didn't pick up on it? Nobody talks that way. I told him to play it straight, but he insisted. Guess he fooled you anyway, huh."

"Oh, Burt. It's not funny."

"You know what your problem is? You have no sense of humor. God, you're gullible. It really cracks me up. Hook, line, and sinker, you swallowed every bit of it."

She turned back to the sink and washed his plate. Her hands shook badly and as she moved the plate to the draining rack, it slipped out of her hand and shattered on the floor.

"Goddamn it!" She leaned her hands on the counter. "Jesus, Burt. You should have told me before."

"Well, you don't have to get *mad*. It was a prank, okay?"

She returned to the breakfast table and sat down. "There's something I have to confess."

"Great. I'm all ears."

Lucy put a trembling hand against her lips, then placed it palm down on the table. "You know how particular I am, how I hate to delegate . . ."

"Jesus, you're telling me? You're a pain in the ass."

"I wasn't sure I could trust Puckett so I came up with a backup plan . . ."

"What's wrong with electrocution? Drop a radio in the bathtub. I liked that."

She leaned forward, clasping his hands in hers. "Don't make jokes. We're in serious trouble here. I thought you were having an affair."

"Nah. The bimbo? I dropped her."

Lucy studied his face with a worried gaze.

"But you told Laird you wanted to rewrite your will."

"Yours, too. It's been ten years since we signed those things. You think our financial situation hasn't changed?"

"Why didn't you tell me? You should have said something at the time."

"Gee, sorry. I didn't realize it was such a big deal."

Lucy sank to her knees beside him. "Listen. You have to trust me. We need to get you to a hospital . . ."

"What for?"

"You need medical attention."

"No, I don't. Are you kidding?"

She shook her head, her voice barely audible. "When I was in Goa the last day on shore, we took a tour of a castor bean processing plant. There's a poison called ricin that's made from the leftover waste. I bought some on the street."

"Ricin? Perfect. I never heard of it."

"I'd never heard of it either so I did a bit of research as soon as I got home. Do you remember that Bulgarian journalist who died in London after he was jabbed in the leg by an umbrella tip?"

"Sure. He turned out to be a spy, offed by the other side."

"Ricin was what killed him. A puncture

46

wound is just one way of delivering a fatal dose. You can also dissolve it in liquid or add it to food. If the ricin's inhaled, it takes longer, maybe twelve hours or so before the symptoms appear. After that, it's quick."

He rolled his hand to hurry her along, as though she were telling a joke and he was impatient for the punch line.

"I'm sorry. Honestly. I planned on leaving the house early, but then you insisted on breakfast and I realized I'd made a mistake. If we can get to the ER, you still have a chance."

He reared back in disbelief. "I can't go anywhere. I'm in my robe."

"You're not hearing me. I'm trying to help you."

Burt studied her, picking up the word she'd used a couple of sentences before. "What do you mean, if it's inhaled? What's that got to do with it?"

"Don't you remember? Last night you asked if the pollen count was high. I said yes and you went straight to the medicine cabinet and took your inhaler out. You sniffed five or six times. I could hear you from the bedroom, even with the TV on."

He tried to laugh, and then stopped. "Seriously. You put poison in my inhaler?"

Lucy wouldn't meet his gaze. "How was I

supposed to know you and Puckett were in cahoots? He said he'd take care of it. I was only being thorough in case he didn't follow through."

"I don't believe you."

"Shit. You're an idiot. I knew you wouldn't take my word for it so I got on the internet and printed out the information from the CDC." She got up and crossed to the planning center, where she took a folded paper from her Day-timer. She flattened it on the table and pushed it over to him.

"You're lying. I feel fine. There's nothing wrong with me."

"Let's hope. This doesn't really specify how much poison you have to use so maybe you're okay."

Burt's face began to flush as his eyes traced the lines of print. It was clear her message had sunk home as he was now short of breath. "For god's sake, quit yammering and dial 9-1-1."

"I can get you to the ER quicker if we take my car. You can read that on the way."

She went to the hall closet and pulled out a coat that she handed him as she passed him. She grabbed her handbag and her car keys and opened the door to the garage.

"I hope you know what you're talking about. I go traipsing in there when nothing's wrong, I'll look like an idiot."

"Oh, believe me. There's something wrong with you."

She activated the garage door and slipped into her Mercedes on the driver's side. Burt paused to close the kitchen door behind him. He'd pulled the coat on over his pajamas and he was buttoning it in haste. She started the car, revving the engine in frustration. "Jesus, would you get in!"

He let himself into the car on the passenger side, the information from the CDC in hand. Perspiration had appeared on his face like a fine mist. He lifted one shoulder, using his coat sleeve to dab at the sheen. His fingers made damp spots on the paper. He glanced down at it. "Symptom number two — excessive sweating." His look full of pleading. "But why would you do this to me?"

Lucy eased through the traffic light at the intersection, and then hit the freeway on-ramp and floored it. "You set this in motion. It wasn't me. Laird told me you were going to change your will. This was all I could think to do. It's only two more exits."

"What if I don't make it? You'll end up in jail. They'll run a toxicology report. Don't you know they test for shit like this?"

Lucy changed lanes abruptly, causing Burt

to brace himself against the dashboard. He yelped as the vehicle next to them swerved just in time. "Christ! Slow down. You're going to kill us. Not that you'd care."

"Would you stop blaming me? I told you I didn't meant to do it."

"Suppose you never told me. Suppose I just died. How'd you expect to get away with it?"

Lucy's tone was reluctant. "Ricin's unusual. I knew it wouldn't show up on a routine screening panel. Anyway, why would it even occur to them? With your history of hypertension, I figured it would look like a heart attack."

"Jesus, Luce. What else do I have to look forward to?" His gaze dropped back to the page. "After the heavy sweating and the respiratory distress, the victim develops a blue cast to the skin." He tilted the rearview mirror so he could see himself. "I'm not blue. Do I look blue to you?"

She glanced at him quickly. "Not that much, really. You're not in pain?"

"No."

"Good. That's a good sign. I think we're okay. When we get there, I'll tell them . . . well, I don't know what I'll tell them, but I'll make sure you get the antidote."

"What a pal." He placed a hand against

his shoulder and massaged his arm. His breathing was heavy and had a raspy sound. "I don't know how to say this but something's going on. Feels like I got an elephant sitting on my chest."

"Burt, I'm so sorry. I know it was horrible, but you really gave me no choice." She looked at him. Sweat trickled down his face, soaking his shirt collar. Two wide half-moons of dampness had appeared underneath his arms.

He began to pack his pockets. "Where's my cell phone? I'll call and tell 'em that we're on our way."

"Your cell phone? Puckett said I should put it on vibrate and throw it in the trash."

He was gasping. He swallowed hard, his gaze turning inward as he struggled with the urge to heave. He used his handkerchief to mop his face. He leaned heavily against the car door, his breathing labored. "Pull over here, I'm going to be sick."

"Hang on. Just hang on. We're almost there."

"Open the window . . ."

She fumbled for the window control on her side and lowered the window, as grateful as he was for the chilly stream of fresh air.

"Luce . . ." He held out his left hand.

51

She reached across the front seat, grabbed his hand, and then quickly released it. "You're all clammy," she said with distaste. Burt was fading before her very eyes.

By the time she pulled into the receiving area at the ER, he was breathing his last. She parked under the ER overhang, prepared, in a moment, to honk her horn, summoning help.

Burt was slumped against the car door. Lucy watched the light drain out of his face.

"Burt?"

Burt was beyond hearing. He gasped once in agony, and then ceased to breathe.

She glanced up as the doors swung open, and a doctor and two orderlies emerged at a dead run. She leaned closer. "Hey, Burt? Talk about gullible — try *this* on for size. You can't buy ricin in Goa or anywhere else. You did it to yourself, you freakin' hypochondriac."

By the time the orderlies snatched open the car door, she was sobbing inconsolably.

■ ■ ■ ■

Ten Years On

BY LAURIE R. KING

■ ■ ■ ■

April 1925, Sussex
A turbaned Sikh with a full beard is an impressive sight, particularly when the gentleman in question takes up most of one's doorway.

"*Sat sri a* —" I caught myself: Why give a friendly greeting to an invader? "Oh, for heaven's sake, what do *you* want?"

Looking back, I was probably more abrupt than he'd been expecting. I was also considerably more female and far less burdened by years. But then, he wasn't what I'd expected to find in my doorway at that hour, either. And considering my degree of irritability that particular day, when an anniversary hadn't gone exactly as I had intended, he was fortunate I hadn't greeted him with a bucket of thrown water. Or a shotgun.

My morning's vexation, already present when I first opened my eyes, had been compounded by my belated discovery of an article in the previous day's paper. I'd spent the day driving down from Oxford via London, reaching Sussex too bleary-eyed for newsprint. By the time I saw the offending story, the sun was up and it was too late to make my escape.

It was a familiar problem, set off every time a paper, local or national, let drop a suggestion of where Sherlock Holmes was to be found. Would-be clients emerged from the crevices like wood lice on a wet day. And the case in the article had involved an aristocratic family, which only made matters worse.

The first fist on the door caught me spreading butter on my breakfast toast. At the second, I was dripping onto the bath mat. My impatience at this, the day's third intruder, might have made a lesser man take a step back, but the Sikhs are a race of warriors, and this one was not about to be driven off by an apparently unarmed English female, not without a fight. "Madam, I have come in search of the detective."

"You and half of Sussex."

"I beg your pardon?"

"You want a detective? Well, you've found one. What can *I* do for you?"

The dark eyes studied me with care, as if

to confirm that despite my short hair and trousers, I was not in fact a male of the species. I waited for his expression to become patronising, or simply confused. Instead, he surprised me by plunging his hand into the canvas messenger pouch slung over his shoulder and pulling out a folded piece of paper, which he held out for me to take.

It was a rough hand-drawn map: the dip and curve of coastline, a squiggle of river, the line of the coastal road from Seaford to Eastbourne, a loop of lesser road around Beachy Head, and an X for our small villa.

No names, no words on the page.

"Yes, that's us. But my husband isn't home. Neither is the housekeeper, who's gone up to Lewes for the day, so I get to answer the door. And because I didn't know that accursed article was coming out, I didn't even keep my farm manager here to wield the dogs. Oh Lord." I'd just spotted another pair of figures past his sturdy shoulders, turning down the drive from the road.

The Indian gent's face had grown increasingly bewildered as I spoke, but at this final exclamation, he turned and followed my gaze. "These are not friends?" he asked.

"Absolutely not. By God, I'm going to murder that newspaper —"

My grumbles were cut off as the man threw back his shoulders and drew his *kirpan* from its sheath, holding it aloft into the morning sun.

The *kirpan,* one of the five required articles of all Sikhs, is a most vicious-looking dagger even in its shorter, modern variation, a twist of gleaming steel all too suggestive of a disembowelling thrust. Certainly it impressed my next set of invaders. They came to an abrupt halt. After a moment, the turbaned head before me moved slowly: first right, then left, and right again.

The two looked at each other, and reversed course down the drive.

The Sikh put away the foot-long dagger, gave a quick flick of the wrist to drop his steel bangle — the *kara* is another of the five requirements — back into place, and turned to face me.

"Well," I said. "I suppose for that you deserve a cup of tea."

I installed my guest in front of the fireplace, where the morning flames had died away but the warmth persisted. He rose when I came in with the tray, but after a glance at his shoes, I asked what he would like to eat.

"Tea is sufficient, thank you."

"You must be hungry. You've walked from

the Seaford station," I pointed out.

"How do you know where I come from?"

"That rough paper could only come from the railway station. And your shoes, which were polished this morning, are dusty now. I'll bring you some bread and cheese." I collected them on a tray. Also some oranges. And a bowl of some walnuts that did not look too stale.

He rose again when I came back, and did not sit until I had.

"Look, Mr — Singh, is it?"

He dropped the bread roll he had just taken from the plate and jumped to his feet yet again. "Anik Singh, madam, at your service."

I held out a hand, which he took so cautiously, I wondered if he'd ever shaken hands with a woman. "Mary Russell, at yours. Please sit. And eat. But honestly, if you're looking for my husband, he may not be back for a day or two." *Which is just fine,* I thought. *It's not as if I'd been asking him for* — "If you want to leave a note, I'll give it to him when he returns."

"But, madam, you said — did you not? — that you were a detective?"

"I . . . yes. Among other things, I am that."

"And a detective is what I need."

With that, the Indian gentleman had my

59

attention. The idea that detectives were interchangeable — that he thought *a* detective was every bit as good as *The* Detective — touched both my sense of humour and my dented self-esteem. I cleared my throat.

"I see. Well, I'm not sure what I can do for you, but how about telling me what your problem is, and I'll see if I can find someone to help you."

I poured tea. He stirred the sugar in his, and sat back with his cup.

"Miss Russell, what do you know of the Brighton Pavilion?"

"The Royal Pavilion? Not much. George IV hired John Nash to turn a pleasant building into a mock-Mughal palace, which he then stuffed full of chinoiserie. When Victoria took the throne, she couldn't bear the place, and forced the city of Brighton to buy it. They used it for balls and exhibitions until the War, when it became . . ."

Ah: the penny dropped.

"A hospital for wounded Indian soldiers, yes."

A remarkably well-equipped hospital, as I recalled, with multiple kitchens, many subcastes of servants, and various places of worship, all of which were geared to the needs of specific Indian subgroups. The Sepoy Rebellion might have taken place well back in Victoria's era, but the memory of it had left the British government, and especially the army, extremely wary of any faint whiff of religious offence to subcontinental soldiers — who, in the early months of the Great War, had made up a third of all Britain's troops. "But that was only for a year or so, wasn't it?"

"Yes. Your European winter killed so many of my countrymen, the next autumn we were moved to warmer Fronts — we in the infantry, at any rate — to face trials other than frostbite. After that, the Pavilion became a rehabilitation hospital."

"But it's been returned to the city, I think. Four or five years ago?"

"Yes. No doubt as worn as the rest of us by its long years of war work."

I eyed Mr Singh. A man in his fifties, who walked with the faint limp of an old injury, was sure to have seen active service.

"Were you there? In the Pavilion hospital?"

"I was among the first, in the early weeks of 1915. An English shell went astray and burst among us. One minute I was shivering and staring out across No Man's Land — and when I woke, some days later, I was gazing up at crystal chandeliers and gilded dragons." I gave a cough of laughter, and his bearded face crinkled into a warm smile.

"I assumed at first that I had died and gone to some Christian heaven, until I began to feel my leg."

"So why do you require the help of a detective, Mr Singh?"

"Miss Russell, do you remember what took place ten years ago last month?"

Did he imagine I might be too young for the War's events to be seared onto my mind? True, I had been preoccupied in March 1915 — fifteen years old, a recent orphan, newly arrived in Sussex — but the headlines would never fade in my mind's eye.

"Neuve Chapelle." I could feel the expression of distaste on my face as I said the words. The Battle of Neuve Chapelle was Britain's first deliberately mapped-out offensive of the seven-month-old war, with detailed aeroplane reconnaissance and a tightly planned sequence of bombardment followed by assault. It would be a paradigm for a new and terrifying kind of warfare — a paradigm, too, for how the sacrifice of the troops would be wasted by the incompetence of officers far behind the front line. The big guns had indeed sent the Germans for cover. The troops had indeed managed to push all the way to the German lines — only to have the attack flounder into chaos and bloody failure when the artillery ran out of shells, the field telephones broke down, and Command's insistence that troops wait for direct orders gave the Germans time to bring up guns of their own.

And as I remembered, nearly half the troops in that attack had been Indian.

"I was just too late to fight in Neuve Chapelle," said my visitor. "I was healed, and received my orders to return to the Front in the third week of March. Two days before I was to go, I passed through the room of new arrivals and heard my brother's voice."

"Your brother was also a soldier?"

"He was. A gentle boy, four years younger than I, and yet he joined the Garhwal Rifles as soon as his beard had grown. Men of my family have borne arms for generations. Mani and I — his name was Manvir — were in the same company nearly the whole time. For fifteen years, we marched together across the north of India, serving the King. And when the Austrian Archduke was killed, they sent us to France. Mani and I reached there in late September. Both of us came down with pneumonia in November, and spent two weeks in a field hospital. When we returned to the lines, we two fought at each other's shoulder and slept at each other's side until the shell landed on me in the second week of January.

"As I said, this was before Neuve Chapelle, but I have talked with men who were at that battle. I know that we began to drop shells into the German lines as soon as it was light enough to see. Thousands of shells from our field guns — a wall of artillery — turning the German wire into an expanse of mud. After precisely thirty-five minutes, the guns went silent and our brigade fixed bayonets to go up the ladders.

"If I know my brother, he would have been one of the first over the top. Once there, the men were as much slowed by the mud as they were speeded by the destruction of the wire, permitting the Germans to retrieve some of their Maxim guns from the debris and get them working. My brother took three bullets before he stayed down. All three were in his front: he did not turn away.

"The two men I talked with said they were surprised that he had survived the trip to the field hospital. But he survived, long enough for the doctors to decide that he should be shipped to Brighton. He lived to reach there, too — although by then, fever had set in. When I heard his voice, he was raving, and did not know me. When I left for the Front two days later, he was still burning with fever. And yet he lived, at least for a time. Many months later, our mother wrote me to say that a field postcard had arrived from Brighton with the message that Mani had been wounded but was recovering. Some kind soul had added a note that his hand was injured and he was fighting an infection, but that he would write when he could hold a pen. Its date was early April. And that was the last we heard, until the telegram came in the beginning of July to say he was gone."

"I'm so sorry."

"Such is war," he said. "In another world, my brother might have been an artist, the father to many sons. But in this world, Mani was proud to fight for his King." He reached into his breast pocket for his notecase, taking from it the photograph of a young man in uniform: slim, dark, bearded (of course) and blessed with shining eyes and eyelashes a cinema star would kill for. I dutifully studied it, then handed it back.

"And yet, you require a detective." Sad as it might be, and interesting in the abstract — something had brought him here, and someone had drawn him a map to find us.

"Mani is dead." He carefully slid the photograph away. "This I have known for nearly ten years. And yet, only recently did

I learn that his death was not as immediate as we thought. When the telegram came, we assumed that it had simply been delayed. Administrative details for Indian troops were not always handled as . . . scrupulously as for white soldiers." There was no bitterness in his voice, merely experience. "And yet, when I came here and asked to see the hospital records, all I found was a brief notation that said, Died of wounds. Not from the spring, but dated June 14."

"Lingering deaths were all too common."

"And so I thought. Until we received this." He bent down for the canvas haversack he'd left on the carpet, taking out a much-travelled cardboard box some fifteen inches by four. The twine around it was new. The front bore English stamps and was addressed, in capital letters, to an army brigade headquarters in India. There was no return address.

I undid the twine and found inside some scrunched-up brown paper padding, on top of which lay a square of quality stationery, folded, with the message:

PLEASE RETURN TO THE FAMILY OF
RIFLEMAN MANVEER SINGH.

I held up the page, and saw that its upper

66

edge had been trimmed away with a pair of short, sharp scissors. The sender did not care to include a home address.

At the centre of the packing material was a knife, a twin to the one Mr Singh had used to chase away the would-be clients: smooth wooden handle with a decorative silver end, encased in a slim, curved leather sheath also tipped in silver. When he laid it beside our teacups on the table, I saw that the leather was far from new, dark with both use and stains.

"May I?" I asked.

"Of course."

When I picked the scabbard up, using my left hand, my fingers came down atop the four darkest spots on its back side. I slid the *kirpan* out. The steel blade was clean and smelled faintly of oil, its cutting side razor sharp. It was also beautiful, in a deadly sort of way, with a complex arabesque etched into the steel near the guard. That design was a part of the manufacture. The blade's other carving was not.

I bent over the weapon to study the marks. Beginning where the blade's point entered its vicious upturn, an amateur hand had carved a series of brief phrases into the steel, using a rounded alphabet descending from horizontal lines.

"This is writing," I said. "Sanskrit?"

"Gurmukhi. My little brother was a romantic. He wished his *kirpan* to bear a record of every battle in which he had fought. Beginning with a duel of honour, one might call it, when he was thirteen years old." He reached out to touch the roughest, faintest words near the tip. "That childhood tussle is represented by the word for *nose,* to commemorate how he'd bloodied his enemy's. The next line says *lathi.* That marks Mani's first active service in the army, when we had to charge a crowd with our batons drawn. But the last one is what brought me here, from India." He laid his finger next to the tenth scratched phrase, close to the knife's guard. "That one you would translate as *three bullets.*"

I looked at him, then carried the weapon over to the window, where it was bright despite the gathering clouds. I dug around in the desk drawer for the big looking glass, and held it above the writing. Considering that proper engraving tools would have been as thin on the ground in the Western Front as they were on the Northwest Frontier, the scratched letters were remarkably clear and controlled — even the last one. And all had been made by the same hand.

I gazed out at the garden, thinking. Ten

years. Ten years ago, my own life had changed, although I would not know it for a time. Not that meeting a man on a barren hillside was comparable to charging, bayonets drawn, toward the German lines, but . . . Ten years ago, for both events.

I smiled wryly down at the artifact in my hand. *Don't be an idiot, Russell.*

Back at the fireplace, I returned the blade cautiously to its scabbard and laid it on the packing.

"I agree, it looks as though your brother lived long enough — and was fit enough — to add Neuve Chapelle to his *kirpan.* But what do you expect me to do?"

The dark eyes blinked in surprise. "I need to know what happened. Why my brother lived for some weeks, yet did not write. Why he was recovering, yet then he died." I studied his face. The embers whispered. And after a minute, Mr Singh slumped back into his chair. "You will not help me. I knew it was unlikely. I merely did not wish —"

"Oh no," I said. "You misunderstand. I will find out what happened, if you truly want."

"Why would I not?"

I could think of any number of reasons. "Not all mysteries have comfortable solutions."

His smile was that of a soldier who has lived with loss too long to remember its beginning. "There is a hole in my life where my brother was," he said gently. "If it can be filled, it must be."

"I'd like —" But my wishes went both unvoiced and unmet. The clatter of the doorbell came just as a face peered around the corner of the bow window, trying to see inside.

I shot to my feet with an oath; the startled soldier came upright an instant later. "Where are you staying?" I demanded.

"I have not yet —"

"Never mind. Mrs Hudson — the housekeeper — she'll be home in an hour or so. Tell her I said to put you in the guest room. Patrick will go for your things, which I'm assuming you left at the station? I shall be back when I have news. No, you can't come with me — that's really not possible. If you want to help, perhaps you could hold this current batch of invaders in place while I make my escape?"

A quick dash upstairs gave me a change of clothing and my still-packed valise. As I trotted back down, I heard my Sepoy troop puzzling over the demands of the people on my doorstep — two of them German, by the sound of it. To my amusement, his

English had deteriorated mightily in the past five minutes.

"Oah, verry sorry," he said, wagging his turban back and forth like a pantomime Indian. "Please, you look for the home of who?"

"Not home, *Holmes,*" the irritated voice enunciated. "*Sherlock* Holmes. Does he live here or not?"

"Shairlock Holmes? The man of the hound story and the pipe? Is he a real man, then? But why would you think he lives here?"

I slipped down the hallway to the study, then out of its window to the ground. The trio at the door heard the car too late to intercept me, and the determined-looking young man marching through East Dean cast me not a glance. I will admit to a degree of satisfaction as the first drops splashed against my windscreen a minute later: every would-be client was going to be very wet by the time they reached the shelter of the village inn.

I drove through Seaford and along the coast to Brighton, scarcely aware of the chalk Downs to my right or the waves to my left.

It had been sunny, ten years ago yesterday. I remembered everything about that day, every vivid detail. All along the coastline, one could hear the rumble of guns from the distant Front. I had been walking with my nose in a book, only to literally stumble across the man who would change my life. Sherlock Holmes: teacher, partner, and for the last four years, husband. A man no less maddening now than he'd been a decade ago, when he'd looked down his long nose at me from his seat on the ground, to deliver a cool and dismissive insult.

On the one hand, does an anniversary matter? Of course not: one day is like another, merely a square on a calendar. And yet, we humans are issued a limited number of days in our lives, and some resonate more than others. Some days — some anniversaries — require at least a *degree* of recognition. More than a puzzled look after a wife's protest, when her teacher-partner-husband suggests that she drop him in London to finish a touch of research rather than —

I tore my thoughts away from that spiral, and scolded my self-centred preoccupations. *A young soldier was horribly wounded in a foreign land, leaving his family bereft, Russell. Kindly keep some perspective on the matter at hand.*

I needed to start with the Pavilion and its brief time as a home for wounded Indian soldiers. Of course, there were the hospital records that Mr Singh had consulted, no doubt composed of endless shelves and cabinets filled with dusty, ill-organised, and often illegible file folders.

In search of a shortcut to save me from the archives, I parked on a wet side street and put up my umbrella, approaching the Royal Pavilion from the south. John Nash's unlikely domes and minarets rose up above the workaday city traffic like something conjured by one of its patients' fever dreams — or like a display of upright spindles in a yarn shop window. What must an actual citizen of India make of this gallimaufry of elements? And this was only the exterior.

As the new southern gate came into view (presented four or five years before by the Maharaja of Patiala, a man of such excellent manners that he'd refrained from bursting into laughter when he laid eyes upon the Pavilion) I noticed a grocer's lorry idling nearby, with several men off-loading crates and canvas-draped trays. Some kind of an event, no doubt. Which gave me an idea.

I stood out of the drizzle to watch for a bit, until I had my man: late fifties, neither labourer nor giver-of-commands, but clearly regarded as an authority both by those doing the off-loading and by the man in charge of the event itself. When the lorry had finished and the sleek-haired figure in the good suit had trailed after the supplies, fussing all the time, the man I'd been watching stepped under the portico to light a cigarette. I moved over to join him.

"Good morning," I said. "Oh heavens, don't let me interrupt your hard-earned break. I was hoping the rain would let up and I could have a wander through the gardens."

"Might not be for a bit, miss," he said.

"Looks like they're having a party."

"Mayor's got a dinner of some kind. Daughter's engagement, I think they said."

"A fine place for it."

"That it is."

"You know, I should ask — have you worked here for a while? That is, I don't suppose you were here when it was the Indian hospital, were you?"

His reply told me I'd judged his amused and proprietary expression correctly: "That I was, miss. Started in the garden here the month the Clock Tower was finished, in time for the Queen's Golden Jubilee. Eighteen eighty-seven that was," he provided, a nod to my youth. "Since then I've done pretty much every job there is."

"Oh good! I'm looking for some of the nurses who were here at that time. Writing an article on, er, women in wartime, you know?" It was an excuse that matched my appearance and my educated accent, and gave him a reason to indulge in airing his memories.

"And a fine lot they were, too," he said. "Though in truth, the girls weren't here for more than a few weeks."

"No?"

"Some idiocy in the papers. The *Mail,* it was, had a picture of some of 'em next to a patient here, stirred up talk about white girls nursing brown men. So they got the younger girls out of here as soon as they could, and even the married ones they replaced with men by the summer."

Clearly, I'd had other things on my mind that spring than the innuendo campaigns of the sensational press.

"Having spent some time as a VAD myself, I can't say the colour of the patient's skin made much of a difference to me. In any event, perhaps you remember one or two of the older ones, who stayed on?"

"You want Mrs Straub," he said promptly. Perhaps too promptly?

"Do I?"

"Well, not sure *want* is the word, but if you can get on her good side, she can tell you anything you need to know."

"A bit of a dragon, I take it?"

"Tigress, maybe. She can be . . . protective." The twinkle in his eyes suggested that he'd like to watch me get anything out of the woman.

"Since I have no interest in stirring up any tabloid rubbish, I'm sure we shall get on just fine. Any idea where I might find her?"

"Last I heard she was at the Victoria in Lewes."

"Lovely. And have you any suggestions? For 'getting on her good side'?"

"Not a one," he said, with no sign of regret.

"Then I shall have to try honesty," I replied. "Thank you for your help, and perhaps you could lift a glass to my luck, later tonight." So saying, I pressed a coin into his palm and opened up my umbrella.

I figured that "Victoria" meant the Lewes hospital rather than the tearoom, and so it proved. She was even on duty. Unfortunately, the judgment of *tigress* proved all too apt.

Beryl Straub: sturdy, scrubbed, and stern, fixed me with an iron gaze through steel spectacle frames, and waited for me to convince her of my need.

Mrs Straub was the Victoria's head nurse.

I had sat in a cool, damp office waiting for her to return from her duties in the wards, and had been greeted by a shake of the hand and the news that she could only spare me five minutes.

"Then I won't waste any of your time. I was told that you were a nurse at the Pavilion when it first began to take in the Indian soldiers."

"December 1914, that's right."

"One of those early patients came to me recently with a problem."

"Yes?"

"Anik Singh, is his name." She did not react. Why would she, after all these years? "I don't imagine you remember him, he was blown —"

"He was in a trench when a shell went off. Among the first intake of patients. I remember him."

"Ah, good. He's fine, by the way. A minor limp, is all."

She waited.

"The problem isn't about him, but his brother. Manvir Singh was wounded in March, 1915, in the battle of Neuve Chapelle. He arrived in Brighton a week or so later. A field postcard was sent home indicating that he'd been wounded and was being cared for. Then in late June or early

July, a death notice was sent out, and his family assumed that he had lost a slow and lingering fight. However, recently they have had . . . a further communication. Anonymous, unfortunately. It suggested that Manvir recovered, for a time — that he was conscious and active before his eventual death."

She waited.

"I know his wounds had become infected before he reached Brighton, and infections have a way of coming back. Or he could have needed surgery, and failed to survive that. But the family wishes to know. And I thought you might perhaps be able to help."

"With . . . ?"

I studied her face. It revealed nothing, very determinedly.

"Information about the young man's death. About his final weeks. Perhaps about the anonymous correspondent." Her face did not shift a hairbreadth, and yet I could have sworn there was a reaction, deep down.

Time to wait her out. For thirty seconds, her mask held. Then a slight change of focus in her eyes betrayed that her thoughts had gone inward. Another thirty seconds . . .

But she glanced at the clock, and stood. "I'm sorry, miss, I'm needed in —"

I made my voice hard. "Mrs Straub, if I

need to, I'm quite capable of digging through the hospital records to find the names of all the nurses on duty that spring, and harassing them for what they know. Manvir Singh gave his life for this country. His family deserves to know how."

Her hand continued to show me the door. However, in the hallway, she paused. "Miss — Russell, was it? My day ends at six o'clock. Come back then, and we shall talk further."

I was in the waiting room at six, but she did not appear. She was inside her office, the stop-and-start of her voice betraying a lengthy telephone call. Her assistant left at half past six. Shortly after, the office went silent.

A long time later, the door opened. She looked older than she had earlier, and not simply because it was the end of a long working day. In her hand was a small piece of paper.

"Miss Russell, there are some things that are not mine to disclose. My strong impulse is to turn you away. But since I know who you are and the resources you wield, I doubt that my refusal will keep you from, as you say, 'digging.' These are the five women who worked at the Pavilion from the time it opened until they were replaced the following summer. There was one other, but she died two years ago. I have not included VAD girls or the nurses who came and went."

She held out the page, but when I took hold of it, her fingers kept their grasp for a time. "I ask you, please, to treat these women with care. They may well still be troubled by their long, hard, noble wartime service. I urge you to think carefully before you proceed. Indeed, I can only hope you decide to go home and assure Mr Anik Singh that his brother died with honour, in the service of his King."

She stepped back inside her office, shutting the door in my face.

Margaret Ainsley, Bristol
Faith Prescott, London
Rosemary Langdon, London
Mary O'Connor, London
Marguerite Winslow, Birmingham

Unfortunately, there were no other details, be it street, telephone number, or even a husband's name. Still, if the telephone directory didn't lead me to them, they would all be old enough — and with luck, either propertied or educated enough — to be on city voting registries. And there was always a way to find registered nurses.

I found a Brighton directory at the hospital's front desk, and saw three entries for the name Ainsley. I checked my watch: too late to call on a strange woman? Not if I hurried. My map showed one address down among the slums — an unlikely home for a trained nurse — and another on the western edges of the city. The third was just half a mile up the London road. However, when the woman who answered the door said that yes, she was Mrs Ainsley, I knew I had the wrong place: she wasn't even as old as I.

"I'm terribly sorry to bother you," I said, raising my voice over the sounds of raging children, "I'm looking for a Mrs Ainsley who nursed at the Pavilion during the War."

"That's my mum," she said, then turned to shout, "Reggie, if you don't leave off tormenting your sister —"

I stopped the closing door with my hand, and asked apologetically, "Would that be Mrs William or Mrs Arthur?"

"Arthur, on Peakside Street."

Mrs Arthur Ainsley was also home, and also about to sit down to her dinner. She was a woman in her midforties, with just the kind of calm, comforting face one would want to have beside one's hospital bed. However, when she heard my question, about an Indian soldier named Manvir

81

Singh, the face closed up.

"I can't help you."

"Mrs Ainsley, please, his brother —"

"I can't. You have to go."

"Who's there?" called a male voice.

"It's no one, dear, just a woman looking for a wrong address."

I looked at the closed door. The porch light went off.

Well, that was interesting.

Either the woman found the mere thought of that period of her life too disturbing to consider, or she knew something she didn't want to tell me. However, I was not going to get anything from her tonight, not with Mr Ainsley in residence. Should I stick around and approach her in the morning — or move on to London and work my way through the three women located there?

Considering the option of returning home to straggling invaders, an irritated house-keeper, and a client in need of explanations, it was not a difficult choice.

My London club gave me a room and a set of telephone directories. Since showing up at doors was not practical here — the number of London listings attached to those three surnames being roughly equal to the entire population of Brighton — I also asked for one of the club's modern rotary telephones. My ear already ached at the thought of how many hours I was going to spend with the earpiece pressed against it, hunting through all those men's names in search of Faith Prescott, Rosemary Langdon, and (my heart sank) Mary O'Connor. Why, oh why did the Post Office not consider the woman in a partnership deserving of a separate entry?

The Langdons did not take me long, the next morning. Unfortunately, they also did not give me a Rosemary, or indeed any woman who had nursed in Brighton during the War. I sent out for the more peripheral London directories, and skipped past the many (*many*) pages of O'Connors to start on Prescott. Where, to my amazement, my eye caught on the name Faith tucked in between an Edward and a Frederick. She might have been married ten years ago, but she appeared to be single, or widowed, now.

I inserted my finger into the rotary, then stopped. She was probably at work; she might be the wrong Faith Prescott — but the address was only a brief Underground trip away. And the sky outside promised a fresh, sunny morning. Who needed husbands and anniversaries, anyway, when a woman had London and an interesting investigation stretched out before her? And tonight, by way of reward, I could simply take *myself* to dinner. I could even go to the cinema: Who was to stop me?

The thought cheered me through the Underground and up a tidy street to the polished bell pull. I listened to its echo fade. The house was as trim as one might imagine from a nurse: scrubbed walk, polished windows, paint that was not fresh, but clean. The sort of house whose resident would use good quality stationery with the address printed thereon.

I did not hear any sound from within, yet . . . Had the curtains shifted a fraction? I spoke aloud, as if to an ear pressed against the door.

"Mrs Prescott? My name is Mary Russell. I was sent by Beryl Straub. Mrs Prescott, I have a couple of questions about your time at the Brighton Pavilion." Nothing moved. "I can come back, if this isn't a good time." Silence, and yet, the sensation that there was someone inside. I waited — and after a minute came the hard quick *clackclackclack* of heels approaching down a hallway. The door came open.

She was in her late thirties, brown-eyed and brown-haired, a streak of grey rising from her left temple. She wore trousers — though she looked the sort who would

84

change to a skirt before leaving the house — and a heavy cardigan with too-long sleeves that covered her hands to the knuckles. She wore thick socks with the noisy Cuban-heeled shoes, and stood as if her feet were pinched.

"Good morning," I said. "I'm looking for a Mrs Faith Prescott?"

"I am she."

"I wanted to ask you a few questions about the Indian Hospital in the Royal Pavilion, in early 1915."

A shadow seemed to pass over her face. Fear? Revulsion? Sadness? "Yes."

"You were there — is that correct? As a nurse on the wards?"

"Only until June. 1915."

"Yes, I heard about the scandal-mongering newspaper. Pity, that. I remember how pressed most places were for nursing help — I was officially too young for anything beyond reading to the wounded and helping them write letters, but even I got pulled in to change dressings from time to time." I gave her a wry smile, to cement this personal connection, then asked, "I wonder if I might come in, just for a bit? Save you from letting out all the heat."

She started to glance over her shoulder but caught the motion. I thought for a mo-

85

ment she would refuse, that she would shut the door in my face — but she seemed to brace herself and step back.

As I followed her down the hall and into the parlour, I saw no indication that some other person had rapidly fled the scene. I did notice that the *clack* of her heels was nowhere near as emphatic as when she'd come towards the door. Which meant she'd wanted me to think the delay was due to her being at the back of the house, not that she'd been tiptoeing along the hall in stockinged feet and eyeing the stoop through a crack in the curtains.

Either the woman was deeply frightened of visitors, or Beryl Straub had warned her I was coming.

The room was quite warm, from morning sun and the remains of a small fire. I took off my coat and hat, chatting all the while — what a welcoming room (in fact, it was); that's a charming desk (which my fingers itched to open in search of stationery); oh, you have children! (three, by the looks of the mantelpiece photos) — but to my interest, she neither removed her own warm sweater nor moved to play the proper hostess and take my coat. I draped the garment over the arm of a settee and sat down, making a brief but thorough survey of the framed photos before raising my friendly face to her.

"How old are your children?"

Even this question had no softening effect on her. If anything, it seemed to raise her maternal hackles before she replied with the most minimal possible information. "My children are sixteen, fourteen, and eight. And a half."

"You and your husband must be proud of them."

"My husband is dead."

"Oh, I am sorry," I said.

"He was killed in the War."

"That must have been hard, to be on your own with three small children."

"My father died when I was young, so my mother was free to come live with us. She still does, which means that I can work nights when I need to." Her right hand came up to encircle her left wrist for a moment, then dropped away with a jerk.

"So you're still a nurse?"

"I am. I was fortunate enough to get a position at Guy's. I've been there now, oh, going on six years."

"You must have started there when your youngest was small."

Her face, which had started to relax as she told me about her mother and her professional life, closed sharply. "Bills to pay."

"Oh, of course, I was sympathising, is all."

"Miss Russell, I do have a number of tasks waiting for me."

"I'm so sorry! Thoughtless of me. Well, I have an acquaintance who is looking for information about his younger brother, who was transferred from the Front to the Pavilion hospital in March 1915. He died later that spring, but the family never received any details. Manvir Singh, was his name. Do you remember that patient?"

The woman was holding herself so tight, I felt that a flick of the fingernail would cause her to shatter. "Half the patients were named Singh. It seemed."

"I imagine so." I kicked myself for not making Mr Singh give me the photo of his brother. "This one would have been in his early thirties. He took three bullets in the battle of Neuve Chapelle. Might have lost some fingers."

She shot to her feet, her right hand clasping her left forearm so tightly, one would have thought she was trying to stop a spurting wound. "Miss Russell, there were so many wounded soldiers, so many horribly mutilated dying, gassed young men, I try not to remember any of them. Please, I have to ask you to go."

To refuse would have been inhuman. I apologised, snatching up my coat and following her to the door. "Thank you, Mrs Prescott — here's my card, please let me know if you think of any —"

But the door was shut, the heels retreating.

Food for thought, as I went down the scrubbed front steps and along the street.

As Mrs Straub had said, nurses, no less than the soldiers they treated, could suffer long-term consequences from the endless grinding months of trauma, day in and day out, over the long years of war. Mrs Prescott could be one of those, repelled by questions that threatened to stir up memories.

Yet if that were the case, would she not have tried harder to leave nursing entirely, instead of returning to a lesser and civilian form of daily reminders? And her responses: easy and forthcoming when it came to nursing duties and helpful mothers, then tightly monosyllabic when asked about children or husband. And wasn't there something about the photos over the fire? The husband, in uniform, was placed slightly apart from the others. And although I had seen his face from the settee, a person seated on the other chairs — including what was clearly her habitual seat — would not.

As for her left forearm, why did she occasionally grip it — and not want me to notice her doing so? Did her old traumas include a physical one like a broken wrist? Was that why she'd worn that thick sweater despite the room's warmth, because of something on her arm she didn't want me to see? Such as . . . What? A scar? A tattoo?

"Oh for heaven's sake, Russell," I said aloud. Women like Faith Prescott didn't have tattoos.

I stood for a minute on the busy pavement, staring down unseeing at the descending steps to the Underground station. Time to search out the other two women in London? Or look more closely into Faith Prescott? She was hiding something — there was no doubt about that. But was it her secret, or that of one of the others?

I sighed, and descended into the dim and smoky depths. I'd give it this afternoon, and if nothing came up I would change my course. And I could always treat myself to the cinema and a nice anniversary dinner when this was finished.

Many dusty hours later, I returned the latest of the file folders to the Somerset House records clerk. I now knew the rough outlines of what had happened, that spring of 1915.

And I knew who could fill in the details.

Outside on the busy pavement, I was surprised to find the sun nearly down. What time was it, anyway? I glanced down at my wrist, finding my watch reversed, and reached over to paw it around — and my hand went still. After a moment, I smiled. Yes.

Back at the Prescott house, I waited across the street beneath an overgrown lilac until the two upstairs windows went dark. A few minutes later, a light went on behind the curtains downstairs.

I crossed over to the nurse's scrubbed steps. This time I knocked softly rather than pull the bell: no reason to wake the freshly sleeping children upstairs. The door came open, and I gave the children's mother an apologetic smile.

"Good evening, Mrs Prescott. I need to know about the steel bangle you wear on your left arm."

It was, as I'd expected, nearly identical to the one encircling the wrist of Anik Singh. It was large for a woman's arm — yet instead of slipping it off before she answered the door, she had pushed it up her arm and pulled down the cuffs of her sweater to hide it.

That told me the bangle was more than an idiosyncratic piece of jewellery to her.

She made tea, reassuring her curious mother that all was well before she closed the older woman out of the parlour. While she poured, I went over to the desk. Her stationery was indeed in the top drawer: same width, same paper, same watermark I'd seen on the other. In a cubbyhole at the desk's back was a pair of scissors with three-inch blades.

I returned the page to its place, closed the drawer, and went to the settee to accept my cup.

"It was the knife, wasn't it?" she asked. "That gave me away?"

"Yes."

"How? I didn't put my address on it, didn't use newspaper to pad it. I even printed it so no one could recognise my handwriting."

I was tempted to tell her that the knot in the twine could only have been that of a nurse, or some such nonsense, but I refrained. "No, it was the knife itself. Manvir Singh was in the habit of etching it with the battles in which he carried it. When his brother saw that its final reference was to Neuve Chapelle, he knew its owner had survived. At least, long enough to carve words into the blade."

She gave a bitter little shake of the head. "I knew I should throw it away. Even if it was important to him."

"Why get rid of it at all? You'd had it for ten years."

"My son came across it in the attic. It's lethally sharp. Not a toy."

"This would be your eight-year-old?"

"My — yes. My first two are both girls."

I knew that from the photos covering the mantelpiece.

"Do you know where he is buried? They didn't send his remains home. His brother might like to know."

"Oh, they only buried the Muslims, somewhere up in Surrey. The Hindu and Sikh religions require cremation, so they built a special place for that out in the countryside."

"There's a burning ghat in *Sussex*?"

"Not anymore. They did make a sort of memorial chapel on the site. Remote, but rather pretty."

I could only imagine what the local farmers had made of crematory smoke drifting over from the next field.

"And the ashes? Are they at the memorial?"

"They were scattered at sea."

So much for a graveside visit, then.

"It sounds as if you were very fond of him."

"I was fond of many of those soldiers. Often young, always in pain, far from home, and in that peculiar setting, yet all were eager to return to the fight. Even those far too badly wounded to be put back on the Front."

"Yes, I understand that Manvir's injuries might have made it impossible to handle a rifle."

"He was certain that he'd be judged fit for duty. His hearing would have been the following week."

"Really? But I thought — Wait. How did he die?"

Her eyes dropped, and her hand came over to turn the bracelet on her wrist, around and around. "There was a fight."

"Amongst the patients?"

She tipped her head, a gesture I took as a shamed yes. And it was true: even discounting her fondness for one of the participants, a nurse might be ashamed of allowing any kind of scuffle to arise between patients, and all the more if it had led to a death.

"So what happened? Was there an arrest?"

She shook her head. "The army had the hospital write down Mani's death as being from his wounds. Which in a way was almost true, since the bullets had left him weak in all but spirit. At any rate, he was cremated and his . . . the other man was sent back to the Front. He died there, a year or two later."

I stared at her, saw a tear start down her cheek only to be wiped away vigorously. She lifted her head, and I saw her bitterness. "By the summer of 1915, they were desperate for soldiers. Remember, conscription did not start until the following year. If it was an accident, not an attack, then they could have their officer back."

Had the dead patient been English, things might have gone differently, but she was right: by June, there was not a man to spare. Even if he had killed another man in a fight.

"What was his name? The man responsible for his death?"

"Does it matter? He died. Knowing who it was could only harm his family."

Holmes would want me to press for the name. But Holmes was not here.

She could be lying, I thought. Certainly she is leaving things out. But perhaps a little more research might prevent my thoughtlessly crashing through the lives of innocent families. Perhaps *not* asking questions might be the better way, just this once.

She noticed the direction of my eyes, which had dropped again to where she worked the steel bangle around her wrist. She took a deep breath, then seized firmly around the circlet to pull it off, handing it to me over the tea things.

It was warm and smooth and heavy in my fingers. The *kara* was as much a part of Sikh doctrine as the *kirpan,* worn by men and women alike. The simple steel bangle, unadorned and never removed, was a constant reminder of God and the strength of the warrior. And sometimes of other things, as well.

I held it out to her. "His brother has Manvir's *kirpan.* This would only confuse matters."

Slowly, listening to the meaning behind my words, she took it.

I stood. "You won't hear from me again. But here's my card. In case you wish to speak to me about anything."

I laid the white card on the table, and gathered my things.

When I left, the *kara* was back on her wrist, and wonder was dawning on her face.

I did not get back to Sussex until the late the following evening. To my considerable relief, Mr Singh was not there waiting for me, having retreated to a guesthouse in Eastbourne: that difficult report could wait until tomorrow.

It was an even greater pleasure to discover that Holmes had returned. He came downstairs to find me slumped into a chair before the fire, coat and hat still on, too tired to move any farther.

He tossed some wood on the embers and fetched us each a drink, then sat in the other chair, legs stretched out to the warmth.

Silence descended. Broken by Holmes clearing his throat. "Er, Russell. I believe I may have neglected to wish you a happy anniversary."

I looked at him blankly for a moment, then laughed aloud. "Oh heavens, I'd forgot all about it. Don't worry, Holmes, you can make up for it next year. Let's say for our fifth wedding anniversary."

He looked both relieved and confused, which is never a bad state for a husband. I put down my glass, shed my outer garments, and went to see what I could find by way of supper. And lunch.

"Was Mr Singh still here when you got back?" I asked around a mouthful of cheese and biscuits.

"He'd just gone. But Mrs Hudson told me you had left a houseguest for her."

So as he took out his pipe and tobacco, I told him about my days: the newspaper article, the Sikh gentleman, the head nurse in Lewes. As often happened, the telling stimulated the reflection, allowing my thoughts to run on two tracks, one aloud and one internal.

In those early months of the War, ten years ago, social niceties had gone the way of the Queen of Hearts' soldiers: up in the air. Anything was possible. Women became bus conductors and police constables, delivered beer, and worked in factories. Women carried stretchers, drove ambulances, and nursed male patients — until a tabloid newspaper stirred up scandal, and the younger of those nurses were tidied away.

Mrs Faith Prescott, however, was too valuable to waste. A trained nurse before she married, with a husband and children, she was no blushing innocent. And with a mother at home to care for the children, she could be kept on at the Pavilion hospital until a full complement of male nurses was brought in.

She was fond of her patients, some — it must be said — more than others. With one in particular, a darkly handsome young man in a turban, she formed a bond.

A bond that in the normal course of

events would have broken when Rifleman Manvir Singh was discharged and shipped home, leaving behind him a degree of heartache and a handful of wistful memories.

"But that's not what happened?" Holmes's prompt startled me into attention.

"No. I spent the day up to my neck in records at the War Office, piecing it together. And even now, I could not say for certain that the 'bond' between Mrs Prescott and Manvir Singh was any more than romantic fantasy.

"However, in the last week of May, her husband, one Captain Jonathan Prescott, stepped on something in the trenches and developed an infection. A minor one, but sepsis moves fast in those conditions, and he was given medical leave before it got to the point that he lost a foot.

"Captain Prescott came home the first week of June, some two weeks before the last of Brighton's women nurses were due to be replaced. He, as many men would, resented his wife not being home to care for him, but it was wartime, she was needed.

"However, either he caught her by accident, or he suspected wrongdoing and went to the hospital specifically to find out. There he discovered his wife and her patient. Mind you, the whole thing took place out of doors in the Pavilion gardens, a very public place, so whatever he saw can't have been *actually* compromising. But he thought it was, and started shouting and threatening and finally attacked Manvir Singh physically. In the fight that followed, Manvir died. An accident, to some extent, although Prescott was fit and Manvir was still weak, with one arm he could barely lift.

"And now I have to decide how much of this to tell Mr Singh tomorrow. Because Captain Prescott was never charged. Not with manslaughter, not even with assault. The police considered it a fight between equals, despite Manvir's condition, and the death an accident. The army was happy to haul Prescott back to the Front, and not lose one of its officers to prison. One does suspect that his superiors knew what had happened and disapproved, because his leave was cut short and he was sent back to France. Where he died the following summer."

Holmes smoked, and we listened to the fire for a time. "So," he said, "what are you going to tell your client?"

"I'm not sure he needs to know. I can't help thinking that the truth will make many people unhappy. Even more unhappy than they are. What would you do?"

"As you know, Russell, I have never hesitated to lie to a client in service to a greater good. Has justice been had, here?"

"The killer is long dead. And honourably so."

"What, then, would be the benefit in further punishment of his family — or indeed, that of the victim?"

"We agree, then. Good."

Having reached that conclusion, Holmes pulled back his outstretched heels and knocked the dregs of his pipe into the fireplace. He dropped the empty pipe into the ashtray, set his hands on the arms of his chair — then noticed that I had not moved.

"Something else?"

"Nothing that affects my meeting with Mr Singh tomorrow. But something that might come back in the future, yes. Not for some years, I imagine, but I left the door open by giving her my card.

"The first time I went to see Mrs Prescott, she'd been warned I might come. She hid the *kara* before coming to the door, and rearranged the photographs on the mantelpiece. One of those showed her two daughters and an infant, who was little more than an armful of white clothing. When I went back to the house that evening, the pictures were back in their original places, and one that was missing had been restored. It showed all three children, and was far more recent.

"She lied to me, early on. She said her youngest child was eight, then corrected herself to eight and a half. Among the dusty papers I sorted through today was a church registry, in the parish where the family lived before they moved up to Mrs Prescott's new position in London. The boy was born in February 1916."

"Nine years old. Not something a mother would get wrong."

"Unless she hoped to lead me away from a scent."

"How far did you pursue matters? Did your day's travels include military records?"

"They did not. Although I would not be too surprised to find that certain of Prescott's superiors breathed a small sigh of relief when his honourable death in battle came before he could be granted another home leave."

"Sometimes," my husband agreed firmly, "ignorance can be the wiser choice."

"Indeed."

He rose, tightened the belt of his dressing gown, and walked through checking the windows and doors before going back upstairs.

I sat for a bit longer, gazing into the last flames among the embers.

That second photograph, the recent one that reappeared on the mantelpiece, had indeed shown a lad rather more mature than eight years of age. It had also shown a boy with remarkably dark, handsome eyes, skin that would tan quickly in the summer, and the shiniest black hair this side of India.

Someday, on an anniversary perhaps, his mother would give him a steel bracelet, and a story.

■ ■ ■ ■

NORMAL IN EVERY WAY

BY LEE CHILD

■ ■ ■ ■

In 1954, the San Francisco Police Department was as good or as bad as any other large urban force in the nation. Which is to say it was mixed. It was part noble, part diligent, part grudgingly dutiful, part lazy and defensive, part absurdly corrupt, and abusive, and violent. In other words normal in every way. Including in the extent of its resources. Now they seem pitifully few. Then they were all there was. Manual typewriters and carbon paper, files in cardboard boxes, and old rotary dial telephones, sitting up straight and proud on metal war surplus desks.

It goes without saying there were no computers. There were no databases. No search engines. No keywords or metadata. No automatic matching. All there was were men in a room. With fallible memories. Some of them drank. Most of them, in fact. Some put more effort into forgetting than remembering. Such were the times. The result was each new crime was in danger of standing alone, entire unto itself. Links and chimes and resonances with previous crimes were in danger of going unheard.

All police departments were in the same boat. Not just San Francisco. Every one of them evolved the same de facto solution. Separately and independently, fumbling blind, but they all ended up in the same place. The file clerk became the font of all wisdom. Usually a grizzled old veteran, sometimes confined to a desk due to getting shot or beaten, presiding over a basement emporium packed with furred old file folders and bulging old boxes on shelves. Usually he had been there many years. Usually he chatted and gossiped and remembered things. Sometimes he knew a guy who knew a guy, in another part of town. He became a database, as imperfect as it was, and the guys who knew guys became a network, even though partial and patchy. Carbon-based information technology. Not silicon. All there was. The same everywhere.

Except in one station in San Francisco the file clerk was not a grizzled old veteran. He was a misfit rookie by the name of Walter Kleb. He wasn't much more than a kid at the time. He was shy and awkward and strange in his mannerisms. He didn't stutter or stammer but sometimes he would need to try out a whole sentence in his head, maybe even to rehearse it on his lips, before he could speak it out loud. He was considered odd. Retarded for sure. A screw loose. Nuts, psycho, spastic, crazy, loony, schizo, freak. In 1954 there was no better vocabulary for such things. He struggled through the academy. He was hopeless in most ways, but his paper grades were sky-high. Never been seen before. No one could figure out how to get rid of him. Eventually he was assigned to duty.

He showed up wearing an overstarched uniform too big in the neck. He was an embarrassment. He made it to the file room in record time. No long previous career. No shooting or beating. But he was happy in the basement. He was alone most of the time. With nothing to do except read and learn and alphabetize and arrange in date order. Occasionally people came to see him, and they were politer than most, and kinder, because they wanted something. Either to return a file, or take one out, maybe without anyone knowing, or to find something that had been accidently lost, or to lose something that had been inadvertently found.

What none of them did was ask database

questions. Why would they? How could a retard rookie who had only been there five minutes know anything? Which was a shame, Kleb thought, because he did know things. The reading and the learning were producing results. True, he had no network of guys who knew guys. That strength was certainly deficient. He wasn't a boy who could call up a grizzled old veteran a precinct away and gossip for twenty minutes on the phone. Or ask a favor. Or do one. He wasn't that boy at all. But he was a boy who made lists and liked connections and enjoyed anomalies. He felt they should have asked him questions. Of course he never spoke up first. Well, except for once. Late in January. And look what happened after that.

A detective named Cleary came down and asked for a file nearly a year old. Kleb knew it. He had read it. It was an unsolved homicide. Thought likely to be political. Conceivably at the secret agent level. There were certain interesting factors.

Kleb asked, "Has there been a break in the case?"

Cleary looked like he had been slapped. At first Kleb thought not slapped as in insulted, but just astonished, that the retard spoke, and showed awareness, and asked a question. Then he realized no, slapped as in rudely jerked from one train of thought to another. Cleary's mind had been somewhere else. Not thinking about breaks in the old case. The only other reason for getting the file was therefore a new case. With similarities, possibly.

In the end Cleary took the file and walked away without a word. Kleb was forced to reconstruct its contents in his head. Homicide by gunshot, apparently at very long range. The victim was an immigrant from the Soviet Union. He was thought to be either a reformed communist gunned down as a punishment by an actual communist, or the reform was fake and he was really a sleeper agent, taken care of by a shadowy outfit with a deniable office close to the inner ring of the Pentagon. In 1954 either theory was entirely plausible.

As always at lunch Kleb sat alone, but that day one table closer to the crowd, to better hear what they were saying. The new case was a baffler. A Soviet immigrant, shot with a rifle from far away. No one knew why. Probably a spy. Then someone said no, State Department back channels were reporting no sensitivity. Therefore no spies involved. Just regular folk, doing whatever regular folk do, with deer rifles in Golden Gate Park.

Kleb went back to the basement, and back

inside his head. He read the first file all over again. He checked every detail. He weighed every aspect. The date of the crime, January 31, 1953, exactly 361 days earlier, the location, also Golden Gate Park, a lonely time of day, few potential witnesses, zero actual witnesses. Bullet fragments suggested a medium caliber high-velocity rifle round. A disturbed patch of dirt behind a tree five hundred yards away was thought to be where it was fired from.

Cleary came back again early in the afternoon.

"You asked me a question," he said.

Kleb nodded, but didn't speak.

Cleary said, "You knew it was an unsolved case."

Again Kleb nodded, but didn't speak.

"You read the file."

"Yes," Kleb said.

"You read all the files."

"Yes," Kleb said again.

"We got anything else like this?"

A database question.

His first.

"No," Kleb said.

"Pity."

"But the two cases are very like each other."

"Why I hoped there might be a third."

112

Kleb said, "I think the five-hundred-yard range is important."

"You a detective now?"

"No, but I notice patterns. There have been many gunshot homicides in the park. Almost all of them have been close range. Easier to walk right up to someone on a twisty path. Long-distance rifle fire is a large anomaly. It would suggest a strong preference. Or familiarity. Or possibly training. Maybe that's the only way he knows how to do it."

"You think he's ex-military?"

"I think it's likely."

"So do I, Einstein. Between World War Two and Korea, half the population is ex-military. That would cover everyone from a hobo living under a bridge to the hot boys working for the back offices in the Pentagon. The President of the United States is ex-military. Ex-military gets us precisely nowhere. Keep thinking, genius. That's what you're good at."

"Is there a connection between the victims?"

"Other than being commies?" Cleary said.

"Were they?"

"They claimed not to be. They spoke out from time to time. They had nothing else in common. They had never met and as far as we can tell never knew about each other."

"That's how it would look, if they were spies."

"Exactly," Cleary said.

"Also how it would look if they weren't."

"Therefore this line of inquiry gets us precisely nowhere, either. Keep thinking, brainbox."

"How would you describe being a Soviet immigrant and a reformed communist?"

"How would I describe it?" Cleary said. "Smart."

"But difficult," Kleb said. "Don't you think? You would have to work at it. Frequent reaffirmations would be expected. As you said, they spoke out from time to time. They must have achieved a small degree of local notoriety."

"Does this matter?"

"I wondered how the shooter identified them as Russians from five hundred yards."

"Maybe being Russians was a coincidence. Maybe they were just walkers in the park. Targets of convenience."

"Not a well-represented national origin here. The odds are against it. But it's certainly possible. Although I feel somehow it shouldn't be. It's almost a philosophical inquiry."

"What is?"

Kleb tested a sentence in his head, and then on his lips. Out loud he said, "There's a second issue that might or might not be a coincidence. Is it too big of a coincidence that two other things might or might not be coincidences also? Or do all three things reinforce each other and make the implication more likely to be true than false? It's an existential question."

"Speak English, loony boy."

"I think the dates might be important. They might explain the Russians. Or not, of course, if it's all just one big coincidence. Then my theory collapses like a house of cards."

"What dates?"

"The dates of the shootings. January 31st, 1953, and today, which is January 27th, 1954."

"What do they have in common?"

Kleb tested another sentence in his head, and on his lips. It was a long sentence. It felt okay. Out loud he said, "I think you should look for a German national in his thirties. Almost certainly a local resident. Almost certainly an ex–prisoner of war, detained back in Kansas or Iowa or somewhere. Almost certainly an infantryman, likely a sniper. Almost certainly married a local girl and stayed here. But he never gave up the faith. He never stopped believing. Certain things upset him. Like January 31st, 1953."

"Why would it?"

"It was the tenth anniversary of the Germans' final surrender at Stalingrad. January 31st, 1943. Their first defeat. Catastrophic. It was the beginning of the end. Our believer wanted to strike back. He found a Red in the neighborhood. Maybe he had heard him speak at the Legion hall. He shot him in the park."

"The date could be a total coincidence."

"Then today would have to be, too. That's what I'm trying to figure out. Does the fact that the dates could be significant together mean they must be?"

"What's today?"

"The tenth anniversary of the lifting of the siege of Leningrad. Another catastrophic retreat for the Germans. Another huge symbolic failure. Stalin, Lenin. Their cities survived. Our believer didn't like it."

"How many more anniversaries are coming up?"

"Thick and fast now," Kleb said. "It was Armageddon from this point onward. The fall of Berlin comes on the second of May next year."

Cleary was quiet a long moment.

Then he winked.

He said, "You keep thinking, smart boy. That's what you're good at."

Then he walked away.

Late the next day Kleb heard Cleary had ordered a sudden change of direction for the investigation, which paid off almost right away. They made an arrest almost immediately. A German national, aged thirty-four, a local resident, an ex–prisoner of war who had been held in Kansas, previously a sniper with an elite division, now married to a Kansas woman and living in California. Cleary got a medal and a commendation and his name in the paper. Never once did he mention Kleb's help. Even to Kleb himself. Which turned out to be representative. Kleb worked forty-six years in that basement, shy, awkward, strange in his mannerisms, largely ignored, largely avoided, and by his own objective count provided material assistance in forty-seven separate cases. An average of more than one a year, just. He was never thanked and never recognized. He retired without gifts or speeches or a party, but nevertheless it was a happy day for him, because it was the anniversary of the moon landing, which meant, same day, different year, it was also

the anniversary of the first vehicle on Mars.
Which was the kind of connection he liked.

■ ■ ■ ■

THE REPLACEMENT

BY MARGARET MARON

■ ■ ■ ■

I shouldn't be here, you know. Not just moving through the house to gather up dirty forks and napkins or to pick melted candles out of cake icing that had read Happy 18th, Matthew!, but *here* here, as in simply existing.

It's after midnight and the party's pretty much over now. The high school friends who came to celebrate and say goodbye before we all split for college next week left almost an hour ago. The only ones still here are longtime friends of my sister.

My *older* sister.

Eighteen and a half years older, to be exact.

Our mother was forty-seven when she gave birth to me, and no, I was not one of those accidental change of life babies. Nothing in their control was ever accidental with either of my high-achieving parents. Within three years of their marriage, they had produced the one son and one daughter they'd agreed on. With that out of the way, they could concentrate on their other goals: a law degree for her and the H. G. Jones Chair in Medieval Studies right here in Chapel Hill for him. Dad's doctoral thesis was on fifth-century Christianity, which he turned into a historical novel that made the *New York Times* bestseller list.

Mom specialized in personal injury suits and litigated obscene amounts of money for her clients. By the time I was born, just knowing she was the plaintiff's attorney was enough to make most insurance companies settle instead of going to trial. I'm told that other attorneys often continued their own cases so they could crowd into the courtroom to hear her closing arguments to the jury.

I hope I haven't made my parents sound like cold workaholics who left their children to the care of others. Yes, there was a nanny until Calder and Jessica started nursery school, and a full-time housekeeper, too, but Dad was there for dinner every night unless he was on a book tour and Mom was usually home in time to read them a bedtime story and tuck them in. Teaching at the university in those early years let Dad devote his summers to family camping trips and once Mom's career was firmly established, she would take a week off to join them. Jess turned into Dad's best research assistant and even began critiquing his manuscripts by the time she was sixteen. Calder, eleven months older, often drove Mom to courthouses and client meetings. During those summer drives, he became a sounding board for some of her closing arguments.

To hear Jess and Dad tell it, they were the perfect family. A mutual adoration society.

Golden.

Then Calder was killed by a hit-and-run driver the summer before he was to enter college. Eighteen. My age.

The police were all over the case, but after a month, there were no leads. Prominent attorney, bestselling author, a huge reward for any information pointing to their son's killer?

Nothing.

Nada.

He was last seen leaving a popular comedy club near the campus where he occasionally took the stage on open mike night. Someone saw him get into the passenger side of a car parked down the block, but hadn't paid much attention and couldn't give any details as to the make or model, although it was thought that the driver was a woman. His body was found on a deserted road a few miles from town out near the lake. He had been drinking and his blood alcohol was such that the police theorized that he might have staggered out in front of a car. My mother was convinced he'd been taken out there and deliberately run over.

"Calder was no saint," Jess told me, "and I'm sure there were guys who resented his good looks, his smarts, the life he was meant to have, but you don't kill somebody just because he might have an edge on you."

"Girlfriends?" I asked when I was fourteen and old enough to be curious.

"By the dozen," Jess said. "But he kept it light, made it clear from the get-go that law school came first."

"But was there really no one special?" I asked on our long flight to Paris this past spring. Jess was going over to accept a literary prize in Dad's name from the French Academy and I was on spring break. Jess never wants to talk about the circumstances that led to my birth, but cars and planes loosen her up a little.

"We all hoped Christa would be the one," she told me.

"Really?"

I've known Christa James from infancy. A reporter for the local CBS affiliate, she's been one of Jess's closest female friends since grade school when her family moved here from Quebec. She has a bunch of Emmys, as well as a Pulitzer for her series on corruption in the state treasurer's office a few years back. Thirty-seven now, she's a beautiful woman. Still unmarried, though, and no relationships that have lasted.

"Because of Calder?" I asked when we were well out over the Atlantic.

Jess shrugged, put the buds back in her ears and closed her eyes to listen to a lecture she'd recorded on her phone.

I had a recording of my own that I'd found on a shelf in Dad's office the week before and copied onto my own phone. I must have listened to it a dozen times since then. It's from one of Calder's appearances at the comedy club. On it, his voice is warm and his pacing is good.

"She was a cheerleader at the local high school, as firm and juicy as a vine-ripened tomato, but she was saving it for Jesus, y'know?"

Okay, so it was a little raunchy and it ended with the girl going, *"Yes! Oh Jesus! Yes! YES!"* I'm sure you can fill in the middle. It got snickers throughout and a big round of applause at the end.

So he had Dad's talent for imaginative narrative and Mom's courtroom flair for drama, and maybe he would even have wound up on the Supreme Court as one of his teachers predicted. We'll never know though, will we? As for Jess, her book on early Christian cults didn't top the best-seller lists, but it did okay because she gave those ascetic desert saints enough humanity that even hedonists of our own time could connect.

Much as I loved our mother, I can't help feeling that maybe it's just as well that she'll never know I'm not golden like Calder, nor scholarly like Jess. That I'm not worth the sacrifice. Law and literature both leave me cold, and the thought of spending my life in a classroom or courtroom is a total no-go. I like math, though, and I'm pretty good with my hands so Dad's getting resigned to the idea that I may wind up in something physical like construction.

He was grief-stricken by Calder's death, but Mom refused to accept it. Even though she was already so far into menopause that she had quit taking her birth control pills, she began hormone treatments that kick-started her ovaries. I was born eighteen months after they buried Calder.

I must have been a disappointment from the beginning. I was colicky, I wasn't cute, I wasn't toilet trained till almost three, and I couldn't read till I was five. But I *was* a boy and as long as I wasn't too cold or hungry, I could sit quietly for long stretches of time. My earliest memory is of Calder's grave, even though I didn't know what it was at the time. *I sit bundled up on a gray winter's day and listen while my mother talks in a low voice. The icy wind stings my eyes, but I don't cry because I am trying to understand her words.*

Only when I was much older did I realize that she was bouncing closing arguments off Calder. It was like listening to one side of a telephone conversation. "You're right," she'd say. "I can't just *tell* the jury that this little girl lost her arm due to negligence. I have to make them see how her whole life is diminished. What if I . . . ?" Then she would pause as if to hear his comments. "Yes, that's a detail that might persuade them."

Those cemetery visits began to taper off by the time I was six and they stopped altogether when I was eight.

"You're not to feel guilty, son," Dad said, putting his arm around me in the limo that took us home after her funeral. "The doctors told her about the risk of hormones and uterine cancer at her age, but she was so determined to have another son that she wouldn't listen."

Mom had explained "uterine cancer" to me but I hadn't connected it to my conception till then, so of course I did feel guilty even though Jess became a second mother to me. She even moved back home so that she could try to give me a normal childhood.

Christa James happened to be passing through Paris at the same time, on her way to visit her sister Amy, who was attached to the American embassy in Geneva. Amy was two years younger than Christa, and such an early Francophile that she had gone to a boarding school in Quebec, studied at the Sorbonne, and joined the State Department as soon as she graduated. I think I was ten the last time she was in Chapel Hill, so I barely remembered that Christa even had a sister.

"Would you have married Calder?" I asked.

"We had barely begun to date," Christa said slowly. "But yes, we probably would have married before we finished college. And then divorced a year later. Monogamy was not in his makeup, Matt. He was a chick magnet and he loved a challenge. I wouldn't have been enough for him."

"He hit on girls?" I asked.

"He didn't have to hit on them, sweetie. They lined up at the door. In fact . . ."

"In fact what?"

Before she could answer, her phone rang. "Sorry, Matt. It's my producer. I have to go."

The next time I saw her, she professed to have no memory of what she'd started to say, back in Paris.

"Leave it, Matt," she said. "Calder's been gone so long there's nothing more to learn."

"But you're an investigative reporter," I said. "Doesn't it bother you that his death was never solved? That no one ever came forward to say who he left the club with that night?"

I admit I had become somewhat fixated. By then, I had read all the online news stories I could find, but the facts were meager and neither Jess nor Dad wanted to keep rehashing it for me.

Most of Calder's friends had moved on, too. All were nearing forty now, and those who hadn't married and divorced a couple of times were settled into careers and parenthood in other parts of the country. Calder's closest friend was Rick Barbour, who teaches English here at the university. He's still around. In fact, he and Jess are a couple. I'm probably the reason they've never married.

Something else to feel guilty about.

Although Calder has come up in casual conversation over the years, Rick and I had never really talked one-on-one about his death until yesterday when he came over to help me set up for tonight's party. Jess and Dad had flown out to L.A. — another one of Dad's books had been optioned for a miniseries — so he was at loose ends.

At loose ends myself the day before, I had looked through the files in Dad's office. None of them were off-limits to Jess or me. Despite electronic databases, Dad preferred print-and-paper records and a bank of oak file cabinets held drawer after drawer of material on early Christianity — and only one containing personal correspondence and family records. He wasn't overly senti-mental, so the folders for our family were pretty basic: birth certificates, medical and dental records. Calder's held his passport, his high school diploma, his acceptance to college, and his death certificate. No cray-oned kindergarten drawings in his folder. No grade school report cards. Jess's and mine were similar, although hers did contain some favorable reviews of her book. Mom's had their marriage certificate, her death certificate and some old snapshots. At the very back of the drawer was an unlabeled folder I'd never noticed. It was stuffed with newspaper articles from the days following Calder's death.

I had read most of these online, but there was one that had been clipped from a now-defunct suburban weekly that I'd never heard of, which is when I'd called Rick.

After we'd hosed down the terrace, cleaned the screened-in side porch, and weeded the flower beds, we treated ourselves to a couple of beers which, according to the state of North Carolina, I was still technically too young to drink.

I had left the folder on the kitchen table and as Rick popped the top of his beer, I said, "Can I ask you about this newspaper clipping I found yesterday?"

He saw Calder's picture and gave an exaggerated sigh. "Christ, Matt! I thought you promised Jess you were going to let it go."

"This says you were the last person to see him alive."

"So? You already knew that."

"No, I didn't. I never heard anyone say it was you."

"Really?" He seemed surprised. "Well, it certainly wasn't a secret."

"You said he got into a car with a woman. You were his best friend, so who was she?"

He shrugged. "It could have been anybody. They came on to him all the time. The car was almost a block away, and I only saw her from behind when he got in and the interior light came on. I thought at first it was Christa. Same long hair. She and Calder had just started seeing each other, but she and Jess were still at a party together around the time I saw him get into that car so it wasn't her."

"What kind of a car?"

Another shrug, but this time he didn't quite meet my eyes.

"C'mon, Rick. You know cars."

"It could have been a Toyota. That's why I thought it was Christa. She had an old beat-up black one. But they were in Jess's car that night and they were both positive about the time. Why are you so obsessed with it, anyhow? You never even knew Calder."

"I'm not obsessed," I protested.

"No?"

"I wouldn't even be here if Calder hadn't been killed. Replacing him was the only reason I was born. Wouldn't you be curious about who made your existence possible?"

"Why?" he asked bluntly. "You want to send him a thank-you note?"

"Of course not, but —"

"Isn't it enough that you're here? Can't you be grateful for that and let go of the how and why?"

From the earnest look on his face, I knew this was something he and Jess must have discussed.

"I'm the reason my mother died," I said, downing the last of my beer. "How can I let go of that?"

"You and Christa," he said, shaking his head.

"Christa?"

"Yeah. Didn't you know? She's carrying a load of guilt almost as big as yours. Calder wanted her to meet him at the comedy club that night, but she went to a party with Jess instead. She thinks that if she'd skipped it, Calder might still be alive. And yeah, your mom, too." He finished his own beer and stood up to go. "Look, Matt, you're leaving for college next week, right? So take advantage of it. Leave the past behind. Concentrate on your future."

"I'll try," I promised. And up until a few minutes ago, I honestly thought I could.

After all my friends left, Dad said good-night, too. Jess and Rick and four or five of their crowd had moved out to the side porch for coffee and brandy, so I left them to it and began clearing away. I took the chips and dips out to the kitchen, stacked the dishwasher, and started gathering up the empty bottles and napkins. My hands were full when I got back to the kitchen and found Christa at the counter. Her back was to me as she reached for a handful of corn chips.

"Still hungry?" I teased.

"Caught me!" she said, turning with a smile.

To my surprise, it was Christa's sister Amy, on leave from the embassy in Switzerland. There's only a family likeness in their facial features. From behind though, both have the same slender build and narrow shoulders.

"Too much brandy," she said ruefully as she popped a dip-laden chip in her mouth. "I need something more in my stomach." She loaded another chip with guacamole. "The others are playing 'Remember when?' and 'Whatever happened to so-and-so?' I've been gone too long to know who or what they're talking about."

After so many years in Europe, there was no trace of the South in her accent.

"Even you, Matt. Last time I was here, you were just a little boy and now look at you. Six feet tall. Eighteen. I wouldn't have recognized you. You don't look at all like —"

She broke off in embarrassment.

"Like Calder?" I asked.

"Sorry," she apologized.

"That's okay. I get that a lot."

She turned to go back to the porch. As I watched her go, I was again bemused by her resemblance to Christa from behind.

And then it struck me.

"You!"

She paused. "Excuse me?"

"You're the one who met Calder at the comedy club!"

"What? *No!*"

From out in the front hall, I heard voices, then Christa appeared with her car keys in one hand and her sister's purse in the other. "The others have left, Amy. You ready to call it a night?"

"Yes!" She reached for her handbag.

"No!" I said sharply.

Christa was puzzled but Amy stared at me

in consternation. Then Jess and Rick were there.

"Matt? What's wrong?" Jess asked.

I focused on Rick. "The night Calder died. It was Amy you saw, wasn't it, Rick? Christa's car, but Amy was driving, wasn't she?"

"Don't be silly, Matt," Christa said. "Amy didn't have her driver's license. She was only fifteen."

"Kids get their learner's permit at fifteen," I said stubbornly. "Rick thought it was your car. Even thought it was you at first because you two look so much alike from behind."

Christa turned to Rick, "Tell him he's crazy, Rick!"

But Rick was looking at Amy as if he'd never seen her before. "I don't know," he said slowly. "I really did think it was your car, Christa. I could've sworn it. But then when Jess said you two were definitely at that party — It never occurred to me that Amy knew how to drive or that she'd be out that late by herself. She was just your kid sister."

With everyone looking at her, Amy backed away, shaking her head. "No. It wasn't me. It wasn't!"

"Leave her alone," Christa said.

"Why?" Jess and I both asked.

136

Whether it was guilt or too much brandy, Amy's defenses suddenly crumbled. "It was an accident!" she whimpered. "I didn't know he was behind the car. He was so drunk I didn't think he had caught up with me."

Always quick off the mark, Jess said, *"You're* the one who hit him? Is that why your parents sent you up to Quebec? To get you away? They *knew?"*

Amy shook her head and tears filled her eyes as she looked at us in hopeless guilt. "Not Dad. We never told him. Mother made us promise."

"But how?" asked Jess. "Why?"

"She and Dad were in Charlotte for the weekend, remember? Christa was supposed to be keeping an eye on me but you wouldn't let her bring me to the party, so I was out on the front steps trying to find the Little Dipper when Calder came by to see if she was back yet. He said he could teach me the constellations but we'd have to get away from town to where it was really dark. I was ready to go right then, but he said to meet him at the comedy club around eleven."

"You weren't supposed to drive without Christa," Jess said.

"And she wasn't supposed to leave me

alone," Amy wailed.

"This was *our* fault?"

"No, of course not. All the same, if you'd let me come —"

Before Jess could reply, I said, "So you met him at the club?"

Amy nodded. "We drove out to the lake and sat down on one of the rocks to look at the stars. He had a bottle and tried to get me to take a drink, but I knew if I got stopped going home, alcohol would up the ante. He pointed out some of the constellations, and then he kissed me. I thought maybe he'd decide he liked me better than Christa. Instead, he took another drink and then he — he —"

"He what?"

"He wouldn't let me go. I told him to stop, that I didn't want to, but he wouldn't listen. He put his hand down my shorts. Asked me what I was saving it for. I pushed him away and ran back to the car. I didn't know he was right behind me. I *swear* I didn't! I was scared and just wanted to get away, but when I put it in Reverse, I must have knocked him over. I heard him yell as I put it in Drive, but I was in such a panic that I drove home as fast as I could and just sat there in the dark and shook till Christa came back."

Christa took a deep breath. "She was in hysterics when she told me what had happened, so I gave her one of Dad's sleeping pills and promised that I'd go out to the lake and see if Calder was okay."

"But he wasn't, was he?" I asked.

Christa shook her head. "He must have staggered out to the road because I found him lying on the edge of the pavement. No pulse and he was cold to the touch. I — I closed his eyes."

With tears in her own eyes, Amy said, "By the time Dad and Mother got home next day, the news of Calder's death was all over town. Everybody was broken up over it, but after the funeral, Mother thought I was taking it harder than I should have. When school started that next week, I was so totally falling apart that we had to tell her. I wanted to go to the police and confess, but she talked me out of it. Said it wouldn't bring him back and my life would be ruined. We had already talked about my going to Aunt Giselle's to finish high school in Quebec so that I'd speak French like a native. I couldn't face you anymore, Jess. Or face your parents. I am so, so sorry." She blew her nose and straightened her slender shoulders. "I'll go to the police tomorrow."

Christa shook her head. "You weren't the

one who killed him, Amy."

"But I shouldn't have panicked. I should have brought him back to town. Sobered him up."

"After what he'd tried to do to you?"

Rick and I stood there in shocked silence but Jess turned on me in anger. "Satisfied, Matt?"

"Me?"

"I told you to leave it alone. I told you that Calder was no saint. Now do you believe me? Amy wouldn't have been his first rape. Mom paid off the girl's parents and got that one suppressed because he was still a minor."

"What?"

"Then she paid off a second girl, as well," Jess said grimly. "The baby was put up for adoption in Tennessee."

"Baby?" I was stunned. "Did Dad know?"

Jess shook her head. "He was too mired in the fifth century to pay attention to what was happening in his own." She reached out and clasped Amy's hand. "I say we leave it there, okay?"

She was looking at Amy, but I knew she was asking me.

"Okay," I said.

And this time, I really meant it.

Except that I've tossed and turned all night, going over and over it, trying to wrap my head around the fact that Amy was the reason I'd been born.

Or no, not Amy. She only knocked him down. She didn't run over him.

It was still some faceless, nameless hit-and-run driver . . . Or was it?

I'm an eighteen-year-old male, but it's not all that hard to put myself into the head of a seventeen-year-old female.

Driving out to the lake that night, Christa must have been furious with Calder. To hear that the guy she was starting to fall for had tried to rape her sister? If he had stepped out into the road to flag her down, would she have braked or would she have floored the gas pedal?

I suppose I could ask her, but what if she says yes? Admits it?

Rick's right. Even if she's the reason I'm here, it won't bring Mom back and I'm certainly not sorry I was born.

When I graduated from high school back in June, Jess gave me a box of thank-you cards and nagged me till I'd written to everyone who'd given me a graduation present.

Maybe I'll send one to Christa.

CHIN YONG-YUN SETS THE DATE

BY S. J. ROZAN

Well, husband. It has been some months since I last came to visit you. Today the weather is hot, but a lovely breeze is stirring the leaves on the trees. These leaves were still new at Ching Ming, when all the family came to sweep your grave. I hope you enjoyed the tea we served you. I have brought more for you today, from Old Liu's shop. Old Liu sends his greetings.

I have also brought the lemon tarts you like so well, as today is the anniversary of our wedding. It was so long ago, yet in my mind it seems like yesterday. Your fine voice growing louder as you sang along the path between our villages. Your friends — some of whose voices were equally loud but not as fine — marching with you, casting fire-crackers to scare envious spirits away. My friends refusing to give me to you until you had paid the bride price. How low that price was, both of us from such poor families! We laughed. I said you had gotten quite a bargain. You said it was your good luck that my friends were such unskilled negotiators.

Weddings in America are not conducted that way, husband. There is no marching from village to village, no bride price. But still, there are weddings. I have come here today to bring you good news.

As you know, I'm not a person who likes to brag about her accomplishments. I thought, however, that you would find what I have to say interesting. Our children lead very busy lives, so I've decided they do not need to take the time to hear this story. Therefore I've come here alone, by bus. This is something our children do not know I know how to do. There are many things the children do not know I know — although now, there is one fewer. The tale is long, husband, so here is your tea.

It begins this way.

On a recent Sunday afternoon I sat at a table at Wo Hop enjoying a bowl of winter melon soup. As this is something I don't often make at home, I do not mind the expense of paying for it, though of course the soup at Wo Hop, though it is excellent, is not as good as yours was. I was with Lin Rui, from the bakery. You remember her? She is a nice woman but sometimes she cannot stop talking. This is not always a problem, as she often doesn't pause for a response. When I am with her, as long as I utter an occasional encouraging sound, I have leisure to observe my surroundings.

That afternoon, we sat at a table in the corner. A family filled that round table in the center of the room. They were an elderly grandmother, a mother, a father, a young man, a young woman holding a baby. Two seats — the places of honor, to the right of the grandmother — were empty when I arrived. They remained empty until another young man descended the stairs. The family's heads all turned. This young man held the hand of a nervously smiling blonde young woman. The family smiled in return, but their smiles seemed tentative.

I realized I knew these people, husband. They were the Chu family, from Eldridge Street. You may remember them. Our three youngest children went to school with their two sons. Our daughter didn't know them well, but the eldest son, Cai, was great friends with our son An-Zhang. They made mischief together. They were always punished, but they were also always forgiven because they were such clever children. The creativity of their naughtiness was especially pleasing to you, as I recall, husband. An-

147

Zhang, as you know, has not changed. In any case, I will have more to say about An-Zhang later.

The younger son of the Chu family is named Li. In school he studied with our Tien-Hua. As neither of them ever did anything except study, they were never in any trouble. In fact, according to our daughter they were boring. Of course, that was not true of our son, but I will admit I did find Chu Li a bit tedious. This, then, was Li at the table, with his wife, who held their child. As elder brother Cai seated his blonde young woman beside his grandmother, Li glanced at the parents. He frowned.

I couldn't hear the conversation as their meal progressed, because of the distance between our tables as well as Lin Rui's ongoing gossip, but clearly the Chus' luncheon was a strained one. As you know, I do not make it a rule to stick my nose in other people's business. I could not help but notice, however, that the blonde young woman was wearing a diamond ring on her left hand. With shy pride she showed it to the family around the table. It appeared none of them had seen it before, which told me she had only recently become engaged to Cai. A family meal after an engagement should be an occasion for celebration, as it was for our family when each of our two oldest sons became engaged. Although you were gone by then, husband, your happy presence was felt each time. Yet an odd air of discomfort prevailed at the Chus' table.

At both tables, we continued to eat. As it happened, I called for our check as the Chus were finishing their meal. Our soup was not quite gone, but Lin Rui had begun to tell me stories about people I don't know. I professed myself quite full, suggesting to her that she take home the remaining soup, which pleased her. "But before we leave," I said, "let me take a selfie of us, for your son."

This offer made Lin Rui beam, even though *selfie* is such a silly word Chinese doesn't have it, so I had to say it in English. Of course, other people in the restaurant appeared in our selfie, but I tell you, husband, so many people are taking pictures like this all the time, no one even looked up from their meal. Lin Rui does not have the good luck to have a family like ours. Her son lives in Texas, so she has no one to show her how to do certain things, such as taking pictures with her phone. Our son An-Zhang, because he is a photographer, thought I would enjoy learning this. He was correct. I now snap many photographs on the street. I show them to An-Zhang when I go to dinner at his apartment. Only one of our children has inherited your talent for cooking, husband. An-Zhang is not that one. However, his roommate, Tony, is an excellent cook, who goes out of his way to prepare dishes I enjoy. So dinner at An-Zhang's home is always a pleasing occasion.

After the pictures, we left the restaurant. I emailed the photos to Lin Rui's son. Then I told Lin Rui I had shopping to do. After one final story about the owner of the eyeglasses store on Mott Street — I don't even know this man's name — she said goodbye.

I stood on the corner enjoying the warm day. Eventually the Chu family emerged from Wo Hop. I took a few steps over, to the shadows under the tailor's awning. Cai said his goodbyes to his family. With his blonde young woman he walked a block up the street. I headed in that direction myself. Cai spoke to the young woman with that look of a man who is troubled but tries to hide it. They kissed on the corner, then parted ways.

I hurried to catch up with Cai. Since he had been such a good friend of An-Zhang's, it was only polite that I greet him.

"Chu Cai!" I said. "Can this be you?"

He turned. "Auntie Chin! What a surprise!" He smiled. "You're looking younger than ever." Cai was a mischief-maker, but always polite.

"I'm happy to see you, Cai. Are you well?"

"Yes, thank you. How's your family? How's An-Zhang?"

"The family is well, thank you. As for An-Zhang, now that he doesn't have you to lead the way, he no longer gets into trouble." This made Cai laugh. "Really, An-Zhang is very successful," I told him. "He is a photographer — of food, among other things. I cannot say I understand why anyone would pay a great deal of money for pictures of food. Sometimes I think this is another clever trick — of the kind you two used to play — that he is now playing on the world. But then, he is not the only one of my children with an odd profession. My daughter is a private investigator."

"Lydia? Wait, Ling Wan-ju, right? She's a private investigator?"

"Yes. She is very busy in her career. She is lucky she has remained living in our apartment, so that I can take care of her. Now, Chu Cai, I must go. It has been lovely to see you." Then, because I had no shopping to do, I hurried off home.

Within an hour, the red telephone in our

kitchen rang. I had expected that, of course, so I was not startled.

"Look at that," Cai said. "I remembered the number after all these years! Auntie, I'm wondering if Lydia — Ling Wan-ju, is there. I'd like to speak to her."

"Come over immediately. Press one long buzz on the bell downstairs so I know it's you."

He was there within ten minutes, bringing a bag of fine oranges. A well-brought-up young man, like our own children. I went to the kitchen for a bowl for the oranges as he removed his shoes. Then I showed him to your easy chair, husband. It is the chair I offer to honored guests. I thought you might not mind if Cai drank a cup of tea there while I helped him solve his problem.

"Thank you," he said when I brought the tea. "Will Ling Wan-ju join us soon?"

"I'm sorry, Cai. My daughter is not available. She was called away on important detecting work. However, since you didn't know she was an investigator, no doubt you also don't know that I often help her with her cases. Please tell me what is worrying you."

He sipped his tea. "Maybe I should wait for her."

"You called within an hour of learning her

152

profession. This must be an urgent matter. Tell it to me. Perhaps there is groundwork I can do." This is a phrase I learned from our daughter. I don't understand it, as I have worked now on several cases but have never had to dig in the ground to solve one. Nor has she as far as I know. However, saying it seems to put people at ease.

"All right, Auntie. You'll tell Ling Wan-ju as soon as you can?"

I picked up my own tea. "Please proceed."

Cai sighed. "It's . . ." He sighed again, trailing off.

"Yes," I said. "It's embarrassing, it's a personal matter, it must be kept confidential, you don't like to ask for help. Fine. Now that is out of the way. I am waiting to hear."

With a smile, he said, "Auntie Chin, you haven't changed. All right, it's this. I just got engaged to my girlfriend, Anna. Anna Powell. She's not Chinese, but she's so nice, so smart, so talented — also, she cooks so well! — I thought my parents would come around to liking her."

"But you no longer think so."

"I don't know. Li — my brother, you remember him?"

"Yes, I do."

"Li doesn't seem to like her. I mean, he

153

hardly knows her. But he worries about my parents, how they feel about me marrying someone who isn't Chinese. Also, about Grandmother. Li was hoping we wouldn't get serious. That I'd break up with Anna, not ask her to marry me. The other day, he came over to my apartment, for a drink. He said Anna — Auntie, he said she's phony. He said she's . . ." Cai seemed to be struggling to find the word in Chinese. Finally he slipped into English. "She's a *gold digger.*"

I don't know if you know this word, husband. It refers to a woman after a man's money. Now, as you remember, I am fortunate to have a rather good feeling for people. I had not gotten any sense of greedy calculation about the young woman when I saw her in Wo Hop. Actually, the opposite. However, I asked, "Do you have gold for her to dig, Cai?"

"You mean, do I have money? I'm doing well enough. Anna's an artist, a painter. Her work is beautiful. But Li says she'll always be poor unless she finds a man to support her. That may be true, but I'm happy to do it. So she can do her work. But Li told me to, quote, 'look out for my stuff.' "

"For his stuff?"

"No, no, for *my* stuff. I guess that's not a

quote. Anyway, Auntie, I would have thought that was just Li, being his usual worried self, but the problem is, some of my things actually have gone missing lately. A diamond tie tack. Some cuff links. An antique teacup my grandmother gave me. Li has a matching one — she gave us each one when we graduated high school." He smiled that same mischievous smile from his boyhood. "If you ask me, they're ugly. But I know they're valuable. Anyway, about the tie tack, the cuff links, I didn't worry too much. I thought I'd just misplaced them. Then I noticed the teacup was gone when I climbed up on a stool to get something from the top cabinet."

"I see. You suspect your fiancée?"

"I would never, except for what Li said. But that's not the end of the story."

"I apologize for interrupting. Please continue."

"I saw the tie tack yesterday. In Golden Journeys Jewelry's window."

"Ah," I said. I sipped my tea.

Husband, I don't know if you remember Golden Journeys, or Cheng Yue, the owner. Cheng is what they call a "fence." That is a buyer of stolen property. I don't know why this word is used. Perhaps because if the police approach, a burglar might throw his stolen goods over a fence. That Cheng was now in possession of Cai's tie tack was ominous.

I asked, "Is there no possibility the tie tack in the window is a different one?"

"I guess it could be, but it's not likely. I got mine from an antiques dealer in Hong Kong. It's fairly unusual. Do you want to see a picture?"

"Of course." When detecting, it is important to be as specific as possible. Cai flipped through photos on his phone, then turned the phone to me. "Anna took this the first time I wore it." He enlarged the photo to feature the jewel.

"You're correct, it's distinctive. Please hold the phone still." I took a photo of his photo with my phone.

He tried to hide a smile. "Auntie, there's an easier way."

"So my daughter is always telling me. Someday I'll learn it. Did you speak to Cheng Yue?"

"Yes. I didn't say the tie tack was mine, just asked about it. He said he got it with other things when he bought up an estate. He's not even sure he wants to sell it, he says. He just put it in the window to attract customers because it's so beautiful."

"You didn't press him?"

"No. I left. I think I was . . . afraid of what the truth might be."

"I see. But now you have decided you must know the truth no matter how unpleasant. You would like me — you would like the truth to be discovered about your stolen items. Really, about your fiancée. Is that correct?"

"Yes," he said, with what seemed to be relief. "I really don't think Anna —"

"Of course not. But you must be sure. Tell me this, Cai. Do you love her?"

"Oh, Auntie! Very, very much."

"All right. Call tomorrow morning at this same telephone number. Now you may go, as I have much to do."

Actually, I did not have much to do to solve the case. It was sadly simple. No doubt, husband, as you are wiser than I, you have seen it yourself. I needed to assure myself I was correct, of course, which would be easily done. Once that was accomplished, the work ahead of me was to think about what to do next.

After Cai was gone I cleaned up the tea things. I organized some things on my phone, which becomes a mess very fast if I do not keep after it. I put on my shoes, locking three of the five locks on the door as I left the apartment. Leaving two unlocked

157

ensures that burglars will lock themselves out as they pick the locks to let themselves in. Our daughter says today's locks are not as easy to pick as formerly. Possibly she's right, because associating with criminals is part of her professional duties. Still, my strategy has kept this apartment safe for the many years since you have been gone. I see no reason to change it.

I hurried to the jewelry row of Canal Street to do the one bit of detecting I needed for this case. I stood outside Golden Journeys's window. In the center under a bright light a diamond tie tack rested on a silk pillow. Ah, husband, how handsome you would have looked wearing such a thing!

A buzzer made an offensive noise when I walked into the shop. Indeed, I found everything about Golden Journeys unpleasant. The lights are glaring, the display cases crowded, the air frigid, the stock gaudy. When Cheng Yue, the owner, came to greet me, he did nothing to dispel my distaste.

"Good afternoon!" he boomed. He is a thick man, of the type who waves his hands meaninglessly as he speaks. "What can I show you this afternoon, Auntie? Or —" as he spied the jade bracelet you gave me at our wedding, which I do not remove — "are you perhaps here to sell?"

"I am not here to buy or sell, Cheng Yue. I'm here to ask about the diamond tie tack in your window."

"Yes, yes." He smiled. "A unique piece. I don't think I want to sell it. I put it in the window to attract customers because it's so beautiful."

"I see. How did you acquire it?"

"It was among other items, in a collection I bought."

"No, it wasn't. A blonde young woman brought it to you. No doubt she brought you a pair of cuff links, also. This woman." I showed him a photograph on my phone.

Cheng Yue looked at it. Then he looked at me. He was no longer smiling.

"It's a good thing you're not planning to sell this item, Cheng Yue," I said. "It is stolen. As you know. Don't worry, I do not intend to inform the authorities. But you must do three things for me."

"I — Auntie, really —"

"I don't have time for your protestations, Cheng Yue. We both know I'm correct. The things you must do are simple. First, you must remove the tie tack from your window. Keep it safe, wherever the cuff links are, until the person who brought them comes back for them. Second, you must tell no one I was here, including the person who brought you these things. If you feel you can't do this, I can call Mary Kee, who is a detective at the Fifth Precinct. She can come here to take the items for safekeeping."

"No, no, Auntie. But —"

"The second thing is, you must confirm that this is the woman who brought them. This woman, in this picture. Here, I have pictures of other blonde young women for comparison." I showed him the photos I had organized earlier. It is so interesting, husband, how many uses this tiny device can have, besides, of course, enabling me to call any of our children at any time from wherever I happen to be.

Cheng hardly looked at the other photos. "Yes. Yes, she's the one. The first one you showed me. But —"

"This situation will be resolved soon, Cheng Yue. Until then, goodbye. But keep in mind — when people throw things over a fence, someone on the other side will often get hurt."

Cheng Yue stared at me. I left his shop. I was happy to return to the heat of the bustling streets.

Once back home, I searched through my old telephone number book for the Chus. My phone knows many numbers, but not the ones from our children's grade school days. My kitchen-splattered book is still useful.

I settled comfortably, then called Chu Mei, the mother of that family. Because we had not spoken in such a long time, it would have been impolite not to ask after her husband, her children, her husband's mother. She then asked after our children. This occupied us for some time. Finally I was able to get to my actual request, which was for her son's telephone number. "My son would like to speak to him," I explained. Though our son had not said that, I had no reason to think it wouldn't be true, if the opportunity arose.

"Of course." She gave me the number.

"Thank you," I said. "Now, Mei, I must ask you something else. Cai has recently become engaged. How do you feel about this?"

"I'm delighted, of course."

"You like his young woman? Even though she isn't Chinese?"

"Oh, Yong-Yun, such old-fashioned thinking. I do admit I have difficulty making conversation with her. My English is poor, as is my husband's. My mother-in-law speaks no English at all. We are therefore perhaps a bit uncomfortable in Anna's presence. But as long as she makes my son happy, I'm happy. Also, she cooks well."

"This is your true feeling? Your husband also?"

"Yes. My mother-in-law feels the same. Although I'm not sure either of my sons believe this. But it is, truly, how we all feel."

"I see. Thank you, Mei."

"It was nice talking to you after all this time, Yong-Yun. We must get together. I would enjoy having tea with you."

"Yes," I said. "That is a fine idea."

After a few moments' rest, I called the number Chu Mei had given me. I reached only voice mail. I identified myself, leaving a message to say it was urgent that my call be returned. Soon it was.

"Come to my apartment in an hour," I said. "Press two short times on the bell downstairs so I know it's you."

"Auntie Chin —"

"This is extremely important."

I have found the only way to insure people will not continue to argue is if you are no longer on the phone, so I hung up.

An hour later I heard two short buzzes from downstairs. I buzzed back. At a knock on the door I peered through the peephole, then unlocked the locks. Into the apartment stepped Chu Li.

162

"Auntie, I don't know —"

"Of course you don't. I haven't told you yet. You may leave your shoes on that shelf." Li handed me a bag of tangelos, for which I thanked him. Putting them in the bowl with his brother's oranges, I showed Li to the sofa.

Of course I'd made tea. It's polite to serve tea to a guest no matter who the guest is.

"I've recently spoken with your brother, Cai," I said. "He's gotten engaged. Congratulations."

Li just nodded.

"Ah," I said. "You don't like his fiancée?"

"I'm not —"

"Or perhaps, you find her acceptable, but you're worried about how your parents feel. Because Cai's young woman is not Chinese. That would be admirably filial of you. It would also be foolish."

"I don't —"

"Did you discuss this question with your parents, Li? Or with your grandmother?"

"I haven't —"

"I thought not. Well, I did. Your mother chided me — chided *me* — when I inquired on this subject. She called such thinking 'old-fashioned.' "

"You asked —"

"You see," I said, "if you'd just spoken

163

with your parents, all this unpleasantness could have been avoided. You wouldn't have had to steal your brother's jewelry or his teacup. Your brother wouldn't have been upset, or suspicious of his fiancée. I wouldn't have had to work out how to make the situation come out well. Luckily, that part was not hard."

"I don't —"

"Don't know what I'm talking about? Chu Li, I don't like to hear lies. I've been to see Cheng Yue. For a man of his type, it appears he is dependable. He said, first, that he had acquired the tie tack in an estate sale. Then when I pressed him he confessed to my charge — that a blonde young woman had brought it to him. I showed him this photo. He agreed immediately that it was this woman."

I turned my phone toward Chu Li, who looked, then frowned. "Who's this?"

"I have no idea. I took her picture on the street because I thought my daughter might be interested in her hairstyle. This was the photo I first showed to Cheng, after which I showed him some others, including one of your brother's fiancée I took in a restaurant. Cheng was emphatic that the woman who'd brought the tie tack was the one in the first picture."

164

I took a sip of tea, but quickly, as I didn't want to give Li time to organize a response. I went on, "Cheng followed your instructions faithfully. You told him to display the tie tack prominently, then wait for someone to demand to know where he got it. No doubt he was surprised it was I, not your brother, who was questioning him, but he did as you said — first pretend to lie, then pretend to admit the truth. The real truth, Li, is that none of this would have had to happen if you had asked your parents how they felt instead of trying to protect them based on your own false assumption."

"I was —"

"Now, here is what we'll do next. You'll go get the jewelry from Golden Journeys so you can return it to your brother's home. I suggest you find a place near the box where he keeps these things, to make it look as though he just absentmindedly didn't finish putting them away. Also, you'll replace the stolen teacup, in the upper cabinet you took it from, but on a different shelf. Or, if you like, on the same shelf, but in a different cabinet. Cai, again, will think the mistake was his. You'll do all this soon. I'll take care of the rest."

"I don't —"

"It's been a pleasure talking to such a

filial, if foolish, son, Chu Li. Now you may go, as I have much to do."

Again, in truth, I did not have much to do. But I had much to think about. After Li left, I drank more tea. I sewed. I made my dinner. During all this, I thought.

The next morning, Chu Cai called, as I had told him to do. "You are lucky, Cai. I've been to see Cheng Yue. He assured me that the tie tack in his window came from an estate sale." You know I do not like to lie, husband, but in order to save a couple's happiness I will stretch the truth. "I compared it to the one in your photo. I believe yours is probably just misplaced in your home. Perhaps you could ask your brother, Li, to help you search for it. Another set of eyes is often useful. Please let me know how things turn out."

Cai sounded relieved, if not completely convinced. I was not worried about him any longer. He would call the next day with the good news that he had found all his items, I was sure.

But I had another call to make. This number was one I have put in my phone. I pressed the button for An-Zhang.

"Ma! Everything all right?"

"Yes, everything is fine. I would like to

speak to you. Is it possible for you to come here?"

"You sure everything's all right?"

"Yes. This is not about bad news."

"Well, in that case, I'm a lucky guy. Can I come for dinner? Tony's out of town. I'm living on sandwiches."

I went about my day, including shopping for the ingredients in An-Zhang's favorite dish. When he arrived in the early evening the air was aromatic with Chinese sausage. He handed me a box of lovely clementines. I'm quite rich in citrus fruit now.

"Smells great in here! Where's Ling Wan-ju?"

"I asked your sister to give us time alone."

"Ma? You said everything was okay."

"It is. Please sit."

"In Ba's chair? You never let us sit there."

"You are a grown man now, An-Zhang. Please, take your father's chair. Here is tea. An-Zhang, I saw Chu Cai recently."

"Cai! How is he?"

"He's very well. He's getting married."

"That's great."

"Yes, it is, though a problem came up that I was required to help him with. His fiancée is not Chinese. Because of this difference, his brother made the error of thinking his parents were not pleased with the young

167

lady. This led to a series of mistakes that threatened the match. Luckily the situation is now resolved."

"That's good."

"Yes, it is. It also started me thinking. If a young man is worried about what his parents think about something, but he hasn't spoken to his parents about it, perhaps his parents ought to speak to him."

"Ma?"

"Cai almost lost his chance for a happy marriage through a misunderstanding brought about by his brother's worry about their parents' feelings. I don't want the same to happen to you. Since your father is gone, I will speak for both your parents." I sipped some tea. "You've been sharing a home with Tony for a number of years. I've been touched by the effort all five of my children have put into hiding from me the fact that you are more than roommates to each other. Because you've been so careful to shield me so I would not be upset, I've said nothing. But I don't want you to lose your chance at happiness through worry about my feelings. So I'll tell you, speaking also for your father, that I like Tony very much. I find him quite dear. Also, he cooks well. Any further affirmation of your friendship is something I would welcome. In fact, I would appreciate

168

having only two, not three, unmarried children to worry about."

An-Zhang sat in his chair with his mouth open. His eyes glowed. He jumped up to hug me. Husband, I tell you, he almost broke my bones.

So this is the good news I've come to tell you. Our son An-Zhang will be married in the fall. I told you weddings are not the same in America, husband. Though they are not entirely different, either. We'll hold a large banquet. There will be singing, wine, red envelopes. Organizing the details of such an event is exhausting. The children say I don't need to worry so much, but the wedding is the responsibility of the groom's family. That this wedding involves two grooms only makes things more complicated.

Luckily, I have Chu Mei to confide in. Her son Cai will be marrying his Anna, also. When we met for tea we exchanged congratulations, then sympathy on the difficulties of wedding planning. Enjoying each other's company, we continue to meet.

So there you have it, husband. Two weddings. A renewed friendship. Our son in good hands. Our children no longer feeling they have to hide something from me.

I know you are as happy as I am with all

this news. Now, as I have tired myself —
likely tired you also! — by telling this long
tale, I will sit quietly with you here on your
hillside, drinking tea, enjoying the breeze,
on the anniversary of our wedding day so
long ago.

AMAZING GRACE

BY MAX ALLAN COLLINS

Grace Rushmore, at eighty, seemed aptly named to those who knew her well. She surely did move with an easy grace — years ago, when she and husband Lem were courting, her dancing particularly suited her name, her movements as fluid as a gentle stream, as lovely as she wasn't.

But those who only knew Grace in her later years, which had begun really around age forty, saw a skinny, sunken-cheeked old woman right out of Grant Wood's *American Gothic,* her countenance severe, her words rare. Perhaps the most graceful things about her, to those who knew her from a distance, were how uncomplainingly hard she worked, how well she had raised the four children who survived (of the ten she'd carried), and how nobly she'd tolerated Lem and his reprobate ways.

In 1909, when Lem had come calling, she already looked like the old maid she seemed destined to become. Lemuel Richard Rushmore had been tall and handsome, tall enough that her bony, lanky frame next to him didn't seem so odd, though he was much too good-looking for her, people had whispered from the start. But no one was surprised by the union, nonetheless.

After all, Grace's father was Jonathan Holding, one of the most prosperous farmers in Polk County, Iowa, and Lem's bad reputation had preceded him. Like Grace, Lem was thirty and unmarried. He had been arrested for stealing horses three times and convicted once, doing a year in the county jail, a sentence her Baptist father considered unduly lenient. Lem was a rounder, it was said, a man married only to drink, but whose good looks and easy charm had brought him plenty of female affection, unmarried and married alike.

But what a smile Lem had. He was fun and he was funny and he wouldn't hurt a fly. People just *liked* him. Even Papa had come to be fond of him, particularly after Lem sat in the parlor, hat in hands, and promised he had changed his ways and wanted only to settle down, have a family, and work hard. He'd never farmed, but was eager to learn.

They had married in 1910, and now it was

1960. Fifty years had passed, that had only felt like one hundred. Not all of it was bad, though. Lem was kind to her, in his way. Brought her flowers on birthdays and anniversaries, though not always on the days themselves. He was good to her children, giving them candy and winning their love, and leaving the spanking to her. She never was as loved by her offspring as Lem was.

His looks had left him by his fifties. His hair had long since turned white and his handsome face became a bucket-headed exaggeration of itself, like something a State Fair caricature artist drew. The tall frame grew a potbelly — beer will do that, and a lot of beer will *really* do that — and his nose spread and reddened.

He never did pitch in at the farm in any way. Sort of pretended to for a while, but not for long. Instead he hung out in the poolrooms of nearby Des Moines and at various saloons and houses of ill repute. After their tenth child died, Lem never bothered trying to have relations with her. She was relieved, because he had bouts of what he called "the French disease," which had played a role in all those miscarriages, the doctors said.

In these fifty years, rewards had been few and far between for Grace. But Lem was pleasant, even kind, called her "Sweet Thing" even now. Just like when they sat on her papa's front porch in the swing and he held her hand and smiled at her. The smile was still nice, thanks to those fancy dentures she'd bought him.

The farm was run by others, since Papa died during the second war and money was coming in. Not as much as Lem would have liked, and he had encouraged Grace to use her skills in the kitchen to bring in a little more.

She in particular had a sweet touch — she could have been a professional baker, Lem always said. They ought to sell the farm and buy a bakery in town and she could whip up those sweet delights, as he put it. Her specialty, what she was best known for, was wedding cakes. She had taken a course in town on decorating, uncovering a natural artistic knack for it, and the golden lemon-touched wedding cake with the delicious cream-cheese frosting was her claim to Polk County fame.

Some people said the only time she smiled was when a bride-to-be and her mother came to pick up their special cake, with its towering tiers, perfectly spaced and arranged like some castle in the sky. The happy clients would *oooh* and *aaah* and a

176

tiny smile would etch itself on Grace's grooved, deep-cheeked face.

She knew this because girlfriends at church (girls in their seventies and eighties like her) would tease her about it.

"You should smile *more,* Gracie," they'd say.

"You're so pretty when you smile," they'd lie.

But what did she have to smile about?

Really, though, when she thought about it, she had plenty to smile about. Four lovely children, grown and successful, Robert and Lucas and Jennifer and Beth, all married, generating twelve grandchildren and two great-grandchildren so far. Not a bum in the batch. No carousers. No loose women.

When she thought about this in church, which she frequently did (Lem accompanying her on Christmas and Easter only), she knew that her brood turning out so well was a miracle.

And she would bow her head and thank God.

Only her oldest, Beth, lived in the area. The others would be coming from hither and yon. That was so very exciting, contemplating it. Not in many years had the entire clan been under one roof. Each little family had its own Christmas traditions, though her kids always made sure one of them brought their family to the big old farmhouse to spend a few days of the holidays with Grandma and Grandpa. Great-grandma and Great-grandpa now, for the two little tykes of Beth's daughter's.

Grace sat in the big cupboard-lined kitchen with Beth, who at forty-eight was quite attractive, if a little heavy, her features echoing her father's, before dissipation. She dressed rather severely, a black-and-gray suit with pink-and-gray pillbox hat today, since as a third grade teacher flashy apparel was not appropriate. They drank hot tea and shared the frosted sugar cookies Grace usually only made at the holidays. This was just September, though, and the Golden Anniversary celebration was the closest thing to a holiday coming up.

In two weeks.

"Where's Pop?" Beth asked.

"At his job."

Lately Lem had been bartending part-time in a little town nearby.

Beth's expression tightened. "I don't suppose there's any chance . . . Nothing."

"What, dear?"

She sighed, summoned a smile. "Is there any chance we might keep him sober at the festivities?"

Grace lifted an eyebrow. "Doubtful. The punch won't be spiked, *that* much I can promise you."

Her daughter glanced away, thoughtfully. "Maybe I could talk to him."

"Welcome to try."

Beth smiled. "You know, Lucy and Sam love Pop to death."

"He's always been good with kids."

"Well, he's always *been* one, hasn't he?" She shook her head. "Mother, how have you managed it?"

"A day at a time."

"Well, of course, but . . . you've worked so *hard*." Beth paused. "That's something I wanted to talk to you about."

"What is, dear?"

She sat forward. "Jenny and Bob's Martha and Luke's Aggie and I . . . we all want to pitch in. We want to make the meal. No, no objections! You tell us what you want to have and just turn the kitchen over to us."

Grace was shaking her head. "Won't hear of it."

"No! Now, listen to me, you stubborn old girl. This is going to be *your day*. You have *earned* it! You let us in here, in your precious kitchen, and we'll wait on you and show you that the good cookin' you've dem-

179

onstrated all these years was catching. We are darn *good* at it, too, thanks to you!"

Grace smiled a little. She could smile. A little. She said, "All right. I want ham and turkey and you'll use my stuffing recipe."

"Of course. You bet."

"Mashed potatoes, brown gravy, green beans *and* creamed corn. Corn muffins."

"Way ahead of you."

Grace raised a finger. "But one thing — *I'll* do the cake. It's my specialty. It's what I'm known for. I'll have it ready before I turn this torture chamber over to you girls. Understood?"

Beth was smiling, nodding. "Understood."

Grace cleaned the old house, every nook, every cranny. No one was staying with them — all her children with their families either went to a motel or bunked in with Beth, who had a big, nice house in Des Moines. After all, the old homestead was terribly run-down, Grace knew — nothing she could do about it. But just the same, every bedroom would be spick-and-span.

For the three days before the 50th celebration, she cleaned like a woman possessed, washing windows, mopping floors, bending here, on tippy toes there, as graceful as the young woman she'd been, dancing. She hadn't been this happy in years. She barely noticed that Lem hadn't been around for three days. Not that such a thing was unusual. Benders, he called them. And he was taking penicillin, so that meant the houses of ill repute again.

Eighty years old and still a rounder.

She didn't get worried till the afternoon before the Big Day. She had spent all morning working on the cake, and it was a masterpiece — towering, tall, white with frosting filigree, guarding the secret of the moist, yellow cake within. Five tiers! The top tier a small cake for her and Lem to share.

She called every saloon she knew of, starting with the one where he sometimes worked. Then the pool halls. Finally her children. Jenny and her husband and kids were already in Des Moines, with Beth. Nobody had seen Lem, but Jenny and Beth said they'd be over.

Beth, in a navy blue suit with white trim, and Jenny, in a more colorful yellow-and-green frock, did not mention their father at first. Instead they gaped at the magnificent cake and clapped and laughed and sang their mother's praises. They were sincere enough, but still, she thought, trying too hard.

The cake was on the table like a confectionary centerpiece, her well-honed cake knife at the ready; but her girls would have to settle for cookies and tea. The women sat at one end of the kitchen table, chattering about who was coming — *everyone!* — and how wonderful tomorrow would be.

Grace said, "I want to ask you something."

"Sure," Jenny said.

"Of course," Beth said.

Her face went to one daughter, then the other. "Why do you love your father more?"

"What?" they both said, smiling in horror.

Both her girls leaned forward and put their hands on hers and looked at her intently, searching for tears that weren't there.

"Oh, Mother, don't be silly," Jenny said. "We love you *equally.*"

Beth said nothing.

"It never felt that way," Grace said.

Silence took the room, leaving nothing but the fragrance left over from baking that cake.

Finally Beth sighed. "We *did* love him more."

Jenny frowned at her sister.

"When we were children," Beth added.

Jenny said nothing.

"He was easy to love," Beth went on, sighing, shaking her head. "He was a big ole teddy bear. He gave us nickels and candy and hugs. He took us to the movies while you were slaving over a hot stove. He was a wonderful father when we were six or eight or even eleven. You were the disciplinarian. *Of course* we loved him more."

Jenny, understanding, said, "When we got older, we knew who to love. We knew who was worthy. Mom, we'll always love Daddy. He's a great big kid. But you were everything to us . . . even when we . . . even when we didn't know it."

Their mother smiled a little. Yes she did. Nodded.

Then Grace said, "The grandkids love him, too. I think I just *scare* them."

Beth smirked. "Why *wouldn't* they love him? He's one of them."

The girls laughed. Grace kept the smile going.

"Mom," Jenny said, clutching Grace's hand, "it's been a long haul, but you made it. Don't spoil your day by thinking about the, uh . . . well, the bad things. The hard parts. No marriage is perfect. Think about the houseful of kids of all ages who will be here to celebrate you and everything you've done for us."

They talked about other things for a while.

Jenny's boy Jimmy, 11, watched too much TV (*Maverick* was his favorite), and her older girl, Kathy, 16, wore too much makeup and hair spray (a Breck girl). Beth's grandkids, Sam and Lucy — seven and five respectively — were a pistol and a little lady, respectively.

At the door, Beth said, "He'll show up. He won't miss this."

"He wouldn't do that to you," Jenny said.

But they all knew he might. Maybe not intentionally, but a drunk out on a drunk? Who knew what he might do?

Her husband stumbled in before midnight, barely able to walk. His clothes were a mess, an unmade bed with a souse in it. His lips were thick and loose. Always seemed liver-lipped when he got really drunk.

Somehow she walked him in and got him to the downstairs bathroom with its shower fixture. Helping him out of his shoes to step into the tub, fully clothed, was tricky. She got the spray going in his face and he drowned standing up for a while, but came around somewhat. Enough to strip himself out of his clothes with only a little as-sistance.

Naked, he was an even bigger baby. Not much hair on him, except that white butch on his skull. Pink like the pigs Papa used to slaughter. She had a bathrobe for him. Got him into it. Walked him up the stairs and into his bedroom. They hadn't slept in the same room for years.

"Sweet thing," he said, and plopped on top of the bedcovers. Clumsily he got his dentures out and dropped them into the waiting glass on the bed stand, *plink plink.* "Sweet thing . . ."

Then he was snoring.

That was when she decided.

When the whole family was gathered, and all the well wishes and speeches were over, she would tell them. She would tell *him.*

"I want a divorce," she would say. Then she would stand and point at him like God Almighty at the world's worst sinner and say, "And I want you out of this house, Lemuel Richard Rushmore, right this minute."

She looked down at the big pink baby in the bathrobe, snoring, his lips flapping over the toothlessness, and clenched her fists and promised herself she would tell him.

Tell them all.

And then the day was everything Grace had dreamed it would be.

After all these years, finally *her* day.

Her girls and the wives of her boys indeed cooked a wonderful dinner, after which Grace's cake was the sensation of the entire event. She served it up herself, and Beth spirited away the top little tier for the hostess and host to share later. Lem had two big pieces but Grace held back, making sure everyone else got however much of the sweet wonderful stuff as they wanted. Then it was gone.

The younger kiddies were running around, having fun exploring the big old house, while the older ones were bored, Grace knew. She showed them to the den where the small black-and-white TV would have to do. The grown-ups danced to some old 78s and even she and Lem cut a rug to "By the Light of the Silvery Moon." Everyone's eyes were big and some teared up when they saw how light on their feet the old couple was.

That was when she softened. She might still throw the old scallywag out, but not today. That would be cruel. That might ruin everyone else's good time.

But she did harden again some, when she saw Lem pouring liquid from a flask into his cup of punch. Five times, she saw that. Still, it only seemed to make Lem more jovial. He had never been a really nasty drunk. That much you could say for him.

And it was fun to watch him caper with the children. The kiddies squealed with laughter, just loving the attention of the big white-haired teddy bear.

Finally, the husband and wife, the Golden Anniversary couple, sat in high-backed chairs with windows behind them streaming sunshine while everybody brought them presents and said kind words. Almost everything Grace received was a kitchen item, green bean slicer, a handheld ice crusher, pots, pans, and a dishwasher that everybody had pitched in on, rolled out by the boys with a big golden ribbon around it (it would be installed later). This got applause. As for Lem, he got tobacco for his pipe, a fancy pool cue, a sweater, a joke book, a few other things. Not as much as Grace. He was half recipient of the dishwasher, after all.

A day that had begun around eleven o'clock was over by sundown, and everyone took their leave. Lem disappeared off somewhere and Grace went to the door and saw everyone out. Thanked each one, squeezed their hands, giving all of them smiles wider than they'd ever seen from her.

She stood on the front stoop and waved and smiled some more as each vehicle drove off, hands big and small waving back at her from car windows, smiles everywhere, then fading with what was left of the sun.

A more perfect day she could not imagine.

All that remained was to have a piece of her white-frosted masterpiece.

In the kitchen, Lem was sitting in his undershirt and suspenders having one last bite of the small final tier of the Golden Anniversary cake. He had eaten every bit. Every morsel.

She sat beside him and he looked at her with frosting and crumbs on his thick smiling lips and she picked up the cake knife and thrust it into his eye.

He sat there with his mouth open, some semimasticated cake within, the handle of the knife sticking straight out, then toppled to the floor. She looked over at the sink, where her children had piled the dirty dishes that would not wait for the installation of the new dishwasher.

But she would clean up later. In the morning.

For now she stepped over her husband and went upstairs to her bed and Bible.

LEMON LAYER CAKE

(FAMILY SIZE)

Cake:

3 cups sifted all-purpose flour
1 tbs baking powder
1/2 tsp salt
1 cup butter, softened
1 and 3/4 cups sugar
4 large eggs
2 tsp vanilla extract
1 cup buttermilk
1 tbs lemon zest, heaping
1/3 cup lemon juice

Frosting:

1 cup butter, softened
8 ounces cream cheese, brick-style and
  softened
5 cups powdered sugar
2 tbs lemon juice
1 tsp vanilla extract
pinch of salt

Cake Directions:

- With an electric mixer, cream the butter and sugar together in a large bowl until smooth.
- Add the eggs and vanilla and beat until smooth. In a separate bowl, combine

189

the flour, baking powder, and salt.
- Add the dry ingredients into the wet mixture.
- Add the buttermilk, lemon zest, and lemon juice and mix on low until there are no lumps. The batter will be a little thick. Pour batter evenly into three round greased 9-inch pans.
- Bake at 350 degrees for 20 to 25 minutes depending upon your oven.
- When done, let cool completely.

Frosting Directions:
- In a large bowl, beat the butter until creamy.
- Add the cream cheese and beat until smooth.
- Add the powdered sugar, lemon juice, vanilla, and pinch of salt and continue mixing until creamy.
- If frosting is too thin, add more powdered sugar; if too thick, add more lemon juice.

Assembly:
- Using a sharp knife, slice a thin layer off the top of each cake to make a flat surface.
- Place one cake on a cake stand, and evenly cover the top with about 1 cup

of the frosting.

- Place second cake on top of the first, and cover with another cup of frosting. Repeat for the third cake, this time covering all sides of the cake.
- Refrigerate for half an hour before slicing.
- *Bon appetit!*

■ ■ ■ ■

Ten Years, Two Days, Six Hours

Days, Six Hours

BY WENDY HORNSBY

■ ■ ■ ■

Before I stood up in front of witnesses and vowed to cherish Herbert Garfield Hardy for better or worse, you'd think that someone, one of his ex-wives maybe, would have clued me in about just how bad the worse parts might get. No one did, but with me, a vow is a vow, so I stuck it out with Herbie for ten years, two days, and six hours before the escape clause, the one about till death do us part, kicked in.

Even after he was gone, Herbie managed to turn what could have been a nice straightforward leave-taking into a grand and complicated cock-up. On his very last day, he was lying in a hospital bed with an IV in one hand and a final directive in the other when I said to him, "Herbie, why don't you buy the cremation package? Think about it. When the time comes I can tuck you into a carry-on, fly you home to Omaha, and put you into the ground, no muss, no fuss."

But Herbie, ever the contrarian, countered with, "Nope. Button me into a good three-piece suit and lay me out in the biggest mahogany coffin my money can buy. Honey, if questions ever come up I want there to be a corpse to dig up." As if anyone would ever question how Herbie Hardy's antique carcass finally came to be inside a box. But it was his own damn corpse to dispose of, so I just held fire one last time and gave him the last word.

Knowing when to hold fire was how I got by with Herbie for ten years, two days, and six damn hours. We met on a firing range, so he always knew I was a better shot than he was. In any ugly situation he could gin up (and there were plenty of those) he always knew there was a line he couldn't cross with me. That, and I cooked for him whatever he wanted just the way he wanted it.

Because of Herbie's need to complicate my life even posthumously, I was out in the middle of the desert somewhere northeast of Las Vegas when Mr. Peters from the mortuary called. After six hours driving Herbie's giant Lincoln Navigator with nothing for company except country classics on the CD and radio preachers promising to save my eternal soul, I confess that a two-way conversation of any kind with a living being, even if it was with Mr. Peters from the mortuary, was a welcome diversion.

"Mrs. Hardy," Mr. Peters said in his silky mortician's voice. "We at the Peters Family Funeral Home want to apologize to you for any inconvenience the failure of our transport equipment caused you and your loved ones this morning. You know that we strive to provide the very best in care and service to families during their time of sorrow."

I rolled my eyes, knowing the reason for his call had nothing to do with any concern for me or my loved ones. Before he could offer some version of *circumstances beyond our control,* I said, "*Inconvenience* may be the understatement of the week, don't you think, Mr. Peters?"

"We are deeply chagrined, Mrs. Hardy. Deeply. The transport vehicle was in perfect running order this morning."

"Until the engine blew," I said. "Explain to me why you couldn't send another hearse to transport Herbie to the airport after the first one crapped out? We missed our flight."

"I am, dear lady, profoundly sorry." Then he said it: "But circumstances beyond our control —"

"Mr. Peters, have you any idea what it cost me to rebook flights at the last minute? As

I'm sure you heard, I couldn't get tickets for the two of us on the same flight. Did you think it was okay for my Herbie to fly all by himself?"

"I — I — I . . ." he stammered, followed by a long pause that I was happy to wait out. After a count of seven and a deep breath he said, "I do apologize again, Mrs. Hardy. You've no idea how sorry I am."

I was trying to dredge up the energy to fake cry a little until he said, "I hate to even bring up the reason for my call, but do you have any idea where our casket buddy might have got to?"

" 'Casket buddy'? You mean Ernie, your crack driver? The guy who was supposed to drive me and Herbie to the airport in time to catch our plane to Omaha, which he did not manage to do?"

"Uh, no, ma'am. And I am truly regretful that you missed your first flight. Unfortunate, and of course totally unforeseeable. But I am referring to the wheeled apparatus used to convey your loved one's casket at the church."

"The wheelie thing under Herbie's casket?"

"Yes, ma'am, the wheelie thing under your husband's casket."

"Why on this green earth would you think

198

I know anything about your damn buddy gizmo?"

"A lovely woman at the church told me that the last time she saw it was while you were waiting for transport."

"That lovely woman at the church was probably the old girl who wheeled Herbie out the back door and threw a tablecloth over him because seeing the coffin upset the ladies who were coming in to set up for a wedding. A pink flowered tablecloth, Mr. Peters. Dignified handling, my ass. I promise that I will forget you ever made this highly inappropriate call if you promise me that you finally managed to get my Herbie onto his plane on time."

"Uh," was his answer. I heard some side conversation but hung up and turned off my phone's ringer before he figured out what to say next. I was fairly certain by the number of times Peters called back after that and the length of the messages he left that he had come to understand that the Peters Family Funeral Home had lost track of the dearly departed Herbert Garfield Hardy, Senior.

What is it with mortuaries that everything involved with preparing a body for burial gets renamed? Flowers are tributes, the dead guy is the loved one, and all his friends and relatives become the bereaved. Casket buddy? The thing certainly is helpful, like a good buddy should be, so okay, a buddy. It folds up like a beach chair. Doesn't weigh much, either.

In no frame of mind to be alone with my own thoughts after that call, I flipped through the radio stations again, found some *banda* music from south of the border and turned it up. But there was no escaping the mental loop that repeated over and over how I came to be in that place at that time.

The cascade of events began Saturday night at the party Herbie's grown kids threw to celebrate our tenth wedding anniversary. A big deal, our tenth, because none of Herbie's previous wives had lasted a full ten years. Herbie, being Herbie, made sure they didn't. The thing was, his standard prenup was for ten years. If his wife, whoever she might be at the time, made it past that ten-year hurdle, the prenup went away and she became Herbie Hardy's sole heir. A rich widow, one day.

Don't think Herbie was cheap, because he wasn't. It's just that he was afraid a wife might get mad enough or fed up enough to throw something at him — like a kitchen knife or a projectile out of the business end of his prized SIG Sauer automatic — unless he set up his finances so that she got noth-ing if he didn't survive to the end of the ten-year term. So call the prenup a life as-surance policy. Out of an abundance of cau-tion, he dumped every one of his wives well before the stroke of midnight on year ten. Except me, though I came close a few times.

The kitchen isn't the only room in the house where a wife can cook, if you get my meaning. Herbie generally seemed piggishly happy with me, so I thought I was safe. Then somewhere toward the end of year eight, or maybe early in year nine, I started getting signals that I might become the next ex–Mrs. Herbie Hardy, no matter how much fun Herbie was having. It was about that time that Herbie started getting sick: stomach cramps, liver problems. From then until the end, every morsel, every drop the man consumed came from my hand. Until the party Saturday night.

Knowing their father was a short-timer, and wanting to curry favor with — they hoped — their future benefactor, Herbie's grown kids decided to throw us a big catered party at the country club. Six-piece band, open bar, sit-down dinner, the whole works. I advised against it, reminding everyone about Dear Old Dad's delicate tummy. Doctors warned that Herbie's former constant companion, Jack Daniel's, was now poison to him, so why tempt with full bar service? If he couldn't drink Jack and he couldn't keep down a heavy meal, why not a quiet dinner at home? I said. As stubborn as their father, the kids were not to be dissuaded from trying to curry Dad's favor. Anyway, Herbie wanted the party so there had to be a party.

The day of the party, Herbie gave me yet another shiny bauble and told me to show some cleavage, and off to the club we went. For most of the evening I managed to keep an eye on Herbie to make sure the glass in his hand held nothing stronger than ginger ale and that no one but me gave him anything to eat. But after all the toasts and bad jokes about what I must have done to hold Herbie's interest longer than any of the five previous Mrs. Hardys, he drifted out of sight. The first call to 9-1-1 logged in at five past eleven.

At the stroke of midnight, when I became his sole heir, Herbie was still breathing. He continued to breathe until Tuesday morning at six. Three days later, buttoned into a three-piece suit and nestled inside a very expensive mahogany box, Herbie made his last trip down the aisle of a church.

The kids, if you can call them kids — the

youngest was a decade older than me —
were ever so helpful during the days after
Herbie passed on to his final reward. Even
Herbie Junior was civil to me. On the morning of the funeral he volunteered to load all
the flowers that came to the house into
Dad's giant Navigator and take them to the
church. I also saw him load a half case of
Jack left over from the wake the night before
into the rear deck along with the flowers. A
chip off the old block, that Junior.

Attitudes among the offspring changed
very soon after the funeral service. When
Mr. Peters's hearse blew its engine and we
were all left standing around in the church
narthex waiting for a replacement car to
take Herbie to the airport, the kids got into
a huddle with Herbie's lawyer. Every once
in a while, from the glances they threw at
me, I understood that the lawyer was explaining the details of their father's will to
them. They each got enough cash, a few
thousand dollars, so that they couldn't challenge the will, and nothing more. After that,
they suddenly remembered that they had
other places to be.

Junior decided that his aunt Harriet, who
looked perfectly healthy to me, was tired
and needed to be driven home. He handed
me the Navigator keys and left in her car.

One after another, the siblings and half siblings followed, the friends and business associates in their wake, until it was just me waiting with Herbie.

Even though Herbie was an unmitigated son of a bitch all his life, I thought it was wrong for him to be left all alone at the church like a jilted bride. Those feelings became more acute when we missed our flight. I called his cousin in Nebraska to let her know we had to postpone the planned graveside service at the family plot somewhere in a cornfield outside Omaha. She said uh-huh a couple of times before she broke in to ask if they could go ahead as scheduled with the catered lunch I'd paid for. Well, why not? Then she gave me the number of the local farmer with a backhoe who took care of graves at the family cemetery and told me to give him a call when I finally got Herbie there. The hole was already dug, better pray it doesn't rain. People had things to do, you know, can't be expected to just hang around until we finally showed up, and goodbye. After I hung up, I patted Herbie's box and told him, "You made your bed, honey. And now you get to sleep in it for long, long time." Still, I felt bad for the old bugger.

The church narthex was fairly cool and

there was a padded bench I could stretch out on, so I was comfortable enough as Herbie and I waited for Mr. Peters to come through with a ride. Pretty soon, though, we were in the way of the florist who arrived to decorate for an evening wedding. With obsequious if insincere apologies, we were moved to a back hallway. Sitting next to Herbie on an itty-bitty chair pulled from one of the Sunday school classrooms, with my suitcase on the cheap linoleum floor beside me and Herbie's sheaf of travel documents — death certificate, health department clearance to transport, airline agreement — clutched in my hand, I felt like an orphan waiting for a bus.

The caterer made it clear that I was in her way as she loaded in. Irritated, hot in my funeral dress, desperate to kick off the high heels, after yet another call to Mr. Peters about the latest estimate on time of arrival for the replacement hearse, I took my suitcase into the ladies' room and changed into comfortable travel clothes, jeans and sneakers. When I came out again I found that someone had pushed Herbie right out the back door. The last indignity was the damn pink tablecloth thrown over him so that the sight of him wouldn't offend.

Now I was pissed, and all the apologies of

all the church ladies, florists, and caterers weren't going to make the situation better. It was hot outside. Embalmed though he was, sitting against a white wall in full sunlight was doing Herbie no good. I called Peters again and got the same answer: soon.

That's when I spotted the Navigator parked under a tree on the far side of the church parking lot. With no place to sit and no place for my suitcase, I walked over and stowed my case in the car. The big SUV was cool inside, a better place for both me and Herbie to wait. So I dumped the last of the so-called floral tributes out of the cargo space onto the pavement to make room for Herbie, backed up to the church door, and opened the rear hatch. That casket buddy made it easy to just roll Herbie inside. I folded the buddy and tucked it in beside the coffin, closed the hatch, and climbed behind the wheel, intending to park the car back under the tree. And then I thought, Fuck it, and just kept going.

Thing was, while I waited, I had started thinking. The best tickets I could get put me on a flight three hours after Herbie. Without me close by to look after things, what if there was a mix-up and he went astray? Or my flight was delayed or canceled? What then? Would the airline tuck

Herbie into unclaimed baggage or ship him out to some local mortuary, where I might not find him for how long? Or, worst of all, what if the airline lost his paperwork and he was sent to the local morgue to who knows what fate?

Considering the way things had gone so far, I had every expectation of yet another grand foul-up. Thinking about all the possibilities, as soon as I put the key in the ignition of that giant SUV, I realized that the only way I could be certain Herbie would get safely under the soil at the old family cemetery was to take him there myself. Messy, yes. Nuts, definitely. The best of alternatives at the moment, I hoped so.

Mr. Peters was still filling my voice mail when daylight faded. The desert scrub that stretched to the far horizon all afternoon disappeared under a black curtain so dense that I could see nothing beyond the reach of my headlights except the occasional beams of oncoming cars and trucks. As I drove, mile after dark and empty mile, having Herbie behind me, quiet as he was, got awfully damn spooky. I began to worry about finding gas on time or having a flat and getting stuck out in the middle of wherever I was. And then answering questions if anything happened. How could I explain?

I had my phone in hand looking for a signal in case I needed to call Triple-A when the glow of flashing neon broke into the black horizon. I crested a low grade and I saw the source, a gas station and mini-mart dead ahead. I pulled in and stopped at a pump. While the SUV's tank filled, I went inside looking for a restroom and something to eat. The option for the first was adequate, for the second skimpy. I took care of business, gathered some basic road trip provisions, and went back outside.

A state trooper had pulled in behind me and stopped with his cruiser kissing my rear bumper. Medium-aged, soft in the middle, shiny on top, the trooper got out and swaggered over toward me. He tipped his hat before he leaned in for a long look at the pink-shrouded cargo in the back of my car.

"Good evening, Officer," I said, dumping my provisions onto the front seat.

"What're ya carrying back there?"

I shrugged, reached behind the seat and gave the coffin a few sharp knocks. "An ugly old antique. A family piece. I'm taking it to a cousin who wants it for some reason."

"Yeah?" The trooper, hand resting on his holstered service weapon, stayed beside the Navigator as if he had nothing better to do.

I didn't like the way he looked me over, top to bottom, eyes lingering where, if he'd used his hands, I'd charge him with assault. "Awful late for a pretty young lady to be out here all alone."

"I'm fine." And not as alone as you might think, I refrained from saying. "I want to get some miles behind me before I stop for the night."

"Next town's across the state line," he said as I replaced the nozzle in the pump and secured the gas cap.

In no mood for chitchat with law enforcement, I smiled and gave him a little salute as I opened my car door. I said, "You be careful out there, Officer," shut the door, and turned the key in the ignition. He stepped aside and watched my tail until I pulled back out onto the highway.

Something about the way the trooper watched me go set me on edge. Ten years with Herbie taught me to always be ready for the next thing that got thrown my way. I popped the hatch under the dash and made sure the SIG Sauer automatic Herbie kept hidden there was in place and loaded. A couple of big rigs barreled past me, and nothing else until I reached the state line. That's when I saw him, staying well back until I was over the Nevada line and into

the top corner of Arizona. Out of his jurisdiction.

I had my hand on my phone when he lit
me up. I pulled over, lowered my window,
and hit Replay on the first of Mr. Peters's
voice mails. The mortician was saying
something about a terrible mistake when
the trooper leaned into the open window.

Phone to my ear, volume down so that
the sound that leaked out was no more than
indistinct male blah-blah-blah. I held my
hand up to the trooper, a signal to wait, and
addressed the phone: "Dad, I don't know
why he pulled me over. I was not speeding,
Dad. Cruise control's on. Maybe it's a tail-
light. What? No, no indicator popped up on
the dash. Just hold on, I'll ask him."

I muted Mr. Peters and smiled up at the
trooper. "Sorry. My dad has a tracker app
on me. As soon as I stopped the car, he was
on the line. So, what's the problem, Deputy?"

"Your father?" he said, scowl lines gathered into a V between his eyes.

"Yeah." I thumbed the volume up a notch
and put the phone back to my ear. "He
looks okay, Dad. I spoke with him when I
got gas. Yes, same guy."

I flipped to the phone's camera and held
it up to frame the trooper's face. "You don't

mind if I take a photo, do you? Dad wants to know what you look like."

The trooper snatched the phone out of my hand, flicked it off, and tossed it onto the passenger seat. "I don't know what you're playing at, lady, but I do know the difference between a new coffin and an antique chest. I need you to come in and answer a few questions. There's an off-ramp about a tenth of a mile ahead. You go ahead and proceed to the off-ramp, turn right at the bottom. I'll be right behind you. Got it?"

"Yes, sir."

I watched him get back into his cruiser as I pulled onto the highway. There were no lights at the end of the off-ramp he signaled for me to take. None nearby and none in the distance. I made the turn at the bottom of the ramp onto a narrow road with weeds growing up between the cracks in the pavement. In a sudden move, the trooper sped around me and stopped at a diagonal in front of me, trapping me between his car and a deep arroyo. I waited for his next move.

His flashlight beam bounced off my side mirror, so I didn't see him approach. Without a word, he yanked open my door, grabbed my left arm and pulled me out onto the ground — rough, no please and thank you. He'd left his Sam Browne belt with his gun in the cruiser and had already undone his pants before he manhandled me into position and knelt between my legs while he ripped at my jeans. As he lowered himself, I got my hand under the small of my back, grabbed hold of Herbie's SIG Sauer, stashed under my waistband, and pressed the business end into his sternum.

"Get off," I said.

There was enough light from my open car door for him to see what I was holding. His confusion, disbelief, whatever, when realization hit gave me time to scoot out from under him and put some space between us. I edged toward his car, putting me and the SIG between him and his service weapon.

Though wary, he managed to say, "Put the gun away, girlie. We'll call this a draw. Just get back in your car and go."

"Uh-uh. No. The minute I drive away, you'll get on the horn and issue an all-points bulletin on me with some bogus charge attached and get every bored lawman in the West out looking for me." I reached into his car and got his weapon, a good-looking automatic, off the front seat. "So, that's not how we end this."

"Put the guns away, honey. You and I both

know you don't have what it takes to kill a man."

"You think not? Why don't you ask the guy inside the coffin?"

His head swiveled toward the Navigator before he snapped his focus back to me. "You shot him?"

"Oh hell no. I needed ten years, 2 days, and six hours to finish off Herbie." I flipped the safety off his service automatic and nailed him dead between the eyes, got off a second shot through the Adam's apple before he fell. Herbie always said that of all his wives, I was the best shot.

A person isn't dead until his heart stops beating. Even when the brain stem is obliterated, as I believed the trooper's was, it takes a few seconds for the message that it's all over to reach the heart. Anyone who's cut the head off a chicken knows that. I waited him out, and then left him as he fell, pants at half-mast, goofy look of surprise on his face. His service weapon, wiped clean, on the broken pavement beside him.

It was raining when I stopped at a motel somewhere in Utah for a few hours' sleep. Thinking about Herbie's open grave and his cousin's concern about rain, I swore at Herbie all over again. If I ever married again, and I doubted that I would, a cremation plan would be the first item on the prenup.

I drove hard all day Saturday and went to ground in another off-brand motel just outside Omaha. Well before dawn, I was back in the Navigator, headed for the Hardy family's ancestral cemetery in a corn patch fifty miles north of the city. The sun was just beginning to brighten the sky when I arrived. A farmer riding a backhoe pulled in right behind me.

"Saw you pull up. My place is just yonder. You have Herbert Hardy back there?" the farmer asked with a nod toward the cargo deck. When I said I did, he said, "First time I knew anyone to get a last ride in a fancy Lincoln like that. Most times the mortuary in town brings folks out in their old Cadillac hearse. Be like old Herb to want something special. Guess the mortuary in town wasn't good enough for him — nothing else here was. Anyhow, I been expecting him to show up. As the elected warden of county cemeteries, ma'am, I need to see Herb's documents. Mortuary send them out with you?"

Clearly, he thought that I was a mortuary functionary of some sort. I did not disabuse him of the notion. I handed over the papers that were supposed to travel on the plane with Herbie. He looked them over, gave me a nod, and stuffed them into a back pocket of his overalls. As if I knew what I was doing, I popped the rear deck and unfolded Mr. Peters's casket buddy, asked for an assist, and got Herbie, at last, out of the car. The warden took over from there. I stood to the side and watched as he lowered Herbie into the ground and covered him over with black Nebraska soil.

Prayer never was my thing, but I admit that I said a little one. Only I addressed it to Herbie. "Bye, Herbie. I got you here, as promised. Six feet under. Now stay there."

Safe at last, I got back into the Navigator and pulled up the GPS, trying to decide what a rich widow should do first.

■ ■ ■ ■

THE ANNIVERSARY GIFT

BY JEFFERY DEAVER

■ ■ ■ ■

"Sir, I am in an extreme situation. Could you possibly help me?"

G. P. Gossett looked down at the woman, about his age of thirty-three and only a few inches over five feet. She was handsome, with a slim figure, and wore a simple tan skirt and stiff white shirtwaist, high to the neck, with billowy sleeves — fashion you saw less in the city than in smaller Midwestern towns. Although the day was not excessively hot — the temperature was around eighty degrees — sweat blossomed under her arms. She wore no color on lip nor rouge on cheek, though her fair skin was colored — with an angry bruise. Her long blond hair was bound into a bun with a thick blue gingham ribbon.

He was intrigued, but cautious. Beggars and con artists in this part of Chicago, the downtown business district, were not unheard of. And Gossett was dressed like the person he was — a well-to-do businessman, a suitable gull to be tricked. "Madam, are you asking for money?"

"My goodness, no, sir. I would never think of such a thing." Her voice was melodic. He wondered if she sang in a church choir.

"What is your trouble, then?" He instinctively straightened his four-in-hand tie. As a nod to the heat, he had chosen a light linen vest, in yellow. His jacket was dark brown and his trousers a complementing brown tweed. His favorite bowler was perched atop his head.

Her desperate eyes swiveled back to the entrance of Hardwick Court, a cul-de-sac off State Street. It was here that Gossett's club was located, and he had been inside taking lunch and a cigar.

"A man has been following me and intends to do me harm."

"Why on earth?" Gossett took in the portion of the street she'd just glanced toward. He saw passersby but no one seemed to be a ruffian.

She choked a cry. "He hasn't seen me yet. I turned down this street by mistake. I didn't see that it doesn't go through. I need to get out of view, only for a moment or two. Please!" She looked up at the doorway of the Bankers and Merchants Club.

Gossett frowned. "I'm sorry, madam, but women are not allowed inside. It's a most serious violation of the rules."

"But . . . Oh no, there he is." She stepped into the shadows of the stairs to the club's entrance.

Gossett noted a large man in a blue suit — too brash to be tasteful — and a bowler hat. He was speaking to a couple and appeared to be haranguing them. The couple walked away and it appeared that the man spat an unkind word or two after them. He gazed about him, as if trying to decide where to go next.

"Please . . ." Her hands, clutching an embroidered bag, were trembling.

The woman's eyes, though troubled, were astonishing blue-green, the color that nearby Lake Michigan assumes when the air and wind and sun all conspire to beauty. On impulse, he said, "What's your name?"

"Annie Fowler."

"And who is he to you, Miss Fowler?"

"It's Mrs. And he's my husband. Please." She touched a bruise on her cheek. "He did this. And he intends to do worse."

Gossett brushed at his thin moustache. "Come inside."

They stepped into the large marble and oak entryway. Gossett removed his bowler, revealing thick dark brown hair, which he smoothed with a palm. The receptionist, John, a bulky man in a brown suit, eyed them with some alarm. "Well, Mr. Gossett. I . . ."

He left Mrs. Fowler at the front, where she gazed out the window, her body hunched forward tensely. Gossett strode across the lobby, his shoe soles echoing in a familiar rhythm.

"Please, Mr. Gossett, you're a valued member here, but you know the rules. This is most irregular." John's voice dipped to a whisper. "It could be a scandal as serious as the Epstein matter." He glanced into the club sitting room to see if anyone had noticed the impropriety. Not yet.

Gossett chuckled. "John, no need to be distressed. Mrs. Fowler here, whom I know, was hoping to inquire about a maid's position with the club. I know the back entrance is for the women and servants but I thought, as I happened to see her on the street, you might accommodate her."

John was nearly wringing his hands. "Mrs. Doyle would be the person to see, but she's not in today."

In a whisper, leaning forward, Gossett spun the tale he'd just concocted. "She's fallen on hard times, John. She's a war widow and has had to resort to scullery work."

The story was more than credible. The War of the Rebellion, which ended eleven years ago at Appomattox Court House, had seen the deaths of hundreds of thousands of young husbands, populating the country with such women. John, a veteran himself, nodded, his face softening as he offered a pen and piece of paper. "Have her write her name and address on this. Mrs. Doyle will contact her. But have her come no farther inside. And, please, sir, be quick about it."

"Thank you, John."

Gossett carried the paper and implement to Mrs. Fowler and explained the sham. She rewarded him with a smile. "You're a clever one, sir."

He tipped his head. "By the way, G. P. Gossett at your service."

She surprised him by shaking his hand firmly. She nodded to the door. "He's past. I saw him walk this way and gaze about. Then he returned to State Street."

Gossett was infinitely relieved. He'd foreseen an incident, possibly fisticuffs — and he knew he was no match for the hulking Mr. Fowler. The woman jotted down her name and lodgings and Gossett returned the sheet and pen to the panicking receptionist. "Bless you, John."

They stepped outside and, donning his bowler, he gestured for her to wait, while he walked to State Street and looked up and down. He waved for her to join him.

She did so.

"At least the fellow wears such a gaudy suit that can be spotted a mile away. What is his name?"

"Thomas."

"He's a big fellow."

"Indeed he is. His fists especially."

"What is the reason he's angry? If that's not too forward a question."

Mrs. Fowler said, "Oh, you've earned an explanation, sir. No, no, I have no hesitation to answer. Matters like this, well, they're always complicated. To cut it short, I tend to be an independent woman. That does not sit well with him. I travel by myself, often to regions that are, we could say, less than felicitous to women. He wanted me to stay at home and dote on him." A scowl. "Like an indentured servant."

"Do you have children?"

"No. The Lord has not blessed us. And a good thing that is, I know now. He would treat a child no differently than he treats me."

"His temper can't always have been this foul."

"No, of course, I never would have married him like this. He changed over time. He was a good son to his mother, and was a brave soldier. He served with the 17th Indiana Infantry and distinguished himself at the battle of Vicksburg. He was a kind husband for some years after, but he made bad business decisions, squandering his parents' inheritance. And much of my parents', as well. It certainly is no help that he has a love for whiskey. Two days ago, when drunk, he delivered this." She gestured toward the bruise.

"And that was one blow too many?"

"I took what I could — just one valise — and fled. Thomas must have terrorized the stationmaster and learned where I went. His temper and the drink get the better of him, but when he's on his game, he's a bloodhound. I came to Chicago, thinking I would get lost in a city of this size. But that hasn't seemed to work." She turned her eyes toward him. "And what of you, Mr. Gossett? You certainly dress smartly, even on such a hot day. And you're a quick thinker. What is your profession . . . if you're not a professional rescuer of damsels in distress?"

"Nothing glamorous. I manage the station

225

operations for a railroad." He hesitated. Then Gossett decided he might as well tell her: "The C&WRR."

She gave no reaction, other than to appear politely interested. Her head scanned about once again.

He added, "The Chicago and Western?"

She focused on him, as she tried to recollect the name. "Yes, an incident, recently? Out West."

"Two months ago. Early May. It caused quite a stir. But in fairness the facts were poorly presented in the newspapers." He felt uneasy, defensive. "We had every right to relocate the village. The savages resisted and our employees and the soldiers merely defended themselves."

"Oh, I have no doubt you were justified. Why, have you heard the rumors about Colonel Custer's regiment at the Little Bighorn? The accounts are saying he and hundreds of his troops were massacred by Sioux warriors. The beasts!"

Gossett was relieved at her words of sympathy. "Exactly. You appreciate the hard spot my company was in. Our mission is to bring civilization to the West, for *everyone's* benefit . . . Ah, but forgive me. It has been a heated topic of discussion and I tend to be defensive about it. I'm glad you do not think less of me." He'd meant to say "less of the railroad," but his tongue had slipped.

"Certainly not." Mrs. Fowler turned her head about, with a faint, anxious frown. No sign of the bully in the blue suit. She said softly, "Mr. Gossett?"

"Please, call me George."

"I will. And the *P*?"

"Pendleton."

"George Pendleton Gossett. A distinguished name. And I'm Annie. I know no one in this city. Other than Mrs. Briggs, my landlady, and the Ginellis, an immigrant family who live beside me and don't speak a word of English. So I don't know who to turn to, to acquire what I need."

"And what is that?"

"A pistol."

"My goodness. Do you know how to use one?"

"I have some experience. Thomas allowed me to shoot a few times in our backyard. It turned out I was quite good — which made him irritated, until I began to miss on purpose."

"I must say, Mrs . . . Annie, I must say my firearms experience is limited to taking bird with shot. I don't own a pistol, but . . . well . . ."

She regarded his face. Gossett knew he

227

was considered a handsome man, and suave in some ways. He knew too that he exhibited a boyishness, in that his face transmitted his feelings as if by the sure hand of a telegraph operator.

She laughed. "You needn't worry, George. You made me a widow in your fiction. And though I wish I were one in this real life, I'm not a murderer. I have no desire to go to prison." Her voice dipped in timbre. "But I will say this. If he does find me and raises his hand once more, I won't hesitate to kill him." She put her long fingers around his arm. "If it troubles you to hear that and you don't want to help me, I more than understand."

"No, no, Annie." He enjoyed the musical ring of her name, as much as he enjoyed the sensation of her hand on his arm. "I'd be honored to assist you. It may take a few hours. I'll make inquiries."

"There's a small park near my boarding house. Jefferson Park, are you familiar with it?"

He was. It was in a not very pleasant part of town. He was going to suggest another location, but decided it might not be a smart idea to be seen delivering a weapon to a beautiful woman in a locale where Gossett's friends, family, or associates might spy him. None of whom would ever take a constitutional through Jefferson Park. "Yes, that's fine."

She lifted a pendant watch and opened the case. His eyes strayed to her bosom. He looked away quickly. She said, "It's now noon. Shall we say three?"

"That should be enough time." He already knew several men who could help him.

"George, I don't know how to thank you."

Again she gripped his hand with as much strength and confidence as any man, though with one very grand difference: the sense of electricity that flowed through him as palm met palm.

Thomas pounded hard on the door of the hardware store.

"Hello!" he shouted. "Hello!"

A half hour ago, he had left the decrepit portion of the city where Annie had taken up quarters, and was now in a modest working neighborhood — the 800 West block of Adams.

The plan was coming together and he now needed some things to bring matters to a tidy conclusion.

His fist slammed into the door again. The glass shook.

Still no response, though he could smell

cooking — the aroma of meat. It was coming from the apartment above the small shop.

Once more, fist upon wood.

A curtain in the back fluttered and then a man in trousers and a wrinkled white shirt pushed through. He was large and balding and he sported an elaborate moustache — not unlike Thomas's own, though he himself was far from bald; his black hair was a mane, and was presently swept back with tonic. He'd learned this gave him an ominous look and made people fearful of him.

"The devil, sir!" the shop owner snapped, opening the door. "The shop is closed." He pointed unnecessarily to a sign that reported that very fact.

"I need something," Thomas said in a monotone.

The shopkeeper sputtered, "Come back tomorrow!"

"I can't wait until tomorrow."

"We.are.closed!"

Thomas unbuttoned his coat. He withdrew his wallet and extracted a bill, held it up. The man's eyes went wide. It was a five-dollar U.S. note, featuring Andrew Jackson gazing inscrutably to the right.

"This is yours to keep. On top of my purchases."

The man blinked. His voice a whisper: "What do you need?"

Thomas said, "I have to put down a swine of mine. It's ill and I'm concerned about contamination. I need lime to reduce the body. A shovel, as well. And rope."

A woman's shrewish voice carried from upstairs. "Henry! Return here this minute. I need more water for the pot. Now!"

The man grimaced, as he looked ceilingward. "All right, but let's be quick about it."

Thomas stepped inside, handed the bill to the man, who stuffed it quickly into his pocket. He selected his shovel and a coil of rope. The shopkeeper walked behind the counter to the place where the chemicals were kept. "How much lime?"

"Ten pounds."

The man hesitated for a moment. "I'd think you wouldn't need that much for one animal. Five pounds should do the trick nicely."

Thomas lowered his head and gazed at the man from under his bushy, black eyebrows — a look that was as much a weapon as the Colt Peacemaker revolver tucked into his back waistband.

The man turned quickly and snagged a ten-pound container of lime. Thomas

231

tucked it under his arm as if it weighed no more than a loaf of bread. "How much?"

"A dollar ten for everything. No, make it a dollar even."

Thomas dug from his pocket two single notes. These he tossed onto the counter, then hefted the shovel and rope.

Irritated that the man didn't seem to understand that their transaction was over, he shot a dark glance at the door and the shopkeeper scurried to open it for him. Thomas stepped into the hot, rank street without another word.

Annie sat on an ancient bench that had not seen a coat of paint for at least thirty years.

The air in Jefferson Park was foul, oppressive. The smells were smoke and manure from the nearby stockyards. The place was bordered by abandoned and burned-out commercial buildings interspersed with squatters' shacks and tents.

Annie divided her time between city and wilderness. On the whole, she probably preferred the more rustic locales. A passion of hers was photography, and she'd had the good fortune to learn not only from Mathew Brady, the famed photographer of the War of the Rebellion, but from the frontier photographers L. A. Huffman and Stanley J.

Morrow. Annie loved those times, traveling on horseback with a small "dark tent," in which she developed her plates and printed the images. Her preference was portraiture and she had perhaps a hundred photographs of a wide variety of characters — good and bad — throughout the Midwest, South, and the territories. They were all black-and-white, not sepia or hand-tinted, as was currently fashionable. Someday, perhaps, an inventor would devise a way to capture and print color photographs. She would wait for that.

"Say there, Mrs. Fowler . . . That is to say, Annie."

She turned and observed George Gossett walking toward her through the park. Annie rose and shook his hand. They sat once more on the bench. Two women walked by. They wore their skirts *above* the knee, as clear an indication of their profession as if they'd been wearing advertising posters front and back. When they were gone and no one else was in sight, Gossett withdrew from his pocket a small revolver, dull nickel in color and with yellow bone or horn grips.

"Ah, thank you!"

She looked down and spun the cylinder slowly. It was loaded with five cartridges. He fished a box from his pocket. "Here are more bullets, though I sincerely hope you don't need a single one, let alone dozens."

She closed the weapon and examined the gun. It was silver and featured a handle that was made of polished yellow bone. His finger touched the grip. "I asked for a pretty pistol for a pretty lady." His skin brushed hers.

A laugh. "Ah, but you flatter me, George."

He withdrew his hand. Slowly.

She put the gun into her bag.

A beggar approached and a stern glare from Gossett deflected him. He gazed about at the troubled neighborhood. "Your accommodations are here?"

"Around the corner. I have a monthly rental for three dollars. I will move to nicer quarters but I have little cash at the moment. When I fled, I took the only thing of value that I had — jewelry my mother left me. It pains me but I'll need to sell some of it. If you know of a reputable jeweler . . ."

She opened her purse and withdrew a velvet pouch. She tugged the top apart and showed him dozens of rings, bracelets, necklaces. The diamonds and emeralds sparkled.

Blanching, Gossett quickly put his hand over the bag and looked around. "My goodness, Annie. Hide that at once. Around here? There are ruffians and burglars and robbers everywhere. And harlots who'd slit your throat for *paste* jewels, let alone for treasures like those. You shouldn't have them at any apartment or hotel around here."

"I'll secure a safety deposit box in a bank tomorrow. I'll take a chance tonight. After all, I have my lovely gun."

Gossett said, "I know a place where they'll be safe for this evening. And, please, let me find you more suitable lodging. I live near north of the river, far nicer. I can make inquiries about temporary rooms there."

"Thank you, George, but I won't have cash until I sell some of my mother's pieces. It could be days."

Gossett waved a hand. "Nonsense. Let me take care of it."

"Oh, but I couldn't allow that."

"You may consider it a loan. You can even wait to repay me until you find proper employment. Of course, my comments about scullery were simply to fool John — that receptionist at my club. You are quite capable of an important job. A department store clerk. Or you might even become a schoolteacher."

"Your generosity is quite breathtaking, George."

235

"And you'll need to buy some new clothing. Have you been to Marshall Field's?"

"The famous department store? No."

"It's on State Street. Not far from here. Tomorrow you can get what you need. I will stand you cash for that, too. Now I suggest we leave. This is quite the dangerous neighborhood."

They rose and waked north. Gossett explained that this, the Cheyenne district, had been so named because it was considered the Wild West of the city. Even the police avoided the neighborhood. It had been somewhat respectable until it was destroyed in the Great Fire, in 1871, and became home to criminals, prostitutes, and drunks. After being rebuilt haphazardly, it was then destroyed *again* in the Fire of 1874. After that, Cheyenne had no aspirations to improve, and it became one large gutter.

The man rambled on about the city, with enthusiasm and affection. He referred to himself, too. His family history spoke to modest means. Gossett, though, was ambitious. He was determined to work his way to the top of the C&W railroad. He'd set his sights on becoming another Chicago millionaire magnate, like Aaron Montgomery Ward, who four years ago created a mail-order retail business. Or Cyrus McCormick, the inventor of the mechanical reaper; and Marshall Field, who had founded the department store that Gossett had mentioned earlier.

They walked for a moment in silence and he appeared to be debating some matter. He sneaked a glance her way. "If I might be so bold . . ." He scoffed and shook his head. "No, forgive me."

"Please," she urged.

"I was about to ask, this evening, after we see to your jewelry and find you some accommodations, would you have any desire to dine with me tonight? But that is very forward of me."

"I don't see it being forward at all. I would be honored to."

Gossett tried to control his pleasure, but wasn't very successful. "There's a hotel downtown, the Palmer House. The poshest place in the entire city. And it has a fine dining room. Oh, and the wine cellar rivals any hotel in Paris."

He told her that the hotel had been completed just last year — it was the *new* Palmer House. The original had burned to the ground in the Great Fire, just days after opening. "The new hotel is even more regal and — better yet — is constructed of stone and steel. They say it's the world's first fireproof hotel."

"Fine food . . . in a conflagration-free environment — a combination I cannot possibly refuse." She offered a smile. "Especially when I'll be accompanied by such a charming host. Though I have to confess that the wine would be lost on me. I avoid alcohol."

"That's probably because you've had no good wine. I'm a bit of an aficionado. Promise you'll try one sip."

"Perhaps I will."

"There we are!" Gossett said. "Now, are you comfortable with walking a few more blocks?"

"Certainly."

They continued north, waiting at an intersection for a trolley to pass, then he directed her east on Madison, toward the lake. Soon they were at the back entrance of Michigan Avenue Station, a massive iron structure, which had largely survived the Great Fire. The smell of coal smoke from the locomotives was nearly overwhelming.

Inside the echoing, cavernous place, he led her down a dim corridor of black-and-white tile to a door marked with the letters *C&WRR Baggage Annex One.* Fishing into his pocket, he removed a key and opened the door. Inside was an ante office, presently unoccupied. Gossett walked to the back door and opened that one, too. In the inner office was a large man in a blue guard's uniform, sitting at a chair behind a desk, on which sat a pen and inkwell, a report of some sort and a well-thumbed newspaper. On the wall were lithographs of various locomotives, a blue Gamewell fire and police alarm box, and bulletin boards on which were pinned dozens of directives and decrees from the railroad's management.

Do not use the fire sand bucket to extinguish cigars and cigarettes!

"Eugene."

"Mr. Gossett. I didn't expect to see you in today. Are you working?"

"Personal matter only, Eugene. This charming lady needs a safe place to keep her valuables for a few days. I told her I had just the place."

"Pleased to meet you, ma'am."

"You, as well."

The guard rose and walked to a chest-high safe. He withdrew a set of keys from his pocket. He inserted one in the lock of the safe and turned it. Gossett did the same with a key he'd produced. He spun the dial in the front and pulled the door open. "Your gems will be in the sure and secure embrace of the Chicago and Western, Annie. More so than in a Cheyenne district boarding house."

He turned back to see Annie take from her purse not the velvet bag, but the bone-handled pistol. She cocked it, pointing it at both men.

Gossett laughed — a sound that faded into silence when he saw that she was serious. Perhaps he could also see the end of his career. It was all a con.

"Gentlemen, I have on occasion shot people and I will not hesitate to shoot you, if you don't heed my instructions. Am I clear enough for you?"

The guard rocked back and forth. His brow was furrowed.

"Eugene. I noticed you eyeing the Gamewell."

The box would send an instantaneous alert to the police via an electric telegraph.

She said in an ominous voice, "The railroad has insurance. They will be made whole. The same cannot be said for you." The pistol moved closer to his chest. He leaned away from the alarm system. "Now take your pistol — with your left hand —

and place it on the desk. Then stand back."

He did so.

While keeping the gun halfway between the men with one hand, Annie used her other to undo the ribbon encircling her hair bun. She set it on the desk and collected the guard's pistol. "George, please bind Eugene's hands with that. And do a good job of it. I know knots quite well and I'll be able to see if you've left slack."

"But, but . . ." His voice was choked.

"George."

He did as she'd asked. She put the guard's gun in her bag. "Help Eugene down to the floor. And do be careful. He's a big fellow and we don't want him to hurt himself."

"But please, Annie . . . How can you do this?"

He may have been sharp earlier, but he wasn't particularly so now. She didn't answer but nodded once more to the guard. Gossett helped him down to the floor.

Eugene said, "You won't get away with this."

His words needed no response, either.

"Now, George, you come with me."

The miserable man preceded her to the door from the outer office into the corridor.

"Open it."

He did and, to his clear astonishment, in

walked Thomas, who nodded civilly to Annie. He carried a leather valise and an envelope, the latter of which he handed to her.

George gaped at the large man's presence. "No, George, he's not my husband."

It was ironic, she reflected, that Gossett had painted her as a war widow to the receptionist of his club. Ironic, because that's exactly what she was. Her beloved husband, Henry Lennox, served with distinction for the North and died at the Battle of Sutherland's Station in April of 1865, a mere week before Lee surrendered at Appomattox. Thomas had been Henry's dear friend and his second in command of the regiment. After the war, he and Annie became close — though not romantically — and found that the loss and carnage had changed them both fundamentally and made them realize that the old rules no longer existed. Hence, adventures like the one they were presently engaged in.

She told Thomas, "The safe is open."

As they'd agreed, they would take only the cash, which would be the railroad's. Annie and Thomas had no interest in the valuables belonging to passengers. He walked into the inner office and chuckled, perhaps at the sight of the large guard bound with fashionable gingham.

Annie said, "George, open this and look at what's inside." She handed him the envelope that Thomas had given her.

He did and gasped. Inside was a photograph that Thomas had taken an hour ago. It was of Gossett and Annie examining the pistol in Jefferson Park, with her face obscured. She had picked a bench directly opposite an abandoned building, where Thomas — no stranger to photography himself — had set up Annie's four-by-five-inch camera. He'd developed the plate quickly and printed the image.

"But, no . . . it will look like I . . ." His shoulders dipped. A defeated man.

"Now, George, what you will do is fabricate a story about who I am and how you were duped by me."

"You're not Annie Fowler."

She was Annie, but Lennox, not Fowler. She didn't bother to respond to the obvious comment.

"If you don't lead the authorities away from me, that picture will be sent to every newspaper in Chicago. And for a further incentive, I should tell you that Thomas earlier today procured some lime, which he scattered over a body in a potter's grave — some unfortunate who died six months or so ago. Before we leave, we will plant a few of the notes we are relieving you of today with the body."

Gossett muttered, "So that if I don't co-operate there will be an anonymous letter sent to the police reporting that I was seen killing someone and liming the body, the implication being that I killed someone who was a witness to my theft. Annie, how can you do this to me? I'm just an innocent!"

"An innocent? That is hardly a portrait of you I would paint, George. Oh, and let me offer my sympathies for your loss."

"My loss?"

"Yes, it appears that sometime during the day, you have lost your wedding ring. It was on your hand in the first few minutes we met, and then it vanished."

His face glowed crimson. He began to sputter some pathetic defense; she cut him off with an abrupt wave of her hand. "Is it unreasonable of me to speculate that tonight at the Palmer House you were going to ply me with wine and suggest we repair to a room upstairs?"

The blush grew redder, the eyes more evasive.

"And that, after I had told you about my husband's drinking troubles?" A wicked smile crossed her lips. "Fictional though both husband and drink might have been."

Thomas appeared in the doorway. He nodded. Thomas preferred less delicate means of restraints than festive ribbons. He pulled from his pocket a pair of hand irons and clamped one on Gossett's wrist and another to a radiator.

Gossett muttered, "This won't work, you know. Employees will come in here soon. The alarm will be sounded. Even if I play the fool, Eugene knows what you look like. The police will spot you in minutes if you take to the streets."

Annie and Thomas shared a smile. In fact, they were about to do just that — take to the streets. They'd be driving a carriage to a south side station. There they would board a train to New York City, where they lived — he in the Wall Street district, she in charming Greenwich Village.

And, yes, on any other day, they would have been easily spotted by the authorities.

But not today. Because as they left their poor captives behind and exited onto Michigan Avenue, they were absorbed into a crowd of thousands, all parading south along the lakefront, amid the sound of marching bands and cheers of "Huzzah, huzzah!" Even the most diligent police or railroad thugs could never locate them.

This was the reason they had chosen to rob the Chicago and Western Railroad now: today was July 4, 1876, the hundredth anniversary of the founding of the United States. Downtown Chicago was awash with celebrants, all conveniently masking their escape.

An hour later, Annie and Thomas were sitting in the dining car of an eastbound train — not one belonging to the C&WRR, of course — perusing the menu and trying to decide what to select for their evening meal.

The heat did not seem so bad this morning. Touch the Sky believed that he and his fellow tribesmen could work through the day. There were still fifteen structures to erect and roof and he wanted the village to be completed by early fall, in time for harvest.

The six-foot-four-inch chief was standing outside his teepee, inside of which his wife, Dark Hawk Woman, was teaching their three youngsters — two boys and a girl — to speak the English language.

He nodded to fellow tribesmen and -women passing by, on their way to the stream or the field. A hunting party, after elk, rode past on ponies. Women ground corn. Children ran with the joyous abandon that only children are capable of.

Another day was beginning.

As he looked about the village, his gaze settled on the east, where a faint trail of dust became a solitary rider on a palomino. He was trotting along at a steady, though not urgent, pace. The man was a White and he was dressed in buckskin. Perhaps a scout. As he drew closer, Touch the Sky observed that he was bearded and in his thirties. There was a military air about him. A veteran, he supposed. Touch the Sky lifted the flap of the teepee and retrieved his pistol, which he put into his belt.

Everyone nearby stared as the man rode into the center of the village and reined his horse to a walk. Looking about, he spotted Touch the Sky and directed the animal in his direction.

The man was not wearing a sidearm.

Dismounting and tying his horse to a post, he approached but stopped a respectful distance from Touch the Sky. He clasped his hands together, with the left hand facing the ground. The Lakota hand signal for "peace."

Touch the Sky did the same.

The man said, "I understand you speak English."

"Yes."

"And you are Chief Touch the Sky." There was little doubt about that, as the chief was a full foot taller than most of the tribe, the rider, too.

"You have business here?"

"I've ridden from Eastern Ridge to deliver a package to you."

The chief was confused. "We receive posts. A wagon comes weekly."

"My instructions were to give you this personally."

"What is it?"

"I don't know. It's sealed." The rider pulled a paperbound package from his saddlebag. He handed it to Touch the Sky. It was heavy and about the size of a large book, which is what he guessed the contents to be. A Bible, most likely. The missionaries simply would not cease their efforts. Touch the Sky found their fervor as irritating as their simplemindedness.

"You would like food or water?" Touch the Sky asked.

"Water for my horse. Only that. I want to get on the road before the sun gets too high. Hottest July in years."

The chief pointed out the stream. The men exchanged Lakota hand signals for farewell, and the White mounted the palomino once more and rode out of the village.

Touch the Sky squatted and withdrew his stained knife from its scabbard and sliced through the string binding the package together. He unfurled the wrapping.

He gasped.

The contents were not a Bible, nor a book of any kind. They were stacks and stacks of U.S. notes. Close to a thousand dollars. An unimaginable sum.

Inside too was an envelope addressed to him. He opened it and read:

Chief Touch the Sky:
We have never met but I know of you. Last May I was shocked to learn of the incident in which the Chicago and Western Rail Road seized your village and relocated your tribe members to an inhospitable place, far from your ancestral land, killing several young men and a woman in the incident. I am somewhat familiar with the area, and it was clear to me that the railroad could easily have bypassed your village, but it chose to drive the railway through it, preferring, I suppose, to avoid the expense of building a trestle. For the petty act of saving money, you have suffered greatly.

I will not burden you with the details, but suffice it to say that a friend and I,

249

from time to time, devise to relieve certain institutions and individuals of resources we decide they do not deserve. We spent the month of June planning how to best make sure that C&WRR paid for its crime against you. We were successful and we now offer this money to you as a gift that will help in improving the lives of your tribe members in this difficult time.

It is, of course, best that we remain anonymous. Accordingly I will simply sign this with the Lakota word for *friend*.

— Kola

■ ■ ■ ■

The Last
Dive Bar

BY BILL PRONZINI

■ ■ ■ ■

Harry had a thing for dive bars.

You know the kind of place. Old-fashioned taverns that have been in business in the same locale for many years, often family owned for generations, where locals regularly congregate and visitors are welcome as long as they respect the rules of the house. Monuments to the past that have changed little over time, each unique in ambience, history, tradition. Some exist in large city neighborhoods, but most are small town institutions — at least one in nearly every town nationwide.

Their diversity was one of the things that drew Harry to them. Another was the fact that he was on the road a lot and had plenty of opportunity to seek out new places. But the main reason was the array of interesting people he met in them, characters of both sexes and all ages, colors, creeds, and personalities — anyone who had stories to tell. You could say that dive bars had become a kind of hobby with him. (He found it amusing that the word *dive* had once referred to a disreputable watering hole, whereas now *dive bar* had become a term of mostly respectful appreciation. That was the evolution of language for you.)

He figured he'd visited a minimum of two hundred different dive bars in the twenty-six years he'd worked for Sutherland Manufacturing. Some were more memorable than others, of course. One of his favorites was a tavern that had once been a flapper-era brothel and that the present owner and several customers swore was haunted by the ghost of the brothel's madam, who every now and then could be glimpsed late at night checking the liquor supply. Another, an Irish pub, had on display a bar stool painted shamrock green that its oldest customer had occupied daily for sixty years. Best of all so far was a 175-year-old former country stage stop, whose low ceiling was thickly festooned with business cards and dollar bills pinned there for good luck by generations of appreciative customers — a tradition so long-standing, the present owner claimed, that if you were to search among the dusty, moldering bills you'd find a few old oversize greenbacks and even a

Confederate States note or two.

In a sense, Harry's job was as old-fashioned as the taverns he frequented. He was a traveling salesman, one of the few remaining members of that dying breed — a sort of modern-day Willy Loman, he was fond of saying, but without that fellow's emotional baggage. What he sold was Sutherland Manufacturing's unconventional line of hardware items — doorknobs and door knockers, faucet handles, cabinet knobs, fireplace grates and tools. The company put out brochures and advertised on the internet, naturally, but Harry's customers were hardware outlets and specialty shops in small, out-of-the-way towns and villages, their owners folks who wanted firsthand looks at product samples and who could be convinced to place an order they might otherwise not by an outgoing, friendly, low-pressure salesman like Harry Murdock.

His territory covered all of Northern California and parts of Oregon and Nevada, so he was on the road two to three weeks a month year-round. But he didn't mind the long driving trips. In fact, he relished them. He had neither wife nor family; his "home" was a nondescript furnished room in Oakland. There was nothing he enjoyed more than discovering a dive bar he'd never been in before, talking to the people who frequented it, adding fresh bits of lore and legend to his memory bank. All things considered, he was a genuinely happy man.

Until he discovered Slattery's Oasis.

It was in a little town called Shelton, in the northeastern part of California near the Nevada line. He'd seen road signs for the town, but had never had occasion to go there until this particular trip. The former owner of Shelton Hardware & Building Supply hadn't been interested in Sutherland's products, but the place had changed hands and a company feeler to the new owner, Sam Peters, had elicited interest. So Harry went to see if he could sign Peters up for a new account. Which he did by showing his samples, making his usual soft sell pitch, and offering a 10 percent new customer discount on the first order.

After they'd finished doing business, Harry mentioned his interest in "old-time local taverns." (You had to be careful using the term *dive bars,* especially in rural areas like this, because not everybody knew or appreciated its modern meaning.) Sam Peters had told him about Slattery's Oasis and where it was located. When Peters added that it had been in business since 1895, Harry was all the more eager for a visit.

He checked into a local motel, emailed the Shelton Hardware Supply order to the company, and ate an early dinner in an adjacent coffee shop. It was a few minutes past six-thirty when he arrived at Slattery's Oasis — a weathered wood frame building on the main drag but not quite downtown. Its name was painted on a big wooden sign across the front, and below the sign stretched a blue banner with white lettering that read: **OUR 125th ANNIVERSARY**. The only external neon was a Budweiser sign in one window.

Harry knew it was his kind of place as soon as he walked in. Dimly lit, the illumination supplied mainly by old hanging miner's lamps and neon beer advertisements. Long mahogany bar with a brass foot rail, carved Victorian backbar centered by a slightly wavy mirror, a row of high-backed wooden booths. In front of one wall was an ancient potbelly stove. That wall and two others were decorated with miner's tools, old framed photographs, deer heads, a dusty moose head. Chunks of one set of the moose's dendritic antlers were missing, the boards behind it pocked with half a dozen splintered holes that looked as if they'd been there a long time. The only modern touches, if you could call them that, were a TV set on a corner shelf, a 1950s era jukebox, and a shuffleboard game that shared space with a pool table in a side alcove.

At this relatively early hour there weren't many customers. Three men in one of the booths arguing good-naturedly about baseball, a man and woman with their heads close together in another. Only one of the red leatherette bar stools was occupied, by an elderly gent sipping from a glass of red wine. Harry's practiced eye took him to be a regular. You could always tell them from the casual drop-ins; they had a kind of anchored look.

Harry considered sitting next to the man, but he preferred talking to bartenders before approaching anybody else; they were often a font of information on their establishments. This one had the appearance of one who didn't mind conversation as long as he wasn't busy. Harry's practiced eye again.

"What'll it be?"

"Draft beer," Harry said, smiling his salesman's smile. "Any kind. I'm not particular."

The bartender drew a pint of Heineken. He was in his forties, heavy-set, his expression good-natured. His hairline had receded two-thirds of the way back on his scalp, leaving a little patch of hair up front like a brown islet in a pink lagoon.

"Don't believe I've seen you here before," he said as he set the mug down.

"My first visit to Shelton," Harry said. "Nice place you have here. Sam Peters at the hardware and building supply store recommended it."

"Did he? Good to hear."

"Yessir, just my kind of watering hole. The banner out front says you're celebrating a hundred and twenty-five years in business. That's really something."

"Oldest tavern in the county by far. Continuous operation since 1895, except during Prohibition."

"The *Ig*noble Experiment," Harry said with a chuckle. "Still owned by descendants of the founder, by any chance?"

"Up until about 1970 it was. My dad bought it when the founder's grandson died. He didn't see any reason to change the name. Neither do I. Jack Zaleski's my name."

Harry introduced himself, handing Zaleski one of his business cards. "Old taverns like yours and their customers and histories fascinate me," he said.

"Nothing too fascinating about this one," Zaleski said. "Not anymore. No excitement to speak of in the past fifty years, other than a few brawls that didn't amount to much."

"I happened to notice those holes in the wall behind the moose head when I came in. They sure look like bullet holes."

"Well, they are. I guess you could call how they got there a historic event. Happened just after Repeal —"

"Hey, Jack. Empty down here."

Zaleski excused himself, went to refill the elderly local's wineglass. Two other people came in just then and also had to be served. Harry sipped his beer, waiting patiently.

"About those bullet holes," Zaleski said when he came back. "Shelton used to be a mining town, and one night after Repeal a couple of hardrock miners packing pistols did a little too much celebrating and made a bet to find out which was the better shot. They picked that moose head for a target and started plinking. Fired half a dozen rounds, chipping off pieces of the antlers before anybody could stop 'em. The Slattery who owned the place back then left the holes unfixed as a warning that he wouldn't stand for any more shenanigans."

That was just the sort of anecdote Harry liked to hear. He asked a few more questions about the Oasis's early days, before and after Repeal, but Zaleski didn't have much else of interest to tell. And business was starting to pick up to keep him busy. The elderly local was still anchored on his stool and the one next to it was still vacant, so Harry picked up his mug and moved down there.

It took a little gentle prodding and the offer of a wine refill to get the old man to talk. But once his verbal faucet had been turned on, anecdotes and reminiscences poured out in a steady stream. His name was Greer; he'd lived in Shelton all of his seventy-four years and worked for Southern Pacific Railroad for forty of them. His stories were entertaining. Informative, too. He identified the ancient potbelly as a Vogelzang cast-iron coal stove, one of the type that once had been a staple in railroad stations across the country.

Harry sat with him for nearly an hour, until Greer decided he ought to be getting on home. When the old man walked across to the door, he was as steady on his feet as though he'd been drinking water instead of wine.

Slattery's Oasis had filled up by this time. In the alcove, the pool table and shuffleboard game were both in use; the click of balls and the thump and rattle of metal tiles added to the sounds of conversation and laughter, sporadic jukebox music, a baseball game on TV that somebody had wanted turned on. Most of tonight's crowd seemed to be couples and small groups. Only one of the few solitary drinkers Harry made overtures to was responsive, a slatternly middle-aged woman, and she had nothing to say worth hearing.

Harry finished nursing his third beer, debated having a fourth. Four was his self-imposed limit; any more than that made him fuzzy headed and led to a mild morning-after hangover. He was still debating when the gray-haired man came in alone.

The newcomer stood for a time looking around, the way Harry had when he entered, then made his way to the bar. The only two empty stools were around on the far curved end; he claimed the closest to the wall. While he waited for service, he did some more looking around. A local scanning for someone he knew, or just another newcomer inspecting his surroundings?

Harry's appetite for camaraderie was still keen. He waited until Zaleski had served the gray-haired man a bottle of Coors Light, then called for a fourth draft. When it came, he went to see if he could strike up another worthwhile conversation.

The gray-haired man glanced at him when he slid onto the adjacent stool, but didn't acknowledge Harry's nod and friendly smile. The fellow was about sixty, he judged, dressed in a nondescript sport coat and brown slacks. Average height, average weight, average features. The gray hair, clipped short, appeared to be the dull color of tarnished silver. He had large hands; otherwise there was nothing distinguishing about him.

No, that wasn't true. He did have one other distinctive feature. When he felt Harry's gaze on him, he turned his head again and their eyes locked. His were deep-set, thick-lashed, penetrating; the irises reflected the backbar lights like polished black stones.

"Something you want?"

"Just wondering if you're local," Harry said, still smiling.

"Why?"

"Well, I enjoy talking to locals, hearing what they have to say about all sorts of things. I'm not one myself. Local, I mean. My first time in Shelton, just here for one night — passing through on business."

The gray-haired man didn't say anything.

"Also just passing through, are you?" Harry asked.

"That's right."

"So we've got something in common right there. Ships that meet and pass in the night, as the saying goes. My name's Harry Murdock. Mind if I ask yours?"

"Why?"

"Just being sociable, that's all."

The gray-haired man poured beer from the bottle into a pilsner glass, carefully so as to keep the foam down. He didn't say anything.

"I'm in hardware sales myself," Harry persisted. "Twenty-six years now. What line are you in?"

"I don't have a line."

"Jack-of-all-trades? Or what I wish I was, a man of independent means?"

"Neither."

"Retired, then?"

The gray-haired man drank some of his Coors Light. "Mostly," he said. Then he said, "Pretty nosy, aren't you."

Harry laughed. "I guess I am. But I like people and I'm just naturally curious. That's one of the reasons I come to places like this."

"Dive bars."

"Oh, so you know the term. Yessir. Dive bars."

"So?"

"Well, they fascinate me. You wouldn't be a habitué yourself, would you?"

"A what?"

"Habitué. A person like me who frequents dive bars."

The gray-haired man slanted him another look. "What do you want to know for?"

"Just wondering, that's all," Harry said. Somebody put a coin in the jukebox just then; the sudden twang of a country-western song made it necessary for Harry to raise his voice. "I guess you noticed the banner out front. Celebrating their hundred and twenty-fifth anniversary — that's pretty remarkable. Of course, Slattery's Oasis isn't the oldest dive bar in the state. There's a former stage stop down in Sonoma County that's been operating for a hundred seventy-five years . . ."

The gray-haired man wasn't listening. He sat peering into his glass. Harry was about to say something else to try to draw him out when the fellow spoke again, almost as if talking to himself.

"Anniversary of my own coming up pretty soon," he said.

"Is that so? Wedding anniversary?"

"What? No."

"Business-related?"

"You might say that."

265

"What kind of business?"

"Mine. None of yours."

"Well . . . can I ask how many years you'll be celebrating?"

No answer for several seconds. Then, "Thirty."

"Must be a special anniversary, whatever it is."

"That's right. Special."

Harry tried another tack. "I've been in more than two hundred dive bars over the years, in three states. No kidding, at least that many, all of them different in one way or another. It's sort of a hobby with me."

No response.

"I'm always on the lookout for a new one. Like this place here. You've been in a lot yourself, have you?"

"Plenty."

"As many as two hundred in three states?"

"More. All over the country."

"No kidding? So that's something else we have in common." Harry was tickled that he'd found a kindred spirit, even a close-mouthed stranger like this. "You must do quite a bit of traveling."

"I get around."

"What draws you to dive bars? The people, the ambience, the local color?"

"No."

266

"What, then? If you don't mind my asking."

Another slanted look. "Why don't you just drink your beer and let me drink mine?"

"I didn't mean to pry. Just being sociable, like I said. How about another round, on me? Or rather, on my expense account." Harry chuckled. "I don't usually pad it with personal expenses, but a few beers now and then —"

"I don't want another beer."

"You sure? I'll be glad to buy —"

"I said I don't want another beer." Abruptly the gray-haired man pushed away from the bar and slid off his stool. Harry thought he was going to leave, but he didn't, not just yet. Instead he leaned close. Even so, with the jukebox blaring and the other customer noise, Harry could barely hear him when he spoke again. "You know something, mister? You're lucky."

"Lucky? How do you mean?"

"I got more driving to do tonight. And I'm mostly retired now."

"I don't understand —"

Those dark eyes fixed on Harry's with an intensity that stirred the hairs on the back of his neck. Seen up close like this, they were flat, cold, unblinking. Like a bird's. Or a snake's.

"You wanted to know why I come to dive bars. All right, I'll tell you. They're good places for scouting, that's why."

"Scouting? For what?"

The gray-haired man leaned even closer, the corners of his mouth twitching upward. He murmured two words into Harry's ear, then immediately turned and walked away, out into the night.

Harry sat motionless, stunned and shaken. He told himself he hadn't heard right, but he knew he had. Just a joke, a sick joke. Only it wasn't. Those creepy eyes, that spectral smile . . . no, it had been the truth.

But what could he do about it? Give chase? He was no hero, and the gray-haired man would be gone by now anyway. Call the police? And tell them what, that he'd had a brief conversation with a weird stranger whose two-word exit line no one else had heard? He didn't know the man's name, or what kind of car he drove, or where he was headed. Couldn't even describe him very well. The gray-haired man was aware of all this, too, or he wouldn't have spoken as he had.

Lucky. My God!

Harry needed a drink now, a real drink. He paid for a double bourbon, drank it in one long swallow. Before he left the tavern, he made sure there was no sign of the gray-haired man outside. Then he drove quickly to his motel and locked himself in his room, those two whispered words and all that they and the thirty-year anniversary statement implied still echoing inside his head.

"Fresh prey."

Harry's hobby ended that night. So did his passion for meeting new people, hearing the stories they had to tell. He keeps to himself now, avoids strangers as much as possible, spends his evenings on the road and at home by himself, or in the company of a few old acquaintances.

Slattery's Oasis was his last dive bar.

■ ■ ■ ■

CASE OPEN

BY CAROLYN HART

■ ■ ■ ■

Peggy shivered despite her thick cashmere sweater. The temperature chilled after dark in August along the rugged Pacific Northwest coast, the tantalizing warmth of the day forgotten. Fog hid the cliff's edge and the steep wooden stairs to the narrow rocky beach far below. Surf boomed, crashing against jutting rocks and massive boulders. She looked toward the stairs even though the wooden railing wasn't visible.

Time didn't help. Evelyn had died a year ago next Friday, but Peggy's feeling of isolation — of suspicion — worsened every day. Damn the sheriff. Of course Evelyn's fall was an accident. She remembered the sheriff's cold gray eyes. "Sorry, Ms. Prescott, there's no way to determine what happened to your sister." How horrid it had been to read the story in this week's *Beacon:* Sheriff Roger Chavez announced the investigation into the death of Evelyn Marlow remains open. Sheriff Chavez said, "We are unable to determine whether Ms. Marlow died in an accidental fall, committed suicide, or was a homicide victim."

When Peggy read the article, fury boiled inside. How dare he do this to her? "Homicide victim." And anyone who knew Evelyn would scoff at the idea of suicide. Cheerful Evelyn. Happy Evelyn. Evelyn with scads of friends and men who loved her and lots of money from two ex-husbands. Everything fell into Evelyn's lap without any effort. She flashed that sunny smile and gave a gurgle of bewitching husky laughter and everything came her way. A year ago Friday.

Peggy listened to the boom as tons of water slammed against the narrow strip of beach at the base of the cliff, swirling over boulders, foaming around jagged pinnacles. Peggy's jaws ached. She concentrated on relaxing the tight muscles.

She wasn't imagining the problem. The latest snub was the worst. She'd chaired the committee for the gala for three years. This year not a word to her. She'd received a letter about a meeting, but she wasn't in charge. And there were the Smiths last Sunday at the club brunch, shying away from her after a sidelong glance. Some clients had left, as well.

Well, at least now she'd faced the problem: that people didn't want to have anything to do with her, and perhaps with others who were here that night. Did the gala committee and the Smiths actually think she pushed her sister over the cliff? Or if not thinking of her as a murderess, they felt uncomfortable, constrained, wondering what happened that night on the terrace, believing there was something unexplained about Evelyn's fall. Anyone could have an accident, including Evelyn. Evelyn fell. That's all there was to it.

No one said anything to her face, but she knew the whispers were out there. Did Evelyn jump? Was she pushed? It was intolerable. Somehow she must dispel suspicion, stop the whispers. She was good at solving problems. That's why she won the class action suit against the mining company that so many lawyers refused to take, took the case, and won millions and millions of dollars, enough to buy this Spanish mansion atop a cliff with a gorgeous view of the Pacific.

She would solve this problem.

Accident, suicide, murder.

People always thought the worst, of course. *Evelyn was graceful. How could she possibly fall? Did something on the stairs make her stumble? I talked to her just the day before and she was so excited about the party. Peggy was tired of having her there. Do you suppose Peggy . . .*

Peggy's jaw ached again. It wasn't fair. Why pick on her? Anyone at the house that night could have pushed Evelyn down the steps. Any one of them. They all had their reasons. Peggy's eyes narrowed. Any one of them. Maybe that was the way to handle it. Get them all together. It would have to be done carefully, very carefully. But she was good at imagining, good at planning. Once they were here, when they didn't expect it, she'd tumble out reasons for Evelyn's murder, dark and twisty, like snakes slithering from an overturned bucket. She'd give the town something to talk about. She felt a surge of satisfaction. All right, if people whispered behind their hands, she'd help them spread malign imaginings. She'd give them suspects: Buddy, Irene, Meredith, Carlson and Jill, Walt. She'd bring everything out into the open. A reunion of those present the night Evelyn fell. What happened on the terrace wouldn't stay on the terrace. The gossip would be too juicy to contain. When the night was done, the town would know about each and every one of them.

A sudden caw rasped against her. Only a seabird, but in it was an echo of Evelyn's scream. So odd that no one had heard, but the surf was always loud, boom, boom, boom. The sheriff said Evelyn died at a quarter after nine. Her watch was smashed in the fall, the time caught and held forever. Peggy wondered where the watch was now. Maybe in an envelope in some kind of file at the sheriff's office.

She canceled all appointments for the day. She found a box of lovely cards with a single red rose against a silver background. Though she always thought fast, moved fast, she took her time. She wanted each of them to come. The notes had to be perfect.

Peggy sat at her desk in the den and remembered that night. They'd had parties almost every Friday during the summer. Evelyn planned them, of course. Peggy was at the office. She'd missed a few working late, but they'd been fun when she attended. It was a usual evening. A fine meal. Games in the den. Wine and whiskey.

Evelyn loved setting a beautiful table, Limoges china, fine crystal for French wine. It relieved Peggy of the chore and pleased Evelyn. Peggy sat at one end as the official hostess since it was her home. Evelyn was simply there between marriages. With her most recent divorce, she agreed to the home going to her ex-husband, accepting instead a heftier settlement. She told Peggy, "Darling, I've had so much fun here with you, I'll stay a while longer. I know you don't mind."

Evelyn was quite striking that night, ebony dark hair short in a jagged cut, oval face interesting rather than beautiful, mesmerizing gray eyes, pert nose, lips ready to curve into laughter, a perfect pearl necklace at her throat, a swirling gray silk dress.

Buddy Hayes sat next to Evelyn, often leaned close. Tall, lean Buddy with his narrow uneven face, one eyebrow higher than the other, wide mouth crooked in a teasing smile, light green eyes that reminded Peggy of a cat, intent, unreadable. Buddy had been her friend first. Until Evelyn came. She hadn't seen him in several months. She'd called twice. It would be nice to see Buddy again.

Irene Porter, brittle, wary, full of herself. Peggy didn't like Irene. She was witchlike, too thin, but a witch in expensive clothes, always the latest fashion, and a necklace with little ivory elephants on a heavy gold link chain. She'd taken the necklace off and passed it across to Evelyn. "My dear, just the finest ivory. Of course, it was smuggled

278

but worth the risk. I'll get one for you if you like."

Peggy spoke sharply, told them about elephants and how they could think and talk and how ivory poachers were destroying them. Softhearted Jill looked at her with tears in her eyes. "Oh please, don't tell us. That's so awful." But Walt immediately checked his phone, found out how much smugglers got paid for ivory tusks, said poaching sounded like a pretty good business to him and hey they were just animals.

Evelyn shook her head, her dark hair quivering. "Walt, you cried when George —" (her elderly basset) "— was hit by a car, so stop pretending to be a tough guy."

Meredith, their young bubbly cousin, often visited. That night she was thrilled because she'd started as an assistant social media manager at a big ad agency in Seattle, which had clients — Meredith told them with huge eyes — from Addis Ababa to Qatar to Iceland. She wasn't making much money and Seattle was so expensive. She was bunking on a houseboat and saving up to move to an apartment. She brought a new boyfriend one weekend. On her next visit Evelyn took her aside and said lightly, "Handsome is as handsome does. Watch that one, honey. He'll be long on promises and short on performance."

Then there was Carlson Carleton. Peggy frowned. Last summer she'd felt a spurt of pride — it showed her stature in the community — that a movie star came to her house often. Carlson and his wife, Jill, lived not far away. The actor wandered over on the cliff path some afternoons and challenged Evelyn to Ping-Pong and then professed great exhaustion and demanded a margarita for solace after he lost. Did his dark eyes hold longing when he gazed at Evelyn?

Jill sometimes bounced in and had a cocktail, too. Was she keeping an eye on her husband? Evelyn and Jill had often spent an afternoon together shopping, seeking out less frequented antiques shops, craft fairs, and flea markets.

Peggy found Carlson . . . odd. Almost like a papier-mâché figure. His face reflected emotions. That was it: the emotions seemed manufactured. But he was an actor. He did grave inquiry or roguish charm or affectionate rebuke beautifully. He was incredibly handsome, tawny thick hair, eyes dark as coal tar, rugged features. Jill was plain, little, and plump, with hair in golden ringlets and a sweet smile.

Peggy had entertained very little since

Evelyn's death. She'd have to change that. Once she took care of this cloud that hung over her, she'd have dinners again. Perhaps Cousin Meredith would like to help. Actually planning meals was a bore. She could always cater. But Meredith was a gourmet cook, her specialty Italian food after a junior year abroad in Florence.

It wasn't long after the fireworks on the terrace ended that the group had begun to disperse. It was Jill a few minutes later who'd looked around the den and asked about Evelyn. "I didn't see her come in." When it became obvious Evelyn wasn't in the house, Jill jumped up and rushed out on the terrace, calling for Evelyn. And it was Jill who looked over the parapet, saw a body sprawled on the rocks below, and collapsed in hysteria.

Buddy, Irene, Meredith, Carlson and Jill, Walt . . .

Peggy enjoyed Walt's bearlike masculinity, his booming voice, his waspish humor, but she didn't trust him an inch. He was a financial adviser to Evelyn. Peggy wasn't amused when Walt boasted about the grand he "borrowed" from Evelyn for a Vegas weekend, but then won big and paid her back with interest. Peggy didn't find jokes about mishandling money funny. Evelyn

281

said Walt made her laugh and in today's world that was worth an extra grand or so. Peggy was thoughtful. She knew Evelyn slept with him sometimes. Did Buddy know?

She picked up the first card and began to write.

Buddy Hayes heard the *clang* of the mailbox on the porch. He clicked off the computer, picked up the spiral notebook with his notes. He carried with him a sense of the oppressiveness and hopelessness in Malinta Tunnel, the heat, the thud of Japanese bombs, the swirls of dust shaken loose from the tunnel walls. How many today remembered Corregidor and the fall of the Philippines in 1942? This was a movie he wanted to make. The script was almost finished. Just a few things to check.

He opened the door, stepped onto the wooden porch. He loved this cabin, simple and remote, peaceful, a good place to work. He could afford to take a year off from teaching because of the inheritance from Evelyn. Evelyn was always telling one or another, "I'll remember you in my will and you have to promise to smile when you think of me." When she sprinkled the idea of largesse in her will on him, he'd grinned, given her a two-fingered salute. "Nice to know I'll have some extra when I'm pushing eighty." Evelyn was in her thirties, quite well, with no reason to believe she'd die soon. He imagined she'd make and remake her will a dozen times before death ever came, and he was under no illusion he would be her last love. They suited each other at the time. He liked new experiences and Evelyn was certainly that for him, a modest history professor at a junior college. He'd been surprised on her death to learn she'd added a codicil to her will and now he was, for him, a well-to-do man, money enough to buy a cottage in the hills outside Seattle, write a script he'd always wanted to write after stories his grandmother told him of her days in the tunnel.

He pulled down the aluminum lever, grabbed the mail. Catalogs. A letter from his sister. Two credit card bills. He frowned when he saw a square envelope, heavy thick paper, his name in Peggy's distinctive printing, her return address. A quick rip, a glance at the rose against a silver backdrop.

Dear Buddy,
I'd looked forward to hosting a wedding on the terrace for you and Evelyn. I wish I could peel back the sad day when that

dream ended and when I lost a sister who was always my best friend.

Although anniversaries are hard, especially anniversaries of heartbreak, I know you will want to lift a glass of champagne in Evelyn's memory.

Everyone who was there that evening will be coming at eight to lift a toast to Evelyn. We can focus on what was fine and good for her.

We also — and I am very sorry to mention a dark reality — may wish to share what has happened to each of us since the sheriff left open the investigation into her death. I'm afraid there are whispers of murder. I hope together we can find a way to stop that kind of gossip.

Sadly — Peggy

The back of his neck prickled. The line from *Macbeth,* "Something wicked this way comes," hung in his mind. Pine needles rustled. A squirrel chittered. Buddy walked slowly inside.

Irene Porter used a part-time secretarial service, but she sorted her own mail at the gallery. She didn't want anyone else handling letters, seeing correspondence. That was one of Irene's rules. She neither sent

284

nor received emails or texts related to what she thought of as special transactions. Letters came from all around the world. She dealt with sophisticated correspondents. Usually there would be a general discussion of a particular artist. Nothing overt. And then a suggested meeting, say at the Pike Place Market or a game at T-Mobile Field. From there, possibly a deal. Or not.

She flipped rapidly through the envelopes, stopped. A rip.

Dear Irene,
Evelyn admired your expertise in art and several times shared with me insights about your amazing ability to offer customers once-in-a-lifetime acquisitions.

I know you recall her with appreciation. Though saddened by her absence, I know you will want to join us to remember her Friday night on the anniversary of her death. Please come at eight and we will toast her memory.

We also may wish to address the status of the investigation into her death. The case remains open.

Until then — Peggy

Irene didn't need to check the calendar.

Evelyn died a year ago. Just in time, actually. Who would have thought Evelyn, always so frivolous, would question the provenance of a painting — tell her with a smile that they'd likely been swindled, must contact the police?

A crinkle. Irene looked down. The card was crumpled in her hand, crumpled into a tight hard ball.

Meredith nodded approval at the mirror. Sometimes her brown hair frizzed in the sea-moist air but today her curls were neat as little lambs in a row and glossy as could be. Maybe that new conditioner was the difference. She smoothed one cheek. Yes, she looked nice. Nice and happy. Some days simply burst around her, bright as pink and green flares in the night sky. She felt a tiny twinge. Evelyn loved setting off fireworks from the stairs. She launched them herself, lighting one and then another and another. There hadn't been any flare evenings since Evelyn died. Meredith had drawn a little heart on her wall calendar to mark the anniversary of her death.

Meredith still felt like a country mouse when she thought of Evelyn and Peggy. She'd grown up in a modest frame house, one of the tract houses put up after World

War II. There was no money in the family until Evelyn became a sought-after model and from there segued into marriage with two rich husbands in a row and Peggy scored her class action triumph. Evelyn was always generous. She helped Meredith's mom in her last illness, sent Meredith to college. Meredith felt a pang. Evelyn had been right about Nate. He was only interested in her because he thought she was rich. When Evelyn turned down Meredith's shy request for a loan for his business plan, he'd dropped her flat.

Meredith popped up from the tufted bench, hurried to the closet for a linen jacket. She'd go down so Jeremy wouldn't have to park. They'd have a glorious day at the zoo. She felt alive to the very tips of her toes.

In the downstairs vestibule, she unlocked her box. She loved living in an apartment house and thanks to Evelyn's generosity she could afford a nice one-bedroom apartment in a lovely area. She pulled out several envelopes, returned all of them to the box to get later except one, a square envelope from Peggy.

Sunlight slanted through the vestibule transom, lighted the card.

Dear Meredith,

I plan a gathering here in Evelyn's memory at 8 p.m. Friday and I'll appreciate your help. We can share memories, offer a toast.

I know how fond you were of Evelyn and what a difference her legacy has made for you.

I hope also we can address an unfortunate result of the sheriff's failure to issue a decree of accidental death. There are insinuations that someone present that evening is responsible for her fall.

I look forward to your coming to remember Evelyn and to confront suggestions of wrongdoing.

Until then — Peggy

Laura Frost wore her black hair in a short uneven cut. She was slender and moved with great energy and she loved her job serving as a buffer/go-to/handle-it assistant to Carlson and Jill Carleton. Who would ever have thought a girl from Walla Walla would end up working for a movie star! It just showed that all her odd jobs during college paid off, working for a catering firm, in a nursing home, in a lawyer's office. She watched and listened and learned and was always willing to do her best. Now she arranged journeys, oversaw the household — including repairs and remodeling — directed the staff from the cook to the chauffeur, dealt with the accountant, made sure Jill's frail mom was well taken care of. Whatever Carlson and Jill needed done, she would do. Her garage apartment, which was quite lovely with a marvelous ocean view, also contained her office, though she spent much of each day in the house.

One of her duties was to deal with mail. She almost added the square envelope to their personal stacks until she saw the return address label. She knew all about Evelyn Marlow and Peggy Prescott. When she was hired last fall, the first thing Jill said was, "Oh, you look so much like a dear friend," and her eyes filled with tears.

Laura immediately thought her hopes of a job were dashed, but overriding that disappointment was her instinctive response. She reached out, touched Jill's arms, gave her a kind look. "I'm sorry to make you sad."

Jill brushed away tears. "Carlson, doesn't that sound just like Evelyn. Oh my dear, I knew today was going to be a good day. When I got up this morning, a goldfinch lighted on the windowsill. You know that's our state bird. Such a thrill. This afternoon here you are and every time I see you I'll

think of Evelyn and how much fun we had."
The job was Laura's.

She held the square envelope in her hand.
Not long after she started to work, Carlson
— that handsome god of the screen —
found a moment alone with Laura. "Thank
you for being kind. That's what I want for
Jill. People think because she smiles and is
cheerful that she's a happy person. She
is . . . fragile. We lost a baby and she's never
been the same. I want you to protect her.
Ever since Evelyn died, Jill's been afraid to
go to the edge of the terrace, look over the
wall at the rocks. Your most important job
is to shield her from sadness. She can't bear
sadness."

Laura enjoyed carte blanche. She determined what mail Carlson or Jill received.
She picked up the silver letter opener, sliced.

Dear Carlson and Jill,
Our dear Evelyn died a year ago Friday.
I know both of you have fond memories
of her. Please come Friday at 8 p.m. We
will raise a glass of champagne in her
memory and share special moments.
There is also the matter of the investigation into her death. I have heard some
unsettling rumors and feel that we
should discuss how such attacks can be

handled.

Warmest wishes — Peggy

Sometimes Walt opened the mail after breakfast. Sometimes a mound grew — especially if there were some big bills coming — and he rushed through a batch on a Friday night with a gin and tonic. This was a gin-and-tonic mail night. Suzanne was in Paris, spending every sou he'd earned this month. She always spent the first two weeks of August in Paris. He came to the elegant envelope, gave a whistle. A card from Peggy? He blinked and the gin fog cleared a little. Yeah, last year. He'd been glad to have some place to go with Suzanne out of town. But it wasn't a fun night. Splat for Evelyn. So what could Peggy want? But he was bored, bored, bored. Maybe this would pop a genie from a lamp. Or maybe a Jeannie.

Dear Walt,
I know how close you were to Evelyn so you will be glad to help us all remember her. Just a small gathering as it was the night she died. Friday night at 8 p.m. Champagne in her honor.

Of us all, you perhaps have the best reason to remember her and will be especially concerned about the ugly rumors that her fall was not an accident. I know I can count on you being here.

Best regards — Peggy

Walt stared at the note in her forceful writing. *I know how close you were to Evelyn . . .* Damn.

Deputy Sheriff Cass Dulaney wished he was at the table. He was feeling lucky tonight. But playing cards on Friday nights stamped his ticket for this damp, ridiculous trek. Buddy Hayes was his poker buddy. Funny to think of Buddy as coming over all sensitive about the invitation to a requiem. Cass thought you never knew what a woman was going to do and this was just a sister coming up on a hard day. The first anniversary of her sister's death. Tough. He looked over the report on the investigation. Yeah, the case was open. Roger said it could have been accident, could have been suicide — unlikely — could have been murder. Roger was a stickler for facts. The dead woman wasn't drunk, clumsy, or stupid. So why would she fall? She was rich. She had a reputation for liking a variety of men. Did somebody push her? Could be. That's why the case stayed open. If gossip was swirling around town as Peggy Prescott claimed, the sheriff's office wasn't in the loop. Was it possible? Sure. Could a rehash a year after the event lead anywhere? In Cass's judgment, the likelihood this clambake would fry any fish was slim to none. But you do what you have to do for a friend and he liked Buddy Hayes. He eased his way in the shadows on the far side of the house, and fetched up in darkness at the edge of the terrace. About half an hour before the festivities would begin. He was grateful for his down jacket and long johns beneath his jeans. Damn cold. Always cold up here right off the ocean.

He felt the quiver of his silenced phone, hauled it from his pocket.

"You have that night camera?" Buddy sounded tense.

"Got everything. Camera. Lights. Action." There was no appreciative chuckle. Probably tough for Buddy, coming back here, exactly one year later.

Buddy dimmed the headlights as he pulled into the circular drive. No other cars yet. He'd wait until someone else arrived. He had no wish for intimate conversation with Peggy. It would be painful. The sisters were both dark-haired, slender faced, attractive, but Peggy was Evelyn without a heart. Over time, any sense of resemblance faded. He'd come to a few of Peggy's Friday soirees, skipped several when he thought she was a little too interested, then become a regular after Evelyn arrived. Evelyn was a mess — flirtatious, pretty, glorying in having and spending money — but something about her fascinated him. An openness to adventure. A disregard for convention. An essential kindness.

Irene Porter cupped her favorite bracelet in one hand, looked at the glow of the rubies in light from the Tiffany lamp. Hers. All hers. She lifted her gaze to a Caravaggio. Color everywhere. Her dress was multihued ripples of silk. She'd built a world beyond the imagining of most. She lived for color, for richness, for possession. Had Evelyn told someone about the painting, her suspicions? Irene looked at her diamond-encrusted watch.

Jeremy turned off the headlights. "Are you sure you want to go in?"

Meredith was already out of the car, looking up at the starry sky. "I have to find out." Her voice quivered. "Peggy sounds like she thinks I pushed Evelyn. I didn't. I loved her." A swallow. "Look. There's a car already here. We'd better go in." How could Peggy think Meredith would hurt Evelyn? Meredith felt dizzy and sick, as if the world were tumbling and she couldn't hold on.

Walt's head ached by the time he turned into the circular drive, his fingers clamped to the steering wheel. Damn scary drive after dark. He'd kept the windows down. Lots of air. Still hard to see.

A rending sound.

Stupid dog statue. He'd knocked it over. Why did anybody have a stone Irish setter on a driveway? If you wanted a dog, get a dog. He wished to hell he were someplace with some swift handsome dog. Dogs liked people. He didn't feel right now like anybody liked him. His head hurt.

Laura drove slowly. She didn't know if people were fashionably late to this kind of . . . She didn't know quite how to think of the evening. A moment of remembrance. A call to arms. Perhaps she'd be the last to arrive. She would murmur excuses for Carlson and Jill. Another engagement, so sorry, sent Laura to tell everyone how often they thought of Evelyn. And of course if there were anything upsetting in the way of accusations, she would tell Carlson. But not

Jill. Never Jill.

She swerved her VW behind a Suburban that was parked on a slant. Uh-oh. Looked like the right front was smashed against a granite block.

Golden lights gleamed in tall post lanterns around the perimeter of the terrace although their glow was scarcely noticeable with the brightness of late summer evening. Peggy wondered if anyone recalled that she was wearing the emerald blouse and silver trousers and teetering heels she'd worn the night Evelyn died.

That night, Evelyn had fluttered bright as a monarch from person to person, and there was the cheerful hum of conversation and laughter. Tonight there was silence, the guests stiff and quiet.

Buddy stood with hands jammed in his pockets. He declined a drink. She almost pushed him, champagne for Evelyn, decided this was not the moment. The moment would come.

Irene held a champagne flute, her face masklike. Peggy thought it might be well to begin her attack with Irene, ask how were things in the art world, that is, the art theft world. That would be entertaining.

Meredith's date stood with an arm around

her shoulders. Peggy felt a flicker of irritation. Yes, she resented Evelyn leaving that much money to a cousin. After all, she had a sister. Even if Peggy didn't need money, family should be preferred.

Peggy fought to control anger. Carlson and Jill weren't here. It was almost a quarter after eight. She would have to begin soon. They were all waiting to say something nice about Evelyn and pepper her with questions about the gossip she'd heard. Well, not yet. Did Carlson and Jill think they were too important to come when invited by Peggy?

Walt was the only one seated. Sprawled, actually, on a wicker chaise. He'd declined champagne, held a tumbler of gin and tonic.

It was time . . . Suddenly she had a wisp of memory from out of nowhere. Evelyn home from college, rushing out the door on a date, turning to smile at Peggy, "Your day will come, sweetie. Remember if you smile a lot, everyone will love you." But they hadn't. She'd smiled. And smiled. But somehow always people moved past her, held out their arms to Evelyn. Even her parents. She blinked. Another memory. Evelyn rushing toward her with a pony-size plush reindeer. A big red nose blinked and blinked. "For you, sweetie." Peggy felt the tears on her cheeks. She'd slept with her stuffed reindeer for years. Now he sat in the corner of her room, minus one ear, his nose no longer red.

Walt pushed up to his feet, lumbered toward her. "Hey, get a drink, Peggy. You need one." He lifted the tumbler, slugged down a big swallow. "Look, you mean well. Trying to do the right thing for big sis. Hell, she's probably quaffing some kind of nectar right now. I'm fuzzy on drinks up there." He gestured with the tumbler toward the red-streaked sky, vivid with the sun splaying below the horizon. "Anyway, let's all get drunk and you can warble out the crap somebody's been sending your way. Who says one of us pushed Evelyn?"

Laura slipped into the shadow of an evergreen and gazed at the people on the terrace. She'd read the stories about Evelyn Marlow's fall, seen the photos in the paper. The sister was upset. She faced the guests with the edge of the cliff a few feet behind her. Laura shivered when she looked at the weathered wooden railing on the steps. That was where the fall happened. Did Evelyn stumble going down the steps or was she standing on the platform, looking out at the sea? Maybe there was moonlight streaking the water. Did she somehow get too close to the edge and lose her balance? Suddenly Laura wished she hadn't come. That heavy guy was drunk. Maybe he was trying to help, but she didn't like the way his words slurred or what he said. A tall, thin woman reminded her of a bird of prey, watchful, dangerous. An older man looked grim. A nice-looking guy had his arm around the shoulders of a pretty girl, but her face was streaked with tears. Maybe this wasn't the moment to say anything.

Peggy rubbed her face roughly. Nothing was going as she'd planned. She wanted heartfelt tributes. "The time Evelyn and I went to Vashon."

"Remember when Evelyn had a divorce party?"

"Did you ever hear Evelyn sing 'I Dreamed a Dream'?"

She could feel the boom of the surf as if the waves crashed over her. None of them would do as she wanted. All right, if that's the way they wanted it, she would attack. Now. "The sheriff thinks one of us pushed her." She heard her own voice, high, thin, harsh.

It was as if statues faced her.

Peggy felt so alone, so hated. She cried out, "We all know the truth. Evelyn was a tramp. A rich, beautiful tramp." She pointed at Buddy. "Did you know she was sleeping with Walt? If you don't believe me, ask him. But maybe you knew."

Walt took a step toward Peggy. "Shut up."

Buddy never moved, but his angular face jutted.

Peggy took a step backward. "Meredith wanted money. She tried to get money from Evelyn — and now she has money from Evelyn."

Meredith gave a cry. "You're awful. Evelyn was kind and good. Not like you."

Peggy wanted to slap her, pull her hair. All of them were against her. All of them. But Carlson and Jill didn't even come. Anger bubbled. "Who's not here? Carlson and Jill. I know why they didn't come. Carlson was always looking at Evelyn. It must have been Jill who was out on the terrace, who ran at Evelyn as she stood looking at the ocean, ran with her arms straight out and her palms slammed Evelyn's back and Evelyn was pushed over the edge of the platform —"

"No." A slight figure burst out of the shadow of the evergreen, ran toward Peggy. "She never ever did. She never —"

Peggy drew in a sharp ragged breath and began to move back, one step at a time.

"Evelyn?" The name hung in the night air, as everyone stared between her and the young stranger with the short black hair and gray dress. *"Evelyn!"* She screamed.

Laura held up her hands. "No, I'm not — Stop!"

Peggy backed away faster now, her face white, her mouth working. "Evelyn, I didn't mean to push you. But you took Buddy away." She looked toward Buddy. The expression on his face, the loathing. "I couldn't bear it, the two of you. It was an accident." She clutched at her throat. "Evelyn was looking down at the water and I don't know how it happened, but I was running —"

"Don't," Laura shouted. "Stop! You're too close —"

Peggy sobbed, "— and she was there, and I pushed and she was gone. I didn't mean —"

"Please." Laura held out both hands.

Peggy was at the edge of the cliff. Suddenly she began to topple backward. Her face twisted in panic. Her scream rose in a crescendo.

Laura rushed to the edge. "Oh God — she's on the rocks — the water's slamming her — oh, someone help!"

Buddy made no move. His eyes held

devastation but no surprise.

Irene folded her arms across her front. Perhaps there was a slight easing of her taut thin face.

Meredith clung to Jeremy and sobbed. He held her hard and tight.

Walt moved unsteadily toward a chair, sank down. "Jesus."

Heavy footsteps thudded on the terrace. Sheriff Dulaney, a camera in one hand, looked over the edge of the cliff. "She must be dead." His voice was calm, authoritative.

There was silence except for the boom of the surf.

■ ■ ■ ■

THE BITTER TRUTH

BY PETER LOVESEY

■ ■ ■ ■

"Do me a favor and read this."

"What is it? Hot news?"

"From *me*?" Tysoe of the *Post* shook with laughter. "It's an obituary. Take a look while I get the drinks."

Mark Peters angled the sheet of paper to catch the light over his shoulder.

Judson Perrin: Forensic Toxicologist
who exposed the Ladybird Killer

Judson Perrin, who died yesterday, was the forensic scientist whose evidence sensationally unmasked the serial killer, Dr. Hugo Burke-Miller, in 1980. Unrivaled in his knowledge of plant poisons, Perrin suggested to the police that the deaths of up to five of the doctor's elderly patients from multiorgan failure may have been caused by absorption of abrin, one of the most fatal toxins on earth. *Abrus precato-*

rius, known also as the rosary plant, is common in tropical countries and produces shiny red-and-black ovoid seeds looking like ladybirds and often strung together to form rosaries. When he heard that the doctor under investigation had lived in Belize, where the plant grows abundantly as a weed, Perrin recommended a search of Burke-Miller's Cheltenham property. A box of the seeds was duly discovered. Even so, proof of murder was difficult to obtain because there were no reliable validation tests for abrin in the body after death. Perrin assembled a dossier based on a close study of the symptoms reported in the final hours of five rich patients who had named the doctor in their wills. The subsequent trial was one of the most sensational of the century and made a celebrity of Perrin. He was steadfast under two days of cross-examination and an unpromising conviction was obtained.

Judson Piers Perrin was born in Bruton, Somerset, in 1935, the second son of parents who between them ran a small private boarding school. He obtained a scholarship to Wellington College, and in 1954 enrolled in the medical school at St George's Hospital, London, where he gained valuable laboratory experience as

a demonstrator in the pathology department. After qualifying as a doctor, he
began to forge a reputation in toxicology,
and published several innovative papers
on plant poisons including ricin and abrin.
He first appeared as an expert witness in
a case in 1963.

In 1969, Dr. Perrin accepted the Chair of
Toxicology at Reading University and
lectured widely on plant poisons. He was
consulted on the use of ricin in the murder
in London of the dissident Georgi Markov
by Bulgarian secret service agents in
1978. Toxicology as a field of study has
increased vastly in complexity as new
compounds are developed and more sophisticated methods of detection em-
ployed. Perrin relished the challenge, and
his 1985 book, *An International Directory
of Poisonous Plants,* is still regarded as
indispensable. He received the O.B.E. in
1992. He married twice, in 1962 and 1974.
His first wife, Marjorie Pelham, was killed
in a motor accident in 1972. He is survived
by his second wife, Jane Deacon. He had
two sons from the first marriage, one of
whom predeceased him.

"What's your reaction?" Tysoe asked when
he returned with two pints of lager. The

Grapes was crowded as usual with journalists.

"I didn't know the old boy had turned up his toes."

"He hasn't. He's still about. Cheers."

Mark had been about to take his first sip. The glass stopped midway to his mouth.

Tysoe said, "Didn't I tell you they put me on the obits desk last month?"

"Ah. Makes sense now." Mark sank some of the lager. "Is that, like, a promotion?"

"Some chance. I'm confined to barracks for my sins, but I'm enjoying it. I've been on the road chasing stories for too long. I'm still busy. People are dying all the time."

"Not Mr. Perrin."

"He's old. He hasn't got long."

"Is that inside information?"

Tysoe laughed again. Not a pleasant laugh. "Be prepared, I say."

"I'm guessing you know something. Your job would depress me."

"Come on, Mark. Everyone who's anyone has an obituary waiting. You know that. I have getting on for two thousand of the undead on file. The point is, you're more clued up about famous trials than any of the staffers at the *Post*. What do you think of this one?"

"Want an honest answer? Not much."

Tysoe wasn't offended. He nodded and waited for more.

"Did you write it yourself?" Mark asked. "No? Then I can be frank. It strikes me as bland. Perrin deserves a better sendoff. I mean, there's sod-all here about his work for the Tobacco Products Directive. I believe I'm quoting him right when he said something like, 'When you get sent rotting guts every day of your life you start to care what humanity is doing to its insides.' "

"Nice one. Exactly the kind of quote I need to inject some life into the thing. Obituaries shouldn't be dull. They should reflect the vitality of their subjects. You could give this some pizzazz."

Giving pizzazz to an obituary was a tough call, but as a freelancer, Mark didn't turn work down. "What's your best offer?"

"I could run to five hundred plus expenses. You might want to visit him."

"I can't do it for less than eight. What do you mean 'visit him'? Tell him I'm writing his obituary? That could bring on a seizure before I get a word out of him."

"Obviously you won't tell him why you're there. You can say you're doing a piece about the trial. We'll send a staff photographer with you to get some pictures."

"You did say you'll pay eight hundred plus

expenses?"

"Did I?"

"It's still peanuts, but I'd like an excuse to meet him." Already Mark was thinking he could get a feature article out of this as well and sell it to a color magazine for thousands, not hundreds. The fortieth anniversary of the Burke-Miller trial was coming up later in the year — a convenient peg to hang the piece on. "Are you sure you don't want a medical man for this?"

"No, it can't be too technical. Leave that to the *Lancet.* You're the ideal choice, or I wouldn't have asked. Get the personal angle, preferably with plenty of quotes and any gossip that's going. Our readers love a bit of goss."

"How long have I got?"

The gallows humor kicked in again. "Longer than Perrin, I hope. End of the month, say, about 1500 words? Oh, and for Christ's sake don't tell him what you're up to, or he'll want a preview. Even Winston Churchill wasn't allowed a sight of his when he asked. You will regard this as strictly *entre nous?*"

Mark tapped the side of his nose and winked. He could get to enjoy this assignment.

That evening, he phoned all the contacts

he knew who were likely to have inside information. He told them he would be interviewing Perrin to mark the anniversary of the much-publicized trial, which seemed to have been a life changer but was all most people knew about the toxicologist. He said he was hoping to discover how the old man's life had panned out in the years since. The facts about his career, the qualifications and the honors, were easily found online and in *Who's Who.* The human side was more elusive.

And this was the bit he really enjoyed — rooting out the little-known personal details.

Piecing together hints from several sources, Mark found the juicy morsel he needed. Perrin was rumored to have used his fame to start an affair with the wife of a senior government minister. The story would need more digging, but, if true, might explain why the high-achieving professor had never received a higher honor than the OBE.

He called a retired journo friend who had once been the mainstay of the political pages of the *Herald.* "Every word is true, Mark. She was the wife of Solly Waterfield, the Home Secretary at the time. Solly would leave his penthouse flat in Chelsea to make a statement in Parliament, and Perrin would be waiting outside like a tomcat. Before the minister's car arrived at the House, Perrin and Portia would be at it, banging like the proverbial shithouse door in a gale."

"Are you certain?"

"The woman who lived underneath listened to Iron Maiden at full volume to drown out the sounds."

"Did they separate?"

"You mean Solly and Portia? No, they soldiered on. She was twenty years his junior and came into a small fortune. He was no better in bed than he was in government, but the Waterfield millions were her consolation after he died."

"Plus her toxicologist lover?"

"Perrin wasn't around by then. The affair didn't last that long. I expect she met other men."

"Was this widely known?"

"Only to a few. Mainly me and the long-suffering neighbor. I could have had an exclusive, but my paper wasn't a scandal sheet in those days."

"Don't you want to use it now?"

"Not really. This has no news value. No one's interested in what ministers got up to in the eighties."

"Solly didn't get up to much by the sound of it. All the action came from his wife and

Judson Perrin."

"Couldn't put it better myself."

Since his retirement, Perrin had lived with his second wife, Jane, in a flat in the Barbican. His voice sounded lively enough when Mark called him the same day. He took the bait. Yes, he answered over the phone, he wouldn't object to being interviewed for a feature if it was going into one of the quality magazines. He hadn't realized that forty years had passed since Burke-Miller was convicted, but he agreed that the anniversary was a good reason for a look back at how the trial had unfolded.

The meeting was arranged for late Friday afternoon. Mark asked if he could bring a photographer with him. "No problem at all. I have a room set up as a lab here," Perrin said. "He can get some pictures of me holding up a test tube or whatever."

"You've obviously done this before," Mark said.

"There was a ridiculous amount of interest at the time. I got used to posing behind a flask of fluid with my face distorted. Nobody wants a toxicologist looking normal."

By Friday, Mark had done his homework. He was feeling confident after a couple of drinks at lunchtime. Dale, the photographer, would drive them both there, so there was no need to watch his alcohol level.

It was apparent from the moment they met that Dr. Perrin would be a good interviewee, delighted to be back in the spotlight. Tall, with watery blue eyes and a florid skin tone, the old man had dressed for the photo session in pinstripes and waistcoat, with a rosebud in his buttonhole. It was hard to picture this dignified old guy as the tomcat Tysoe had described. He introduced his wife, Jane, a sweet-smiling lady in her seventies who offered coffee, but they decided to do the photography first. Just as Perrin had predicted, Dale wanted shots of the toxicologist in his home lab, peering into a microscope and then holding a test tube close to his face so that light was refracted onto his features.

"Is this ghoulish enough for you?" Perrin asked, entering into the spirit of the occasion.

"You terrify me," Dale said.

"You could try a knowing smile," Mark suggested, thinking of the revelation to come in the obituary. "That's nice. Get that, Dale."

"Anything else?" Perrin asked.

Dale looked around the room. "Would

you have a picture anywhere of the ladybird seeds?"

"I can do better than that. I can show you some of the little beauties. I still have a few in my poisons cabinet."

"Brilliant. It would be wonderful to get a close-up of them in your open hand."

Perrin unlocked the wall cabinet and reached for a box at the back. He gave it a shake and it rattled. "The shells are so hard that they're sometimes used inside maracas." When he opened the box, the abrin seeds really did look like ladybirds, shiny red, each with a jet-black spot at one end. He gave a mischievous look. "Hold out your hand."

Mark was cautious. "Are they safe to touch? They look innocent enough."

"They're not alive." Perrin poured some into his own palm. "In this state, they can't hurt you. The outer shell is a protection, but I wouldn't advise breaking into one."

Mark held out his hand and allowed Perrin to pass the seeds over.

"Are they still potent after so long?"

"They will be. Variations in temperature don't affect them. The people who string them together as rosary beads run a risk by drilling into the casing. There are stories of pricked fingers and nasty consequences."

"You'd better take them back for the picture."

Dale used a fish-eye lens that would exaggerate the size of Perrin's hand. When he'd finished, he asked, "Are the seeds really so dangerous?"

"Have you heard of ricin? Thirty times more toxic." Perrin returned them carefully to the box and used a wipe to clean his hands.

"Immediate death, then?"

"I was talking about the degree of toxicity, not the speed. The uptake in the body isn't rapid. Anything from eight hours to three days, and then the symptoms can be confused with a severe stomach upset. Vomiting, diarrhea, dehydration. That's the beauty of it for a poisoner. For the victim, it's all downhill from there. The effects are unstoppable. There's no antidote."

"Nasty."

"It is when your liver, spleen, and kidneys stop working. Would you like one of me in profile looking over my shoulder? I'm told that's quite sinister."

With the photography over, Dale retired to the kitchen to chat with Jane Perrin while Mark invited the toxicologist to share his memories of the Burke-Miller trial.

Perrin's powers of recall were excellent,

and the quotes would have fueled a lead story in any paper. "The judge is dead now and I haven't got much longer, so I'll say whatever I please. I didn't rate him at all. I wouldn't have let him judge the pumpkin competition at the garden club. As for the rest of the lawyers, they were pig-ignorant, as well as unpleasant. The prosecution chap kept me in the witness box for two days thinking he could trip me up. By the end, he'd chewed his fingernails to the quick. You asked about Burke-Miller. Funnily enough, I felt some pity for him. Fellow doctor and all that. They decided not to put him on the stand. He was a loose cannon, you see. His greed was the finish of him. He should have stopped when he was ahead. No one is going to question one elderly widow dying from multiorgan failure, but five — to misquote Oscar Wilde — sounds like carelessness."

Mark was making rapid shorthand notes. "The families must have been grateful to you. Plus any other old ladies who had a lucky escape."

"Not at all. I had a nasty letter from one old duck who missed the point altogether. She'd arranged to leave him a few thousand. She said he was a lovely man, worth six of me, and she wouldn't be changing her will just because I'd put him in prison. He needed something to look forward to when he came out. People's stupidity never ceases to amaze me."

"But even if you didn't get much thanks, you had the satisfaction that the law had been upheld and a guilty man got his comeuppance."

"Didn't get me a wealthy widow, did it?"

Mark laughed. "Can I quote that?"

"Why not? It's the truth."

Perrin was so full of himself that Mark decided this was his opportunity. "I read somewhere that you met plenty of people in high places."

He watched the body language, the puffing up of the chest and the hands meeting across it, fingers touching, making a steeple. "A few. Who are you thinking of?"

"Wasn't there an invitation to the Home Office?"

"Not exactly. A few drinks at a private address in Chelsea."

"But you knew the Home Secretary, Solly Waterfield?"

"True."

"And his wife, Portia?"

Perrin's show of swank stalled suddenly. He was frowning. "They were there, yes. Speaking of drinks, you're a lager man, aren't you? I smelt it on your breath when you came in. Help yourself to a can from the fridge. I won't join you. I'm on medication." A blatant change of subject.

"Thanks," Mark said, as he crossed the room to the small fridge under the window. It was stacked with chemicals in glass containers of various sizes, but several cans of a familiar brand of lager were stored behind the door. "You became good friends with the Waterfields, I heard."

"Lager is safer than beer," Perrin went on as if Mark hadn't spoken. "Did you know beer once contained unhealthy amounts of arsenic? A royal commission was set up in 1903 to investigate a spate of poisonings in Manchester. They used glucose in their brewing, you see. And now you're wondering how glucose can be tainted with arsenic. This glucose was. It was made from contaminated sulphuric acid. And there was arsenic getting into the beer from another source. They liked their drink to have a smoky flavor, so they dried the malted barley over a fire. Coke and coal contain appreciable amounts of arsenic."

To show confidence, Mark removed the ring pull from the can and drank deeply. "You were telling me about the Waterfields."

"No I wasn't." The mood had changed

dramatically. "You asked me, and I confirmed that I met them. There's no more to
be said."

"Aren't you going to tell me about your
affair with Portia?"

Perrin's face reddened and his free flow of
words changed in a heartbeat to abuse.
"You're a muckraker. That's why you're
here. You're not a serious journalist."

"It's a simple question."

"And I'm not answering it."

Mark was stung into saying, "It can't be
ducked, you know. You might as well confirm it for the record. The truth is so much
better than innuendo."

"What do you mean — 'for the record'?"
Perrin's eyes widened. "Ha, I see it now. All
that stuff about the magazine feature is
bollocks. You're writing my obituary, and
you want to juice it up with scandal, you
shit."

"Your obituary?" Mark said as if it was a
foreign word. "How could I, when you're
still alive?" An evasion, if not an outright
lie. Mark hoped it carried conviction.

"Barely alive. I've been given three to four
weeks. A tumor as big as my fist."

What could he say to that? Tysoe, damn
him, must have known about the tumor.
Mark remembered the ugly smile when

inside information had been mentioned.

Working for the press toughens anyone. He was there to do a job, but in good conscience he couldn't trade insults with a cancer patient.

"Who put you up to this?" Perrin demanded. "The *Telegraph* or the *Post*?"

"I'm freelance. I didn't know about your tumor, or I wouldn't have troubled you. Like I said, I'm here mainly to do a piece to mark the anniversary of the trial." The truth still sounded insincere and was.

"My private life has fuck all to do with the trial. You mean to smear my reputation — a lifetime of high achievement — by skewing my obituary to make me into some kind of stud."

"Mr. Perrin, we wouldn't have taken all those pictures for an obituary. One mugshot would have been enough."

"Mugshot. You couldn't put it more clearly. I'm the mug. I've been set up."

"Okay," Mark said as the weight of his conscience bore down, "I'll admit it. I was asked to prepare an obituary, but believe me, Mr. Perrin, that's a minor task compared to the magazine feature I want to write."

"Go to hell, you prick."

There was a limit to the flak Mark would

take from most people, but he simply wanted to extricate himself from this mess. Any chance of more useful quotes had ended.

Perrin was clearly of the same mind. "You can leave right now. I haven't any more to say to you except if you insist on shaming me after I've gone, my wife will be heartbroken."

"That's not the point."

"No? You hacks call it collateral damage."

"Fine, I'm out of here if that's what you want. But before I go, I'll clean my hands. I noticed when you'd finished with the seeds you wiped your own hands, but you didn't offer a wipe to me."

"Is this symbolic, washing away your guilt?"

"No, it's being careful."

Perrin picked up the pack of wipes and pulled out a handful. "Dry. I'll moisten them." He reached for a bottle and dampened the wipes before handing them to Mark.

Mark made sure every pore of the hand that had held the abrin seeds was wiped clean.

Perrin changed his tone. "When do you file your copy? Please don't write anything about the affair. I don't want Jane reading after I'm dead that I was unfaithful."

"But it happened."

"I have a son, as well."

"Oh? Who with?" The words were out of Mark's mouth before he sensed their force.

The old man's anger erupted again. "That's vile. I invite you into my home, pose for your pictures, answer your questions, and all I get in return is trickery and insults. Don't you have any respect at all? Piss off, will you? Get out of my house."

Mark didn't need telling. He was ready to go. He called out to Dale that they were leaving.

Perrin still had a parting shot. "Scumbag."

After driving away, Dale said, "Got overexcited, did he?"

"Only towards the end when he cottoned on that I was writing his obituary."

"What does he expect?"

"He thinks I'll skewer him."

"And will you?"

Mark thought deeply before answering, "There's a saying of Voltaire's I learned when I trained as a journalist: 'To the living we owe respect, but to the dead we owe only the truth.' "

■ ■ ■ ■

Ten days later, the *Post* contained a news item on an inside page:

SUDDEN DEATH OF JOURNALIST

Freelance journalist Mark Peters, 44, was found dead at his Fulham home on Thursday morning. It is not known how long his body had lain undiscovered. Apparently in good health until recently, he is thought to have succumbed to a severe gastrointestinal disorder leading to multiple organ failure. A postmortem examination was inconclusive, and further tests are being conducted. Mr. Peters was an occasional contributor to this newspaper. An obituary will follow in tomorrow's edition.

Judson Perrin read the report with satisfaction. The muckraking journalist hadn't died from a mystery illness. He'd been poisoned with abrin, but not from contact with the seeds. Abrin is water soluble, and can be absorbed through the skin. The moisture sprinkled on the hand wipes had been lethal.

And when Perrin himself died a week later, his obituary said nothing about the affair with Portia. It was unchanged from the bland version Tysoe had shown Mark.

UNKNOWN CALLER

BY MEG GARDINER

The package arrived on a stormy autumn day. A padded manila envelope, it had no return address. But the sender's handwriting made Evan Delaney smile as she walked from the mailbox to her front door. Inside the house, she kicked off her pumps. She'd spent a spirited afternoon arguing motions in Santa Barbara Superior Court, and wanted to change and go for a run. Outside the French doors, a crimson-edged sunset cut through the clouds.

Evan tore open the envelope. Inside was a hard object roughly the size of a cigarette, thickly wrapped in layers of newspaper.

The newspaper was what stopped her.

She unwrapped the package slowly, layer by layer, reading the headlines. They were old news, and familiar. ARRESTED, one said. SCHEME EXPOSED, said another. She smoothed out a photo of a muscle car smashed through a storefront's plate glass window. PLEADS GUILTY.

The final layer of newspaper contained no shocking headlines, just an Odds 'n' Ends column. CHURCH BAKE SALE. SCHOOL CAR WASH. DOG FOUND. It was dated November 26, three years ago.

A chill inched up Evan's back. Three years ago exactly.

Heavily, she sat down at the kitchen table.

The knock on Evan's apartment door had come late on a Monday afternoon. It was fall semester, her second year in law school, and she was barefoot in the Northern California heat. She opened the door and did a double take. The woman on the porch wore a flannel shirt and hiking boots. Her long ponytail was pulled through the back of a Giants baseball cap. Her cheeks were flushed, and not just from riding her bike across Palo Alto to campus. The distress on her face made Evan's breath catch.

"Gram, what's wrong?" she said.

"Kid, I hate to bother you. But I don't know where else to turn."

Kath Wheeler put a hand to her mouth. Her eyes were bright and brimming.

Evan pulled her into the cramped student apartment. Kath was a former army nurse, and didn't do tears. Even when she'd lost

Evan's grandfather three months earlier, she'd tried not to break down in front of her grandkids.

In the kitchen, Evan poured her a glass of water. Kath briefly eyed the bottle of vodka by the sink, then accepted the glass and drank it down.

Evan took her hand. "Gram."

Kath held back, uncharacteristically. Kathleen Evan Wheeler lived full-steam-ahead. Evan had been named in her honor. Her mother called her K.E. version 2.0. It wasn't always a compliment.

"Your brother's in trouble," Kath said.

For a moment the kitchen turned so bright Evan couldn't focus. Fear coursed through her. Brian was a navy fighter pilot. *Trouble* could mean his F/A-18 had drilled a smoking hole in the ground.

"What happened?" Evan said.

"He begged me not to tell anybody," Kath said. "Especially not your mom or dad. But it's getting out of hand."

Evan's fear changed to confusion. "Wait. What kind of trouble?"

"He got arrested. In Mexico."

"Oh my God."

The room seemed to throb. Kath leaned against the counter, as though she had no energy to stand up.

"He drove down to Ensenada this week-end for a bachelor party. He and his buddies were driving back from a bar when the car wrecked." She pinched the bridge of her nose. "Brian was driving. He was drunk."

Evan put a hand to her forehead. She led Kath to the sofa and sat beside her. Arrested for drunk driving — in Mexico. *Conduct unbecoming an officer.* It meant the end of her brother's naval career.

"That's not the worst of it," Kath said. "One of his friends got hurt — somebody from his squadron, I think. He's in the hospital."

Evan's chest tightened. "Marc Dupree?"

"That sounds right."

"Is he going to be okay?"

She nodded. "But Lord knows how much the hospital's going to cost." She wiped her eyes with the heel of her hand. "Brian wasn't injured, but sounded awful."

Shaken, Evan put an arm around Kath. "We'll help him. Help them both." Her throat caught. "We have to tell Mom and Dad. They can —"

"Absolutely not." Kath straightened. "Brian was adamant. He does not want your parents involved."

"Does he have a lawyer? We need to call him —"

"We can't. He called me from a pay phone at the jail."

"Then how . . ."

Kath set a hand on her arm. "I sent him money for bail. That's what I need to tell you."

"You what?"

"I paid his bail. And I was happy to help. But bailing him out didn't solve his problems, so I think it's time to bring in more troops to fight this fire."

"Money." She frowned. "How much did you pay?"

"Three thousand dollars."

"That's not as bad as it could have been." It actually sounded like a bargain for bail on an injury accident DUI, whether in the U.S. or Mexico. But it was nevertheless a substantial amount for a widow on a fixed income to pay. "Still, it was a lot to ask. I'm surprised Brian called you."

"Your brother's good for it — I don't doubt that. But he phoned an hour ago and said he needs five thousand more, as bond, to get his passport back."

A new chill settled on her. "That doesn't sound right."

"Brian's my grandson. I have to help. But another five thousand dollars — I can't raise it."

"Stop." Chilled to her fingers, Evan grabbed her phone. "This doesn't add up."

"You can't call him. The police confiscated his phone. They're holding it with his passport, as collateral."

Kath's fear and deep sadness were palpable. The look in her eyes was desperate. But this whole thing smelled wrong. Evan hit Brian's number.

He answered on the second ring.

"Ev, great photos from your Halloween party. Good *Alien* chest-burster outfit."

"Where are you?" she said.

He didn't need to answer. The background whine of jet engines told her he was exactly where he was supposed to be: on duty with his Carrier Air Wing at Naval Air Station Lemoore, near Fresno.

"What's that sound in your voice?" he said.

"I'll call you back."

She hung up. With a glance at Kath, she phoned the police.

The Palo Alto Police Department was bustling. Outside, live oaks swayed in the breeze. The view was cozy and slick: the shiny Spanish-style architecture of Silicon Valley. Detective Hector Mendoza was sympathetic but steely.

334

"It's even called the Favorite Grandson Scam," he said.

Kath looked shrunken to half size. Evan's heart ached. She'd been clenching her fists since she spoke to Brian.

"The caller ID was 'unknown caller,' " Kath said. "I should have known, but when he said Mexico . . ."

"Did the caller identify himself to you by name?" Mendoza said. "Did he say, 'Hi, Grandma, it's Brian'?"

She shook her head. "He said, 'Hey, it's me.' And I had to think for a sec, but I said, 'Brian?' And he said, 'Right.' "

Mendoza wrote it down.

"His voice sounded rough. But I thought, he's been in a car accident." Kath lowered her eyes. "It was stupid of me."

Evan said, "No. It was logical."

She was thinking that when Kath had told her one of Brian's friends was injured, she'd done exactly the same thing: filled in a blank, with the name Marc Dupree.

"How did you send the money?" Mendoza said.

"A wire transfer. From the Western Union in the shopping center, to Brian Delaney at the Western Union in Ensenada. Can you trace it? Find out who picked it up? I know it's outside the U.S., but . . ."

"Mrs. Wheeler, I'm sorry. But no matter the name and address on a wire transfer, it's possible for anybody to collect the money anywhere in the world. He didn't have to be in Ensenada. He could have been in the East Bay. Or Estonia."

Kath's face paled. It looked like the last of her hope and self-respect draining away.

"What can you do?" Evan said. "How do we track these bastards down and get my grandmother's three thousand dollars back?"

Mendoza's sympathetic expression seemed to say, *Really?*

She said, "How do these people know who to target? They apparently knew that Gram *is* a grandmother. Do they cold-call random numbers?"

"Sometimes. Mrs. Wheeler, can you remember telling anybody in town about your grandson?"

Her eyes went soft. "I tell everybody about my grandkids."

Evan put an arm around her shoulder. "Can you think of anybody in particular?"

"The people at the bank. And the post office. And the library."

Mendoza said, "Sometimes they target people when there's been a bereavement. They'll look for funeral notices, or public records and court filings."

"My grandfather died in August," Evan said. "His estate is in probate."

She could hardly swallow. Her rage was so blinding, the detective seemed to shimmer.

She wanted her mother there, but Angie Delaney was a flight attendant, and was in Rio. Her dad would have broken legs for Kath, but he was in Washington, D.C. She dreaded telling Brian. His anger would be incandescent.

"We have to do something," she said.

With a cheerful chime, Kath's cell phone rang. Everyone fell silent. Kath pulled the phone from her pocket, and her jaw tightened.

The screen said *Unknown Caller*.

She looked at Mendoza. He nodded sharply. She set the phone on his desk and answered on speaker.

"Hello." Her voice held firm.

"It's Brian," a man said.

Acid rose in Evan's throat. It wasn't Brian. But with the noisy, staticky connection, it didn't sound too far off. She stood and leaned over the phone.

"Hey, it's me," she said.

He paused a long beat. "Cool. You get the cash?"

"I got something better," she said. "I'm at

the Palo Alto Police Department. Detective Mendoza thinks he can help clear things up with the Ensenada cops."

The call went dead.

Mendoza gave her an inscrutable look. "Proactive. That's a tactic."

Evan's pulse was thumping. Kath put the phone away. She looked even paler than she had before.

Mendoza's tone softened. "They won't call back again, Mrs. Wheeler. They're done going after you. Your granddaughter just saw to that."

"And we have no way to go after *them*?" she said softly.

His eyes were concerned, and pained. "If you remember anything else, or come up with more evidence, let me know. I've got your report. Until then . . ."

Evan took Kath's hand, and they left.

Outside, in the cheery California sunshine, she said, "I'm sorry."

"My fault entirely," Kath said. "I'm a grown woman, and I should know better."

But the loss of Evan's grandfather was still raw. Kath wasn't herself yet.

"We won't give up," Evan said. "We'll figure out a way."

Day by day, it festered. Evan could see that

the crime, coming on top of her grand-mother's grief, stuck Kath like a splinter: a sharp, outsize pain. Brian was horrified when Evan told him. It jabbed her, too. Scamming a widow — the psychopathic *balls* on these guys. Detective Mendoza got used to her phoning and stopping by to ask if there had been any breaks in the case.

Weeks passed, and her paltry hopes shriveled. But she couldn't let it go. Let it go, and she felt she'd be letting Kath down.

Then, on her ninety-fifth call, Mendoza went quiet for a moment. "I'm heading out for coffee. Starbucks on University, if you're in the neighborhood."

She got there in ten minutes, and Mendoza didn't waste time.

"We don't have probable cause to arrest him for scamming your grandmother, but we think we know who did it."

"Tell me."

"Man named Roger Inke. Runs a pawn shop on El Camino."

Evan was already steaming. "Why can't you arrest him?"

"Insufficient evidence. Inke's a low-level con man, persistent and clever. The Favorite Grandson Scam is rumored to be his specialty. We arrested him for pulling it on another senior citizen, but last week his attorney got the charge dropped on a technicality."

"Roger Inke."

"We have no evidence tying him to your grandmother's case. However, if you do . . ."

"Are you asking? Hoping?" she said. "What are you saying?"

"I'm telling you that as much as I hate this guy, as of today I can't get him. But if you have the resources to pursue this on your own, it could be worthwhile. If you could substantiate your grandmother's claim well enough to file a civil suit, it might be possible to obtain a judgment against Inke."

If they had the money to hire a lawyer, and a private investigator, Mendoza was telling her. Which they didn't. It was a lesson not taught in class: the law didn't guarantee justice.

"The only evidence we have is what we've given the police department," she said.

"So far," he said. "Think you could come up with more?"

Icarus Jewelry & Pawn sat on a barren patch of El Camino Real, the main business street that ran through Palo Alto. The display windows were stuffed with tat. On the second floor, a blue neon sign blared BAIL

BONDS. It hit Evan again why the scammers had claimed Brian was in Mexico: to keep Kath from calling a California bondsman. The scam was as slick as grease. Anger filled her again, like an abscess.

A buzzer rang when she opened the door. The shop's interior was both shiny and dim. *"We buy gold!"* it promised, and it did, great dripping necklaces of it.

At the back, Roger Inke sat behind the counter, beneath walls mounted with electric guitars and velvet Elvis paintings and laptops available for the price of a steak dinner. He was a thin man with a thin grimace and thinner eyes, reading *Today's Pawnbroker* magazine. At his feet lurked a greyhound. The dog didn't exactly sit, but hovered nervously over a dog bed, looking ready to bolt if anybody so much as smacked their lips. Judging by a photo behind Inke, it was a former race-winning greyhound. But as guard dogs went, a hamster would have been more threatening.

Inke eyed her with disinterest. "What are you after?"

She hesitated. What was she going to do — scream *Vengeance!* and leap on him like a banshee? She pointed at a painting and asked how much.

"Forty-five dollars," he rasped.

341

"I'll give you fifteen."

Behind her, a mailman slid a stack of letters through a slot in the door. Evan jumped at the sound. As the letters dropped to the floor, the dog sprang to its feet. It pranced down the narrow aisle and picked them up, daintily, with its teeth. It primped back, nails ticking on the tile, and Inke took them.

"Good girl, Tyche." He glanced at Evan. "Twenty."

The painting made her eyeballs ache, but she didn't care to linger. She paid and left, her nerves vibrating.

Half an hour later she picked up Kath. In her decrepit Honda Civic, they drove along El Camino past Icarus Pawn. Kath was unfamiliar with the shop. Evan wasn't surprised.

But a hundred yards down the street, Kath swiveled, eyeing a used car dealership.

"That's where I sold your granddad's Volvo after he died."

Evan did a double take. PINKY'S PRE-OWNED PARADISE.

"Did you talk to anybody there about your family?"

Kath huffed. Of course she had. Her grandkids were the shiny red apples of her eye. And of course she had given the dealership her name, address, and phone number.

She glared out the car window, deadly silent for a minute.

"How many people do you think they've ripped off since they got to me?" she said.

"I don't know. But one's too many."

"We can't let this go on. And we don't have forever, do we?"

"What do you mean?"

"There's a cutoff for prosecuting a crime. For suing."

"The statute of limitations," Evan said. "I think for fraud, it's three years. There's still time."

"Not for the people they're targeting while we cruise around. People who may not be able to take a three-thousand-dollar hit to their wallets. For them, the clock's ticking. Loudly."

Evan wrung her hands on the wheel. Kath was right.

"Turn around," Kath said. "Drive by again. I want to get a solid look at these human skid marks."

"You're not going to do something. I am," Evan said.

"You think I'm too old to kick some ass?" Kath said. "Fine, I need a knee replacement, but don't underestimate me."

Evan tried to laugh. Kath sighed.

"I know," Kath said. "I just don't want

anybody else getting conned."

The next day, Evan started staking out Icarus Pawn.

Evan didn't know what she was looking for, but sitting across from the pawnshop on El Camino in her rusting Civic proved a good way to study. She found it helpful to be away from the law library and all its angst and lust. She read casebooks and highlighted her class notes, drinking lukewarm coffee and scrutinizing everybody who went into the shop. It convinced her she never wanted to be a cop.

On the third day of her stakeout, a car rumbled to a stop in front of Icarus. It was an orange Camaro with a price soaped on the windshield — $9,999. A young man climbed out and lit a cigarette. He looked like Roger Inke's younger, even skeevier incarnation. He walked into the pawnshop without extinguishing his smoke.

Only family would so casually stink up a store, Evan thought.

Five minutes later, the young man came out of the shop with the greyhound on a leash. The dog popped up and down at his side as though the sidewalk was a hot skillet.

The man looked half-bored. He had an

envelope in his hand. The dog jumped and tried to nip it away from him. He teased her, holding it out of reach, before finally letting her grab it. Jerking the leash free from his hand, the greyhound bolted along the sidewalk toward a mailbox on the corner. She accelerated like a Lamborghini. The man ran after her for a few steps, then threw up his hands and slowed to a saunter in frustration.

Roger Inke leaned out the pawnshop door and yelled at him. When the man shrugged, Inke put two fingers to his lips and whistled. The streaking dog pivoted, ears pricking, and stopped. The younger man raised his middle finger, as if trained to flip the bird on command, and kept strolling.

Evan watched him mosey into the distance. She fired up the Civic, U-turned, and drove to the used car dealership. Amid a profusion of American flags, salesmen patrolled the lot like predatory squid. It took four seconds for one to approach her.

"You look like you're in the market for something fast and hot," he said.

"I'm looking for one of your sales associates. Mr. Inke."

The salesman deflated. "Wayne's on a break. I can help."

"I have a yen for an orange Camaro. I'll

come back when he's here."

She left, nerves sizzling.

Wayne and Roger Inke. The two of them had thieved and humiliated Kath. She felt certain. She just had to get evidence that proved it.

How? The Inkes wouldn't easily talk and incriminate themselves. She wasn't a black hat who could hack their texts or bank records. She didn't have the burglary skills to plant bugs in their wall sockets. She had snark and a talent for provoking people into talking smack.

That was when she first thought of tricking Roger Inke into confessing. Detective Mendoza wanted her to do something about him. Wanted her to take the initiative. What other choice did she have?

This was called rationalization, and she was a pro at that.

From there, it seemed simple. It seemed necessary and righteous. A little voice said it also seemed risky. She flicked the little voice off her shoulder.

She knew she couldn't simply walk into Icarus Pawn and demand a confession. She needed to be subtle and sneaky. Unfortunately, she also knew that she was in-your-face and a lousy liar.

"Use that," said her roommate, Nikki Girard.

It took her a fevered week to work up the idea. She gamed it out. She drew a map of El Camino and a floor plan of Icarus Pawn. She rehearsed it. She ran it by Nikki.

"It's basic," Evan said. "Get in, maintain a clear line of sight to the door, keep the recorder running, lure Inke into tripping over his own tongue. Get out."

Nikki hated it, even more than she hated the painting Evan had bought at the pawnshop: *Cats at the Last Supper.* As an art history major raised in the AME Church, she objected to the painting on both aesthetic and theological grounds. But beyond all else, Nikki hated the fact that Kath had been scammed.

"There's no honor among these thieves," Nikki said. "Because they have no honor, period. Count on that. Screw with their heads."

Evan phoned Brian to warn him what she was planning, in case she needed exfil from her own missteps.

"Unlike you, I might end up needing bail money for real," she told him.

She didn't tell Kath.

A cool wind was blowing the next afternoon

when Evan walked through the door of Icarus Pawn. Her throat was dry. Roger Inke sat behind the counter polishing a tarnished wristwatch. The greyhound huddled near his feet. They both glanced up listlessly.

Inke smirked. "You're spoiled for choice today." He nodded at new paintings on the wall. "Decorate your boudoir."

He swept a hand. LeBron James. Sasquatch. The Little Mermaid.

Evan approached the counter. In her front pocket, her phone was recording a voice memo.

"I know it was you and your nephew," she said.

"Say what?"

She pressed her hands to the counter to keep them from trembling. "You and Wayne are the people who conned my gram out of her money."

Inke's eyes went cold and cloudy, like ice chips. "If you ain't buying, you need to go."

She jabbed the counter with her index finger. "She sold a Volvo to Pinky's used car dealership. Wayne overheard her explaining that it was her late husband's car. She gave the dealership her address and phone number — which was all Wayne needed to call her up anonymously and pull her in."

348

Evan was playing a hunch. Roger Inke could have been the one who phoned Kath, but his voice sounded old and worn, unlike the voice she'd briefly heard on the phone — the voice of the man who'd convinced Kath he was Evan's brother.

Inke's eyes stayed opaque. "Get out."

"She and I went back to the dealership. She saw Wayne," Evan said. "She heard him talking to a customer and recognized his voice. He was the caller."

Inke stood and came out from behind the counter, shoulders tight. "I said, get out."

Evan backed toward the exit. "Wayne had already phoned her four times — she wasn't going to forget what he sounded like."

He was stalking after her, pointing at the door, but when she said that, his expression tightened with surprise and what seemed incipient suspicion.

"Why'd you have to be so greedy?" she said. "The first five thousand bucks Gram paid was bad enough, but then another five, and when Wayne called back *again* for even more?" She sneered. "Pigs shoving your snouts into the trough over and over because you can't get enough."

That may have been too much. The look in Inke's eyes turned poisonous. *Crap.* Evan spun and took a sharp step toward the door.

Inke jumped in front of her, blocking it.

"Move," she said.

He stayed put. "You tell me Wayne's ripping people off, and expect to just waltz out of here?"

Clinging to a thin thread of bravado, she tried to see past his shoulder out the door. "I said you're both ripping people off. Don't act aggrieved."

"Prove it."

"Which part?"

"That he took her for ten grand. Prove it right now."

She could have kneed him in the groin and run. Her nerves were screeching. But what he'd just said was better than a confession. It told her that Inke already had doubts about young Wayne, who treated him with casual disrespect and who brought his dog back from her walks exhausted, with dirty paws.

"You think I'm going to show you a receipt, with her personal information and account numbers?" she said. "Forget it. You scammed my gram — you're not going to scam me."

"I can check this," he said. "Real quick."

He turned the sign on the door to *CLOSED*. Pointed at the counter.

She hesitated, then walked to the back of

the shop with him breathing on her neck.

At the counter he got on the computer and brought up Western Union. The site said "MONEY IN MINUTES. 500,000 locations worldwide for cash pickup."

Bending over his cell phone, Inke scrolled through photos. Evan got just a glimpse. He was perusing snapshots of credit cards. Belonging to customers, she'd bet — his or the used car dealership's. After some thought he chose one. He checked the card number carefully as he typed it into the computer. And he checked the cardholder's name and spelling with equal care.

He hit *SEND.*

"Now we'll see," he said darkly. He picked up the store phone and punched in a number.

A few seconds later, Wayne apparently answered. Inke said, "Got one."

Evan's heartbeat kicked up.

"Get over to the cashpoint in Mountain View and pick it up," Inke said. "Yeah, right now. I had to reel this one in. And I get the sense they might be on the verge of figuring it out."

Evan fought the urge to fidget.

"Just do it," Inke said. "Name on the money order —" he checked the credit card image on his cell phone "— Arthur Mann-

351

heim." He set the cell down. "Then get over here straightaway."

Another pause, more annoyance. "Because I said so. I have something to show you. You'll like it. Just hurry."

Win. That's what Evan was thinking: *a complete win.* This was evidence of intent to commit fraud. She took a step away from Inke.

He reached across the counter and grabbed her wrist. "Where do you think you're going?"

It didn't take long before the door buzzer rang and Wayne strutted in. He looked flushed. The wind gusted and paintings battered against the wall.

Wayne marched down the aisle, jerking a thumb over his shoulder at the door. "Sign blew the wrong way round. Says you're closed."

"But you didn't bother to fix it, did you?" Inke said.

"What's your problem?" Wayne reached the counter. "What do you want to show me?"

Inke nodded at Evan. "She says you been shortchanging me."

And she realized her mistake, and inexperience. They had her outnumbered. She wasn't a good undercover operative. Or even a wily lawyer in training. Just stupid.

"What are you talking about?" Wayne said.

"Just want to make sure you're giving me the full amount," Inke said. "You better have brought five thousand dollars."

Wayne's eyes flared, and his face reddened. "What kind of stories has she been telling you?"

Evan really needed to get out of there.

"You don't trust me?" Wayne said.

"Show me," Inke said.

"On her word? The word of a stranger?"

"A stranger whose grandmother paid out," Inke said.

Wayne glared at Evan. Then he reached into his back pocket, pulled out an envelope, and slapped it down on the counter.

"Count it." He cut a glance at his uncle, then leaned toward her, hulking. "She's pulling something. On you and me."

The door buzzed again and blew open in a violent gust of wind. Papers swirled from the countertop. Wayne was inches from her face.

In the doorway, two men appeared.

Inke said, "We're closed."

"Good."

They were in their late twenties, lean, fit, slide rule straight, with eyes trained to sight enemy fighters from fifty miles away while flying at the speed of sound. One white, one black, both deadly, and beloved. Evan's brother, Brian, and his friend Marc Dupree filled the aisle. Side by side, they walked toward the counter.

Wayne turned. "The hell are you?"

Marc said, "I'm the guy who was in the hospital in Mexico."

Brian said, "I'm the one who was in jail. Looks like I busted out. Oops."

He smiled, like a shark. Roger Inke had gone absolutely still.

"What is this?" he said.

The wind blew hard through the open door. A set of chimes rang off-key.

And the envelope with the money lifted off the counter. Inke swiped at it but the envelope caught air and swooped to the floor.

"Wayne, get it," he said.

Wayne attempted to stomp on the envelope with his boot, but missed. It scooted along the floor. Evan lunged for it.

The greyhound beat her to it.

Tyche grabbed the envelope and streaked out the door like she'd been catapulted.

Inke and Wayne charged after her, shouting insults at both the dog and each other. At the door, they shoved and grappled to get out first, then ran down the sidewalk.

Brian put an arm around Evan's shoulder. "You okay?"

"Oh yeah," she said. "More than."

Nikki phoned while Evan was walking to her car with Brian and Marc.

"I got it. All of it." Her roommate's voice was fizzing. "Got photos of Wayne. I followed him from the used car dealership to the Western Union cashpoint. Got pics of him going in, signing the receipt, collecting the cash. And I talked to the clerk after he left. She let me snap a photo of the receipt. He signed it 'Arthur Mannheim.' Evan, we've got them."

"Sensational," Evan said. "Nikki, you're a star."

She kept thinking: *that close.* The money had been within her reach.

When they reached her car, a white piece of paper was stuck beneath the windshield wiper, fluttering in the wind.

It was a blank envelope. It was the envelope that had held the cash. It was empty.

Evan and Nikki took all the information to the police. Detective Mendoza was amazed to get it. And he scolded them severely for taking such a risk. But he was happy to download the conversation Evan had recorded with Wayne and Roger, and to copy Nikki's photos and take her statement.

He walked them out. At the station door he paused, looking stern, then smiled broadly.

"I'll be in touch."

He called that night, after hauling the Inkes to jail.

Their arrest featured on the local TV news, and in the next day's paper. The fallout featured in later reports. Wayne and Roger turned on each other during interrogation. Once out on bond, their blame casting turned ugly. Arguments and insinuations escalated to accusations and threats. Two weeks later, on the sidewalk in front of Icarus Pawn, Roger challenged Wayne to come at him. Unfortunately, at the time Wayne was at the wheel of the orange Camaro he'd borrowed from the used car lot. He came straight at Roger and kept going, through the front window of the pawnshop, and the car had to be marked down from $9,999.

Tyche, apparently, was the sole mourner at Roger's funeral. By then, Wayne was back in jail, being held without bail. It was a rough, shocking end to a nasty episode, and for Evan a pointed lesson in how the world worked.

Later, she stopped by Kath's house, to toast their bitter half victory. She talked to her grandmother about filing a civil suit to recover her money — they could sue Roger Inke's estate, she suggested. They could try to attach the proceeds from the sale of the pawnshop. Arthur Mannheim's credit card company had done exactly that to recoup its missing five thousand dollars. Or they could sue the cashpoint that had let Wayne collect Kath's money without asking for a legitimate ID.

Kath shook her head. "You've done more than enough."

"But, Gram . . ."

Kath took her hand. Her eyes were bright. "It's done, Evan. Let it go."

That was the image shining in Evan's memory as she opened the newspaper-wrapped package. Just over three years since Kath had been scammed. Exactly three since Evan had faced off against the Inkes. Graduation, a job, a move to Santa Barbara. Kath finding herself again, traveling. Confident, since that day. Evan unwrapped the last layer of newspaper and saw what was inside.

She stared. Her laugh, when it came, was

sharp with shock. She understood now. About that day at Icarus Pawn, and how an envelope that had been emptied of cash ended up on the windshield of her car.

There had been an unknown caller.

Three years to the day. This wasn't just any anniversary. Three years was the statute of limitations for grand theft. As of today, no prosecution was possible. She ran her fingers across Kath's handwriting on the envelope, and picked up the item that had been wrapped in the headlines.

A dog whistle.

■ ■ ■ ■

April 13

BY MARCIA MULLER

■ ■ ■ ■

April 13. Anniversary number five. A ridiculous ritual, I admit.

Normally I'm not a superstitious individual. Black cats don't bother me — I have two. I skip happily under ladders, don't eat an apple a day, and have broken more mirrors than I can remember. But I couldn't get loose from this April thirteenth obsession.

It was eleven in the morning. I'd cleared up all my paperwork, held a staff meeting, and conferred one-on-one with various of my operatives. Hy Ripinsky, my husband and partner in McCone & Ripinsky Investigations, was back east at our Chicago field office, and I had nothing urgent to share with him anyway. I wasn't currently working a case myself. No reason to remain in my office in the M&R building. After all, I was the boss!

But still I remained at my desk and turned

to my computer, opened up the older case files section, and scrolled down to "Voss, Judith." And there it was — the cold case that I'd reviewed obsessively every April 13 for five years now. Maybe this year something would stand out — a fact or scrap of information that I had somehow missed or failed to internalize before.

Judith Voss, according to her parents, had been one of those too-good-to-be-true daughters: the kind who make good grades — in her case, at SF State — never cause trouble in the home, date the appropriate boys, have ambitions appropriate to their family's station in life. In fact, for them *appropriate* was a good word to sum up her character. She was conventionally pretty, excelled at soccer and swimming, wanted to be a physical therapist. In order to finance her higher education, she banked money from a part-time job clerking at a small flower shop near the home she shared with her parents in the inner Sunset District near Golden Gate Park. She claimed she loved San Francisco and would never leave it, but apparently she had.

Five years ago on April 13, Judith had left home at 7:00 p.m., supposedly for a French club meeting. She went out the door calling

362

out, "Goodbye, Mom, goodbye, Dad," instead of her usual "See you later." When she didn't return by the time her parents normally went to bed, they didn't think much of her absence. They assumed she had decided to stay over with a friend from the club, as she sometimes did. But when she hadn't returned by late the next afternoon, Mrs. Voss called the friend and found there had been no club meeting; in fact, the friend hadn't seen Judith in a month or more.

The officers on SFPD's Missing Persons detail hadn't seen much cause for alarm. Young people disappeared in the city all the time; they usually turned up unscathed. Detectives went through the motions, which included contacting outlying jurisdictions, but finally concluded that Judith had left the city of her free will. She was over eighteen and had every right to come and go as she pleased — not like the decades-long plague of underage runaways who flocked to such places as the Haight, Taos, Seattle, New York, and Florida. The parents were referred to me by their attorney and they asked me to see if I could find something the police had missed. I tried for two weeks, but the record was straightforward; we finally terminated our professional relationship, and Judith remained missing.

I've never considered any of my agency's relatively few unsolved cases closed. Years ago when I'd been changing offices, I'd unearthed an open file that dealt with the disappearance of a young couple. I read it, put a couple of neglected facts together, and by night the couple were reunited with their families.

That was why, every April 13, I picked through the Voss file. An exercise in futility so far.

All the transcripts of my interviews were there, starting with my clients, the parents. Emily Voss was blonde, thin, and nervous; her fingers picked at her clothing and she constantly twisted her wedding ring. I suspected the nervousness was habitual rather than related to the problem at hand. When she spoke of her daughter, I heard a wisp of envy in her voice: "Judy was so smart — she could achieve whatever she wanted to in her life. She wouldn't be ordinary . . ." At that point she let her words trail off and glanced at her husband. His thick lips twisted, acknowledging the unsaid, "Ordinary like me."

Doug Voss, stocky in his neatly pressed chinos and checked sport shirt, was a high school basketball coach. His big hands swooped around as he talked. "That girl,

364

there's no way she's in serious trouble. I trained her well. She's strong, got her head together. Whatever she's up to, she's got a reason."

"You think she disappeared deliberately?" I asked.

He nodded. "That girl, she's up to something, is what I say."

Judith hadn't had many friends — "Too competitive," her father claimed — but I interviewed them all. And they all offered opinions that conflicted with her parents' views.

Nancy Melton told me, "Judy could be a lot of fun. She had a wild side. Nothing dangerous, just pranks. Like stealing her boyfriend's jock from his gym locker and leaving it on the math teacher's desk."

"Judy dated a lot," a former boyfriend, Gary Cramer said. "You wanted some, you knew where to get it. She loved to fuck, the more the better."

"She was a very spiritual person," Cindy Stafford remarked. "It was always up to God. 'God's gonna get me for this.' 'God'll handle this problem.' "

Art Gallo commented, "Girl knew — and used — more swearwords than I do."

The friend who had the most penetrating insights into Judith Voss was classmate Barbie Jennings, a big, graceless woman in bib overalls and a T-shirt who, in the course of our talk at her apartment, tripped over a hassock, bruised her upper arm on the corner of a bookcase, and knocked over a tall stack of paperback books.

From the Jennings transcript:

BJ: If you asked me to come up with one word that described Jude, I'd say it would be *wanting,* as in aching for stuff. She needed . . . I don't know what she needed. But whatever it was, she wasn't going to get it on a physical therapist's salary.

SM: She wanted something in a monetary sense?

BJ: Yeah. It's like what we used to do on Sundays sometimes when the real estate ads came out. Jude would go over the open homes section and circle ones that looked good. Then we'd go tour them.

SM: You weren't thinking of buying or renting?

BJ: God, no. Even back then, the prices were outrageous. And the places she wanted to look — Cow Hollow, Pacific Heights, Russian Hill — were out of sight. I asked her once why didn't we look at inexpensive condos or apartment rentals. Maybe something nice would turn up and we could go halves on it. She said no. The way things were, she'd have to go it alone.

SM: The way things were?

BJ: Yeah. I asked her what she meant, but she just smiled like I was supposed to know.

SM: Did she have a boyfriend — this Gary Kramer, for instance — whom she might've been planning on moving in with?

BF: Did she have a boyfriend? Who-eee! Guys were calling all the time, but as far as I knew she didn't go with any one for very long. And she didn't talk about them.

SM: No one steady at all?

BJ: No. She'd say, "He's strictly temporary" or "I can't be bothered with him."

That was it. Once, not long before she disappeared, she found a house she really liked on Russian Hill. It was an odd little place, but she was very taken with it. As she was looking around I heard her mutter, "This would be perfect for —" and then she saw me looking at her and smiled in that weird, secret way she had and refused to talk about it. After that . . . well, I decided she wasn't much of a friend, and we saw less of each other. Then suddenly she was gone, and I never heard from her again.

Next I looked at the transcripts of my talks with Judith's teachers.

Lynda Holman, English literature, found Judith "very studious. Most of the kids, well, you see vacant stares and you know they're far away, into something else entirely. But I'd be giving a lecture on Chaucer — which even bored me — and I'd catch Judy watching me with an intense look, almost as if she wanted something more from me. But the few times I called on her and asked, 'Yes, Judy?' she waved the question aside."

Mark Bolton, statistics, had a similar take on her: "Most students take my courses to satisfy a requirement for a program like the MBA, but Judy was into them for the content. She wanted to know what statistics could do for her, personally. It's hard to say why, but it was as if she was working on a problem and needed proof of the solution."

Emma Carpenter, biology, said, "When she disappeared, I thought, 'Well, isn't that just like her.' I mean, she was so remote. She performed the class and lab work all right, but she was . . . well, mechanical. Just filling up space until she could get to what was really important to her."

Valerie Mott, women's athletic director, commented, "God, could that girl run." Then she smiled and shook her head. "Sorry, the pun was unintentional. But I guess that's what this is all about — she ran, and nobody ever knew why."

More transcripts. Older people, friends and associates of Judith's parents, all of whom had widely varying opinions of her.

"I wish I had a kid like her."

"Sneaky."

"Sincere."

"Very helpful to her mother."

"I don't think she was very close to her father."

"Physical therapist? I thought she wanted to be an interior decorator, or do something in real estate."

"She wouldn't just up and run away. She's

got to be dead. Someday they'll find her body in a ditch someplace."

"She gave off a strange sexual aura."

"She went out with my son Jeff. Just a few dates. He found her boring."

"I never caught her in a lie, but she sometimes seemed untruthful."

"Gossipy — but most of what she talked about was untrue. I wouldn't be surprised if she made it all up."

"She made me uncomfortable."

"I'm not sure that there wasn't something abnormal about the girl."

"Flirtatious? Yes. But a lot of girls like to flirt with older men. And we like them to flirt."

"Bright. She could hold up her end of conversations on many complicated issues."

"Poised and socially at ease."

More of the same from the Vosses' neighbors:

"She'd sneak out of the house in the middle of the night," Mrs. Polly Gilbert said. "I know because I'm unwell and sit up in my chair next to our bedroom window most of the time. There'd usually be this man waiting for her."

"A man, not a boy?" I asked.

"I'm sure I'd know the difference."

"Can you describe him?"

"Not very well. Just tall and well built."

"Did you hear them talking? Maybe she mentioned his name."

"Talk? The two of them? Not hardly."

"Yes, I'd see Judy slipping out of the house all the time," an elderly woman who wouldn't give me her name told me. "Out the window, and gone. It's lucky that's a one-story house. If she'd had to climb down a drainpipe, she might've broken her neck."

"Men? Nonsense!" Mrs. Olivia Johnson shook her head vehemently. "They weren't all men. Some of them were teenagers, too."

"Do you remember any of them?"

"Well, the man who came the most, he had a red Porsche — one of the old ones that look like an upside-down spoon — that he'd park down the street, and then he'd lean against the car, bold as brass. She'd go to him, and they'd take off. I can still hear the sound of that car growling away into the night."

"When was this?"

"It went on for four months, right before Judith disappeared."

"Did you ever overhear any conversation between them? The man's name, for instance?"

371

"No."

"What about the car's license plate?"

"It was in-state. But I didn't notice the numbers. I've never been good with numbers." She shook her head and added, "I warned my Margaret to stay away from the Voss girl. Her midnight escapades set a bad example. Let's just say that Judith Voss never came around here selling Girl Scout cookies."

That first April 13, the grown man with the red Porsche had seemed my only starting point. From my contact at the Department of Motor Vehicles, I learned that there were twenty-three such models in the Greater Bay Area that had been licensed over five years previously. Nine of them I could rule out because they were registered to women. Two were on planned nonoperation. Another had been in a wreck and consigned to the junkyard.

Ten cars, then, in various locations around the area.

I'd begun by phoning.

Owner #1 had been deceased for over a year. "I just can't get around to selling that Porsche," his widow said.

Owner #2 had been in Thailand on sabbatical five years ago. "Car was up on blocks in his garage," his secretary told me. "He made me go over and check on it once a month. That's how much he loved that car."

Owner #3's phone was disconnected.

Owner #4 had moved to Utah.

Two more deceased owners. At the second number a woman said, "I always told my husband that car would be the death of him."

Owner #7 was annoyed. "I sold it to a kid a year ago. Don't tell me he didn't reregister it!" Apparently he hadn't.

Three owners to go. None of them answered the phone. I decided to wait until evening, then show up at their addresses.

Eldon McFeeney lived in a bad section of Oakland: men wearing gang colors congregated around a corner drugstore; most of the dilapidated houses had security gates on the doors and windows, while others were boarded up. I parked in front of the McFeeney garage and mounted the rickety stairs to knock. In a few moments, when I'd just about given up on getting a reply, a skinny black man on crutches answered. His skin was dry and clung to his fragile-looking cheekbones; his hair had receded to two small spots above his large ears; a strong odor of alcohol surrounded him.

"Yes, what is it?" he asked.

I handed him one of my cards. He looked at it, shook his head, and muttered something that sounded like, "What next?"

"I'm interested in the Porsche 912 you have registered under your name," I said.

"The Porsche . . . that's not mine. Can you see an old wreck like me driving that baby?" He smiled faintly. "It's my younger brother's, registered in my name because . . . well, Donny has trouble with traffic cops. They took his license away permanently years ago."

"How many years?"

"Seven? Eight? My memory's not so good."

"Does Donny live here with you?"

"No, ma'am. I don't know where he crashes these days. The car lives with me — he's too messed up to drive it."

"How long has the Porsche been living with you?"

"Five years. It needs a lot of work, but since I don't drive it, I'm not putting any money into it."

"Does your brother drive it at all?"

"Not since he parked it in my garage. I suppose I'll get around to selling it when he . . . goes."

I knew what he meant by "goes." I myself

had had a brother who died of drug addiction.

Arthur Harris, the next Porsche owner, was an entrepreneur of sorts. His office was a cubicle in a shared workspace in an old building on Fourth Street south of Market. The lettering on the door said Entertainers Collective.

The cubicle was tiny: a single desk and two chairs, one of which was piled with files, and a bookcase full of reference works that were mostly collapsed on one another. Harris himself was fifty at the outside and energetic, judging from the way he sprang from his chair when I entered. His blond handlebar mustache twitched as he examined my card, and he then studied me with keen blue eyes.

"I don't believe this," he exclaimed. "A private eye masquerading as an entertainer. What is it you do — act, sing, play the xylophone?"

"None of the three." I took the chair he indicated. "Actually, this is an inquiry about a disappearance. Are you familiar with the name Judith Voss?"

Pause. "Can't say as I am. Does she act, sing —"

"No, and she doesn't play the xylophone. I understand you own a red Porsche 912, license number —"

"So what if I do?"

"And you've owned it since . . . ?"

"Oh, maybe seven years. What the hell does that matter?"

"Judith Voss had a friend who owned one. She was seen with him shortly before she disappeared last month."

"Well, that friend wasn't me."

"I see. I'm curious — what exactly is it you do, Mr. Harris?"

He began fiddling with objects on his desk — a stapler, letter opener, calculator. "I'm an agent — I put my clients together — actor with director, scriptwriter with producer, that sort of thing."

"And you take a fee from them?"

"Of course."

"Sounds like interesting work. How long have you been doing this?"

"Forever, it seems. At least fifteen years."

"Would I know any of your clients?"

He hesitated. "Well, there's Sandra Adams and Kiki Charles and Lissa Sloane."

I'd never heard of them.

"And Sam Sills."

Sam was an artist; I knew him slightly, in the way you become familiar with someone you bump into around clubs and galleries and gatherings associated with the art world. I hadn't seen him in quite some time.

I mentioned as much, and judging by the look on Harris's face, he hadn't, either.

Getting back to the subject, I asked, "Are you sure you have no recollection of Judith Voss?"

"No, sorry but I don't." His gaze avoided mine. I was sure he was lying.

The last red Porsche owner was Evan Draper, what the newspapers used to call a metrosexual: trendy, stylish, and thoroughly caught up in his own appearance. When he answered the door of his high-rise condo in the SoMa area, he automatically pushed back an errant curl of his dark hair and straightened the jacket of an expensive pin-striped suit. "Yes?" he said.

I gave him my card and explained my reason for being there.

He motioned me into a stylized modern living room — sling-back chairs and glass tables with spindly metal legs, carefully placed globes that caught the light from recessed fixtures and spread varicolored beams in all directions. Large uncurtained windows afforded a view from the Ferry Building and Alcatraz to the Oakland shipping terminals.

Draper was a gracious host: he offered tea or coffee and, when I refused, settled me into one of the chairs, which proved to be surprisingly comfortable.

"A missing person case, you said?" he asked, perching on the edge of a sofa.

"Yes. Are you familiar with the name Judith Voss?"

"The woman who disappeared recently?"

"That's the one. How do you know her?"

"I've been following the case in the papers. Disappearances fascinate me — Judge Crater, Hoffa, you know. But why have you come to me, a stay-at-home accountant?"

I explained about the red Porsche.

"Amazing how you can trace people. Detective work is so compelling. I watch all the TV shows."

Just what I needed, a detective junkie.

"I've been thinking," Draper added. "This Judith Voss — did she have money?"

"Only what she earned at a part-time job."

"Too bad. But she could've saved up and left the country."

"Passport control says she didn't."

"But she could've gone to Mexico or Canada. I read someplace about how there're places along the Canadian border where you can just hike up a trail, open a gate, and be in Canada scot-free. Or there's always the old trick of stowing away in a moving van or a UPS truck. They say FedEx apprehends dozens of free riders a month."

His eyes were bright and his face was turning red; Draper was really getting into his game.

I said, "Those are two interesting takes on the situation. I'll have to think about them."

"What about her parents? What does her father do?"

"He teaches school."

"Too bad. I was thinking he might be connected, you know. She could've been taken hostage by the mob —"

"I doubt it."

"Well, kidnapped by somebody."

"There's been no ransom note."

"But there could be a conspiracy. A friend of mine, he's very into conspiracies. He has a fine collection on the subject, and I've read a lot of it."

God save me from conspiracy theories! Next we'd be talking alien abduction.

"Mr. Draper," I said, standing up, "our conversation has been very enlightening. I'll get back to you if —"

"Do you want I should send you some of the literature?"

"Sure, why not?" I headed for the door. It would make interesting reading by the fireplace.

So there I was: three red Porsches, their

owners claiming no connection to Judith Voss. During the next few days I ran more checks on possible owners but came up with nothing useful. Second interviews with Judith's friends and neighbors proved equally fruitless. Finally I had to admit I was wasting the Voss family's money and my time.

File closed.

Late afternoon, April 13, five years later. My eyes were burning from reading off the computer screen, so I hunted up the paper file and took it to my comfy leather armchair next to the window. The chair, which had been with me since my days at All Souls Legal Cooperative, had been shabby and butt-sprung for most of those years. But then, in honor of M&R's splendid new offices, Ted Smalley, our office manager, had smuggled it out to an upholstery shop. When it returned, it was outfitted in soft brown leather and had acquired a matching footstool; now both resided in front of the broad window of my corner office beneath a ficus tree, also a gift from Ted and, appropriately, called Mr. T.

Okay, I told myself, *go over the file one more time. If you don't find anything, there's always next April 13.*

The impressions of Judith I'd gathered

from friends, teachers, and other adults varied widely: studious, sneaky, poised, highly sexed, spiritual, a lot of fun. Who was she, really? After a moment I turned back to my lengthy interview with her former best friend, Barbie Jennings. The word she'd used to describe Judith was *needing*. Needing in terms of "aching for stuff." Stuff she was unlikely to acquire on a physical therapist's salary.

Then the red Porsche came into the picture. A man had frequently met Judith, a man who could afford a classic car. Much as my friend at the DMV had searched — and much as the lunch I bought her every year as payment for her services would cost — only the three individuals I'd spoken with had matched the time frame.

Eldon McFeeney. Could the brother or someone else have taken it out of McFeeney's garage without him noticing? I'd doubted it five years ago and I still doubted it; McFeeney might be disabled, but he was mentally sharp. It was something to check on, though, and I called McFeeney's number. The woman who answered told me she was his niece and that her uncle had died the previous year. The Porsche was still in the garage.

"Nobody ever showed up looking for it,"

she said, "and since it wasn't taking up any space I needed — I don't have a car myself — I just left it there. I keep thinking I ought to have it fixed up and sell it. How much do you think I could get for it?"

I referred her to her local Porsche dealer.

Evan Draper. A "mere stay-at-home accountant" and detective buff, to say nothing of conspiracy theorist. He knew of Judith's disappearance, had advanced his ideas on what happened to her. A very enthusiastic man, Mr. Draper. But what if his enthusiasm was manufactured to mask other, darker motives? Might as well see how Evan was doing this year. I left a message on his voice mail.

Arthur Harris. The agent who had named clients I'd never heard of. I'd checked on Harris on past April 13s. Harris was no longer listed in any of the Bay Area directories. How long had he been out of the agenting business? None of the clients he'd mentioned except for artist Sam Sills were listed, either. In the entertainment section of last Sunday's *Chronicle* I'd noticed Sills was having a showing at a gallery in Dogpatch this week. Had Harris set that up for him? Well, why not go to his showing tonight and ask him? I had nothing better to do.

■ ■ ■ ■

The NewSpace Gallery occupied part of an old warehouse in the eclectic Dogpatch neighborhood. A trendy part of the city between Potrero Hill and the Bay, the former shipbuilding center had been transformed by live-work lofts, cafés, specialty shops, brew pubs, and wine bars. Although it was early — only five — Third Street, its main artery, was crowded with strollers and shoppers. I stopped to admire a Peruvian cape in a window, imagined its outrageous price tag, and pressed forward.

The gallery was doing a brisk business. Sills's space was a large one at the front and there were tags affixed to some of the paintings indicating a sale had been made. I couldn't say I liked them much: he must have been in his gray period, because most of them were muddied, with occasional splotches of bright primary colors peeking through. They struck me as real downers.

"That painting," a voice said over my shoulder, "does it speak to you?"

I turned. Sam Sills hadn't changed at all. Short, brown-haired, with a fluffy beard and a thick mustache that someone had once opined made him look as if he was "trying to eat a cat."

"Sharon McCone! I haven't seen you since . . . when?" he exclaimed. "Forget my words — I wouldn't attempt to sell you any of this tripe."

"Tripe?"

He took my arm and drew me aside. "That's just what it is — folks like it, buy it, keep me in food and drink. Fuck 'em if they can't take a joke."

"In the interviews I read you used to seem so serious about your work."

"I used to be serious about a lot of things. But I was only publicly serious. When I stopped with the self-praise I took a good look at my work and realized I'd better get a real job or go broke. Real jobs and going broke have never appealed to me, so I altered my technique and aimed for a less sophisticated audience. That's why I don't praise my work anymore. But you, I hear about you and your agency all the time. What brings you here tonight? Just slumming?"

"I wanted to talk to you about your agent, Arthur Harris —"

"Former agent. He took me on when I was a starving artist and kept me poor by stealing from me. I left him as soon as I could attract better representation. Is the old bugger still in the business?"

"Apparently not. He's no longer listed anywhere."

"How come you're interested in him?"

I explained about Judith Voss.

Sills smiled knowingly. "You should've come to me five years ago, darlin'. I can't tell you where your missing woman is now, but I can make a pretty good guess why she went missing. Along with his agenting career, Artie Harris was a pimp."

For a moment I was taken aback. "A pimp!"

"Right. And not your small-timer. He set his ladies up in fancy places, trained them in the high-class call girl business. He had half a dozen or more in his stable at one time."

"What happened? His agent's office was pretty downscale when I saw him five years ago."

"That was his cover. He figured the law wouldn't suspect anybody that unsuccessful could have been doing so well in an illicit trade."

A blonde woman in a black dress with an official-looking name tag came up behind Sam. "Mr. Sills, I have a customer who's serious about purchasing *Summer Dawn*."

"All right!" To me he said, "Good luck

with your search, Sharon. If you need anything else, call me." He hurried away with the blonde woman.

Okay, I thought, *now maybe I have the lead I need to finally solve the April 13 cold case.* The probable scenario: Judith Voss, a woman who reputedly "loved to fuck" and "wanted stuff," had somehow encountered Artie Harris, a high-class pimp and the owner of the red Porsche she'd been seen in, and he'd set her up in luxurious digs. When Harris was forced to quit pimping, if Judith was smart — and I knew she was — she would have continued with her clientele and kept the fees for her services for herself.

The question was, where was Judith now plying her trade?

Somewhere here in the city that she'd vowed she would never leave? It was entirely possible. She'd surely changed her appearance — dyed and restyled hair, expensive cosmetics, expensive clothes — and would be living a lifestyle far removed from her former one. San Francisco is a big city; she could have been lucky enough not to have crossed paths with any of her former acquaintances.

As soon as I left the gallery, I called Barbie Jennings, who expressed surprise at hearing from me. "Is this about Judith after all this time?"

"Yes. I have a few questions for you."

"Okay, shoot."

"You mentioned a house on Russian Hill that Judith fell in love with on one of your excursions. Where was it?"

"I remember the house, but . . . Wait a minute. I kept a diary back then. I'll hunt it up."

It took her a few minutes to get back to me. "Here it is," she said somewhat breathlessly. "End of March. Yes. Sunday. The house was on Taylor Street. It was unique, set way back from the street. You had to approach it down a little alley."

There couldn't be that many such houses in a district where millionaires had been putting up mansions since the Gold Rush days. "Do you recall what the cross streets were?"

"Umm . . . I'm pretty sure it was between Filbert and Union. Why is this important —"

"I'll get back to you."

The house was an original, for San Francisco. Tucked halfway down an alley between two looming redbrick apartment houses, and overgrown by tough old wisteria vines that looked as if they were reaching for the sun. Probably a converted outbuilding for one of the mansions that had once crowned the hill. There were lights on inside.

The woman who answered my knock at the front door could not possibly have been Judith Voss. Too old, too tall, with long red hair tied in a ponytail and trailing down her back to her waist. She wasn't unattractive, but she didn't strike me as the call girl type.

"Yes?" she said pleasantly.

I showed her my ID. "Do you have a roommate, by any chance, Ms . . . ?"

"Kelly. No, I don't."

"May I ask how long you've lived here?"

"Six months. Why do you want to know?"

"I'm looking for a young woman who may have been a former occupant —"

"You must mean Jennifer Vail. She lived here for about five years before I took over the lease."

J.V. — same initials.

"And she moved out six months ago?"

"Closer to eight. But she didn't exactly move out."

"Oh?"

"She disappeared just before the lease came up for renewal. Here one day, gone the next."

"Do you have any idea where she went?"

"No. Nobody does, apparently. Not even the police."

"The police?"

"Somebody called them and reported her missing. One of her johns, I suppose."

"Then you're aware of her profession. Did you know Jennifer?"

"No, I never met her. Her profession became apparent almost as soon as I moved in. Men kept coming by, asking for her. I finally contacted the police, and the detective I talked to confirmed that she was a call girl. He didn't seem particularly interested that she'd disappeared."

I didn't suppose he had been. People are prone to disappear in a big city, and unless they're prominent in one way or another, or there's evidence of foul play, it's just business as usual.

"Did she take all her possessions with her when she went away?" I asked.

"No, and it's kind of odd that she didn't. She had a lot of jewelry and clothing that she left behind."

"Do you know what happened to it?"

"It's all still here. The real estate agent had it boxed up and put it in the storage closet. It'll all be sold if she doesn't claim it after a year."

"There was nothing that might indicate where she'd gone or why?"

"Not according to the agent or the police," Ms. Kelly said. "But you're welcome to look through the boxes, if you'd like."

"I would."

There were three big boxes full of carefully folded underwear, lounging outfits, formal dresses, and informal wear. A velvet pouch held earrings, rings, bracelets, and necklaces. I wasn't any expert on jewelry, but it all looked expensive to me.

I thanked Ms. Kelly and walked down the alley, but stopped midway, staring at the little vine-covered cottage. My search for Judith Voss had ended here tonight. And so had my April 13 obsession. I had found her at last, only to have her elude me again, and there was nothing more I could or wanted to do to find her a second time. Nor would I share what I'd discovered with her parents. They must have come to terms with their loss by this time; I was not about to bring more hurt to them by revealing what their daughter had chosen to do with her life.

Maybe her disappearance had been a willful one, and if so, she'd found what she was looking for someplace else. But a call girl's existence is precarious at best. And it seemed out of character that a successful one with expensive tastes would abandon her material possessions on a sudden whim.

It just might be that Judith had found her Mr. Goodbar.

■ ■ ■ ■

WHODAT HEIST

BY JULIE SMITH

■ ■ ■ ■

November 2018

"I've been thinkin'. This is the year." Forest nodded for emphasis, although Roy wasn't even looking at him. "This is definitely the year."

"*Thought* you were thinkin', ol' buddy. The whole place is shakin'."

"Well, actually, that could be the music." Forest and Roy, his crime partner, were holding down a couple of bar stools at the Cat's Meow on Bourbon Street, where some idiot was trying to channel John Fogerty. The crowd was singing along to "Proud Mary."

"This is definitely the year the Saints win the Super Bowl."

Roy belted out the verse about the wheel turning.

"Goddammit, this is important."

"I'm listening." And to signal that he was, Roy followed up with "Whodat?," the shorthand version of the Saints chant, "Who dat say dey gonna beat dem Saints?" Then he went right back to guzzling his beer and devoting himself enthusiastically to the chorus.

It might have been annoying, but Forest didn't let Roy bother him. They'd had been best friends since they were six — grew up together in Pascagoula, Mississippi. But everybody in three states knew Roy didn't have the sense God gave him. "See, it'll be the second time, after that epic win in 2010. So you know what we're gonna do? We're gonna trademark 'Two Dat.' And sell T-shirts and hats and stuff."

"Or maybe we could just sell the name to a company that makes ball caps."

"Yeah. For a million dollars, maybe."

They could have cleaned up, except it turned out that someone else had already done it. Shame, too, 'cause it was looking more and more like the Saints were going to the Super Bowl.

"Know what I've always said?" Forest mused. This time they were at Molly's, sitting right in the open window.

"Sure. Perfect time for crime is during a Saints game. 'Cause ain' nobody on the street, so there's not gon' be no witnesses. And no cop in New Orleans is gon' tear himself away from the tube long enough to work a lick."

"You ain't so dumb," Forest said approvingly, even though he knew different.

What Roy was was handsome. He looked just like the Kennedy kid who crashed his plane, one of his primary attributes as a crime partner. Only one woman on earth — who might or might not be named Heidi, and might or might not be Dutch — didn't fall for that perfect mug, but that was probably only because Roy hated her. Forest was about half in love with her. "Heeeey, baby," Roy said, as some skinny redhead in a fur coat and shorts the size of Barbie clothes sat on the bar stool next to him.

He was going to be busy for a while, but Forest didn't care — he was used to it. He scrolled over to nola.com to get some scores, but something else caught his eye. He was always on the lookout for stuff he could steal, and here, right before his eyes, was a dream score — a freakin' pot of gold, just waiting for him barely ten blocks away. This was the headline: "For the Birds: First-edition Audubon prints coveted by collectors — and thieves."

"Thieves 'R Us," Forest mumbled, and scrolled ahead hungrily. Two items had particularly caught his attention. One was the name of a museum in the French Quarter; and the other was this figure: 11.65 million dollars. That was for a four-volume set of prints — not even originals, just prints! — called *Birds of America.*

There were a bunch of these books, two hundred originally, but the right one, the Havell Edition, was worth a fortune. That was the one with the "double elephant folio." He had no idea what that was, but it sure sounded cool. The main thing was, the museum had it.

He got sort of puffed up, absorbing the double elephant part, and wondered what Roy would make of that. He shook his head. Roy was not going to get the hang of it at all, but he knew who would. The only problem was, Roy wouldn't work with her.

This was a heist made in heaven. There was even a movie about someone who'd tried something like it once — *American Animals.* A gang of frat boy amateurs had ended up first getting the wrong edition, then trying to sell it at Christie's. Just walked in with stolen merch and offered it up for sale. Dumbasses. Everyone knew you had to get the insurance company to ransom it. You'd never get your ten or twelve million, maybe just one or two, but Forest could live with that. And he was pretty sure the Dutch Treat could figure out how to do it. Roy would kill him, but Forest needed her. Okay, he'd worry about her later.

First he had to get Roy on board. When the redhead was gone, he said, "See, the thing is, the Super Bowl's different from a regular game. When the Saints win, I mean."

Roy said, "Well, yeah. Somebody beat you with a genius stick?"

"No, I mean it's different for crime purposes. Remember how it was last time? Everybody in the whole freakin' city out in the street? I mean, *everybody.*"

"Oh yeah. All these chicks were kissing everybody, and high-fivin' and everything."

"Well, they were kissing you. But, yeah, everybody was high-fivin' and hugging. *Everybody.*"

"Some reason you keep saying *everybody*? Like it means something special?"

"It does. Think about this part — do you remember how traffic came to a standstill? You literally couldn't drive anywhere."

Roy pulled at his tongue, like he was trying to remove a stray piece of tobacco. "Yeah. Yeah, I do. I was stayin' with some girl at the Royal Sonesta and we had to walk all the way back from whatever party we were at, somewhere Uptown. In the Bentley-Benz district. Waaaay Uptown. Took about an hour, but *what* an hour." His face got all dreamy. "All that kissin' and high-fivin'. Wouldn't trade that for nothin'."

"So the point . . ." Forest said.

"Oh, wait! I see what you're getting at. *After* the game is even better for a crime than during. 'Cause even the cops can't go anywhere. Yeah, I see it now." His whole torso was in motion. "It's a beautiful thing. A real beautiful thing." Then his face fell. "But only if the Saints win. If they lose it's off. Whatever *it* is."

"No, see, I've got that figured, too. What we do, see, is we bet on the other team. Then if the Saints win, we make a big score. And I mean a *humongous* score. If they lose we still win something. Like a consolation prize."

"Excuse me. Did you just say bet *against* the Saints? No! Not going to do it. That is flat against my religion."

"Roy, you don't have no religion."

Roy laughed, and tapped his cigarette, looking down ruefully. "Okay, you got me. So what's the hustle? I'm pretty much up for anything so long as The Treat's not involved."

"Awww, Roy. I don't even know how to get ahold of her. Anyhow, would I do that to you?"

400

"Yeah, you would, ol' buddy."

He was right, and Forest knew it. They ought to have a Twelve Step Program for that woman. Neither of them had any business even being in the same state with her.

Funny thing was, Roy had been the one to find her, not Forest. She was so far out of Forest's league he wouldn't even have tried to talk to her. He was your average sweaty redneck with dirty-blond hair and love handles, whereas Heidi was not just attractive, but a lady. Pretty, sure, in that classic blonde round-faced way that was almost innocent, the kind of face people call "all-American." But there was something special about her.

And she *wasn't* American. She said.

The first time they'd met her, she'd said she was Dutch, and they didn't have any reason to think different now, because they still didn't know a goddamn thing about her. And she had that tiny trace of an accent that Forest found so appealing. Sometimes. Other times she kind of sounded like she came from the Gulf Coast, like they did.

She was Heidi Van Eyck that first time, and Heidi Handshaw, or possibly Mrs. Ben Inglesby the second, but another time she'd been Renee something, and once even Rosa Klebb, but Forest knew she was just joking around with that one.

Three times — three completely different, entirely unrelated times she'd made fools of them. Totally fucked them over, left them more broke than a windshield in a wreck, and lucky not to be arrested or shot. Roy would probably kill her if he got the chance and would definitely kill Forest if he ever proposed working with her again.

But Forest? He'd kill to hear her laugh again. She had the goddamndest laugh he ever heard, like water from the deepest cave on the continent rippling its silvery way over sunbaked rocks, all the way to the ocean. Or the Nile or the Congo, or maybe Alf the sacred river in the drug poem he had to learn in high school. God, what a laugh she had!

Also she was far and away the most adept criminal he'd ever seen, on or off the screen, and you had to respect a fine talent. Forest flat-out worshipped her. Even though he understood perfectly that she was what would happen if sarin gas and ricin had a baby.

How they'd met was, Roy'd somehow struck up an acquaintance with her in a seaside town they were planning to knock over — a town called Seaside, matter of fact — and brought her over to the beach to

402

meet his good buddy Forest. To this day Forest didn't have a clue why, except that Roy had so many women he usually didn't even want the next one. Maybe also because Forest had just finished a two-year stretch in an Alabama prison, and she was Roy's idea of a coming-out present.

If he'd been that presumptuous, the gods of feminism had gotten their revenge. Although they were probably goddesses. It wasn't but half an hour before she'd gotten them involved in some caper so ingenious no way it could screw up. And it hadn't. It worked perfect. Just the way she planned it. Which meant Forest and Roy got screwed.

The next time, they asked *her*. They thought of it as kind of the rematch where they got their revenge, and they were right about the first part. They could have walked away with two million dollars. The Queen of Crime did instead. That was how Forest thought of her.

The third time was . . . Well, who the hell knew? Seemed like they'd just kind of accidentally run into her when she was about to get killed by her current crime partner (who she fucked over just as bad as them), but maybe it wasn't an accident. Maybe she had some kind of magic power, and had summoned him there. Not "them," meaning Forest and Roy. Just Forest. Because maybe they were meant to be, somehow or other.

Heidi and Forest, sittin' in a tree, k-i-s-s-i-n-g. *Sure, dream on,* Forest told himself. Meant to be, like a wolf and a rabbit. He didn't even know her freaking name.

He told Roy what the hustle was. "We boost this ten-, maybe twelve-million-dollar item from a museum and walk away in the crowd. That simple."

"Ten million dollars, huh?"

"Maybe twelve."

"Forest, Forest, Forest, you're such a dreamer." Somehow, that wasn't the reaction Forest had expected. Roy was usually up for anything. "That cannot happen this year," Roy continued.

"What the hell you talkin' about?"

"Hail," was how he said it. "It *cannot*? It wouldn't be any miracle, bro'. They're *this* far from the play-offs. All they gotta do is get in the play-offs, which is practically a done deal, and then win the play-offs."

"And the game. They've gotta win the game. I don't know. I don't have a good feeling about it."

"Why not?"

"Because next year would be the perfect Two Dat— the tenth anniversary of their first win ever." He got a dreamy look. "Now that's symmetry."

Forest didn't know Roy even knew that word. "Well, I get that. I can see that. Okay, you're right. That can't happen this year, 'cause it's only the ninth anniversary. But nine's better than ten, you know? Because they can still go ahead and win next year, too, and then you get your symmetry. Just a year late."

"I don't know. I gotta have somethin' to believe in."

"Well, believe in this — think of it as a dry run. Sometime it's gotta happen, am I right? *Sometime.* You agree?"

"Well, sure, it's gotta happen sometime."

"And that book's always gonna be there. So if it doesn't happen this year, then you know what? We're ready for next year. We've already had a dry run and we've ironed out all the glitches. And then next year we go the whole nine yards!"

"That's it! Dude, that's it."

"That's what?"

"That's the symmetry. This year we go the whole nine yards. 'Cause it's the *ninth* anniversary. Yep, that's it! Okay, it's meant to be. You were right all along."

Forest shook his head. Sometimes he had trouble following Roy, who seemed to have dropped a stitch there, but who cared? "Works for me," he said.

"What's the next step?"

"Let's go case the place."

"Now? It's almost midnight."

"Not now, dumbass. In the morning."

This was Forest's favorite part — the planning was almost better than the money, which was a good thing, because so often that didn't pan out. But making a perfect plan was a payoff in itself. It took an artist to figure out these things, and Forest was practically a Picasso. The Picasso of planning, he called himself. And he had all the time in the world to get this one right. Maybe he could even get a job at the museum. Hey, that was a thought. Heidi'd once gotten a job as a security guard to pull off a heist. How clever was that? It was the perfect fox-in-henhouse dodge.

Oh, wait. Probably no one would hire a guard with a rap sheet as long as an alligator. So maybe not that. Maintenance was a thought, though. Everybody needed janitors. And delivery guys! Maybe he could get a job with a business that serviced the museum. Like FedEx, only local. A deli, maybe. Maybe the real guards ordered out. Yeah, something like that. He was getting excited. He could do that. For once he had time.

Figuring it might be a quiet part of the day, he and Roy ambled over just before lunch. No guard at the front door, and none just inside. Just an ordinary counter with a cheery lady behind it. "Goooood morning," she said. "Would y'all like to see the museum?"

"We sure would, ma'am."

"That'll be twenty dollars for two."

Well! Forest hadn't counted on that part, but sure, why not?

"You can go right through that door."

So far so good. Not a single guard. They walked into a large room where a group was taking a tour, and someone was asking a question. Something about it must have been funny because everyone laughed, including the tour guide. It was a group titter, nothing much, but when the tour guide laughed, it was the silvery sound of the purest water in the world crackling its way over stones worn smooth over centuries on its way to . . .

Wait a minute!

Forest froze. Roy said, "What the fuck?"

Forest didn't think Roy'd ever even noticed Heidi's laugh. "Be cool now," Forest whispered. "We gotta just keep a low profile and everything'll be cool."

Roy's answering whisper was like a desperate cry. "What the fuck is *she* doing here?"

"Shut up and watch her, okay? Whatever you do, don't let her out of your sight."

They stalked her at a distance, taking note of the way she'd once again reinvented herself. Her hair was dark, with heavy straight bangs, and it was long, so her face looked longer. She wore huge black-rimmed glasses, very fancy, Forest imagined, and meant, he supposed, to make her look like a student of Louisiana history, to which the museum was devoted. Her clothes were different, too. He'd only seen her in bathing suits and sarongs. And shorts and summer dresses.

Today, she had on a long black skirt — what chicks called a "maxi" — and a matching turtleneck thing with a big ol' pendant necklace. He noticed with trepidation that the pendant was a gold fleur-de-lis. The Saints' logo. Half the town was wearing Saints gear these days — Roy himself had on a gray hoodie bearing the word *Saints* and a smaller version of that same fleur-de-lis. But Forest didn't like the idea that the looming play-offs were so clearly on her mind.

She saw the two of them, he was pretty

sure, but she never lost her train of thought, never faltered in her seemingly off-the-cuff lecture, which, to his mind, was very polished and learned, although slightly accented. One thing about the Queen of Crime, she never did anything halfway.

When she had said goodbye to her history class, Forest called quietly to her, "Howdy, Miss Heidi," making the "howdy" part sound almost like her name. She shot him a caustic glare, clearly designed to shut him up, and turned away. So he got a little louder: "Now, is that any way to treat your ex-husband?" This wasn't entirely off-the-wall — it was one of the parts she'd once duped him into playing.

When she turned back to him, she was smiling, ready to play. "I beg your pardon. I think you may have confused me with someone. My name's Sasha. Sasha Orloff."

"You sure do like those foreign names, don't you?"

She ignored that. "And you are?"

"Forest McElroy, at your service. As usual."

"We're the plumbers," Roy said, "You left a note for us . . . ?"

She shook hands with them, so that anyone watching would think they'd just met. "Ah, yes, we spoke on the phone. Shall we go outside to talk?" He could see she was getting rattled, looking all around to make sure no one overheard them. "Wait for me. I'll be out in a minute."

Now it was Forest's turn to laugh, and Roy joined in, creating a raucous redneck chorus, just what you wouldn't want in a place like this. "Not a chance."

They stopped by the desk, where she told the resident sweet apple-cheeked lady that she was taking lunch now.

"Good," Forest said. "You're buying. I think you owe us."

They were barely on the sidewalk before she spluttered, "What the hell are you two cretins doing here?"

"I *could* say we're trying to collect a debt — wait! Make that three debts. Pretty sure you owe us at least a couple million by now — but let's let bygones be bygones. We didn't exactly expect to see you today. And we're seriously hoping never to see you again. This is *our* play, got it?" He hated saying the part about never seeing her again, but he had to shut her down. Right this minute! Even though he felt her pulling him in all over again. She always did that. She'd be the perfect crime partner, a whole lot better than Roy, if she'd just quit fucking him over.

She said, "I have no idea what you're talking about."

"Hey, baby, this is Forest and Roy. That fancy museum guide thing ain' gonna fly with us. We know you."

"Docent," she said.

"What?"

"Not guide. Docent. It's a volunteer job."

Oh yeah, of course she'd done that. Just what he'd been about to do himself — gotten a job that would let her case the museum without causing suspicion. "A volunteer job," he said, "that you got when you realized the Saints were going to be in the play-offs."

"What does that have to do with anything?" She stared at him through the elephantine spectacles.

But her face changed as she thought it through, the Super Bowl possibility clearly presenting itself for the first time. Forest realized he'd blown it. Ray elbowed him. "You dumbass!"

Forest sighed, defeated. "Buy us a sandwich and let's talk."

They took the sandwiches to the river for an impromptu picnic in Woldenberg Park, where no one could overhear, or if they did, they'd either be tourists or too drunk to remember, or both.

Forest slammed her with it: "What's your game, babycakes? You look real nice in black, by the way."

"You're not so bad yourself."

Just like her. Deflect, flatter, reduce him to a puddle . . .

Finally she said, "I'm just interested in history."

"So are we gonna have to talk to the museum about *your* history — Hey, come to think about it, one gig even involved a museum. That little thing over in Biloxi?"

"You know about that?"

"We were your patsies, I seem to remember. Us and that guy with the weird hair."

"Sol. Poor guy, someone snitched on him."

"Heidi. Or whoever you are . . ."

"Listen, let's team up. I've already cased this job, and I was just about to call you anyhow." Woo-hoo! Just like he hoped. No need to have The Heidi Talk with Roy.

"Sure you were," Forest said, but Roy pretty much drowned him out with a heartfelt, "No way, Jose!"

"Guys, it's a three-person job. Too many cameras in there. But if we could create a distraction . . ."

"Uh-uh," Roy said. "Negative. Red light. Over my dead body."

412

Forest spoke softly. "Let's just hear what the lady has to say. We've already got a pretty decent plan and she's got . . ."

"An inside track," Heidi said, looking smug. Like she knew she'd won. "You want to know the name of the museum's security company?" And then she laughed, that silvery, melodious, seductive laugh filling up every inch of Woldenberg Park.

The next day she quit her docent job, saying that, as a professor at Nicholls State, she needed to devote more time to the book she was writing.

Now she could come and go as she wished, to all appearances "doing research" without being tied to any schedule, and she could put to use her good relationships with the guard and other employees. (According to her, there was a daytime guard, though none at night, but he tended to roam all over the museum.)

That same day Roy scouted bars near the offices of Castletower, Inc., which provided security for the museum. He was going to be hanging out there a lot the next few weeks, making friends with any Castletower guys he could. Women, better yet.

Forest, meanwhile, went shopping. Although first he established a few new email addresses and opened accounts that would make his purchases difficult to trace. Not that anyone would ever get that far.

Among items he needed: one convincing-looking NOPD uniform, with all the accoutrements — gun, radio, and badge; a foldable art portfolio, about forty by thirty inches; more Saints gear; black and gold glitter; and a truckload of good luck charms. (After all, the team still had to get through the play-offs.)

The Play-offs, January 27
None of the charms worked. As history has shown, although the Saints easily dive-bombed the Eagles, they were robbed, raped, pillaged, injured, insulted, royally screwed, and scarred for life in the Rams game. The now-famous pass-interference no-call that cost them the game elicited howls heard round the world, some of the loudest from Roy: "Fuuuuuuuuck! Fuuuuuuuck! Fuckety-fuck-fuck! That wasn't just pass interference, it was helmet-to-helmet contact. Double goddamn insult!"

On and on like that, for about five minutes.

Forest was almost as loud. The heist of the century, blown — just like that.

Of course Roy had to rub it in: "I told you it was a long shot."

But Forest just couldn't give it up. They had such beautiful plans.

He was seriously regretting the fortune they'd blown on Super Bowl tickets for key employees at the security company. Damn! Sure would like to have that back.

He had no idea in hell where Heidi lived, but at least he had her phone number.

"You okay?" he said, and was rewarded with silvery chimes. That made it almost worth the loss.

"Forest, Forest, Forest! Thinking of little me at a time like this. Really, I'd marry you if I had time. And inclination."

"Okay, sure."

"Okay what?"

"Let's get married."

Once again, water crackled merrily over warm rocks. Forest was flat-out enjoying this conversation, but, delightful as it was, he took the laugh as a no. "What do we do now?" he said.

"Do now? It's over, babe. We fold our tents like the Arabs."

He loved the way she talked. How in hell did she come up with that one? Arabs! "It can't be over."

"I gotta think." She hung up, leaving him to brood about their beautiful blown plans.

They'd known they couldn't disable the

alarm, due to backup systems, so the next best thing was to disable the company that had to deal with it. Roy, by now, had fulfilled his job admirably: befriended the two people, Alice and Tony, who, to their utter consternation, were going to be working at Castletower Security on Super Bowl Sunday.

They were the ones who'd been surreptitiously gifted with Super Bowl tickets that arrived in mysterious ways.

The gang was betting that nobody, but *nobody* was going to want to work that night, no matter how much overtime it paid. And that whoever ended up stuck with night duty was going to be fuming, inattentive, and watching on their phone or laptop anyhow. Maybe drinking. And with any luck, not having any idea in hell how to handle a real alarm. Maybe that would get them five minutes, which was all they needed.

The museum's Sunday hours were 10 a.m. to 3 p.m., and the plan was for Heidi to enter around noon and stay until the game was over, when she'd walk out with the first volume of *Birds of America* tucked away in her foldable portfolio. (She could only handle one of the huge books — they'd worked that out — but even one was at least a million-dollar score, probably more like three.)

Her part was by far the trickiest, and was hugely shored up by the inside track she'd cultivated. If she pulled it off, she'd have really earned her cut, Roy and Forest decided. They even made a pact not to rip her off once they had the book. Although they knew they couldn't trust *her* for a millisecond. Still, they felt it was only honorable.

It was a masterpiece, the way they'd set it up! Maybe they should do it, anyhow — maybe drunk fans would riot, and that could be the distraction.

But in his heart, Forest knew New Orleans wasn't that kind of city. It was the kind of city that held hurricane parties with a Category 5 on the way.

Three days before Super Bowl Sunday, Roy and Forest were drinking at Shaggy's in Pass Christian when Heidi called. "Hey, looks like the Boycott Bowl is going to be big."

"The what?"

"It's an impromptu music festival, right in the middle of town on Super Bowl Sunday. How's that for a distraction?"

"Game on!" Forest said.

Heidi walked into the museum as scheduled, promptly at noon, dressed as Professor Sasha Orloff and carrying a Saks shopping bag heavily lined in tissue paper. What happened after that Forest had to wait to find out. Soon after 2:00 p.m., she texted, Feet down. Finally.

That meant she'd checked the bag with the nice lady behind the desk, said hi to her buddy the wandering guard, read for a while in the Louisiana History room, and waited for the guard to go to the bathroom. When he did, she first signed herself out, then reentered the museum, and used her insider privilege to retrieve the bag herself, rather than asking for it. Then, instead of leaving, she went to the ladies' room, where she locked herself in a stall and took out of the bag her burglary outfit, a hammer, and the folded portfolio, which she unfolded and used to hold the hammer and the Saks bag. Then she changed, a chore that had to be done now to avoid setting off a motion detector. After that, she sat down and waited, feet up in case someone came in.

"Feet down" told Forest that all had gone according to plan and everyone was gone, including her buddy the guard. Instead of human beings, the museum relied solely on their alarm system at night. Which Roy and Forest had disabled — the human component anyway.

During her tenure as Sasha, Heidi had worked out where the cameras and motion detectors were, so she knew the only immediate problem she had was a motion detector in the ladies' room, which would set off an alarm too soon if it found her. But if she sat on the floor until time to pull the job, and commando crawled to the door, she could stay under it.

Meanwhile, Forest and Roy were holed up in the hotel room they'd rented a block from the museum. They were following the action, a lot of which they could see from their own window. It was way better than they'd imagined — the Blackout and Gold Second Line Parade was jamming Jackson Square, the Boycott Bowl was *raging,* and just about every bar in town — on the ninth anniversary of the one great Saints' Super Bowl victory — was running video of that game instead of the Stoopid Bowl. The streets were teeming.

Even for a cop, getting from one place to another was going to be tough. Forest loved that.

Everything had been rehearsed and rehearsed. All they had to do now was get dressed.

Forest put on the cop outfit, with all its attendant gear. Roy's goal was to look like every peckerwood out on the street. He wore a pair of tired-looking jeans, a #9 Saints jersey with quarterback Drew Brees's name on it, half his face painted black, the other half gold, with glitter applied on top, and the whole thing topped by a black ball cap, with this fleur-de-lis thing Heidi'd made attached to it. The fleur-de-lis stood up on his head like antlers. The idea, she explained, was that people would look at that instead of his face.

The Quarter was so jammed Forest had to move like someone chained to a cement block. Reaching the front of the museum, he started his crowd control act. But he wasn't controlling anything; he was just messing around — the whole idea was to have a large unruly crowd on hand.

Meanwhile, Roy texted Heidi: Now or never! That meant she was about to commando crawl, portfolio and all, to the large gallery where the book lay open in a glass display case.

In his mind's eye, Forest could see her doing that and everything else they'd practiced: she removed the hammer from the portfolio and broke the glass, no doubt setting off the alarm. But no matter, so long as the cops didn't get there before she was gone. Because all the cameras would catch was a somewhat overweight guard wearing a Drew Brees mask bought from the NFL's own website.

The guard outfit had been easy to find, complete with a cop hat that completely hid her hair. They'd bought the shirt in a men's medium, so she could bundle her loose-fitting Sasha Orloff dress under it, tied in place with an old black scarf to give her a believable paunch. A pair of gloves completed the ensemble.

Once she was outside, she'd look like any other off-duty guard going home, wearing a festive mask like half the other fools on the street. Forest knew if it was him, he'd definitely flip off a few cameras on the way out, but Heidi was a pro. She'd just keep her head down and get where she was going.

She texted that she was at the door.

Showtime!

Roy shouted, "Whodat!" like the kind of drunken birdbrain who'd fire a gun in a crowd, and he shot out the museum's camera.

Everybody shut up and got real still.

"Hey," Forest responded. "Give me that gun."

The crowd gasped and fell back, some people bolting, some staying to catch the drama. Forest held out his hand for the gun, and Roy pointed both hands in the air, kind of in surrender mode, but still holding the gun. At that exact moment, the museum door opened and — from the point of view of onlookers — a guard in a Drew Brees mask stepped out, assessed the situation, and stuck a gun (or maybe just a finger) in the shooter's back, yelling, "Drop it!"

Terrified, the guy dropped the gun, and the cop handcuffed him. Those close enough heard him thank the guard and say something like, "Mind coming in? We gotta fill out a report." Then the cop hauled the handcuffed guy away, with the guard trailing along. The most observant might even have noticed the guard was lugging an art portfolio.

At least, that's what *should* have happened. They'd planned it that way on the theory that if Heidi tried to make a run for it, they could take her down easy — there were two of them, one in very good shape (Roy, of course), and neither was carrying a heavy object.

But it all went south the minute Heidi

stuck her finger in Roy's back.

Instead of dropping the gun and letting Forest arrest him, Roy collapsed on the sidewalk. Instinctively, Forest ran to him, realizing the Satan spawn had probably shot him, very likely killed him. But no, Roy could speak. "Tased me," he said. "Damn, that hurts."

Forest didn't even wait to help him up, just jumped the hell up and started asking people where the guard went. Not a single person knew. All eyes had been on Forest and Roy enacting their drama.

She could have escaped in any of four directions, all of them affording plenty of crowds and cover, so Forest picked one, and started elbowing people aside. Roy did the same, but neither of them found a trace.

Later, changing direction, Forest did find a fireplug that someone had playfully decorated with a cop-type hat and a Drew Brees mask. Encouraged, he forged ahead, finally spying an incoherent gutterpunk wearing gloves and a too-big guard's shirt, but he was too stoned to say anything other than "Fuck the N-Fuckin'-L!"

Forest walked for hours, it seemed like, all elbows and anxiety, but finally had to concede that once again, the Dutch Treat had worked her evil magic. He half loved her for it — she was so damn good at her job!

He wasn't bad either, he thought. But somehow, in the excitement and the crush of people, he never even glanced at a Muslim woman with a black hijab covering her hair. Those who did noted with approval that she wore a modestly fitting dress and a fleur-de-lis pendant proudly proclaiming her loyalty to the Whodat Nation. Not a single soul even thought to wonder why she was hauling around a humongous art portfolio.

"Told you it wouldn't work," Roy fumed in the rehash, from his favorite bar stool at Checkpoint Charlie's. "It shoulda been the *tenth* anniversary."

"To next year," Forest said, hoisting his beer. "Did you know they got Napoleon's Death Mask in one of these museums? Gotta be worth *somethin'.*"

BLUE MOON

BY WILLIAM KENT KRUEGER

Once again, they met for the last time and, as always, it was under a blue moon.

They walked toward each other, he from the north, she from the south. The bridge was wooden, the planking sturdy under their feet. Far below, the river was a thread of silver in the moonlight. Mountains rose sharply on either side, blacker than the velvet of the night sky against which they pressed. Her gown was green satin with white lace at her throat. He wore riding breeches and high leather boots, polished and gleaming in the moonglow. When they met, he took her hands.

"I was afraid you wouldn't come," he said.

"You always say that, yet here I am, always."

"That doesn't mean I don't worry. You're so beautiful. The most beautiful woman in the entire county."

"And you the handsomest man."

He kissed her, his lips like firebrands against her own. She yielded for a long moment, then drew away.

"A blue moon," she said. "Are they always this bright and beautiful?"

Her face was upturned, and he saw how soft and pale her skin was, like sweet cream.

"I expect," he said. "But even more so, just for us. It's so quiet and peaceful here."

"And isolated. I wish it didn't have to be this way."

"A love like ours was never meant to be. Footloose gambler, wealthy married woman."

"I married him long before I met you." She gazed into his eyes and her own eyes shone. "But oh, I remember the first time we saw each other across the dance floor."

"You wore a dress the color of a summer sky and a red bow in your hair, a flame amid all those lovely tresses. You were radiant, as if the sun itself burned inside you."

"Even across that filled dance floor, I saw you eyeing me. It sent chills down my spine to be looked at so frankly."

"So lovingly."

"So lasciviously."

"I was on fire," he said. "I thought if I didn't kiss you that very night, I might as well be dead."

"It was that very night. And you did a good deal more than just kiss me." She took his hand and placed it on her breast.

"Dear God," he said. "I want you. Right here, right now."

"I don't know if this bridge will hold up under our passion."

"Then let's go somewhere more comfortable."

"What did you have in mind? I'm tired of barns and haylofts and sneaking into your rooming house. I want . . ."

"Yes?"

"You've asked me a dozen times to run away with you."

"And a dozen times you've said no."

"Ask me again."

There was something different in her eyes, a look of resolution he hadn't seen before.

"Why?" he said cautiously.

"Maybe I know something now that I didn't before."

His hand, which had been softly kneading her breast, paused. "And what would that be?"

The color of her face in the moonlight changed, became instantly like snow, soft still but cold. "Annabelle," she said.

"Annabelle?"

"Don't pretend. It's a small county. I hear things."

"A dalliance. She means nothing."

"Not to me."

Like hers, his voice now took on an edge of ice. "Every night, I know you're sharing another man's bed."

"That's different. It's not because of love. It's duty."

"How can you stay with him? He treats you like one of his prize mares. Like one of his acreages of tobacco. A possession."

"I am, in a way." Her face changed again, the cold melting. "But not all of me." His hand had not left her breast, and now she put both her own hands over his, pressing his palm desperately against her bosom. "Not my heart. What if . . . ?"

Through the satin of her dress, he could feel the rapid pulsing deep within her. "What if what?"

"What if I really did leave him and we ran away together?"

"Every time I ask, your answer is the same."

"What if I told you I've finally left him?"

"You've teased me this way before."

"I mean it this time."

"You would really come away with me?"

"Tonight. Right now."

"In that dress?"

"I'll shed the dress. You can buy me traveling clothes."

"With what? You know I have nothing. We'd live as paupers. Is that what you want?"

"Every time we meet you beg me to leave him," she said, the cold descending once more. "Now, when I finally say I'm willing, you show me all the backbone of a scarecrow." Moonlight glinted off her eyes in arrows of ice. "I can see exactly what's in your heart."

"Can you?" He dropped his voice to a soft croon, and once more took her hand. "Then what you must see there is a love so burning, I know it would consume us both. That's what I'm afraid of."

"A burning love? There's a fire in your heart, yes, but not for love." She lifted the hem of her dress and led his hand beneath. "As long as you have that and no responsibility, you're happy."

"It's more," he insisted. But his hand remained where she'd placed it.

She closed her eyes. The moonlight pressed against her lids, and she let his expert fingers ignite the familiar fire inside her.

"It's true this time. I have left him. I'm

431

yours now. Forever," she whispered. "We'll be together for all eternity."

He quickly drew back, and she opened her eyes and saw his look of terror.

"You're joking," he said.

"I've never been more serious."

"In God's name, what are you thinking?"

"That I can't live anymore with a man who equates me with his horses and his tobacco fields."

"He's the most powerful man in the county. Do you really think he'll let me take his wife? He'll have me strung up from the nearest oak tree."

"You've had his wife many times already."

"Not like this."

"You mean not forever. There's no turning back. I left a note. Come morning, he'll know."

"You wrote a note? You told him?"

"Everything. I wanted him to know how vile his touch is. How I can't look upon his face without feeling wretched. How every moment of every hour of every day feels like a long, slow descent into hell."

"Are you mad?" He took two steps back, distancing himself from her. "I have to get away."

"*We* have to get away."

"I can't take you. I don't have the means

to care for you."

"I've brought money, lots of it." She held up a knitted handbag that had hung from the crook in her arm.

"What good will it do me if I'm dead? He'll kill me if he catches me, and you'll only slow me down."

"He'll kill me if you leave me behind."

"I doubt that. A good beating, maybe."

"Like one of his rebellious horses? And you'd leave me to that?"

The winter look descended on her again, even colder this time, as if her heart had frozen entirely.

"I thought you were my way out," she said.

"Ah, I see now." His tone became every bit as icy as hers. "That's all I've been to you this whole time, the possibility of a way out of a loveless marriage."

"And what have I been for you but an elegant sheath for that sword between your legs?"

"You must be desperate, to choose a poor gambler as your hope for escape."

"Do you want to know what hell is? It's lying in bed every night, repulsed by the man next to you. Yes, I chose you. At least you're handsome. And I do love your touch."

"Which you'll feel no more. Madam, I

wish you luck."

He started to turn, but she said, "I have something for you."

She reached into her knitted handbag and drew out a little pistol.

When he saw it, he tried to smile. "You won't shoot me. I'm the man who makes your heart beat like the wings of a butterfly."

"Your words have always been so smooth, always kept you out of real trouble, I imagine. I suppose I always knew that beneath that beautiful skin beat the heart of a coward." She raised the gun level with his chest, the barrel gleaming blue in the moonlight. "The note I left him was not exactly as I described it to you. It was more in the line of a ransom demand."

"Ransom?"

"It will simply look as if you've kidnapped me. In case he caught up with us, I thought it best to give myself a way out."

"And now you plan to shoot me?"

"If need be, to save my reputation and to save me from that beating you were so willing to have me suffer."

"He'll never believe it."

"He will if I shoot you, and if I pledge my love to him in the same way I pledged it to you."

434

"Wait." He raised his hands as if to shield himself from the bullet. "I'll take you with me, I swear it."

"Another promise you would never keep."

She let out a long, exasperated sigh and pulled the trigger. But nothing happened.

"Misfire," he cried, and lurched for her throat.

She had writhed in his arms before but always with pleasure, never with the desperation she displayed now. They struggled only a few moments, locked in a fatal embrace, their black, moon-cast shadows entwined on the planks of the bridge beneath them. Then, with all the thoughtlessness the struggle engendered, he threw her against the low railing and she tumbled over. But as she fell, she grasped the sturdy material of his coat in a death grip and pulled him with her into the dark abyss below.

The night was silent once more, the blue moon high overhead, the place where they'd met once again for the last time brightly illuminated and tragically empty.

He parked the Harley near the bridge. They dismounted, and he removed his helmet.

"So, this is the place?"

She took off her own helmet and shook

her gold hair free. "According to Mongo."

He eyed the ancient planking and the gorge beneath that plunged into darkness. "You're sure it's safe, babe?"

"It's old, but Mongo swears it'll hold. Come on, Woody."

She took his hand and led him to the middle of the bridge, where they stood with their shadows puddled under them in the brilliant light of the full, blue moon.

"It's beautiful," she said.

"Awful quiet and isolated," he noted.

"Mongo says that's why they met here. She was married to a wealthy man who had a heart cold as ice. But her true love was a gambler. They knew if they tried to run away together, her rich old man wouldn't rest until he caught them and strung her lover up from an oak tree."

"So they threw themselves off the bridge? Kinda drastic, you ask me."

"Romantic, Woody. Tragically romantic. They did it so they could be together forever. They were found down there beside the river, locked in each other's arms. A beautiful sacrifice."

"Hell, I'd've just whacked her old man."

She lifted her face to him in the moonlight, her eyes glistening. "I'd jump off this bridge for you. Would you jump off for me?"

"You're kidding me, right?"

"Or is it Doreen you'd jump for?"

Her eyes, he saw, were pale chips of ice. "How many times I gotta tell you, babe, she don't mean anything. It was just, you know, a big mistake. You're my lady. Always will be."

She put her hand on the old railing. "Mongo says the legend is that they return to this bridge on the night of every blue moon."

"You mean like ghosts? Like they're doomed or something?"

"The anniversary of their sacrifice. He says if you listen real close, you can hear them swear their love."

"Is that why we came? You didn't have to bring me all the way out here for that. You know I love you, babe."

"What about Doreen?"

"Hell, can't you just forget about Doreen? What do you want from me?"

"I want to believe in the kind of love that would make two people sacrifice themselves the way those lovers did."

"Fucking waste, you ask me."

"Coming here?"

"That's not what I meant," he said quickly, hearing the chill in her voice. "Killing themselves."

437

"I want to believe in that kind of love, Woody. And I want you to believe in it, too. That's why we're here." She took his hands in her own and said, "So, shut up and close your eyes and just listen."

He started to tell her the whole thing was nuts but saw her lids flutter closed and figured he had no choice but to do the same.

And he heard. To his great amazement, he heard. When he opened his eyes, he saw a beautiful look of absolute amazement on her face.

"It's true, Woody. You heard them, too, didn't you? Like an echo or something. He told her the love in his heart was so burning it would consume them both."

He spoke slowly, as if stunned. "She swore that she was his forever, that they would be together for all eternity."

"There was more, but I couldn't catch the rest. Did you, Woody?"

"No, that was all. But it was real, babe. Mongo wasn't fooling."

"They were with us, really here with us, for a moment anyway. And we heard what's important, right, Woody? Exactly what I wanted to hear, what a couple of lovers like us need to hear." Her eyes were huge and wondrous as she gazed at him.

"Jesus," he said, feeling overwhelmed

himself. "And I thought it was just bullshit."

In that surreal moment in which two worlds connected, a moment repeated with every blue moon, these two hopeful lovers kissed long and passionately. When they separated, their faces were illuminated with promise.

"Mongo says according to the legend, if we swear our love here on the night of a blue moon, just like they did, we'll be together forever. That's the whole reason I brought us here. I love you, Woody," she said.

"And I love you, babe."

"Forever," she said.

"Forever," he echoed.

They kissed again, then turned and peered into the dark beneath the bridge, where far below a thread of water ran silver under the moon.

She gave a deep sigh of envy. "Oh, Woody, their love for each other must have been something terrible."

"Yeah, babe," he said with a grave nod of agreement. "Fucking terrible."

■ ■ ■ ■ ■

AQUA VITA

BY PETER ROBINSON

■ ■ ■ ■ ■

It was when the waiter handed him the "Water Menu" that Gerald thought he might have made a mistake in taking Cheryl to Mystique for their fifth wedding anniversary. The choice had been based on the recommendations of friends — mostly Cheryl's friends, and no doubt biased in terms of the kind of food and attention that *she* liked — so he realized that it would be best all round if he feigned a certain level of enjoyment and kept any negative comments to himself. Even so, he couldn't help himself from responding, "Water's water, isn't it? Tap water will do just fine for me."

The waiter seemed disappointed, and Cheryl gave Gerald a reproving glance. When it was her turn, she said, "I'll try the black water, please."

The waiter beamed. "Yes, madam," he said. "Certainly. Black water. From Canada." He then asked about food allergies, and they said they had none.

"What on earth is black water?" Gerald asked when the waiter was out of earshot. At close to ten quid a shot it ought to be something special. It was almost as expensive as the glasses of champagne the waiter had brought them without asking when they first sat down.

Cheryl smiled. "No idea," she said. "But it sounds interesting. Live dangerously. That's what I always say."

Gerald grunted.

"I don't know about yours," she whispered, leaning forward over the table, "but my menu doesn't have any prices listed."

"Mine does, unfortunately," said Gerald. "From what I can see, I should imagine they don't want ladies fainting at the tables."

Cheryl laughed and put her hand on his, giving him a gentle squeeze. "Oh, darling," she said. "I know you'd prefer fish and chips, but put a brave face on it. We were lucky to get a table here."

"I'll try," Gerald muttered, returning the squeeze. "For you." He gestured toward the floor-to-ceiling windows beyond which the lights of the city skyline glittered like Christmas decorations, the Gherkin and the Cheesegrater standing out dramatically, side by side. "At least we can enjoy the view."

"I think I'd like the tasting menu," said Cheryl after a sip of champagne.

Gerald looked at the price and swallowed. "But it says we *both* have to have it."

Cheryl pouted. "But you'll do that for me, won't you, darling?"

Gerald felt her foot brush his ankle and smiled. She was wearing his favorite black dress tonight, the one that showed off her graceful neck and shoulders to best advantage, with just enough cleavage to hint at the delights below. "Of course. How could I refuse?" At the age of sixty-five, he knew he was a lucky man to be married to a beautiful woman twenty-five years his junior. Certainly lucky enough to spring for two tasting menus.

When the waiter reappeared with their respective waters, Gerald saw that Cheryl's really *was* black. "Can you tell me about the tasting menu?" he asked.

"It's Chef's choice," the waiter said.

"Naturally. What are the courses?"

The waiter shrugged. "That depends on the ingredients available, on what Chef wishes to create."

"And what ingredients *are* available today?"

"I'm afraid I can't say, sir."

"Can't or won't?"

"Each dish is a surprise. That is part of the experience."

"You can't give us any idea?"

"I'm afraid not. It is different every day."

"Let's take a risk, darling," said Cheryl.

"Very well. We'll have the tasting menu."

"Excellent," said the waiter. "And the wine?"

"It's a little difficult to choose the wine when we don't know what we'll be eating."

"If I may suggest, sir, perhaps you might begin with a bottle of Chablis, then move on to a Bordeaux, shall we say? We have an excellent selection. If I may recommend —"

"I'll choose myself." Gerald scanned the list and picked two bottles from the mid-price range.

"Excellent choice, sir, if I may say so," said the waiter.

Not long after he had disappeared, he was back again, this time with a trolley. "Your wine will be here momentarily," he said. "But first, perhaps sir and madam would enjoy a little fresh bread?" He held out a basket and named the contents. Gerald got lost after sourdough and went for a straightforward mini baguette. Cheryl picked something yellow with dark seeds embedded in it.

Like a stage magician, the waiter then took

446

a small squat bottle with a fitted blue glass top from his trolley, poured in a few drops of viscous gold liquid, then held it between his palms, gently rolling it back and forth. Finally, he lifted out the stopper with a flourish and stuck the bottle under first Cheryl's nose, like a dose of smelling salts, then under Gerald's. All Gerald could tell was that it was olive oil. The waiter didn't seem much interested in their reactions, but quickly poured more from the bottle into the dainty little bowls beside their side dishes.

After the wine arrived — happily, Gerald thought, without a fanfare of brass — there followed numerous amuse-bouches: essence of scallops; finely shredded crab and lobster mousses; concentrated drops of gooseberry, lime, pear, and God only knew what else. All were excellent, Gerald had to admit. His palate wasn't quite as bland as Cheryl liked to make out.

Cheryl seemed in her element, and he couldn't help but feel a burning sense of pride as he watched her enjoying the little delicacies and the fussy attentions of the waiter. It was true that they had their problems — what couple didn't — and sometimes Gerald felt he wasn't dynamic or adventurous enough for her. Which was why he was careful to give her space. If she wanted her own room to be alone in, and even to sleep alone in sometimes, who was he to argue? If she liked to stay with old university friends up in Manchester for a night or two, where was the harm in that? It wasn't as if he didn't have enough to keep him occupied at the bank. Sometimes he wondered why she had married him in the first place, but he tried his best not to dwell on it too much. Perhaps it was his kindness and gentleness that had attracted her, the very order and stability of their life that she sometimes found so dull. It certainly wasn't his money or his looks, though he had enough to keep her in reasonable style and ensure that she didn't have to go back to work.

He tried to keep up with the courses when they began to arrive: stuffed calamari (a little rubbery); a psychedelic scrambled egg concoction served with the ubiquitous black water on the side in small earthenware jugs (just like his tap water, only a little more bitter); a wild mushroom risotto (rice overcooked and mushy). There was no beef, nor even a shred of pork, lamb or chicken; the only real meat dish was sweetbreads, which Cheryl didn't like. She did, however, approve of the meal as a whole and asked the waiter to compliment the chef, then insisted that Gerald leave a larger than usual tip, even though, he noticed, the twelve and a half percent "service charge" had already been added.

When they went back to their hotel room, after a couple of substantial cognacs out on the balcony, Gerald hoped it might be his lucky night. Cheryl had been smiling and flirtatious all evening, but when they got to the room, she said she was very tired and wanted to go straight to sleep. Gerald realized that he had probably drunk too much, anyway, so he gave her a good-night kiss and sat up watching some rubbish on TV after raiding the minibar for another cognac. Since they had a suite — it was their celebratory anniversary trip, after all — he didn't have to worry about disturbing Cheryl. After a while, the cognac had its effect, and Gerald found himself drifting to sleep on the couch.

Gerald didn't know what time it was when he woke up, but the television was still on, and it was dark outside. His watch face was blurred, but he thought it said a quarter to five. He wasn't feeling at all well. It wasn't just a hangover, he was certain. The terrible burning sensation in his chest and stomach, like indigestion only ten times worse, had awoken him. He even thought for a moment that he might be having a heart attack. Didn't they start with something like heartburn? Or maybe it was an ulcer. He hadn't been careful enough with his diet.

He tried to get up off the couch but doubled up in pain and fell on his knees to the floor. It was getting quickly worse. He needed to get to the telephone. No. Wake Cheryl. She was a heavy sleeper, especially after a few drinks, but he would have to rouse her somehow. *She* would take care of him and call the ambulance.

He tried to shout out, but the sound wouldn't come. With almost superhuman effort, he got to his feet and pushed over the little table beside him. The carpet was thick, though, and the table didn't make much noise when it fell. He suddenly needed to be sick and staggered to the toilet, where he bent over the bowl and retched. No sooner had he finished with that, than he felt his bowels explode and maneuvered himself onto the toilet just in time. After he had emptied himself, he made his way shakily back to the couch just in time to see Cheryl coming out of the bedroom rubbing her eyes as she felt for the light switch.

"Gerry! Darling!" she said, dashing toward him and helping him back to the couch. "What is it?"

Gerald shook his head. It made him feel dizzy. "Don't know," he said. "Feel sick. Aaarrrgghh!" And he retched again, this time on the carpet.

Cheryl stepped back. "My God," she said. "It's all bloody."

Gerald was sweating and his breath was coming in short gasps. He could barely get the words out, but thought he said, "Thirsty. Water. Please."

Cheryl disappeared for a moment and came back with a glass of water.

"Please call someone," Gerald gasped. "Doctor." He drank the water, but it didn't do much good. His stomach lurched, and he retched again. He felt like he imagined the John Hurt character in *Alien* must have felt before the creature burst out of him. Was something trying to burst out of *him*? He clutched his stomach and moaned, feeling dizzy and faint.

When he looked up again, Cheryl was standing over him. The expression on her face puzzled him. She didn't look worried or afraid. If anything, she seemed *curious.*

"Cheryl," he said, struggling to get the words out. "Please . . . doctor. Ambulance."

451

Cheryl took his hand. "It's all right," she said. "They're coming."

He could have sworn there were tears in her eyes. He couldn't understand what she was saying now, what she meant. He tried to get up, but a terrible pain shot through him. He felt paralyzed. "Cheryl," he whispered. "Can't move. Too weak. Please help me. Dying."

Cheryl kept hold of his hand and lowered her head so he couldn't see her face.

"Please! Hurry!"

But Cheryl kept on kneeling there, head bowed, and Gerald lapsed into unconsciousness, felt her recede further and further away from him until she was nothing but a tiny image at the wrong end of a telescope.

The next few weeks were a terrible ordeal for Cheryl. First came the doctors, desperately trying to save Gerald and discover what it was that had afflicted him. She told them about their meal, the drinks they had consumed. Could it be a heart attack? No, they said. It was something else, something that attacked his organs and caused them to fail one by one. They did tests and took samples, but it was all too late. Gerald died, without regaining consciousness, of cardiac arrest caused by multiple organ failures at eight nineteen the following morning, just over twenty-four hours since the ambulance had arrived at the hotel. The doctors were no wiser then than they had been when he was admitted.

After the doctors came the police, of course, and she told them the same story. She and Gerald had been celebrating their wedding anniversary, and she had gone to bed early, having had a bit too much champagne, leaving her husband on the sofa watching TV. When she had awoken in the morning, he still hadn't come to bed, and she had found him lying on the sofa, comatose. At first she had thought he was dead, but discovered that he was still breathing, though he didn't seem able to tell her what was wrong with him. She had immediately phoned reception and asked them to send an ambulance, that it was an emergency. The rest was . . . Well, something of a blur.

For a short while, she believed that they suspected her of murdering Gerald, though it was never spoken out loud. They just kept coming back, asking more and more questions, often the same ones, over and over. How would she describe her marriage? Were there any problems between her and her late husband? What time did she wake up and find him? The facts worked in her favor. It appeared she had acted quickly, and the ambulance had arrived in fifteen minutes. Also, though she was adequately provided for in Gerald's will, and she inherited the mortgage-free detached house they had lived in, it was hardly a vast fortune, and it spoke greatly in her favor that Gerald had never bothered to take out a life insurance policy. The police, therefore, lacking any other evidence to the contrary, soon concluded that she lacked a financial motive for wanting him dead. And what other could there be? These days, if you wanted rid of a husband, whatever the reason, you simply divorced him; you didn't need to resort to murder.

And then came the stories of several others claiming they were sick after eating at Mystique that same night. That also helped convince the police that there was no foul play. One elderly woman died in much the same way as Gerald had, and two others were seriously ill, though expected to recover. Naturally, the restaurant had been closed and inquiries were underway. Of course, the police returned with more questions. Why hadn't she been sick, too, if they both had the same tasting menu? She had felt a little ill, she told them, but only to a very minor extent. As it happened, she wasn't particularly fond of mushrooms and, as she didn't know that they were on the menu, she hadn't been able to avoid them. So she had left most of them. She was pretty full by then, anyway.

Cheryl took the train home a few days after Gerald's death. Her mother came down from Durham to stay with her and comfort her for a while, and the neighbors all rallied around and helped her through the funeral and its aftermath.

But there was no postponing that dreadful moment when she was finally alone in the large house.

Except that it wasn't dreadful; it was as if a great weight had been lifted off her shoulders. The burden of having to play the grieving widow. That role would have to continue in public for some time, of course, but in private she could unbutton, as one might say, put her feet up, and dream and plan for the future. For there was most definitely a glittering future ahead of her.

Hot on the heels of the doctors, the police, and the undertakers, came the lawyers. As it turned out, they said, the restaurant was owned by a wealthy international chain, and the question of compensation had arisen. A preliminary investigation had concluded that the item responsible for the Gerald's death was *amanita phalloides,* a deadly fungus which could grow beside, and easily be mistaken for, the more edible variety of mushroom. Despite the rigorous checks and balances to which all the restaurant's ingredients were usually subject, these had somehow slipped in among a supply of nonpoisonous field mushrooms, bringing about the possibility of a tidy sum in compensation for those affected. Most of the people who had eaten the mushroom risotto that night had swallowed such small amounts that they had been only mildly sick, but Gerald and the other fatality were older than the rest, and therefore more susceptible. Gerald also drank too much, which rendered his liver already fair game for the first predator that approached it — in this case, a poison known as phalloidin, which targeted the kidneys, liver, and cardiac muscles, ultimately causing death.

The money finally came through several months after Gerald's death, by which time Cheryl had adapted to her new single life. Though the amount wasn't quite as much as she had hoped for, it was enough to raise her standard of living a notch or two and to ensure that she wouldn't have to go back to work. She had served as a bank teller at the local branch, which was where she had met Gerald, the manager. Though the #MeToo movement was unknown at the time, it was still frowned upon for senior management to form liaisons with the clerical staff, but Cheryl had as little regard for that idea as Gerald did. No man was ever going to force her or persuade her to do something she didn't want to do just because he happened to be her boss, but if *she* wanted to marry *him,* why the hell shouldn't she?

Of course, Gerald wanted her to stay at home in the hope of children, but she saw to it that nothing like that was going to happen, especially as he would be in his seventies by the time any progeny of theirs entered his or her teens. Cheryl was damned if she was going to end up either changing nappies or playing single mum to a sulky teen. And so life had gone on without any particular highs or lows.

Until Marco, that was.

Cheryl would be the first to admit that it had started as a purely physical affair. Gerald had liked the bottle rather too much, and his performance in bed, if it occurred at all, often wasn't up to snuff. With Marco it was sex, sex, and even more sex. Cheryl was thirty-nine at the time they met, and

Marco was twenty-four, a waiter at Mystique. The poisoning had all been his idea. He knew the owners of the restaurant had millions. He also knew his poisons — he had had grown up in the countryside and had started, though he hadn't finished, a university course in pharmacology — so he even knew how the deed could be done. Cheryl had taken a bit of persuading. After all, she didn't *dislike* Gerald. Life with him might be dull, but it was comfortable enough. Even so, lust and passion had won out over reason and common sense in the end, as they so often did, and she had become as excited by the idea as Marco was.

Forever cautious, Cheryl and Marco had decided it was safest to have no contact whatsoever for a year after Gerald's death — no letters, texts, emails, or phone calls — after which time they would meet at a remote Cornish bay and plan their future. So until then, she was on her own.

After a suitable period of mourning, Cheryl had taken stock of herself and concluded that she was an attractive woman, just turned forty, with the sort of gamine looks and svelte but curvaceous figure that attracted men. One or two of Gerald's old pals made passes at her, which she found easy to resist. Her female friends told her she could get out more. After all, why should she simply sit at home and watch television while she waited for the time to pass? There was excitement out there, a life to be enjoyed, to be savored. So she did get out.

The first time she went alone to a busy bar accompanied only by her newfound freedom, she went home with a football player — only championship league, not premier, admittedly — who proceeded to demonstrate that kicking a ball around a large field for ninety minutes wasn't the only skill he used his stamina for. After that, it became a regular thing — not with the footballer, whose name she couldn't even remember — but with other fit-looking young prey she came across in bars and shops and cafés.

Time passed. She had some work done on the house, putting in an exercise room with all the usual accoutrements, including a personal trainer, and having her bedroom redecorated more to her taste, including a mirror on the ceiling, and an en suite bathroom installed. She also developed a taste for cocaine. It wasn't hard to spend money, she soon found, after paying out a small fortune for a luxury stateroom on a top-of-the-line South Pacific cruise that winter.

The cruise provided no interesting distractions except the gorgeous weather and some delightful excursions to exotic locations on shore. Most of her fellow passengers were well into their seventies, which meant more groping on the dance floor, and when she was flying back home, she decided to postpone any further cruising activity until she reached that age herself. She would see who tried to grope her then.

And so life went on in a delightful hedonistic whirl of money, booze, coke, and sex.

But there remained one nagging problem, and every day it was getting closer, beginning to throb like an aching tooth. What was she going to tell Marco when it came time for their meeting?

As Marco settled into the train's soothing rhythm, he thought of the ups and downs of the past year. What a year it had been.

Needless to say, when the scandal of the tainted mushrooms broke, the entire staff of Mystique had been fired and the restaurant closed, and though no one had been singled out for blame — it was regarded as a failure of the system as a whole — the kitchen staff had certainly come under suspicion. Nobody suspected Marco, a waiter, though it was he who had introduced the *amanita phalloides* into the store of perfectly edible mushrooms, and he who had added an extra dash to Gerald's dish before serving it. Everything had been meticulously planned. Marco had already managed to ingratiate himself with the kitchen staff, just as he had in his previous jobs, so access during the hours when the restaurant was closed was not difficult. Nor was it hard for him to get in there unseen when no one else was around. He also knew that the sous-chef drank too much and tended to be sloppy, which meant he was unlikely to check the spore print and gills of the mushrooms he prepared. And he knew that mushroom risotto was on the tasting menu that night.

When he thought about it afterward, he was not only amazed at the audacity and sangfroid with which he had carried out the murder, he was also appalled — appalled that he had let himself be so carried on a tide of lust to the madness of murder. For that was what it had been. And innocents had died. He had their blood on his hands. Though he had instigated the poisoning, and persuaded Cheryl of its financial benefits, he hadn't expected such a sudden attack of conscience.

There was a long agonizing period when he had yearned for the release and relief of confession. On a number of occasions he had even found himself loitering outside a police station — on one occasion, during a particularly tense period of terrorist activity, being told to move on. He knew the facts, the method, things they would be able to tell that no one but the true killer could know, and that would convince them. But he had never got farther than the front steps.

And then he had met Alice.

When Marco had got over the guilt and the urge to confess, he felt that he had finally come to his senses, emerged from the vile spell of Cheryl's domination and begun to see things as they really were. And Alice had a lot to do with that transformation. What was it about Cheryl that had so drawn him in and corrupted him? Girls his own age had often seemed silly, brash, crude, and shallow to him, but he had thought Cheryl had class. She was the sexy, sophisticated older woman: elegant, sensual. She had style. She wore expensive silk underwear and subtle perfumes. Their first meeting had been an across-a-crowded-room moment, and Marco had been emboldened by the power of his attraction to her. She hadn't rejected his advances or reacted as if she was doing him a favor, like the most attractive girls his own age usually did. She was a real woman, and when they were together they fulfilled one another in every way. Or so he had felt at the time. Exotic as Cheryl had seemed at the start of their relationship, when he thought of her now, from a distance, he realized how she had used him. What a witch, an enchantress, she really was! And how much *older* than him. She was forty, for crying out loud. She'd be well into her fifties before he reached that age, and by the time he was fifty, he'd probably be pushing her around in a wheelchair.

He had started working again out of financial necessity, lying about his references, saying he had been unemployed for the past year and a half. And that was how Alice had come into his life — at a gourmet burger café in Lowestoft. She was sitting alone at a table, long hair tied back, little makeup, the sleeves of her black sweater pulled down over her hands the way some young girls wore them. Looking back, Marco realized there could hardly be anyone more different from Cheryl. Alice was his own age — a month younger, as it turned out — and she was on her lunch break from the bookshop across the road. They started chatting casually. Alice was rather shy, and Marco had reverted to his old awkwardness around girls. But there was definitely a spark, and as she came in two or three days a week, they were able to strike up some sort of relationship before Marco dared to invite her out for a drink after work. Alice accepted, and before long they were inseparable. This was true love, Marco felt. Not the head-whirling, kaleidoscopic illusion of love with Cheryl, which had led him to murder. No, that part of him was gone now. Alice was the genuine article. She had brought freshness and clarity to his life, and they were going to get married, have children, and live a normal life, with his past far behind him. The only problem was that he was a murderer. Alice was an innocent, and he couldn't risk her finding out what he had done.

He realized that what he had done for Cheryl — all right, for the two of them — wasn't really anything to do with money. That was entirely *her* perspective. No. He had done it because he had wanted Cheryl all to himself, for always. But now that he had Alice, he didn't want Cheryl at all. In his memory, she had become coarse and crude, little more than a cheap whore, and nothing she did would surprise him. The thought of her repelled him — however, he had to go to Cornwall. He had to meet with her just this one more time and tell her he no longer wanted her or her money. She would be relieved about the latter, but as for the first, he wasn't so certain. Hell hath no fury like a woman scorned, or so they said.

The announcement that St. Ives was their next stop came over the PA and the train started to slow down. The change in rhythm jolted Marco out of his memories. He reached up for his suitcase. Time to meet with his destiny.

Cheryl was waiting outside the station in her new green racing sports car. The cottage she had rented was on a hillside overlooking a secluded bay farther west. It was an idyllic location: perfect for watching the sunset and close enough to the sea to hear the waves breaking on the shore at night.

As Cheryl had expected, things were a little awkward at first. The hug seemed perfunctory, the kiss a little hesitant. A year is a long time without any contact at all, she realized, and Cheryl was aware that they may have drifted apart to some extent. It was a beautiful day. She had planned a barbecue at the cottage, and perhaps after that they could take a sunset stroll on the cliff path above the beach. It was very wild and romantic. *Poldark* country. Marco would love it.

He put his suitcase in the boot and got in beside her. She wore dark glasses against the glare of the sun and felt the warm wind ruffling her hair as she drove. They passed no other cars and saw only the occasional distant farm laborers working in the fields.

Finally she pulled up outside the cottage, a rambling old structure with three large bathrooms, an open-plan kitchen complete with cookware, cutlery, and dinnerware, and a large garden out front, looking over the bay, complete with wicker chairs and low tables. Cheryl had been enjoying her breakfast coffee there, looking out over the sea, for the past couple of days. There was no Wi-Fi or mobile phone reception, but that wasn't much of a drawback as far as Cheryl was concerned.

She changed into shorts and halter top and busied herself with the barbecue in the garden while Marco freshened up. First, she wrapped a couple of potatoes in foil and put them on the grill, then tossed the shrimp in oil and spices and rubbed the steaks she had bought to go with them. Surf and turf. She threw the salad together as the potatoes cooked.

Marco came out wearing rather tight garish shorts and a yellow T-shirt. He was carrying a bottle, which he handed to her, and something wrapped up in gift paper.

"Presents," he said.

The first was a bottle of fine cognac from the duty-free shop, but the second, she saw when she had peeled off the wrapping, was an earthenware jar.

"Black water," said Marco, beaming. "I finally managed to find some."

Cheryl thought it a bit insensitive of him to present her with an obvious reminder of the night of her husband's death on the day of their reunion, but she let it go. No sense making a fuss about it. "Thanks," she said. "I haven't seen any since . . . you know. We'll have it with dinner."

Marco stretched out on a lounger while Cheryl barbecued.

"Mmm," he said. "This is the life. I could get used to it here."

Cheryl laughed, standing over the barbecue, keeping an eye on the steak and shrimps. "Come to the table," she said finally. "Dinner's ready."

Cheryl served the meal with all the requisite condiments, and put out the bowl of salad for them to help themselves. A couple of bluebottles and a pesky wasp started to show an interest. Cheryl waved them away.

"We'll save the cognac for later," said Marco, opening the earthenware jar and pouring them both a glass of black water. They clinked glasses and toasted themselves. Cheryl took a sip. It was good, she remembered. Like ordinary water, only slightly bitter and more full-bodied. "So, tell me what you've been up to this past year," she said as they settled down to eat.

"Oh, this and that," Marco replied between mouthfuls. "It was hard just after . . . you know. We all got fired."

"It was pretty hard for me, too," said Cheryl. "I'd just lost my husband, remember?"

Marco gave her a cockeyed look. "It's what you wanted, isn't it?"

Cheryl shrugged. "I'm not saying I didn't. Just that it was a tough role to play."

"Well, being unemployed was no great shakes, either. Not to mention being a murderer."

"But you got over it."

"You do, don't you? Especially when you get away with it."

They lapsed into silence for a while and carried on eating. When Cheryl could stand it no longer, she asked, "What are we going to do now?"

"I don't know," said Marco. "Depends on what you want."

He sounded strangely hesitant, Cheryl thought. "Got cold feet?"

"About what?"

"Us. Being together."

"Oh, that. No. Course not."

But there was still something about his tone. "Is there something you want to tell me?"

"No. Just that it was hard, that's all. Making ends meet, being alone and everything."

"But you got another job?"

"Eventually."

Cheryl pushed her empty plate away. "And you don't have to worry about money now, do you? I've got plenty for both of us."

"It wasn't about the money. You know that."

She was about to respond that it was for her, but held herself in check. "Of course not. But even so . . . it helps."

"Helps what? Salve our consciences?"

"I don't know about you, but I can't say I give my conscience much thought." What was wrong with him? Cheryl wondered. They used to be able to talk so easily. Now it was like pulling teeth. "Come on," she said, reaching over and taking his hand.

"The sun's going down. Let's go for a walk. We wouldn't want to miss it."

The path followed the cliff edge around the jagged bay. Marco took Cheryl's hand as they walked. One of the rock formations below had a keyhole in it, and the waves gushed through with a loud whooshing sound, then retreated with a sound like an indrawn breath. To their left, the sun was setting in a deep orange and lilac glow, light fluffy gray clouds on either side, as if they were little dogs nipping at the edges of the fading light.

"It's beautiful," said Marco, pausing to look.

"I knew you'd like it," she said.

"How did you find it?"

"Mostly good luck," said Cheryl. "And newspaper adverts."

They walked on.

Soon the sun had sunk below the horizon and tinged the underbellies of the clouds with its dying light. "It'll be dark soon," Cheryl said with a little shiver. "We'd better be getting back."

But Marco didn't move. "Look," he said, standing with his back to the fading light. "I want you to know that I've found someone else."

The words seemed to burn their way into Cheryl's consciousness. *"I've found someone else."* This wasn't supposed to happen. True enough, she no longer felt any need for Marco in her life, and in fact, he seemed immature and vain to her now. But it wasn't supposed to happen this way. "*Someone else?* How could that be?"

"I met her at work," he went on, though she was hardly hearing him. "We want to get married, have children. I'm sorry. I wanted you to know. I can't let anything get in the way of that."

The sea was roaring in her ears, and before she knew it, she had pushed his chest. He flailed his arms as he fell backward, as if trying to fly, a surprised expression on his face. Then he went over the cliff edge and fell all the way down, his scream harmonizing oddly with the noise of the sea, and crashed onto the rocks below. Cheryl held her breath, put her fist to her mouth and looked over the edge. He lay broken on the rocks, arms out like a scarecrow. He wasn't moving. Then a huge wave came rushing over him, and when it went out, Marco's body was gone.

Cheryl practically ran the whole way back to the cottage, and when she got there, she was breathless and shaking like a leaf. She had never killed anyone before. Well, true, she had been involved in Gerald's murder, but not like this. Besides, Marco had done all the actual work; he was the poison expert. This time she had actually shoved a man to his death. And not just any man. Her lover. But she had known even before she saw him again that she didn't want him back. She had got used to living by herself, got to enjoy the freedom, and the last thing she wanted was to be involved in a relationship again. She wanted the life she had made for herself after Gerald's death, the money, too, and she would share it with no one.

She hadn't been sure what she was going to do about him once she had told him she didn't need him anymore, but she knew she couldn't risk having him on the loose, liable to turn up at any moment or, worse, feel the need to confess to Gerald's murder. Perhaps killing him had always been her intention, though she hadn't realized it until that moment when he opened his mouth and told her there was *someone else.* Only then did she know for certain that she had to do it. Marco could implicate her. She would never have been truly rid of him while he was alive. He could have turned her life into a living hell.

In retrospect, she had been very careful in planning their meeting. She had convinced herself it was because they mustn't be seen together, but what if it had really been so that she could kill him and get away with it? There was no one for miles around. Nobody had seen them on the cliffs, and if anyone had noticed her with Marco at the station, it was hardly something they would remember. With any luck, his body would never turn up, and even if it did, the authorities would just assume he'd had an accident. It happened all the time on dangerous cliffs like these.

She went into the bedroom and found he had left his case open on the bed, his jacket beside it. She would make a bonfire on the beach later. She went through the pockets and found little of interest. The was a photo in his wallet of a pretty young woman about Marco's age. So that was her. Cheryl felt another surge of anger. Then she told herself to calm down and not be so stupid. He was dead now. It didn't matter that he'd found someone else, someone younger and prettier. She wouldn't be so pretty when her precious Marco never came home again. She opened the case and was surprised to find it almost empty. Where were his changes of clothing, his toiletries and so on? Hadn't he planned on staying more than one night? Perhaps not, given what he had told her earlier. So why bring a suitcase at all?

Cheryl felt exhausted, and she lay back on the bed. She couldn't think clearly at all, didn't want to think anymore tonight. She had just killed a man and she couldn't process what she had done.

But she must have fallen asleep, because it was going on for four in the morning when a sharp pain in the stomach woke her. She'd had acid reflux before, so she thought nothing of it at first as she went downstairs to find the Zantac she carried in her handbag. Maybe it was something to do with the shellfish she had eaten from the barbecue.

The pain struck again on the stairs, almost doubling her up, and by the time she got down she was feeling nauseated, and the agony had become even harder to bear. She clutched her stomach and groaned. God, she had never felt like this before.

She staggered through the kitchen toward the downstairs toilet to be sick, and on the way she passed the dishes from their dinner. She hadn't noticed before, but she saw that Marco hadn't touched his glass of black water.

The bastard, she thought, as another spasm twisted through her gut like a burning corkscrew, then she finally collapsed, gasping for air, on the bathroom floor.

■ ■ ■ ■

THE LAST HIBAKUSHA

BY NAOMI HIRAHARA

■ ■ ■ ■

Mas Arai hated his wheelchair, but might have hated his cane even more. It was his cane, after all, that had forced him in this jail on wheels. The rubber end of his cane had gotten stuck in between two bricks in a walkway at his wife's care facility, launching him forward into some camellia bushes. He felt something pop around his side and it was as he suspected: he had fractured his hip. Up to this time — ninety years old, sixty of which had been spent tending lawns — he had not broken even one bone. He went off to surgery and was now recuperating. He vowed to himself that he would be back on his feet without the wheelchair or the cane in a month's time.

The worst thing about the wheelchair was, once his daughter, Mari, or son-in-law, Lloyd, got him in it, he was under their full control. Today, however, he was a willing prisoner of Dr. Rin Fujii, his physician for the past six years. Mas didn't care much for women doctors, but Dr. Fujii was different. Her smooth face was usually expressionless, whether she was treating an ingrown hair or a cancerous tumor. She was no-nonsense and she delivered difficult diagnoses unadulterated but still with humanity. She did so with Mas's second wife, Genessee. "You're in stage two Alzheimer's, but you have time," she said. Two years later, Genessee's mind began to really slip, tiles of memory coming loose and disappearing. Dr. Fujii, not Mas, was the only one who seemed able to mitigate this loss. Sometimes Genessee was fully aware of what was happening to her and the doctor's self-assured, calm voice served as her only guide through the maze. Genessee had been the young spouse, the professor. She wasn't supposed to go first, and especially like this. Mas was used to surprises, however, and met this tragedy in the same fashion that he initially dealt with other ones in his life: to dig a deep hole and bury it.

"We've arrived," Dr. Fujii announced in Japanese. She parked her car in front of a tiny building in a residential area in a nebulous neighborhood in between the Arts District and East Los Angeles. Mas was immediately suspicious. He didn't go anywhere

480

unless he was forced to, like today, but he knew enough about Los Angeles's Hiroshima Peace Flame. It was housed at a Buddhist temple in Little Tokyo accessible from First Street through a narrow driveway. They were at least a mile from where they should be.

Dr. Fujii read Mas's confused expression. "They had to do some seismic retrofitting at the main temple. So the Peace Flame is being brought here."

Moving a flame from one location to another was absurd. But that was the legacy of this flame, whose fire had somehow been transferred from the cenotaph in Hiroshima Peace Park to Southern California by the Los Angeles mayor at the time, a commanding and distinguished African American man, the former LAPD chief. Mas wrinkled his forehead imagining the gangling mayor holding a heated block on his lap in the plane. This was years before 9/11, of course, a time when people actually lit their cigarettes and smoked on planes. Considering the late mayor's feat, perhaps moving the flame in a lantern at a distance of one mile for today's anniversary may have been inconsequential.

Mas waited for Dr. Fujii to get out of the car, unload the wheelchair from the trunk, and open the passenger door for him. The thing that he hated the most about getting old was waiting. It was as if his body had lost all of its proactivity. Everything now was about responding to someone else's action. It infuriated him, but what did the old-school Japanese say — *shikataganai.* It could not be helped.

Dr. Fujii had not only brought out his chair but her black medical bag that reminded him of a prop in that old medical television show *Marcus Welby.* Mas's arms were still strong enough to help steer his body into his wheelchair without his doctor's help. More than six decades of gardening in the hot Southern California sun had gifted him that much. He was also able to get his loafers onto the footrests by himself, another physical accomplishment. Perhaps that was a sign that today, the 75th anniversary of the first atomic bombing, might be a surprisingly good day.

Dr. Fujii pushed Mas along the concrete path to the small building, which was essentially a house, a bungalow like the others next to it. The only thing that seemed to distinguish its purpose was a rock garden that bordered the house. Placed amidst the sea of smooth stones were three *jizo,* simple carved statues with infantile round, bald heads and closed eyes. Dressed in little red aprons and knit hats, the *jizo,* the protectors of dead children, traveled in the spirit world where the living parents of the deceased could not.

The door of the house temple was open and a Japanese man, his head as bald as the *jizo*'s, bowed in the doorway. He was wearing a black robe with a woven purple sash around his neck and Mas presumed that this was the minister. "Dr. Fujii, it's so good of you to come in such heat," he said.

Dr. Fujii bowed from the bottom of the steps. *Chikusho,* Mas cursed in his mind. *Again, no ramps.*

"*Sensei,* this is Arai-*san,* the *hibakusha."*

"Maybe the last one," Mas replied in Japanese. The last atomic bomb survivor, at least maybe the oldest one in California.

He meant it as a semijoke, but the minister didn't laugh. He instead bowed, awkwardly flashing a quick smile before murmuring to himself. He assisted in pulling Mas's chair up the two steps. Mas felt as though he was a sack of potatoes being carried in a wheelbarrow.

Once in the building, Mas saw the living room had been transformed into an intimate sanctuary. Since they were early, the three rows of padded chairs, maybe five in each row, were all empty. A Butsudan, the Buddhist altar, was up front. It was encased in a black lacquer box, its doors open to reveal an ornate gold interior. In the middle was a screen with the image of the Buddha. In front of the Butsudan was a long covered table, which held the familiar Hiroshima Peace Flame lantern, a small container of black incense ash, and an incense burner encased in a gold urn.

Mas was wheeled to the front row, where one of the chairs was promptly removed to make room for him. He grimaced. His place was usually in the back row, but with his recent disabled status he often found his broken body on full display. As the minister and Dr. Fujii engaged in some nonsensical small talk, Mas took in the small room. A light blue floor rug had been laid over the hardwood floor. Thick curtains covered the long wood-framed windows. The white walls remained unadorned, giving Mas the impression that he could as well be in an insane asylum instead of a makeshift house of worship.

There was one doorway to the right-hand side that led to a darkened hallway. He then noticed the small handwritten sign in both Japanese and English, TOILET, and an arrow pointing down the hall.

What a peculiar space, Mas thought. This sanctuary must have once been the dining and living room. Usually in old bungalows like this, there would have been access to a kitchen. He assumed that there was a kitchen someplace, perhaps connected to the hallway to the right.

More people entered the room. Mas recognized the photographer of the local Japanese American newspaper, a burly Mexican man named Mario. He entered with a young Asian woman wearing a T-shirt with the message, No More Nukes. Two other chairs in the front row had been taken away to make room for two more wheelchairs.

"Arai-*san*, it is so good to see you again." An elderly Japanese woman with an unruly bush of hair stood in front of Mas. Her cheeks were sunken and gray. She did not look well.

He couldn't remember the woman's name, but he recalled her story. She had been in her mother's belly when the bomb fell. She was Dr. Fujii's longtime patient — perhaps a distant relative.

"Miiki," she said, her surname, and Mas appreciated the reminder.

He lowered his head and managed the best bow he could sitting down.

"Mom." A woman who might have been his daughter's age, in her fifties, addressed Miiki-*san*. This woman, however, didn't have a middle-aged paunch. She was all skin and bones. A walking skeleton. Mas didn't want to jump to conclusions, but there was something about her that he'd seen before.

Mas had known addicts in his day. Those who were strung out on *hiropon,* heroin, during the Occupation, and also more recently the children of his close friends, who had succumbed to the easy relief from psychic pain. Mas himself was not into relief. If he chased after relief, that would be admitting that he was in pain.

Miiki-*san* didn't seem happy to see her daughter, but she still managed to introduce her to Mas. "Arai-*san,* this is my daughter, Stacie."

He again bowed toward the woman, but Stacie didn't seem interested in making Mas's acquaintance. Instead, her attention was focused on getting her mother situated in a chair in between two others in wheelchairs in the front row.

"Stacie." Dr. Fujii approached, and Mas couldn't help but notice that the daughter's jaw immediately tightened.

"Hello, *Obasan,*" she said. *Obasan* was an honorific that could mean aunt, but as far

486

as Mas knew, the two were not closely related. Dr. Fujii was originally from Hiroshima before making her home and practice in Los Angeles. She might be in her early sixties, barely that much older than the emaciated Stacie. Dr. Fujii was obviously a respected figure in Miiki-*san*'s family circle.

The priest sat on a stool next to the open Butsudan, a sign that the ceremony would start. Stacie took the seat next to Mas. Another man in a wheelchair sat on her other side.

The chanting commenced. Because of Genessee, Mas had converted to Christianity, but Buddhism and a bit of what he referred to as Mother Nature were still in his blood. The smell of incense transported him to a lonely space in his mind, where he ran barefoot on the tatami floors of his childhood home in Hiroshima.

An usher directed people, starting with those in the back row, to offer incense. They went up, one after another, bowing in front of the altar, taking a pinch of incense from a round container, dropping it into the burner, and bowing again.

Finally it was Mas's row. The first one was a woman in a fancy motorized wheelchair that she operated with controls on the machine's arm. She wore a wide-brimmed hat, sunglasses, and gloves, which was unusual for a Japanese woman inside of a Buddhist temple, but to each her own. Mas could not see her well enough to judge her age, but he wondered if she might be a fellow *hibakusha.* Going up with a large pocketbook in her lap, she clutched at a large handkerchief as big as a napkin. In Mas's opinion, these kinds of memorials attracted the most dramatic individuals.

Miiki-*san* was next. She bowed deeply in front of the altar and the Peace Flame lantern. She brought her *ojuzu,* her Buddhist rosary, with her. She seemed especially touched by today's proceedings, the 75th anniversary of the bombing of Hiroshima. Was that a tear running down her wrinkled face? Mas could have sworn that he saw her gnarled hands trembling as she pinched a large dab of the incense and then released it into the urn.

Next was the man in a wheelchair. He wore a newsboy cap and also gloves, in spite of the August heat. He even had a blanket on his lap. Miiki-*san*'s daughter, Stacie, got up to wheel the man to the table, and Mas wondered how they knew each other. After they exchanged words and readjusted his blanket a number of times, they offered incense together.

Dr. Fujii got up from the second row to push Mas to the Peace Flame. The lantern itself was a single gold cylinder with a scalloped top reminiscent of the petals of the lotus blossom. It was extraordinary that it still flickered light after all these decades. It wasn't from 1945, but the 1960s, when the Peace Park in Hiroshima had been constructed. That was still something. Mas went to pinch some incense, but the container had been pushed back — it was almost hidden behind the Peace Lantern — and he could not reach it. Dr. Fujii, without expression again, calmly pulled the bowl closer to Mas. He pinched and then threw the powder into the burner. That's where such memories of horror should go — into the incinerator.

After they returned to their places, the minister began to speak. He spoke in both English and Japanese, and Mas, who usually tuned out when moments became too somber, could barely follow what he was saying in either language. Something about they must pray for peace and never forget.

While the minister continued, a strange wind blew into that tiny room and Mas, his eyes on the eternal flame, watched it as it flickered in and out. He pointed at it with his grizzled index finger, shaped like a dying branch, attempting to alert the others about the dying light.

There was a commotion at his side, and a scream.

"Please, someone help my mother!"

Mrs. Miiki had collapsed onto the floor.

Dr. Fujii quickly came to her assistance with her black medical bag. "Call 911!" she called out. As the minister pulled a cell phone from his robe and began tapping on the screen, she added, "And please give me a little privacy with my patient."

Those in the front, aside from Mas, moved quickly away. He watched as Dr. Fujii removed a stethoscope from her black bag and began to check her patient's heartbeat. She put on a pair of gloves, then seemed to hold something underneath Mrs. Miiki's nose. Did Mrs. Miiki's body heave slightly? Mas couldn't trust what he was seeing.

Finally Dr. Fujii rose. "Miiki-*san* is dead. No one leave!" She said it with such authority that no one dared disobey.

The crowd was in a state of disbelief and a murmur circled the small room, escalating into actual words: "What?"

"Nani?"

"I can't believe it."

"She was standing right in front of us a few seconds ago."

Dr. Fujii quickly peeled off her gloves and put them in a plastic bag that was returned into her black bag. She seemed surprised to find Mas beside her, and she quickly wheeled him away toward the back row, where everyone else had congregated.

"Mr. Mario, please photograph the body."

The photographer first hesitated; he obviously did not come here to record a corpse, but he reluctantly snapped the shutter of his camera, barely looking at his subject.

"We will wait until the police come," Dr. Fujii said.

The small crowd was too traumatized to make a fuss. The daughter's reaction was odd. She seemed shocked, as she well should. But she didn't seem bereaved. She sneaked a glance at the man in the newsboy cap; he responded by awkwardly turning his head toward the other direction. Mas watched the other stranger in her motorized wheelchair. She hadn't snapped her purse shut, and it had come open to reveal that it was completely empty. *How curious,* thought Mas.

The man wearing the cap was becoming extremely agitated. "I need to get out of here," he murmured. Stacie bent down, whispered in his ear and rolled him toward the TOILET sign.

"I needsu to go to bathroom," Mas announced in English, loud enough for Mario to hear. He gestured toward the hallway.

The photographer responded accordingly and pushed Mas to the closed bathroom door.

Loud voices began to sound from the bathroom. Were the couple fighting?

Mario frowned and bent his head toward the door. Obviously his busybody journalistic instincts were kicking in.

The door swung open. The man was the first to run out, abandoning his wheelchair, followed by Stacie, who was spitting out a string of obscenities.

Mas saw the blanket on the tile floor covered in some kind of dusty ash, which looked like incense. In fact, the incense container lay in the corner. But hadn't Mas himself offered incense from that same container, the one beside the Peace Flame lantern? The photographer was now in full paparazzi mode and furiously snapping pictures.

"You two get out of there." Dr. Fujii chased Mario away and swung Mas's wheelchair away from the bathroom door.

When they reentered the sanctuary, the paramedics and police had arrived. A woman and man in blue jumpsuits and white masks were checking Mrs. Miiki's prostrate body, while Stacie and her male companion were yelling and were being subdued by police officers. The crowd was told to evacuate the building and wait in the front yard.

Eventually Stacie and the man, their wrists secured in plastic ties, were taken out of the building by police escorts and placed in black-and-white squad cars. By this time three fire trucks, a hazardous waste unit vehicle, and coroner's van were parked outside the humble temple, while a couple of bicycle cops stood by the *jizo* statues. This anniversary had turned into an Armageddon.

"Do you think it's sarin?" Mas overheard the no-nukes girl ask Mario.

"You got me." Mario looked sick to his stomach as he told her he'd called in the story to his editor, who was attempting to get more details from the LAPD watch commander.

Mas himself wasn't feeling too good. Had the daughter intentionally killed her mother, with some kind of toxin? For what purpose? It probably involved money, and perhaps money to feed her drug habit.

How did they get the poison into Miiki-*san*'s body? Mas pictured the incense container on the floor of the bathroom. Stacie had been the one who had strategically placed her mother in a seat in between the two in wheelchairs. That had been no accident.

The woman in the wide-brimmed hat had steered her wheelchair to the far end of the walkway, near the sidewalk. As Mas watched, she seemed farther and farther down, as if she was making a very slow and discreet getaway.

"Police!" Mas was surprised at the volume of his voice. He didn't think that he could yell that loud. "Watch her." He again pointed, the second time today.

A female bicycle cop pedaled toward the woman in the wheelchair, who, in response, activated the control's acceleration mode. The broken sidewalk barred her fast exit and in fact the wheels skipped and bounced, leaving her literally stuck in a concrete hole. She must have really been disabled as she didn't get up to run like Stacie's male partner. She was soon surrounded by a handful of uniformed officers.

Mas waited in the walkway underneath the shade of the porch roof by the stone *jizo* for what seemed like hours. He did a staredown with one *jizo* that was dressed not only in an apron and knit cap, but also a scarf. Staring was futile, of course, as the *jizo*'s eyes were already closed.

During the course of the afternoon, he overheard a number of theories of how the murder had been committed. Mas had a good idea which one was correct. The woman in the big hat had carried the drug in an identical incense pot — standard issue among Buddhist temples — inside her large pocketbook and set it down when she was supposed to be offering incense. She pushed the other pot farther in back of the lantern. After Mrs. Miiki exposed her skin to the drug in the poisoned incense, her daughter and coconspirator went up and hid the incense pot underneath his blanket in the wheelchair. It was indeed a ridiculous plan that only individuals with clouded and warped thinking could come up with.

The crowd thinned out as the afternoon wore on. The coroner's staff carried Mrs. Miiki's covered body on a gurney into their van. Trudging in rubber boots, the masked firefighters and hazmat specialists left the premises with covered containers. Mario, the photographer, eventually went to make his deadline.

Soon it was indeed just Mas and the *jizo* out front of the temple. He felt like a fool, but there was no one breathing to hear his complaint.

Finally the minister and Dr. Fujii appeared from the back through the driveway. The minister offered a bottle of water to Mas, which he accepted even though it was room temperature.

"Miiki-*san* recently kicked Stacie out of the house," the doctor was telling the minister. "She staged this so she could have access to her mother's estate as soon as possible."

"What a complicated scheme." The minister dabbed at some beads of sweat on his forehead.

Finally it was time for Dr. Fujii and Mas to clear the crime scene. The minister helped the doctor fold Mas's wheelchair and place it and the medical bag in the truck.

Mas sat quietly in the passenger seat. Once Dr. Fujii had gotten into the car and closed the door, he told her, "I knowsu you killed her. I saw you take sumptin' out from your black bag and put it in Miiki-*san*'s nose."

Dr. Fujii stared out the front windshield. "Miiki-*san* found some notes in her daughter's room about this convoluted plot to kill her and get the house before she gave it all away. The man in the wheelchair is Stacie's boyfriend. Both very troubled."

"And the lady in the hat?"

"I don't know where they found her, but I'm sure that she was well compensated. Miiki-*san* didn't think that they would be able to successfully carry it off."

Mas didn't understand.

"She was dying of pancreatic cancer. It was only a matter of weeks. She was regularly giving large donations to medical research on radiation exposure, but her daughter was contesting the gifts, saying that Miiki-*san* had temporarily lost her mind. Miiki-*san* was in such distress and so much pain. She wanted her assets to go to charity and not be in limbo in probate courts. This morning she transferred the deed to her house to UCLA Medical Center. She was ready to go, and I didn't want Stacie and her partner to abuse her in any way once they found out." Dr. Fujii took out a pair of sunglasses and replaced her regular glasses with them. "So I brought some carfentanil with me just in case they didn't get the dosage right. It's the same substance that they brought over in the incense holder."

"Maybe police coulda have done sumptin'."

"What? I'm sure that they would have just laughed at me if I told Miiki-*san*'s story. I told her not to come. She's been a recluse, anyway. But she was insistent.

"She was tired. She wanted to let go of life. And she wanted to do it on the 75th anniversary of the Bomb. In honor of what her mother had gone through. How could I put a stop to it? This was Miiki-*san*'s desire."

"Why'zu did you bring me?"

"Because I knew that you would figure it out. You would be the one who would have suspected the daughter and solved the case. And I guess you did more than I expected."

Dr. Fujii turned the key in the ignition. "Ready to visit with Genessee, Arai-*san*? I can drop you off at the care facility."

Mas nodded. The doctor knew that he wouldn't say anything. Because what would happen if he did? She would be arrested and Genessee would be panicked without her trusted medical counsel. There was no doubt in Mas's mind that his wife would become even more paranoid than she already was.

As Dr. Fujii pulled away from the curb, Mas realized that he had forgotten to check on the peace flame. Did it indeed go out, or had that been just his imagination? Just like for Genessee, how many fragments from their past could he collect, like scooping out

498

seaweed from the sea with a net? And how much would remain on the bottom, in the darkness, never to be retrieved again.

30 AND OUT

BY DOUG ALLYN

The sign on the door read Sergeant Charles Marx, Major Crimes. I raised my fist to knock, then realized the guy at the desk wasn't just resting his eyes. He was totally out, slouched in his chair, his grubby Nikes up on his desk, baseball cap tipped down over his eyes, snoring softly. Looked like a class C wrestling coach after a losing season. Edging in quietly, I eased down into the chair facing his desk. When I glanced up, his eyes were locked on mine like lasers.

"Can I help you?"

"I'm Jax LaDart, Sergeant Marx. Your FNG."

He frowned at that, then nodded. "The fuckin' new guy?" he said, massaging his eyelids with his fingertips. "Ah, right. You're the homeboy the chief hired, straight out of the army. I was reading your record. It put me to sleep." He spun the Dell laptop on his desk to show me the screen. "According to the Military Police, you've closed a lot of felony cases overseas, but the details are mostly redacted, blacked out."

"The army'd classify 'Three Blind Mice' if they could. You don't remember me, do you? Jackson LaDart?"

He glanced up at me again, looking me over more carefully this time. Not a comfortable experience. I was in my usual leather jacket and jeans. Not dressed to impress.

"Nah, sorry, I got nothin'. Did I bust you for something?"

"No, but you could have. When I was fourteen, you had me for grand theft auto."

"No kidding?" he said, curious now. "What happened?"

"My cousin and I were working after hours at the Shell station by the freeway, tuning up an old junker Norton motorcycle. Managed to get it running, took it out for a test drive. We made it a few miles, then a tire blew and we cracked it up."

He nodded, didn't comment.

"I banged my face up pretty seriously," I said, jerking a thumb toward an old scar on my forehead. "I'm bleeding like a stuck pig, we had no phone. My cousin runs to the nearest house. Nobody's home, but a pickup in the yard had keys in it, so Jimmy piled me in, drove me into Samaritan Hospital, pedal to the metal. You spotted us on the road, chased us the last few miles with lights and sirens. But at the hospital, you took one look at my face, hustled me inside, and got me some help." I shook my head, remembering.

"Thing is, Jimmy and I were only fourteen, neither of us had a license yet, and we'd wrecked a bike and stolen a truck. You could've come down hard on us, but you stood up for us instead. When the pickup's owner came stomping in, yelling he wanted our asses arrested, you took him outside, straightened him out."

"Curly Beauchamp." Charlie nodded slowly. "I remember now. He was half in the bag, all bent out of shape about you two borrowing his piece-of-shit ride. Needed an attitude adjustment, is all. No big thing."

"It was to us."

"I was new to the badge back then," he said with a shrug. "Young and dumb and full of myself. Threw my weight around a lot. Till I learned not to."

"How do you mean?"

"What's that rule about unintended consequences? Something about butterflies?"

"Butterfly Principle," I said. "A butterfly in China flaps its wings, and Hawaii gets a hurricane."

"Except butterflies don't know any better. Cops are supposed to be smarter, but sometimes we're not. That's what the law's for. Draws hard, clear lines, the ones we don't cross."

"You crossed a line for me back then. If you hadn't, maybe I'd be talking to you from a cage."

"And the world might be a better place."

We both smiled at that. He was probably right. But his grin morphed into a frown as he cocked his head, listening to the loud music wafting up from the street. Rock and roll at concert volume. "Sweet Home Alabama." Lynyrd Skynyrd.

Easing stiffly out of his chair, Charlie moved to the tall window behind his desk and cracked the blinds. I stood at his shoulder, looking down on Valhalla's Main Street, three stories below. Northern Michigan in mid-December. Snow and sleet mixed, stinging like BB pellets in the winter wind.

Down on the street, a funeral cortege was crawling past, a flatbed truck in the lead, carrying a small coffin, escorted by a long queue of pickups and motorcycles, revving their engines, adding to the din of Skynyrd blasting from the flatbed's sound system.

Battle flags were flapping wildly in the wind, some trucks flying Old Glory, others flying red rebel flags, the Stars and Bars. The flatbed was flying both, full-size banners at the head of the small casket.

"What's all that?" I asked.

"What we were talking about," Charlie said. "How bad things can wind up when you cross a line."

"In a funeral, you mean?"

He nodded without speaking, which was answer enough.

Eyeing the long cortege, I noticed an old man on the flatbed staring up at me. He was maybe sixty, salt-and-pepper beard, wrinkled black suit from Goodwill. I wondered if he was somebody I knew from back in the day. I tilted the blinds for a better look, but the truck was already passing out of our sight.

"Crossing a line can definitely go sideways," I conceded. "But sometimes bending a rule or two is the only way to get a bad guy into a cage. Or in the dirt."

"What was your date of separation, La-Dart?"

"A few weeks ago."

"From where?"

"Afghanistan. Why?"

"You're back in the world now, troop, and

507

here we call 'em cells, not cages. And dirt naps —"

"Strictly hyperbole, Sarge," I said. "Just kidding."

"Right," he said, eyeing me doubtfully. Because I wasn't kidding. And we both knew it. I'd come home from a war without rules, where I learned to live by my own. He let it pass.

"Chief Kaz tells me you grew up out in the county."

"I'm a woodsmoke kid." I nodded. "Raised in the deer woods."

"Still know your way around out there?"

"Some, sure, but nobody knows it all. There's eighty thousand acres of state land spread over the five counties, Sarge. Daniel Boone could get lost."

"Which is why our brother officers in the DEA have asked us for a guide. They got a call on their tip line about a motor home parked deep on state land. Their GPS coordinates put it somewhere inside this red circle, but they've got no idea how to get there."

He tapped a computer key, then swiveled his laptop to face me again.

I leaned in, scanning the screen. It took me a moment, but then I recognized a few landmarks. "Their circle's just beyond the north fork of the Black. It's swampy ground, but there's an old logging road just east of it. That road is the only way an RV could make it in. I can get them there."

"Won't be easy. The DEA strike team will be mostly newbies, recruits fresh out of Quantico. We'll have our hands full with 'em."

" 'We'? You're going?"

"Why wouldn't I?"

"The chief said you're short. Almost out the door."

"Eight days to my anniversary," he said with a broad grin. "Thirty and out. Thirty years from the day I signed on the Valhalla force as a rook."

"It'll be rough going out there, sir, and I owe you one. Why not relax, put your feet up for once. Let me handle it."

"You think I'm ready for a rocking chair, LaDart? You're the FNG here, not me."

"I didn't mean it that way."

"Then let's get something straight. A couple weeks back, I got called to the Samaritan Hospital emergency room. Three kids had been dumped off in their driveway, overdosed on meth. They were foaming at the mouth, like *dogs*! *High school* kids! So if the DEA thinks some lab rat's cooking crank on our turf, I'm all over it. If that's okay with you? FNG Sergeant LaDart?"

"Absolutely, boss." I raised my hands in mock surrender. "It's totally fine by me."

But it wasn't totally fine. The raid was the diametric freaking opposite of fine. Charlie and I met up with the DEA crew at first light, at an abandoned motel parking lot just off the interstate. Charlie knew the Agent-in-Charge, Ken Tanaka, but the others were green kids, decked out in full battle rattle, body armor and helmets, M4 automatic weapons, night vision gear clipped to their helmets like snorkels. Looked like fucking starship troopers. They even brought a dope dog along, a black-faced Belgian Malinois bitch half again the size of a German shepherd. She looked more wolf than dog, but she definitely seemed to know her business — cool, calm, and collected. Which was a lot more than I could say for her crew. The young agents were practically jumping out of their skins with excitement, first raid, first action. I was getting a very bad feeling about this.

We divided up into two squads, then scrambled into a pair of camouflaged Humvees to head into the back country. As the guide, I was riding shotgun in the lead vehicle with the DEA boss, Agent Ken

Tanaka at the wheel, a hard-eyed oil drum of a warrior, shaved skull, Fu Manchu. Ken would have looked at home on a steppe pony, riding to war beside Genghis Khan.

Only the Belgian dog was totally calm, alert, and aware, but not a bit hinky. Like she'd done this a hundred times before. Which made me wonder about her.

There was no time to quiz her handler about her history, though. The logging road twisted through the hill country like a rattler with a broken back. We stayed with it until we were roughly a half mile from the DEA's red ring. Then I called a halt to dismount. Our target should be straight ahead, at the end of the road, but we were in a cedar swamp now. If the meth cooks heard us coming and scattered into the woods, we'd be chasing them all damned day. We needed to locate the lab, encircle it, then tighten the noose.

Good luck with that.

Out of the vehicles, we formed a long firing line, stringing the young DEA agents out for seventy meters on both sides of the road, with Charlie and me holding down the center. It's a Tactics 101 maneuver, should have been easy, but the line has to stay absolutely straight to give everyone a clear field of fire.

No chance. A hundred meters along, we had to stop to realign, then twice more as we made our way through the snowy swamp. The young agents were unconsciously edging ahead, eager to put first eyes on the target. Unfortunately, they were also increasing their chances of getting their heads blown off by their own crew. There's no such thing as friendly fire.

After our second stop to realign, I was seriously wishing I could turn the lot of 'em into dogs. The Malinois maintained her position perfectly, always aligned with the center, her eyes front, sniffing the icy breeze —

"Contact!" one of the agents yelled. "Ten o'clock, straight ahead!"

He was right! A hundred meters down the road, a battered Coachmen motor home had been pulled off the road into the trees. It was well hidden, crudely camouflaged with rattle-can paint, then covered with brush.

Even at this distance, we could smell the rank bite of crystal meth on the wind. For the young agents, it was red meat thrown to a pack of wolves.

Battle tactics required us to extend our line, then surround the motor home. Instead, the agent on the far end totally blew off his training and headed for the RV at a dead run. A few others raced after him, joining in the chase. Only the rough country and the foot or so of snow on the ground slowed their rush —

And saved their lives.

I dropped to my belly on the road, pulling my weapon, screaming "Down, down, down! Take cover!" into my lapel mike. Tanaka and Charlie Marx dropped instantly, but the younger agents froze in confusion, uncertain as to *why* I was warning them.

For a split second, I wasn't sure why I was yelling either, then it registered. The Belgian! When we'd first smelled the meth, the dog had frozen in place, her tail twitching slowly, alerting us . . .

But then she suddenly dropped to her belly, which sent a far more serious signal. Explosives! IED!

WHAM!

A massive blast smashed the motor home into flaming splinters, lifting it off its frame, raining fiery debris down around us like a hailstorm from hell! I rose to my knees, dazed, glancing wildly around, trying to make sense of what the hell just happened.

Most of the agents were down, flattened by the blast, but a few were already collecting themselves. Thanks to the Belgian, we were still far enough out that the explosion had roughed us up, but no one seemed to be badly hurt. No one was screaming for a medic or —

A shattered door in the motor home burst outward as a guy came hurtling through it, sprawling in the snow, shrieking, his face a bloody shambles, his clothing on fire. Scrambling to his feet, he was off to the races, trying to outrun the flames burning through his clothes.

"Red light! Red light!" Tanaka shouted. "Hold your fire!"

But the dog handler had lost his leash, and the Belgian instantly gave chase, racing after the runner like a rocket. And after her warning before the blast, I knew what she was, knew what she'd do if she caught him and pulled him down.

She'd tear him apart!

I was up and running, knowing I was already too late. She'd be on him in an instant —

"Hond!" I shouted after her. *"Auf! Auf!"*

The Belgian dropped like she'd been shot. Down flat on her belly, but still taut as a drawn bow, teeth bared in a silent snarl, ready to resume her attack on command, her eyes were locked on the runner like rifle sights. I tackled him a few steps later, holding him down as he thrashed around in the snow, which actually helped smother the flames.

Tanaka and Charlie caught up and joined in, grabbing fistfuls of snow, smearing it all over the kid. And he was a kid, a freakin' teenager, bleeding from a half-dozen cuts, and clearly in shock. I tried a few questions, but he could barely remember his own name. Had no idea why the RV had been blown to hell. One of Tanaka's newbie DEA agents had EMT training, and took over for us, rendering first aid. The Belgian was still crouched, watching. I picked up her leash, but she didn't even look up, totally focused on the kid. One wrong move and he'd be gone.

Her handler trotted up, a fresh-faced redhead, Kelly on his name tag. He reached for the leash, but I held on to it.

"Where'd this dog come from?"

Kelly glanced a question at Tanaka. "Better tell him," Ken said.

"Overseas," Kelly admitted. "My brother was her handler in the 'Stan. Worked with her for two tours, but he got orders to Iraq and she's maxed out agewise. They were gonna put her down."

"Do you know why?" I asked.

"Her age —"

"— has squat to do with it," I snapped. "She's a war dog, Kelly. I've worked with Belgians, attack dogs, trackers, bomb sniffers. Once they've tasted blood? Chewed up an intruder or tackled a runner? They change, up here," I said, tapping my temple. "After that, they're as dangerous as a brick of C-4. When their handlers rotate back to the States, their dogs stay behind. They retrain with new handlers and go straight back to the war. Over and over, until we get too old or too crazy."

"We?" Kelly echoed.

"It's a running joke over there. Guys who pull multiple tours? Like me? We're called Belgians, too. This dog can't be in the field here, Kelly. I'm taking her."

"The hell you are!"

"Jax is right," Charlie said, stepping between us. "Look at her, son. One wrong word and she'd tear that kid's throat out before you could —"

A supersonic crack split the air, opening a fist-size wound in Charlie's throat, lifting him off his feet, slamming him to the ground.

"Down, down!" Tanaka roared as I crawled on top of Charlie, covering him with my body as the rifle report echoed over us, instantly drowned out by the thunder of return fire as the young agents opened up, loosing a hail of lead toward the tree line, whacking down branches, chewing up brush. In the winter wind, they couldn't spot the muzzle blast or gun smoke, had no idea what they were shooting at.

But maybe it had some effect. No more shots came.

Kneeling beside Charlie, I put pressure on the wound, but I could feel the disconnect from his spine, an unnatural flexing, and read his empty stare. He was dying before my eyes.

"Help me!" I roared at the EMT. "We've gotta get him out of here!"

Our flying column roared into Valhalla Samaritan like the invasion of Iraq. We'd called for an ambulance, but Charlie couldn't wait for it. We loaded him aboard the lead Humvee and tore out of the forest, leaving the young agents to sort through the wreckage and hunt for the shooter.

At the hospital, the emergency team quickly loaded Charlie onto a gurney and rolled him away. Tanaka and I found a bench in a waiting room, but neither of us had much to say, both of us trying to sort out what the hell just happened.

We weren't the only ones asking. A State

Police team showed up a few minutes later. Officer-involved shootings are always investigated by another department, but this didn't feel like standard procedure to me. Two uniformed Staties quickly led Tanaka away to question us separately.

I stayed in the waiting room with two detectives in civvies: a heavyweight sergeant, Haskey, square and gray as a cement block with an attitude to match, and his boss, Lieutenant Sharon Keenan. Haskey's tweed jacket was JCPenney off-the-rack. Keenan was in black slacks, black jacket, black turtleneck. Blonde, no makeup, her hair cropped short as a boy's. Haskey had a mouse under his right eye. It looked fresh.

I gave them a quick briefing on what happened, our approach, the blast, the kid running out, then Charlie's shooting.

"So, right after the blast, you, Agent Tanaka, and Sergeant Marx were bunched up?" Haskey asked. "Not too smart. Made a pretty sweet target for the meth cookers."

"I'm not sure it was them. The RV was already blown, the shot came from the other direction and it was definitely a long one. Charlie was already falling when I heard the report. The shooter had to be seven or eight hundred meters out. Helluva long ways for a head shot."

"Actually, the round struck Sergeant Marx in the throat," Keenan said.

"Think center mass, Lieutenant. Normally, you zero in on the heart, but Charlie was wearing a vest. The shooter moved his bull's-eye up to the bridge of his nose and only missed by a few inches. I think he hit what he was shooting at."

"Why cap Charlie?" Haskey asked. "He's at thirty and out, about to retire and everybody knows it. There was even a write-up in the paper about it. If somebody wanted him gone, they only had to wait a few days. But you? You're brand-new on the job when the DEA tip line gets a call about a lab they need your help to find? Did you make that call, LaDart? Or maybe one of your backwoods relatives, trying to make you look good?"

I stared at him. "Me? Where's that coming from?"

"Same place you came from, sport — Afghanistan. Only a trained marksman could make a shot like that. Or maybe a woodsman. Did you make any enemies over there, LaDart? Maybe one who followed you here?"

"You think a vet did this?"

"We've been having a lot of problems with Afghan vets," Keenan put in. "Sergeant

Haskey mixed it up with one last week."

Which explained the eye, and maybe the attitude.

"We're seeing substance abuse, domestic violence, even suicides —"

"I'm aware," I interrupted. "We call it going Belgian, the same as the burned-out war dogs. A vet would have no reason to kill Charlie."

"Maybe he missed by more than a few inches," Haskey said. "Maybe he missed by a couple of feet."

"Missed me, you mean? How long have you been on the job, Haskey?"

"A lot longer than you, sport."

"Maybe that's your problem," I said, standing up. "This is a lazy interrogation, guys. You're asking me questions without doing fieldwork first, ergo, you don't know if I'm lying or not."

"Are you lying to us, Sergeant LaDart?" Keenan asked.

"Lady, somebody just capped the guy who saved my life, years ago. I want him a lot more than you do."

"This is a State Police investigation, LaDart," Haskey said. "Stay away from it."

"I know the rules, guys. If I accidentally trip over anything useful, you'll be the first to know. But right now, unless I'm under

arrest? I need to get some air before somebody gets his other eye blackened."

I half expected an argument, but they let
me go. No choice. We all knew they had no
cause to hold me.

Out in the corridor, I took the stairs, two
at a time, up to the burned cooker's room.

Agent Kelly was on guard out in the hall.
"Any news about Charlie?" I asked.

"In surgery, last I heard, Sarge."

"How's the kid doing?"

"Still unconscious. He was a mess before
he got burned. Meth head, bad skin, rotten
teeth. He'll be a zombie in a year."

"Did he talk at all?"

"Nothing coherent. Between the painkill-
ers they gave him for his burns and the bat
shit he's been snorting, I doubt he knows
what year this is."

"Did he say anything about the shooting?"

"No, but I've spoken with the guys who
searched the wreckage of the motor home.
The only weapons they found were sawed-
off shotguns plus a few handguns, strictly
street quality. Mismatched calibers, none
bigger than a nine."

"No long guns? Anything with a scope?"

"Nah. Tanaka thinks these punks are
downstate bangers, Sarge, learned to shoot
by watching TV. They don't aim, they pose.

Probably couldn't hit a barn from the inside."

"Somebody did," I said. "Last question. Where's your dog, Kelly?"

She was down in the parking lot in one of the Humvees, patiently waiting for her next assignment. I gave her some water from the Hummer's canteen, then sat beside her, stroking her great, scarred head as I tried to sort everything out — the raid, the dog, Charlie's shooting, and the Staties' focus on vets.

Hell, maybe they were right. Maybe we all do come home a little crazy. Trying to make sense out of the 'Stan could definitely send you around the bend.

Maybe they should lace our Alpo with arsenic like they'd do to this lady — Damn.

That's exactly what would happen if they found out she was here. Kelly's brother would get jammed up over it, and Kelly, too. And the Belgian would definitely be put down. Poisoned, or just shot in the head. And thank you for your service, ma'am.

To hell with this. I'd lost enough friends for one day.

Firing up the Humvee, I headed south out of Valhalla, into the Black River hills, eighty thousand acres of rough country, an area bigger than most nations in the U.N. It was a good fifty-minute run, and I needed four-wheel drive to make the last ten miles after the gravel road I was following petered out to a dirt track.

The old farmhouse sat atop a long rise, with a magnificent view of the rolling forest on all sides. From the front porch, Fifi Dumont can watch the morning sun rise, and then see it set again at the end of the day. He can also see anyone approaching a good half hour before they pull into his yard.

He was waiting for me on his porch, a grizzled beer barrel of a woodsman in a checked flannel shirt, cork boots, and hard eyes. He had a long rifle on his lap, an old '95 Marlin, I think. Used to be his dad's.

"Hey, Feef," I said, climbing out of the Humvee. "Long time."

"Jax? What the hell, I thought you was the law."

"I am, bro, but I'm strictly local. Are you and your brothers still growing high grade weed out in the bush?"

"Who's askin'? My high school buddy or Five Oh?"

"Your old bud. You're not in my jurisdiction out here, anyway. Do you still fence in your grows?"

"Some. Chain link keeps the deer off the reefer, but it don't stop the meth heads. They cut their way in to rip us off now and again. Why?"

"I brought a present for you. *Hond! Volg rechts!*"

The Belgian sprang out of the Humvee and immediately took up a position beside me. Eyeing Fifi hungrily. His eyes went wide as saucers.

"What the hell is that?" he asked uneasily. "Cross-wolf?"

"No," I said. "She's the answer to your prayers."

I explained exactly what the Belgian Malinois was, and that I'd brought her here because woodsmoke boys treat their dogs like family. He could turn her loose inside his enclosures, and she'd guard his crops with her life, running free in the forest while she did her duty. It wasn't a perfect solution, but it was the best I could do.

I gave him a list of commands in Dutch, the language she was trained in, and we practiced his pronunciation until the dog clearly understood him. And at the end of things, I asked for a favor in return.

"You know Charlie Marx, right, Feef?"

"I heard he got shot," Fifi nodded. "It was on the radio. How is he?"

"Bad. Maybe gone by now. Whoever capped him did it from seven hundred yards out. I've been away awhile. Who could make a shot like that?"

"I could." He shrugged. "You could. Hell, half the woodsmoke kids we grew up with could do it."

"But why? Charlie was at his thirty and out, almost done being a cop."

"Don't know why it would happen now," Fifi said. "Maybe years ago, but not no more."

"How do you mean?"

"Back in the day, Marx had a rep for roughhouse. If he busted you for beating on your wife or abusing a kid, you might trip and fall a few times on your way to jail. Or get your head slammed in a door."

"Charlie told me a bust went bad," I said. "I need a name."

He chewed that over a minute, then shrugged. "Broussard," he said. "Or maybe Guthrie."

"Who?" The names meant nothing to me.

"There's a junkyard out on 41, Guthrie's Auto Salvage?"

I shook my head.

"I think the Guthries moved up here around the time you left for the army, ten years ago or so. Bunch of 'em, rednecks from Alabama. Came up to Detroit to work in the auto plants years back, but when the shops closed, they moved up here, to the backwoods. Fit right in. Outside of town, the county's pretty redneck."

"Woodsmoke," I said, shaking my head.

"What's the difference?"

"Not much," I admitted. "Where does Charlie come in?"

"One of the Guthrie girls, Janiva? Gets in a family way with Leon Broussard. Wasn't married, but they're livin' together. But when Janiva gets knocked up, Leon starts knockin' her around. About the third time Charlie gets called out to their place, he beats the livin' hell out of Leon, kicked his drunk ass across his front yard like a dog, I heard."

"Sounds like he had it coming."

"Sure enough. But after Charlie leaves, Leon staggers into the house, grabs a shotgun and paints the kitchen with his brains."

"Damn," I said.

"Yeah. Naturally, Janiva blames Charlie for it. It's all his fault her drunken boyfriend offs himself because he got his butt kicked. She's blamin' Charlie while she's still wearin' the shiner Leon give her."

"What happened?"

"There was some kinda investigation. Charlie got suspended a week, that was it. But he definitely calmed down after that. Didn't go on the muscle so much."

"What about the 'Bama rednecks? How'd they take it?"

"The Guthries? No problem, far as I know. Leon wasn't family, just Janiva's boyfriend, and a bad one at that. Left 'em a little something to remember him by. A kid, a boy. Never had no luck with him neither."

"Why?"

"He passed away last week. Ten years old. Cancer. Heard his funeral cortege was a mile long. Damn shame."

"Funeral," I echoed, remembering. "Flatbed truck in front, long line of pickups, a lot of rebel flags?"

"That's them Guthries. You know 'em?"

"No, I just saw it pass," I said. "From Charlie's office."

I thanked Fifi for the info, warned him again about the lady Belgian, and headed back to town, still chewing over what he'd told me.

Fifi was right. Whatever happened was over and done with way back when. No reason for it to crop up now, years later.

And it wasn't my problem, anyway. It was a State Police case, they'd warned me off, and the lines were clear. I'd been an army cop for most of a decade. I knew all about the lines you shouldn't cross.

But Charlie Marx had crossed a line for me once, and maybe saved my life. If I'd taken a fall for grand theft auto at fourteen, God knows where I'd be now.

Maybe dead. Or doing hard time. Not much difference to a backwoods kid.

I knew I should hand over Fifi's information to the Staties, but I decided to check it out first. At this point, it was only hearsay anyway. An old story told by an old friend. Probably nothing to it.

I headed back to the station, but didn't bother to check in. I parked on the street out front instead, waited for a break in traffic, then walked out to the centerline and stood there, looking up. Cars were whipping past on both sides, horns blaring, drivers yelling stuff about my mother.

But it was worth it. Because there was nothing to see.

Looking up from the street, I was standing roughly where I'd seen the flatbed pass with its flags and small coffin. At the time, I thought the old man on the truck was staring up at me, even adjusted the blinds to get a better look at him.

528

But from down here, with the building in sunlight? I couldn't see squat. The windows were completely opaque in the reflected light. So the old guy hadn't been staring at me at all. From here, all he could see would be the blind windows of Charlie's office.

And when Charlie said that crossing the line can end up in a funeral, he didn't mean just any funeral. He meant this one. The boy's. Which made no sense at all. Because Charlie'd quit muscling suspects years ago. And the sod on this kid's grave probably hadn't taken root yet.

Whatever happened between Charlie and the kid's drunken, wife-beating father went down before the boy was born. Why would it crop up again after all this time?

A horn blared behind me, a garbage truck this time. I crossed the street to the station, but didn't get past the front desk. The duty sergeant had two messages for me, one from Tanaka. Charlie was gone. Never regained consciousness.

It wasn't a surprise. Hell, I'd known from the moment I saw the wound. But it still drilled me like a kick in the belly. Which did surprise me. I've lost friends in combat, once saw a best bud get blown in half. I hadn't seen Charlie Marx in years — we weren't really friends, but he'd had a huge impact on my life. Far more than I'd realized until this day.

The second message was from my boss, Chief Kazmarek. The two Staties had more questions for me. I wadded up that message in my fist, tossed it in the trash.

"Damn shame about Charlie," the desk sergeant said. "Only a week from his thirty and out, you know? Crazy."

"It is," I agreed. "And you didn't see me, okay?"

He frowned at that, but only for a moment. "See who?" he asked.

Route 41 leads northwest out of Valhalla, past the hardboard plant and used car lots, definitely the seedier side of town. Guthrie's Auto Salvage was a sprawling junkyard set back from the main road, acres of rusty cars half-hidden behind a galvanized metal fence. Compared to the 'Stan, the yard looked prosperous. They call it vehicle recycling nowadays. Late model wrecks are worth more for parts than the cars cost new. I guessed this yard held two to three thousand units on a hundred acres. Probably worth a million or more. Wrecks they might be, but junk they ain't.

A few cars were parked in front, with a row of rusty wreckers off to one side. The flatbed truck from the funeral was on the far end, still flying its flags, American and rebel. The only thing missing was the bier. And the small casket.

The office/showroom was built like a fortress, concrete block walls, windows narrow as gun slits, a muddy, rutted driveway that stopped at the front door, the end of the line in more ways than one.

Inside, the lighting was dim, overhead fluorescents winking and buzzing. The room was filled with long rows of shelving units piled high with car parts, some rusty, some new, still gleaming with lube. The air was rank with the stench of burned metal and motor oil. A long counter ran the width of the building at the back of the room. A young guy in greasy coveralls was behind it, Latin from the look of him. Jumpy as a cricket on a griddle.

I headed for the counterman, but veered off when something caught my eye. A rifle rack was bolted to the back wall beside a door that opened out to the yard. The rack held a half-dozen long guns, most with scopes. A security chain ran through the weapons' trigger guards, but its padlock was unclasped and the last slot in the rack was empty. A framed display hung beside the rack, and as soon as I saw it, I knew.

It held a long row of medals for expert marksmanship, plus red and yellow combat medals from Vietnam.

The guns in the rack were a serious collection of military sniper rigs. The oldest was a .30-40 Krag that dated from Teddy Roosevelt's charge up San Juan Hill, 1898. Then an '03 Springfield from the War to End All Wars, and a scoped Garand and an M14 from the wars after that. If the logic of the collection held, the missing weapon would be the most modern, a Winchester Model 70 from Vietnam, or maybe an M16. It didn't matter which. Either way, with only my sidearm, I was totally outgunned.

I turned to ask the counterman about the missing weapon, but he'd vanished. I was on my own.

I knew I should call for backup — it was a State Police case now — but I didn't. I wasn't here as Sergeant Jax LaDart, the FNG. I was the kid Charlie Marx stood up for all those years ago.

And however this went down, it wasn't police business anymore. It was personal. I thought about taking one of the rifles in the rack, but the magazines were empty, and I didn't see any ammo at hand. I left them.

Instead, I gently eased open the door to the yard and edged out to face Harland

Guthrie. And if I'd had any remaining doubts, they disappeared.

It was the old man from the funeral flatbed, the one I'd thought was staring at me when he'd looked up at Charlie's office. Same black suit, same wild white hair and beard. Looked like he'd been sleeping in his clothes. His rifle was in much better shape. A Vietnam era Winchester Model 70, a bolt action rifle chambered in 30-06, deadly out to fifteen hundred yards. He was holding it at port arms across his chest, not aimed in my direction, but it didn't have to be. He was leaning against a wrecked Chevy Blazer, maybe sixty meters across the yard from me. If I drew on him, I might get off a round or two, but it would take a miracle for me to score a hit at this distance. Guthrie wouldn't need a miracle. With a scoped Winchester, he could cap me like swatting a fly.

"I know you," he called. "Saw your picture in the paper when you signed on to the force. A war hero, it said."

"We both know better, don't we? The real heroes are buried in Arlington. I just did my job, same as you, back in the day. Vietnam?"

"Two tours," he nodded. "Sniper with the Airborne. More than sixty confirmed kills. You?"

"Afghanistan, the Sulaiman mountains. Nowhere near sixty, but way too many, I think now."

"You'd better figure on doing one more, if you're here for me."

"I'm here for Charlie, Mr. Guthrie. I owe him, big. And I've figured out *what* happened, I think. But not the why of it."

"It ain't complicated. Ten years ago, Charlie Marx got called to my daughter Janiva's place, because her live-in, Leon Broussard, was roughing her up. Marx had been there before, but it was different this time — she was pregnant with Leon's child. I guess Charlie figured Leon had a lesson coming, and roughed him up pretty good. I got no problem with that. I'd have beaten the bastard myself if I'd known. Leon was a drunk, mean as a snake when he had his load on. But Charlie crossed the line. Kicked Leon across his own yard, like a damn dog. But he misjudged how drunk and crazy Leon really was, and after he left . . . ?"

"Leon offed himself, like the psycho asshole he was. And you blame Charlie for that?"

"Not then, I didn't. I figured my Janiva was better off without him. And when her boy was born, Todd? I almost forgot where

534

he came from. Todd was Guthrie to the bone. His mother's son. My blood. None of his dad's. Or so I thought, until two years ago . . ." He looked away, swallowing hard. But the gun never wavered. And my heart sank like a stone, as his meaning, and maybe his intent, sank in.

"The cancer," I said.

"The worst kind," he agreed. "In his bones. Couldn't cut it out, chemo hardly slowed it down, drugs couldn't help much with the pain. Todd's only hope was a bone marrow transplant, but he had a rare blood type, AB negative. Like his father. None of us were a match."

"Even with matching blood types, there's no guarantee Leon would have been a match."

"I know — they told me that. But he could have been. That boy needed a miracle, and he deserved one, but he didn't get it because Charlie Marx wanted to feel like a big man. And he put Todd's last, best hope — his only hope — in an urn on his grandma's mantel."

"Charlie didn't kill your son-in-law, sir."

"He killed my whole damn family! That boy was the last of my blood, last one entitled to bear my name. I'm the last Guthrie now, and I'm going to lay it down a long damn ways from home."

"It doesn't have to be that way —"

"Don't blow smoke at a smoker, son. I don't plan to die in jail. I've killed plenty before, overseas, for my country, same as you. I've thought about that a lot since, same as you, I expect. We killed them on their home ground, in wars that didn't mean spit, in the end. I didn't hate them people, wouldn't take their damned country as a gift, but we dropped 'em anyway, didn't we? They sent us there, and we did what we did. But your Sergeant Marx? He crossed the line, shamed Leon so bad he took his own life, and took away my grandson's last hope. And when I'm suiting up for Todd's funeral, I see this article in the paper, how Charlie's gonna retire on his anniversary, thirty years from the day he signed on."

"Thirty and out." I nodded.

"He's gonna go fishing, maybe sit and rock on his front porch of an afternoon, while the worms are chewin' into my grandson. He done what he done. It was time to pay up for it. Now it's that time again."

"It's not what I want," I said.

"In case you ain't noticed, son, this world don't give a rip what you want —"

And I was off, sprinting straight at him, full tilt, pulling my weapon as I came, trying to close the distance between us, my only hope. Guthrie froze, staring, startled, but only for a moment. Then he shouldered his weapon, snugging it in — to his right shoulder. Right-handed. Harder to swing to his right. I dived to my left, landing hard, then rolling back to my right.

He fired! The slug whistled past, so close it cut a notch in my ear, burning a groove where my head had been a split second before. He racked his Winchester — but I was already returning fire, shooting blindly, not aiming, just trying to throw him off stride. But I grew up hunting in the back country. I have gunman's instincts, and serving in the 'Stan made me better. And I was fresh out of a war, much sharper than the old man. On pure reflex, I'd zeroed in on center mass, ripping off a dozen rounds as fast as I could pull the trigger —

And got lucky. Or maybe my desperate run had gotten me just close enough to score two solid hits out of a dozen shots. In center mass.

Dead center.

Guthrie's legs buckled, and he dropped to his knees, staring at me the whole time, as he toppled and fell. Surprised, I think.

So was I, but I didn't waste time on it. I was up and running again in a heartbeat. I knew damned well he was dead, but I kicked him hard in the chest anyway, furious at what he'd done, and what he'd made me do. As he rolled off the rifle, I grabbed it up, racking open the action to make it safe —

But it was already safe. The magazine was empty. He'd fired the only round he had. And missed me. At forty yards. A guy with sixty confirmed kills. Who'd dropped Charlie Marx with a head shot at seven hundred.

Goddamn it! I eased down slowly, kneeling beside his body, trying to read an answer in his glassy, empty eyes.

Had he missed me on purpose? How the hell could I know? All I know is he put me in a situation, and I did what I had to. It was his play; he called it, and if I was just a puppet in the old man's swan song, well, so be it.

Fuck him.

He's the one taking the dirt nap.

And in the end, I squared things for Charlie the best I could. He'd gotten his thirty and out, though not the way he'd planned. Or hoped.

Not like this.

Not like this.

They buried old man Guthrie the following

Saturday. No flatbed truck or "Sweet Home Alabama" this time. A private ceremony, family only. I was definitely not invited, but I was there anyway, watching, from the far side of the cemetery, still brooding about what happened.

I know damn well it could have been me in that box, dropping down into the deep, dark tunnel to forever. I had a bandage on my ear, covering the notch his bullet put in me, as a reminder.

But that notch wasn't my only cause for thought. That Saturday was an anniversary. They buried Harland Guthrie thirty years to the day that Charlie Marx signed onto the Valhalla force. Thirty and out. He came close, but didn't quite make it.

Nor will I, I think.

My hometown on the north shore isn't the same country I grew up in. It was a quaint little vacation village then. People came to get away for a few weeks in summer, or for hunting season in autumn, or skiing over Christmas break.

The web has changed all that. Why live in a cramped, dirty city when you can do business from a laptop on your patio? Why not vacation year-round, sell shares from a beachfront cottage or a cozy condo looking out over a glittering lake? Valhalla's population is exploding, and crime's keeping pace with it, and everything is moving so much faster than before.

I have Charlie's job now, boss of Major Crimes. But I won't see my thirty and out.

I'll be lucky to make twenty.

Or ten.

■ ■ ■ ■

THE FIXER

BY ALISON GAYLIN AND
LAURA LIPPMAN

■ ■ ■ ■

Now

There's a rhythm to the signing line. Smile, fleeting eye contact, sign, next. Smile, fleeting eye contact, sign, next. The eye contact is essential — she will forever be "Doe-Eyed Dawn" to the men and women who line up for her autograph — but it has a downside. Held even a second too long, her gaze invites conversation, confidences. The con's attendees know they aren't supposed to slow the line, but there is always someone.

And it is always a man.

An older man, too old for the show in its heyday, much too old to have read the magazines, *16* and *Tiger Beat,* that dubbed her Doe-Eyed Dawn. If she allows her eyes to rest on such a man, he will insist on trying to engage her with what he believes is a stunningly original comment. Something about the platform-soled boots or the miniskirt, how silly it was for her to have long hair in space.

Her hair is shorter now. Sometimes, they comment on that. "Why did you cut your hair?" If she still wore it long, she would be criticized for that, too. "Aren't you too old to be wearing your hair like that?"

Dawn's autograph goes for forty dollars. Then it's fifty dollars for a photograph, sixty if it's an item that the fan brings to the con. This puts her in the middle of the pack at the regional comic cons, which are the ones that invite her. Baltimore, Minneapolis. This year, it's San Antonio — Alamo City Comic Con. She has always been reluctant to do events in Texas, for fear that her appearance will be pegged to her last time here, twenty-five years ago to the day tomorrow. But memories are short and — money is long. She's done okay — nice little house in Santa Monica, lots of tiny checks every month that add up to a decent income — but she can make as much as $10,000 at a good con. When her agent called with this offer, she was about to say no, and then the agent said, "It's bluebonnet season," and she said yes in spite of herself.

It was bluebonnet season twenty-five years ago, too.

Eye contact, sign, eye contact, sign, eye contact, sign. Maybe a little chitchat, as long as she keeps her eyes down. *No, I don't talk to the rest of the cast much from* Moon-Watch. *Yes, I'm very proud of my work in that film. Yes, it was an honor to work with an actor of that caliber. Yes, it's a shame that we didn't get to work together again. No, we didn't keep in touch. His son? That was a tragedy, a real tragedy.*

She's on autopilot, her mind registering every signature. Even with conversation, she's making about five hundred dollars a minute. Whereas her quote right now for acting work is SAG minimum.

The next person in line says: "Hi, Dawn." Oh-so-familiar, but aren't they all?

Only this woman actually knows her — or thought she did, twenty-five years before.

"Hi, Corinne," Dawn says. "What a surprise." She tries to make it sound as if she thinks it's a pleasant surprise.

Then
"Hi, Dawn. Hello, Dawn. Nice to meet you, Ms. Darling. Miss Darling. Hi, Miss Darling, I'm Corinne and I'll be your —"

Corinne winced at her reflection, the way the flat light in the airport bathroom picked up the sweat stains on her silk blouse, the spray of acne across her forehead that had cropped up just this morning, like a rash of dandelions on a freshly mowed lawn.

Her first week working McNally Stark PR, her first out-of-town assignment — arranging interviews for Dawn Darling, *the* Dawn Darling, for goshsakes. *Millie from* Moon-Watch — and here her body was betraying her the way it always did when it mattered most, her stupid period one week early, complete with bloating, zits, hair that kept frizzing out like insulation material, even though she'd dumped an entire bottle of Clairol Herbal Essence conditioner on it this morning.

At least she smelled okay.

When Corinne was eight years old, she and her sister used to pretend their rec room was the *MoonWatch* outpost. They spent hours there, every afternoon imagining that Millie's father, Commander Jim, had been captured by Martians and it was up to her to save him. Corinne was always Millie — the part Dawn Darling played — even though her blonde, big-eyed sister Katie was more of a physical match. Corinne was older and stronger, and so she always got her way, and her way was to play Millie — beautiful, smart, shiny-haired Millie — leaving poor Katie the boring role of Commander Jim.

You're too little to be the teenager, Corinne

would huff at her sister, as though it made more sense for Katie to be the male, middle-aged commander of an outpost on the moon. *I'm Millie. I need to be Millie because I am her, deep down inside.*

So when Mr. McNally informed Corinne she'd be flying out to San Antonio, Texas, this morning, where she would wait at the airport for Dawn Darling's afternoon flight, it was all she could do not to scream as though it was fifteen years ago, and Millie from *MoonWatch* had crash-landed in her family's front yard.

"Are you familiar with her TV work?" Mr. McNally had said. "You're a little young." Corinne had said yes, but he'd slapped a file folder on her desk anyway — Xeroxes of Dawn's old interviews in *Seventeen* and *16* and *Tiger Beat.* "As a refresher," he'd said. "Read these on the plane. Dawn hates flacks who don't know her life story."

"Really?" she'd asked.

"Don't let the America's Sweetheart shit fool you, babe. Doe-Eyed Dawn has a nasty temper and a big fat ego. It's our job to make sure we're the only people in the world who know either of those things. Bad for the optics, otherwise."

This was big. Huge. The shoot in San Antonio was for Dawn Darling's first big-budget feature since she was fifteen, and made *Runaway* with Mick Sinclair. In the new movie, *Comanche County*, she would be reunited with Sinclair — but as his widowed twenty-four-year-old daughter-in-law.

"Can I ask one question?" Corinne had said, pretending she didn't feel McNally's meaty hand brushing against her waist in a you're-not-supposed-to-notice-this kind of way.

"Sure thing."

"Why me? I mean . . . Shouldn't someone with more experience be her press escort?"

At that, the hand had tightened to the point where Corinne had pulled away, forcing a girlish laugh in order to take the sting out of it.

"Because, sweet cheeks," McNally had said, a leer spreading across his tanned face, oiling up his features. "Doe-Eyed Dawn asked for a woman. And you're the closest thing we got."

Corinne had stood at the gate as Dawn's plane arrived, her heart pounding, her hands full. She carried the file of clippings in a briefcase, along with some extra Dawn Darling headshots, directions for the waiting driver, and a press itinerary for the next few days. She also carried a clipboard with today's schedule printed out on it. Her own overnight bag rested next to her feet. She wasn't sure whether or not she'd be staying here in San Antonio for *Comanche County*'s entire six-week shoot — that felt a bit excessive — but she'd packed well regardless. A few good separates in neutral colors that didn't wrinkle easily, one cocktail dress, heels, a pair of sneakers, a bathing suit just in case. Lots and lots of underwear. She went over each item in her suitcase in her mind, one by one. It calmed her.

And then she caught sight of that long, silky, pale hair.

"Hi, Miss Darling, I'm Corinne, and I'll be your press —"

"You can call me Dawn." She said it warmly, a sparkle in her huge brown eyes. Her face was thinner than it had been in her teens, her body rangier and more sinewy. There were a few lines around her eyes and mouth, from sun or cigarettes or maybe a little too much concern. But otherwise she looked the same. Those impossibly long lashes, that rosebud mouth, and that hair — the hair Corinne used to long for, patient and smooth and perfect as it streamed down her back, reaching nearly to her butt without a single tangle or split end, the same way it had on *MoonWatch.*

She rested her hand lightly on Corinne's. It was tiny and cool as a porcelain doll's. "Thank you so much for making the trip out to San Antonio. I know this isn't exactly Monaco or Cannes."

Corinne thought about what Mr. McNally had said about Dawn's big ego, her nasty temper, and heard herself say, "You're just as nice as Millie."

Dawn was kind enough to ignore it.

She looped an arm through Corinne's, and the two of them headed for baggage claim, travelers and airport personnel turning to stare at them. Dawn stopped to sign an autograph for an older couple in matching Hawaiian shirts, asking for the spellings of their names and proving, for Corinne at least, that big egos and nasty tempers were in the eye of the beholder.

"What's first on the agenda?" Dawn asked once they reached baggage claim.

Corinne checked her clipboard. *"Movieline,"* she said. "Looks like it's a group interview with you, the director and your costars. Brenda Johnson, Earl Casey, Mick Sinclair and his son —"

Dawn Darling held up a hand, a hardness creeping into those big doe eyes. "I've got a better idea." She said it quietly, carefully, less a suggestion than an order. "What do you say you and I get a drink?"

"I'm not sure I know where —"

"Don't worry. I'm good at finding bars."

Now

Dawn looks around the bar. "This can't be the same place."

"It's not," Corinne says. "Casa Contigo doesn't exist anymore, I checked."

"What about the pizza place, the one with the belly dancer and the really good white pizza with rosemary? Or that bar where the nasally busboy sang those strange songs?"

"They're all gone — although that busboy actually ended up being quite successful," Corinne says, naming a name that she clearly expects Dawn to recognize. Dawn widens her eyes and nods solemnly, but she doesn't have a clue. She doesn't keep up with music, once so vital to her. She doesn't go to movies, seldom watches television. It's painful to be reminded of the career she might have had if *Comanche County* hadn't been scrapped four weeks into production.

"I remember this strip as being fun, full of life and music."

"Places change," Corinne says. "Like people."

"But a snake never changes its spots."

"Leopard," Corinne says. "It's leopards

who don't change."

"Right. Snakes shed their skins."

When Corinne had asked in the signing line if she and Dawn could grab a coffee later in the weekend, it had seemed best to say, "Sure, sure," and hope that Corinne would have the manners, the *antennae,* to realize Dawn was just trying to keep the line moving. She remembered Corinne's antennae, even after all these years — that uncanny ability of a natural-born "fixer" to understand what Dawn wanted and needed, to play the bad cop, to extricate her from an interview or even a party. *Early call!* she would carol, and they would go back to Dawn's room, where they would drink and smoke, giggle and gossip. Perhaps because she had lived so long inside a fake world full of cheap monsters cobbled together from ridiculous materials, Dawn sometimes imagined she could *see* Corinne's antennae, thin and not particularly long, lost in her frizzy hair. She knew what made them prick and perk. They couldn't sense everything, and they overestimated some threats while missing others completely. But overall, Corinne's antennae had been very good, back in the day.

They're probably even better now.

Dawn sips her Virgin Mary. Corinne had

been oh-so-solicitous when Dawn suggested they meet on the strip where they had spent so much time. "Maybe a coffee would be better?" Everybody's always expecting to find her on the edge of a relapse.

But all Dawn wanted was to get away from the hotel, to find a place without fans or industry people. It was perverse of her to suggest they go back to St. Mary's Street, the place that had been the center of that brief time of her life. At the end of each week, while most of the cast and crew rushed back to LA, she, Corinne, and Mickey Junior would drive out to play around in the bluebells, and then at night come down here and — what had M.J. called it? *Whoop it up. Let's go whoop it up.*

When Dawn had spotted the sign for Casa Contigo, she'd expected a mechanical bull, line dancing, men in cowboy hats, but the music had been varied and raucous. Charlie Sexton, the Texas Tornados, Johnny Reno and the Sax Maniacs. A band called The Perpetrators with a tall, gangly man on harmonica. Mexican bands driven by the unexpected engine of an accordion.

They call it conjunto *music,* M.J. had told her. *It means 'together.'* And he reached for her hand under the table. When Dawn said it had to be a secret, the two of them "hook-ing up again," he had agreed readily. It was hotter that way, and M.J. liked whatever was hottest. Of course, Corinne wasn't fooled for a minute, but that didn't matter. In fact, it helped.

Corinne watches Dawn lift the glass to her lips. Dawn can sense her every twitch, every instinct. She's trying to see if Dawn's hands shake. She's wondering if Dawn has staked out this place, made an agreement with the bartender to sneak her true Bloodies, not this watered-down version.

"It must be hard," Corinne says, "being back here."

Improvisation has never been Dawn's strong suit, but she knows the character she's playing right now. "There are some bad memories, yes. But it was an accident. Remember, Corinne? It was an accident."

Then

The first bar Dawn found — the first one open at two in the afternoon anyway — was called Casa Contigo. "Home with you," Corinne had translated for Dawn when they had stopped out front — an attempt to impress her with what little she'd retained from her two years of high school Spanish.

Dawn, however, insisted on calling it Casa Contagion — a name that became funnier and funnier with each Bloody Mary. *Two Bloodies.* Dawn had said it before Corinne could order the Diet Coke she'd planned on, before she could even get adjusted to the darkness of the place — completely windowless, what little light there was flickering out of the electric votive candles on the tables and one sad string of party lights behind the bar, shaped like chilies. *Never trust a bar with no windows.* Someone had said that to Corinne once — she couldn't remember who.

"Just one," she had said when her first Bloody had arrived, the celery stick jutting weakly out of it, like a surrender flag.

Dawn laughed, her laughter magical, musical. "There's no such thing as just one Bloody Mary."

She was right. At some point, Corinne started measuring time in Bloody Marys, but that had been at around three or five of them ago and now she wasn't measuring anymore. It must be dark out by now. Sometime around Bloody Mary #6, Dawn switched to something clear — straight vodka, maybe? — but Corinne stuck to the original plan.

Corinne was laughing now, so hard that tears were spilling down her cheeks and her breath was coming out in fitful snorts.

Dawn had just told her about a one-nighter she'd had with "the smart one" from a boy band Corinne used to love in junior high.

"I am telling you the complete truth," Dawn was saying. "A tentacle, coming right out the side. I had no idea what he expected me to *do* with that."

Corinne fell over onto one side, her face smacking the sticky banquette seat Dawn had so graciously offered, taking the hard chair for herself.

"Are you okay?" Dawn said.

Corinne had to catch her breath before she could respond, and even then it was just a "Yeah, yeah fine" floating out of her slack mouth as she pushed herself up to sitting, Dawn smiling at her from across the small table, perfectly composed, chili lights glimmering behind her like a backdrop.

"This is fun," Dawn said. "You're fun." Her face blurred in and out of focus and her features in the dim light softened into Millie's.

"You've got the best fucking hair," Corinne said.

They both started at a loud metallic ringing. It took Corinne a few moments to recognize her portable phone, McNally Stark's phone, actually, a sleek little Motorola. She had been so proud when Dick

McNally gave her that phone that she had tried to ignore his hand on her ass.

"The cops?" Dawn said.

Corinne nodded solemnly, all the laughter wrung out of her. She took what she hoped was a sobering breath, lifted the phone from its cradle and pulled out the antenna, willing the words not to slur. "McNally Stark, Corinne speaking."

Dick McNally's voice was like a bucket of ice over her head. "Are you high?"

"Excuse me?"

"I just got a call from the editor of *Movieline*. What the fuck, Corinne? You have one simple job and that's to take her to the fucking interview, and you can't even do that? What the —"

"I'm sorry, Mr. McNally. I . . . Um . . . Dawn had some things she needed to attend to."

"I'm so fucking close to firing you right now."

"What's he saying?" Dawn said.

Corinne waved her off. "I'll call the editor myself. I —"

Dawn grabbed the phone from her. "Dick?" she said. "Yeah. It's me. You say one more word to this girl other than, 'Sorry,' and I'll pull my business so fast it'll make your brain spin. Yeah? Well I don't care about my image. How's that? And you know what else I don't care about? Telling your wife why my last personal assistant quit."

Corinne felt her eyes widen.

"Great. Now hang up. And don't call her again." Dawn handed her back the phone. "How about another round?"

"Thank you," she said. "Thank you, Dawn."

Dawn waved at the bartender. She held up two fingers, and just as she did it, the door opened, bright light spilling into the bar, hurting Corinne's eyes. It was earlier than she had thought.

"We've got so much time ahead of us." Dawn said it as though she was reading her mind.

Maybe she can, Corinne thought. *Maybe she is.*

Their driver took them to the resort where they would stay during filming. It wasn't more than twenty miles from downtown, but it looked more like that other Texas, the one Hollywood had re-created in Utah, Pasadena, soundstages, you name it, and actually felt more familiar. After all, Corinne had never been to San Antonio before today, but she'd seen a lot of Westerns.

Corinne had a room in the hotel proper,

while Dawn and the other stars would be staying in the resort's bungalows — casitas, the staff called them, adding to that John Wayne flavor.

A bellhop in boots and a cowboy hat was piling Dawn's four pieces of luggage on his cart when a silver-haired man walked into the lobby.

Dawn looked up at him, her face breaking into a bright smile. "Mr. Sinclair!" she said. "I'm sorry I missed the *Movieline* presser. My flight was late."

"Not a big deal. You know the drill. Same ole, same ole. Any message for your fans."

Dawn asked if he wanted to have a drink, shocking Corinne; Dawn couldn't weigh more than 110 pounds; she'd had a dozen drinks and had been sipping from a tallboy on the drive up. Yet she hardly seemed affected at all by their afternoon, whereas all Corinne wanted to do was to take a preemptive handful of Tylenol and crawl into bed.

"Maybe later, darling. I'm not young like you, you know." He winked.

As he turned to leave the lobby, Corinne had a flash of déjà vu, but it was only from a film she'd seen him in — one of her dad's favorites.

"Mr. Sinclair," Dawn said, before he reached the door.

"Yes?"

"Is M.J. here yet?"

He nodded. "Should I let him know you've arrived?"

She smiled brightly. It didn't quite reach her eyes. "You better," she said.

Now

The second day of Alamo City Comic Con, Dawn has a panel. It's not the biggest ballroom, but it's the second biggest and it's almost full. She can't remember the topic — Something Pioneers Something Future — but the topics never matter at these conventions unless you're Making News. It's been a long time since Dawn made news. She's here to charm more people into coming to her signing line. She flips her hair, does her patented scream, really more a yelp.

About midway through, she sees Corinne come in, take a seat in the back row, and it's like she drops a stitch in the discussion. By the time she picks the thread up again, it's as if the whole conversation has unraveled. The audience is asking questions now.

"Dawn?" prompts the person who's roaming the hall with the microphone. "She asked about the tragedy on the set of *Comanche County*."

"Well, yes it was — tragic."

Whispers, rustling. Great, soon there will be rumors that she's drinking again. Dawn surveys the room and does the only thing she can: she bursts into tears.

No one could cry on cue like Dawn Darling.

"I'm sorry — it's still so hard. Such a young life, wasted. And his father was never the same. Understandably. It was a *good* movie — or would have been, if we could have finished it. But no one had the heart to do it without Mr. Sinclair and he was wrecked, just wrecked. An accident like that —"

The woman who asked the question is not done. "I have it on good authority — *good* authority — that it might have been a suicide. Or a drug overdose. He was very experienced with guns —"

Dawn studies the woman through her damp lashes. Does she really know something? She remembers Corinne bustling about. *Close the perimeter,* she kept saying. *We have to close the perimeter.* Dawn had almost burst into hysterical laughter, but Corinne was right as usual.

But even a closed perimeter has people inside it. The resort staff as anxious as Corinne that it be reported in the most benign way possible. A justice of the peace, who ruled it an accidental shooting death. Dawn had known that justices of the peace married people. She hadn't known they could pronounce people dead, too.

Could this be Sophia, twenty-five years later and as many pounds heavier? No, Sophia's slinky body was the kind that got mean as it aged, dry and brittle. Like a snake's. All these years, Sophia has never tried to get in touch with Dawn. Still, she worries.

In the back of the room, Corinne motions for the microphone and asks: "Vampires, zombies — what do the panelists think will be the next big breakout character in supernatural stories?"

Even from here, Dawn can almost see Corinne's antennae twitch.

Then

The good news was that Dawn insisted Corinne stay in San Antonio.

The bad news was that meant keeping up with Dawn and Mickey Sinclair Junior when he arrived.

Dawn and Mickey Junior — he made it clear that he preferred M.J. — had met on the set of *MoonWatch,* where he had a small part as a lustful alien who appeared to be a handsome Earth boy, but was really a many-tentacled monster in search of a mate. He claimed now that he was the one who pushed his father to cast Dawn in *Runaway,* her breakout film. "She was young, but I could see her potential."

His own career had fizzled out while Dawn's soared. He was almost too good-looking, his face more like his French model mother's. So his father found him some kind of work on whatever picture he was making, tried to coax directors into throwing him a line or two.

But M.J. said he didn't care about acting. He wanted to party. *If he could act as well as he could hold his liquor and his drugs,* Corinne thought, *he'd have a bigger career than his father's.*

When the weekends came and others (including Mick Senior) flew back to LA, M.J. persuaded Dawn to stay behind. (Corinne had to stay; she was on call.) "Let's go to St. Mary's Street and whoop it up," he said. Corinne had hoped for an Urban Cowboy experience, but apparently that was out of date, even in Texas.

On this particular Saturday night, they had gone back to Dawn's discovery, Casa Contagion. Corinne was the designated driver, or supposed to be since the rental car was in her name, but she could barely keep her eyes open by 1:00 a.m. while M.J. wanted to keep going, to someplace he swore never closed.

"The night is young," M.J. said. "And I like 'em young."

He was staring hungrily at a dark-haired woman in white pants. Pretty enough, but not prettier than Dawn, and certainly not that much younger. Yet Dawn glared at M.J., eyes narrowed with hate — until she realized Corinne was watching her.

"You go home," she said to Corinne. "You don't need to babysit us."

"But the car —"

"Oh, I bet M.J.'s new friend has a car."

He was already across the room, chatting up the girl in the white pants.

Corinne was grateful to have the night off, although she realized on the drive home that she was less sober than she should be. How did Dawn outdrink her five-to-one and stay so centered? And never a trace of a hangover when she had to work. Corinne fell into bed, grateful for the chance to sleep as long as she liked.

The phone erupted at 5:00 a.m., apparently uninformed of her plans. She started to let it go, then remembered that the cost of staying here in San Antonio was that she was always on call. She put the receiver to her aching head, but there was nothing but the bleat of a dial tone. It took her a few moments of utter confusion to realize that it wasn't the hotel phone ringing. It was the McNally Stark cell phone.

Corinne stumbled out of bed with her eyes half-closed, following the sound to the corner of the room, stubbing her toe on her suitcase. Pain shot through her. "Hello?" she yelped.

"Hello." It was a woman's voice, smoky/scratchy like Demi Moore's. "Is this Corey?"

"Corinne."

"Whatever. I wanted to call the police, but Dawn told me to call this number so I'm calling."

"Dawn? The *police*?"

"Yep."

"Why?"

"Probably best you jus', like, come over here?"

"Where is 'here'?"

"The . . . what are they called? Casita."

"Dawn's casita?"

A muttered conversation. "No, the other one. The guy's."

Corinne swallowed, her throat closing in on itself. She longed for water, and when she spoke, her voice was scratchy and unfamiliar, a pale imitation of the caller's. "Who am I talking to?"

"Sophia," she said. As though that was supposed to mean something. And then she hung up. She didn't even give Corinne a last name.

Then

Corinne noticed Dawn first. The door to the casita was unlocked, and when she stepped into the living room, her eyes went right to her, curled up in the corner of the room clutching her legs, small as a child, blond hair draped over her knees.

"Dawn?" Corinne said. And then she saw the dead body.

Corinne opened her mouth, but no sound came out.

Dawn let out a whimper.

Corinne took a few deep breaths, her eyes on what was left of his head. "What . . ." she said. "What . . ."

Dawn looked up, her cheeks red and glistening. "I was in the other room and he . . . I heard him say something about Russian roulette and he . . . Oh God . . ."

"Who is this?"

"Mickey."

"Who?"

"M.J."

Jesus, no. Oh God no. Not Mick Sinclair's son. "Are you serious?"

"Does it look like I'm joking?" Dawn's voice pitched up, like a frightened child's. And then she started to cry.

In Corinne's mind, a switch went off — as though she were outside of herself, viewing the whole scene from the scope of a camera. "Oh my God," she whispered. The words ran through her head, but she didn't say them out loud. It was bad enough to be thinking them, but still. Still. It was why she was here, wasn't it? She was the fixer — that was her purpose. To fix the optics.

Dawn Darling. Millie from *MoonWatch*. America's interstellar sweetheart, Corinne's very first and *most important client* curled up in the fetal position in the corner of the sleaziest crime scene imaginable. The beer cans on the floor. The empty bottle of Jack Daniel's. The condom wrappers. The smeared, full-length mirror at the center of the room dusted with the remnants of a cocaine binge. The optics.

"We've got to get out of here."

"I have to go to the bathroom."

"You can go to the bathroom in your — your casita."

"I need to wash my face."

"Look, Dawn. We need to get you away

from this place as quickly as —"

"Did you fucking hear me?"

Corinne stared at her. The dead calm of her features. Her voice smooth and steady, despite the tears on her cheeks.

Without another word, Dawn stood up, turned, and left the room.

Hysteria. She's traumatized. Who wouldn't be traumatized after seeing something like that? That was it. Trauma. Hysteria. And yet —

Corinne moved closer to the body, the dank, coppery smell of it. The ruined, bloody face. *M.J. Handsome M.J. . . . Russian roulette. Jesus.*

The gun in his open palm. A revolver. Black dust on his fingers. *Russian roulette.* Corinne thought of Dawn's hands.

Of Dawn in the bathroom, washing them clean.

Then

It wasn't until they were back in Dawn's casita, optics averted, that Corinne was able to breathe again, to think. And what she thought of was not the dead body on the floor, not her client either, though she was well and truly a murderer. It was not even her own reaction to what she'd seen, the person she had become. No: what she

568

thought was what a fixer would think.

"Where's Sophia?" Corinne said. "The one who called me?"

"Long gone," Dawn said.

"Jesus Christ."

"I'm never going to drink again," Dawn said, but not to Corinne. She was staring at the ceiling, promising whatever God she believed in. "Never."

Now

"Bloody or virgin?"

Dawn had thought she could hide in another hotel bar along the Riverwalk, but here's Corinne, yet again. It feels like that episode of *MoonWatch,* the one on the planet with the invisible creatures that track humans by their smell. Everywhere she goes, there's Corinne, waiting to take little bites out of her.

"Virgin," she says. "Not that it's any of your business. I haven't had a drink for —"

"Twenty-five years ago. Today. Though I have to wonder, when did you really quit drinking, Dawn?"

"I've never fallen off the wagon, not once. I had a reaction to some pain meds one time, but I never drank after that night."

"You weren't even drinking then, were you?"

Dawn just looks at her.

"The drinks, the drugs — it was all very convincing. At first, I thought you killed him because you were jealous. Jealous and drunk and high."

Ah, but it was M.J. they made jealous, Dawn and Sophia. It wasn't really Dawn's thing, but she was an actress, after all. *Here's what you're going to do,* she had told the girl. *We're going to kiss a little, just to tease him. And then we're going to tease him some more.*

"M.J. died playing Russian roulette, Corinne."

"I know that's what you told me at the time, Dawn. Doesn't mean I believed it, even then."

"*You* were the one who said that wouldn't fly — that no one played Russian roulette alone, that they would want to find witnesses. You also knew that his father, the whole production really, wouldn't want it to be reported as a suicide. So the official ruling was an accidental shooting, even if the gossip rags whispered for years that it was a suicide. Good diversionary tactic."

"It was a murder. I've always known that."

"Really."

"What really happened, Dawn?"

"I'm afraid we've run out of time for questions," Dawn says. "Catch up with me at my next signing."

"I've kept your secret for twenty-five years. I think I'm entitled to the answers."

She feels a surge of rage. "*Entitled?* Everyone thinks they're *entitled* to what I have. My mother took my money, 20 percent of my salary to be my manager, which was a joke — not like she was finding me new work."

"She drove you to set, she was your guardian —"

"Aren't guardians supposed to guard? Watch? She barely did anything. Hell, she thought it was a good career move, being raped by Mickey Sinclair Jr. She all but congratulated me."

Corinne stares at her. "Raped! You acted like his girlfriend, the whole time. You weren't raped."

"Not in Texas, Corinne. I'm talking about the set of *Runaway.* Late rehearsal. He sneaked me a few beers."

"You were fifteen years old," Corinne says, her eyes wide.

"Still fourteen, actually. Not that it made any difference under the law. And the law never came into it."

For a few seconds, the years peel back and Corinne's transformed, looking like that

571

trusting young publicist again. That sweet, frizzy-haired *MoonWatch* fan who couldn't hold her liquor and spent her days hunting down patches of bluebonnets.

Her reaction feeds Dawn somehow, pushing her to tell what she'd never given anyone before. "When I told my mother and my agent what happened, they said I shouldn't make a big deal out of it, that it would torpedo my career. Well, here I am, career essentially torpedoed. I'll never know what would've happened if *Comanche County* was produced. And you know what? I'd still do it all over again."

"Shoot M.J."

"I. Did not. Shoot. M.J.," she says, watching Corinne's face change even more. Twenty-five years of self-assurance dropping away. A fixer who knew the answers to everything, realizing that all she'd ever had was a partial script. Corinne was younger than Dawn. She'd always be younger than Dawn.

"We did goad him," Dawn says. "Sophia was an extra, wanted to be an actress, so I gave her a scene. Told her to cozy up to him in the bar, then start fooling around with me back at the casita. M.J. wanted to get with both of us, of course, but we told him he wasn't man enough for two women. We told him he couldn't be with us until he proved he was a man. We said we'd do his father before we'd do him because his father was a real man."

And, Dawn remembers, she'd made sure to call him Mickey Junior, the one thing M.J. could never stand.

"Who suggested Russian roulette?"

"Does it matter, Corinne? An accident is an accident is an accident. It's like what parents say to little kids. *If Dawn told you to go jump off a bridge, would you do it?* No one could prove anything."

"I could have," Corinne says. "I checked the gun while you were in the bathroom. I grew up around guns. My dad taught me how to shoot."

Dawn almost admires that long-ago Corinne. Almost.

"But you didn't."

"No."

Dawn leans against the table and gazes into Corinne's eyes. "If you had it to do over again —"

"I wouldn't do anything differently. Not then. Not now."

Then

"I want to be famous," Sophia said.

Corinne blinked at her. She'd expected

Sophia to say something else. She wasn't sure what. But standing, as she was, in the woman's trailer home at 1:00 a.m., the line seemed from a different, more glamorous script.

It hadn't been hard to find Sophia. That morning, during the press conference announcing M.J.'s death, Corinne had seen her in the back of the crowd in a different pair of tight pants — red this time — a smirk on her face, as though all this was some terrific joke and only she knew the punch line.

A tragic accident, the *Comanche* publicist had said, Corinne and all the other personal flacks forming a grim line behind him. *No one knows . . . He was a happy young man . . . No other cast members involved . . .*

And there she'd been, that bad penny of a bad actress, smirking away.

After the group of reporters had dispersed, Corinne had approached her, heart pounding. "I'm —"

"I know who you are."

"We need to talk."

Sophia had pressed a piece of paper into her hand, an address scrawled on it. "Meet me here," she said.

"It will have to be late. Dawn's flying back to LA and I have business to attend to."

"That's fine," she'd said. "I like late."

And late it was. The lights had been out in all the trailers except Sophia's. Corinne had arrived to find the door unlocked, Sophia standing in her sty of a living room — with a gun in her hand, aimed straight at the door. Corinne's thoughts careened around in her head: *A Western, that's what this is. The OK Corral.* Sophia spoke again. "You hear me? I said, I want to be famous, like Dawn."

Corinne's gaze stayed on the gun. Calm. In control. "And how do you expect to accomplish that?"

"You're going to help me, Corey."

"How am I going to do that?"

"You're going to call your boss. You're going to tell him that you've met the next Dawn, and you need to fly me out to LA for a screen test and you won't take no for an answer."

"My boss runs a PR agency, not a studio."

"You can still make it happen."

Corinne swallowed, her gaze fixed on the barrel. "And if I don't?"

"Then I tell. I tell everything about what Dawn did, and how you covered it up. I tell the cops. I tell the tabloids. Either way, I'm famous." She smiled. "It's win-win."

Corinne felt light-headed, her thoughts

traveling back to the morning. Dawn in the bathroom. That moment, right before she'd knelt down and plucked the gun out of M.J.'s hand with a room-service napkin, right before she'd opened the cylinder and looked inside and saw every chamber except that one filled with a bullet.

"Poor innocent me," Sophia said. "Taken in by those awful debauched celebrities. Witness to a murder. Hell of a story for the *Enquirer.* I bet they'd pay good money for it, too, and I'll be . . . you know —"

"Famous," Corinne said. "Okay. You win. I'll fly you out. I'll get you a screen test and an agent."

Her face brightened. "You will?"

"Just put the gun down."

Sophia laughed. Spun the cylinder. "No bullets. I put them all in the other one." She laughed. "It's almost like a nursery rhyme, innit? Or the Three Bears. The first gun had too many bullets, but the second gun had no bullets —"

Corinne stared at her, this laughing woman who would always be a part of her life. Of Dawn's life. Sophia was standing on a chair now, brandishing the gun and going on about some stupid scene she'd seen on *One Life to Live* . . .

And Corinne went for the gun in her

purse, given to her just a few hours ago by the oiliest of the local teamsters in exchange for the rest of her per diem and an act she'd rather forget.

"See, I'm good, right?" Sophia said. "I could make it, right?"

Corinne shot Sophia until every chamber was empty.

As Corinne ran back through the trailer park to her rental car, she thought of all the sheriffs she'd seen in those old Westerns she used to watch with her dad. How they never hesitated before shooting someone dead because they knew they were in the right, and right always wins. *Just doing my job, ma'am,* those sheriffs would say. Then the movie would end, and the sheriffs would tip their hats and would walk off into the sunset.

And never think on it, ever again.

ACKNOWLEDGMENT

Special thanks to Laurie R. King for her invaluable editorial assistance.

ABOUT THE AUTHORS

Doug Allyn is the author of eleven novels and more than a hundred and thirty short stories. He has been published internationally in English, German, French, and Japanese. His most recent, *Murder in Paradise* (with James Patterson), was on the *New York Times* bestseller list for seven weeks. More than two dozen of his tales have been optioned for development as feature films and television. Career highlights? Sipping champagne with Mickey Spillane and waltzing with Mary Higgins Clark.

Lee Child worked in television until he was fired in 1995 due to corporate restructuring. Deciding to see an opportunity where others might have seen a crisis, he bought six dollars' worth of paper and pencils and sat down to write a book, *Killing Floor,* the first in the Jack Reacher series. It was an immediate success, and launched the series which has grown in sales and impact with every new installment over twenty-three novels — the most recent being *Past Tense* — and various short stories. He currently lives in New York City.

Max Allan Collins is an MWA Grand Master. He is the author of the Shamus-winning Nathan Heller historical thrillers (*Do No Harm*) and the graphic novel *Road to Perdition,* basis of the Academy Award–winning film. His innovative '70s series, Quarry, revived by Hard Case Crime (*Killing Quarry*), became a Cinemax TV series. He has completed fifteen posthumous Mickey Spillane novels (*Masquerade for Murder*) and is the coauthor with his wife, Barbara Collins, of the Trash 'n' Treasures cozy mystery series (*Antiques Fire Sale*).

Jeffery Deaver is the *New York Times* bestselling author of numerous suspense novels, including *The Blue Nowhere* and *The Bone Collector,* which was made into a feature film starring Denzel Washington and Angelina Jolie. He has been nominated for five Edgar Awards from the Mystery Writers of America and is a two-time recipient of the Ellery Queen Reader's Award for Best Short Story of the Year. A lawyer who quit practicing to write full-time, he lives in California and Virginia.

Meg Gardiner is the bestselling, award-winning author of fifteen novels, including *China Lake,* which won the 2009 Edgar Award for Best Paperback Original, and *UNSUB,* which won the 2018 Barry Award for Best Thriller. She is the 2019–2020 President of Mystery Writers of America. She lives in Austin, Texas.

Alison Gaylin's tenth novel, *If I Die Tonight,* won the Edgar Award in the Best Paperback Original category. A graduate of Northwestern University and Columbia University's Graduate School of Journalism, Alison lives with her husband and daughter in upstate New York.

Sue Grafton (1940–2017) was a #1 *New York Times* bestselling author, published in twenty-eight countries and in twenty-six languages. Books in her alphabet series, beginning with *A is for Alibi* in 1982 and ending with *Y is for Yesterday* due to her death in December of 2017, are international bestsellers with readership in the millions.

Sue was a writer who believed in the form

that she had chosen to mine: "The mystery novel offers a world in which justice is served. Maybe not in a court of law," she has said, "but people do get their just desserts."

Carolyn Hart is the author of sixty-two books and two collections of short stories. Her work includes sixteen suspense novels and the Death on Demand, Henrie O, and Bailey Ruth mystery series. She has been a member of MWA since the publication of her first book in 1964. She was named an MWA Grand Master in 2014. She is a past president of Sisters in Crime.

Naomi Hirahara is the Edgar Award–winning author of two mystery series set in Southern California and one in Hawai'i. Her Mas Arai series, which features a Hiroshima survivor and Los Angeles gardener, ended with the publication of *Hiroshima Boy* in 2018. The books have been translated into Japanese, Korean, and French. The first in her Officer Ellie Rush bicycle cop mystery series received the T. Jefferson Parker Mystery Award. A former newspaper editor, she has also published noir short stories, middle-grade fiction, and nonfiction history books. For more information, go to www.naomihira hara.com.

Wendy Hornsby is the author of fifteen novels and a collection of short stories, *Nine Sons,* that includes the Edgar Award–winning story of the same title. Several of her short stories have been selected for inclusion in annual best story collections. Her most recent book is *A Bouquet of Rue* (Perseverance Press, April 2019). A professor of history emeritus, Wendy lives with her husband in California's Gold Rush country.

Laurie R. King is the author of twenty-seven novels and other works, including the Mary Russell–Sherlock Holmes series which began with *The Beekeeper's Apprentice,* named one of the twentieth century's best crime novels by the IMBA. Her books are regulars on the *New York Times* bestseller lists, and have won an alphabet of prizes from Agatha to Wolfe.

William Kent Krueger is the author of the *New York Times* bestselling Cork O'Connor mystery series, set in the great Northwoods of Minnesota. He is a five-time winner of the Minnesota Book Award.

Among his many other accolades is the Edgar Award for Best Novel for his 2013 release *Ordinary Grace.* He lives in St. Paul, a city he dearly loves, and does all his creative writing in local, author-friendly coffee shops.

Since the publication of her first novel in 1997, **Laura Lippman**, the *New York Times* bestselling author of the acclaimed stand-alone novels *After I'm Gone, I'd Know You Anywhere,* and *What the Dead Know,* has won virtually every major award given to U.S. crime writing, including the Edgar Award, Anthony Award, Agatha Award, Nero Wolfe Award, Shamus Award, and the Quill Award. Her latest book is *Lady in the Lake.*

Peter Lovesey's crime writing began with the Sergeant Cribb novels, set in Victorian times and later made into a TV series. His many awards include the Gold Dagger of the Crime Writers' Association for *The False Inspector Dew.* More recently he has written about Peter Diamond, a modern detective based in Bath, and the first of the series, *The Last Detective,* won the Anthony Award. In 2000, he was awarded the CWA Cartier Diamond Dagger in recognition of his career and in 2018 he was honored as Grand Master of the Mystery Writers of America.

Margaret Maron lives and writes in North Carolina where she is an inductee into the North Carolina Literary Hall of Fame. A founding member of Sisters in Crime and its third president, she is a past president of MWA and an MWA Grand Master. Her novels have won her the Edgar, the Agatha, the Anthony and the North Carolina Award, the state's highest civilian award.

Marcia Muller was named MWA Grand Master in 2005. She has published fifty novels, thirty-two in the Sharon McCone series, as well as six short story collections and numerous articles, stories, and book reviews. Her other honors include two Edgar Award nominations, three Shamus Awards, the Lifetime Achievement Award (1993) from the Private Eye Writers of America, an RT Lifetime Achievement Award (1999), the Bouchercon Lifetime Achievement Award (2005), and a Western Writers of America Short Fiction Spur Award (with Bill Pronzini, 2008). In addition, her character Sharon McCone received the PWA Hammer (2010) for her longevity and contribution to the genre.

Peter Robinson is an English Canadian crime writer best known for his crime novels set in the fictional Yorkshire town of Eastvale and featuring Inspector Alan Banks, which encompass twenty-six volumes and have been translated into nineteen languages. He has also won nearly every major mystery writing award there is, including the Ellis, the Macavity, Le Grand Prix de Littérature Policière, the CWA Dagger in the Library Award, the Martin Beck Award, and the Edgar.

S. J. Rozan is the author of sixteen novels and more than seventy-five short stories, and the editor of two anthologies. She has won multiple awards, including the Edgar, Shamus, Anthony, Nero, Macavity; the Japanese Maltese Falcon; and the Private Eye Writers of America Life Achievement Award. She speaks and teaches widely. S. J. was born in the Bronx and lives in lower Manhattan. Her most recent book is *Paper Son.* She can be reached though her website: www.sjrozan.net.

Bill Pronzini was named MWA Grand Master in 2008, making him and Marcia Muller the second pair of married mystery writers to be so honored. (Ross Macdonald and Margaret Millar were the first.) He has published ninety novels, including forty-six in his Nameless Detective series, four nonfiction books, and numerous short stories. Among his other accomplishments are six Edgar Award nominations, the Grand Prix de Littérature Policière for the best crime novel published in France in 1988 (*Snowbound*), three Shamus Awards and the Lifetime Achievement Award (1987) from the Private Eye Writers of America and the Bouchercon Lifetime Achievement Award (2005).

Edgar-winner **Julie Smith** is the author of twenty-two mysteries, most set in New Orleans and starring one or the other of her detective heroes, a cop named Skip Langdon and a PI named Talba Wallis. (Both female, both tough and wily.) Her novel, *New Orleans Mourning,* won the Edgar for Best Novel. She is the owner of the digital publishing company booksBnimble and also operates bbnmarketing, a marketing service for indie authors.

The employees of Thorndike Press hope you have enjoyed this Large Print book. All our Thorndike, Wheeler, and Kennebec Large Print titles are designed for easy reading, and all our books are made to last. Other Thorndike Press Large Print books are available at your library, through selected bookstores, or directly from us.

For information about titles, please call:
  (800) 223-1244

or visit our website at:
  gale.com/thorndike

To share your comments, please write:
  Publisher
  Thorndike Press
  10 Water St., Suite 310
  Waterville, ME 04901